The Oath

Patricia M Osborne

White Wings

Books

Published 2023 in United Kingdom
by White Wings Books

ISBN 978-0-9957107-3-3

British Cataloguing Publication data:
A catalogue record of this book is available from the British Library.

This book is also available as an ebook.

In Memory of

my dearest mum,

Lila (1932-2014)

and Sister,

Heather (1956-2009)

Two courageous and inspiring women.
A light went out in my heart when you both left this world

PART I

Chapter 1

Françoise

23ʳᵈ March 1895

Where were they? I paced the floor, my pulse quickening. Something must be wrong. Papa never called formal meetings. Four o'clock, he said. It was ten past now. What was it they wanted to tell me?

Papa finally hobbled in and sank into the armchair by the inglenook fireplace. 'I trust your birthday tea with Geneviève was enjoyable?'

'I had a wonderful afternoon, Papa, but you wanted to speak to me?'

'All in good time.' He coughed into a handkerchief.

'Papa, are you ill? Is that what you wanted to tell me?'

Before he had the chance to answer, Maman entered the parlour, her once dark hair now iron-grey. Pressing the middle of her back, she eased down on the tan Chesterfield. André followed her in. He strode over to the fireplace, poked the embers, and added a few pieces of coal. 'Come, Françoise' – he ushered me to the couch next to Maman – 'sit with me.'

Trembling, I asked, 'What is going on?'

Papa lit his pipe, coughing and spluttering. 'Ma fille, we must discuss your future.'

'You are ill.' I sat forward. 'What is wrong? Is it serious?'

'Sit back, ma soeur. Let Papa speak.' André's bright blue eyes twinkled.

Papa cleared his throat. 'Remember how when you were little, I would tell you the story of a prince who lived far away who would one day send for his princess?'

'Oui, Papa, but that was just a game. Mais oui?'

'Non, ange, not a game.' He coughed again. 'One hundred years ago there were two brothers, Henri and Willeme, our ancestors. Henri emigrated to England but before leaving he drew up a contract with his twin brother, Willeme. Henri vowed to support Willeme and his descendants for evermore. We are Willeme's descendants.'

I frowned. 'Contract?'

'Oui. The contract was written in our family bible.' Papa shuffled over to the mahogany sideboard and patted a tattered leather embossed book. 'In here.' He flipped the page. 'Willeme also swore an oath to his brother that if ever a male descendant of Henri's, during any time era, required a bride to provide an heir, they could call on Willeme's line for the pledge to be fulfilled.'

My heart beat faster. 'What has that got to do with me?'

'Because my dear, you are the princess and your prince has sent for his bride.' Papa blew wispy clouds of smoke from his pipe.

'I still do not understand.' I stood up and strode across the room.

'Sit back down, my child, and I will try to explain.' Papa took a deep breath. 'Lady Elizabeth Dubois, widow of Henri's descendant, has called in this promise. She is keeping to her late husband's wishes that if their son Charles had not settled in marriage by the age of twenty-four, she must intervene and ask for the pledge to be fulfilled in order that Charles provides an heir for the Dubois name. This means as our only daughter, you must wed Charles.'

'But I do not wish to marry someone I do not know.'

'That may be, dearest, but we cannot always have what we want. Playtime is over. Seventeen is old enough to wed and bear a child.'

'Non.' I stamped my foot. 'I will not.'

Papa furrowed his brow. 'Would you see us destitute?'

'I do not understand why the Dubois' in England support us? Did Henri take all our money when he emigrated?'

'Non, my dear.' Papa smiled. 'Our family would have become penniless had it not been for Henri stepping in. He saved the Dubois household by marrying an English baronet's eldest daughter.'

'And now I am supposed to step in and do the same?' I looked at André hoping he would come up with a solution but he stayed silent, stroking his dark moustache. 'André is older than me. Why can he not marry to help the family instead?' By twenty-five he should have settled down. An attractive man, with such a trim physique, was a perfect choice for any mademoiselle.

'That will not help. All this' – Papa spread out his hands – 'is because of Henri.'

'Why do I have to fulfil a stupid oath from one hundred years ago?' I pleaded.

'Because we will become paupers if you do not. Is that what you want?'

'Non,' I whispered, easing myself down next to Maman. She was looking tired. 'When is this supposed to happen?' I asked.

'You and André are to leave for England in six weeks. Lady Elizabeth has booked ship passage in May for you and your brother. She has also sent funds for your trousseau.' Papa closed his eyes.

'But Maman' – I rested my hand on hers – 'I do not wish to leave you and Papa and what about my friends?'

'You will have André. Papa has arranged for him to stay with you for at least six months. The wedding ceremony will take place in August, allowing time for you and Sir Charles to get acquainted. You will want for nothing, my child.'

'You both keep calling me a child yet you expect me to marry and provide a son.'

Father pursed his lips. 'It is time to grow up, Françoise. You will become a Lady and once you have borne Charles an heir you will fill your time with motherhood.'

'Maman, s'il te plaît, do not make me.'

She patted my arm. 'Shh, child.'

'Shh indeed. Do you want your father to be ruined?' Papa scratched his head. 'We need you to do this. The betrothal was signed long before any of us were born. It is in here.' He tapped the bible. 'There is nothing to be done. Maman and I are too old for la prison des pauvres.' He took a deep breath. 'You will have a good life. A chance to travel. Become Lady of the House. Why can you not see this is for your benefit as well as ours?'

I leaned forward. 'But what about my friends? My family?'

'You will make new friends and you will have André for a time.'

*

Maman pulled open the drawers in the mahogany tallboy. She winced as she held her back.

'Are you in pain, Maman?'

'It is just my lumbago.'

'Perhaps I can help.'

'Non, you sit down. I have something to show you.'

A warm breeze touched my face from the opened windows running across two of the walls as I perched on the edge of Maman and Papa's huge wooden bed. I brushed my fingers across the exquisite eiderdown Maman had stitched herself.

Rainbow shades of red, pink, green, blue, and yellow made up the floral design, and a pattern of a young couple and elderly gentleman were interspersed by a cherub and birds. Maman had promised to teach me to quilt but how would that happen now? I would never get a chance to learn this wondrous craft.

Maman closed the drawer and eased herself down by my side. 'This was my maman's. You can have it as part of your trousseau.' She placed a piece of jewellery in my palm. 'It will be your something old.'

I examined the diamond-leaf brooch with pearls in its centre. 'It is beautiful.' I closed my hand around it. 'Maman, do you not agree that fulfilling a one-hundred-year pledge is a little foolish?'

'It does not matter what I think. It is written in the family bible. Papa does not see this as foolish and will not break the vow. He explained to you how we will be cut off financially if the oath is not fulfilled.'

'But why now?'

'Because your distant cousin, Sir Charles, needs to wed a female of good breeding.' Maman closed the drawer. 'We must go shopping, and arrange a couturière for your bridal gown.' She wiped away a tear. 'My only regret is that I shall not see my only daughter walk down the aisle.'

'You and Papa will not be there?'

'Regrettably no. Papa, with his health, would never manage the journey.'

'But, Maman, I have an idea. Perhaps I could marry a rich Frenchman. Think about it. Would that not be a good solution?'

'Now, child, we have been through this. Papa explained. I have just explained. The oath must not be broken. The marriage is a good match. I have heard Baronet Charles is an exceptionally handsome man and *Highwood Hall* has much more extravagant grounds than here at *Vue de Jardin*.'

It was useless to protest. Maybe I could convince André to stay in England with me forever. What about my best friend, Geneviève? What would she think about me leaving her?

*

Maman's femme de chambre placed the gown over my head. 'You will make a belle mariée, Mademoiselle Françoise. Regardez.' Marie gestured me towards the mahogany full-length mirror.

My reflection showed an alluring young bride. The dress was indeed beautiful. Pure white taffeta flowed to the floor. Its tight bodice accentuated my small waist and a demi-train draped behind. Marie adjusted the tight sleeves which puffed out at the upper arm making me look like I had wide shoulders. My chestnut brown hair piled high in a knot made me look older. Tight curls brushed across my forehead.

'And now this.' Marie placed a small coronet fixed to a long silk tulle veil on top of my head.

It did not look like me at all. I was a woman. My childhood days were over and I would never be able to wear my hair loose and free, caressing my shoulders again. I squeezed my eyes closed to stop myself from crying.

Maman entered the room. 'Françoise, ma chérie. You look divine.' She moved closer and wiped my eyes with a handkerchief. 'Ne pleure pas, mon ange. I promise you will thank Papa and I for this.' She took a coin from her purse. 'This is a sixpence. Lady Elizabeth sent it over as part of your trousseau. On your wedding day you will put this in the bottom of your shoe. It ensures future wealth. Try it now.'

I slipped off the white slipper from my left foot and placed the coin inside. 'It is rather uncomfortable.'

'I am sure it will be fine. English brides do it all the time. If it were painful then they would not have such a custom.' Maman smiled. 'Now, I have more treasures.' She gave a nod to Marie to leave us alone. Once Marie had left, Maman said, 'I have given you the brooch which is your something old but you need something new.' She opened a box and showed me the contents.

'It is divine, Maman. Merci.'

'It is not from Papa and I but your betrothed. Sir Charles chose this himself for his beautiful bride.' She placed the necklace around my neck and clasped it closed at the back. I stroked the diamond choker.

'This is just the beginning. Once you are married your husband will bestow wonderful gifts on you all the time. But we have not finished yet.' She returned to her purse and this time passed me a white handkerchief with a blue embroidered motif.

I looked in the mirror again. I did indeed look beautiful. Surely, I could be a prize for any wealthy Frenchman. Why did I have to go all the way to England? 'Maman…'

'Now, Françoise, you are not going to start again, are you? This is what we must do.'

Chapter 2

Françoise

My trunk was loaded onto the post-chaise. I was dressed in a dull-grey flannel dress but at least I had chosen a small green hat complimenting my emerald eyes. André helped me into the carriage before settling down next to me. Maman was crying. 'Look after my child for me.'

'I will, do not worry, Maman.' André patted my hand.

Maman sniffled. 'Françoise, write to me every day.'

'I will, Maman.' I dabbed my eyes with a handkerchief.

The boy had already flicked the reins to let the horses know to proceed when Papa came hobbling down the steps from the house. He raised his cane and the driver held the horses back.

Papa put his hand to his chest, catching his breath. 'I thought I was too late. Stay safe my children and write often. Maman and I will miss you.' He opened the carriage door, leaned in to kiss my cheek, and shook André's hand before banging the door shut. 'Go now,' he said to the coachman.

Maman moved over to Papa and linked her arm in his. The horses slow trotted picking up their pace. I looked behind, watching Maman and Papa turn to black dots as we rode out of *Vue de Jardin* towards Calais.

André took my hand. 'It will be fine. Look on this as an adventure. I know I am.' He smiled.

I laid my head on his shoulder and closed my eyes.

*

André shook my arm. I jumped, forgetting where I was.

'It is morning and we have arrived.'

I yawned, stretching my arms and legs.

'What do you think?' André asked. Brown curls peeped from his top hat.

I looked ahead at the enormous ship. 'It is huge.'

Two men barged past, one of them knocking me with his cane.

André frowned. 'Mind the mademoiselle.'

The taller one turned around and tipped his hat. 'Veuillez accepter mes excuses, mademoiselle.'

The boy unloaded our trunks. A ship's porter retrieved them and hauled them on to the boat as crowds moved closer. Nausea crept into my stomach at the thought of maybe never seeing Maman and Papa again. Especially as Maman had hinted Papa was poorly and that cough did sound bad. And now we were far away from Penketh, our home, and closer to England.

'Come.' André linked his arm in mine. 'Let us board and find a seat quickly. It is not safe to linger with all these people about.'

I felt proud to be on André's arm as we embarked the vessel and I let him lead me down the steep steps to the lounge where I sat down by a window.

André dipped into the small hamper our cook, Juliette, had packed for us. 'We should eat something for breakfast. It has been a long journey and a while yet to still go.'

'Merci.' I took the portion of wheat bread filled with cheese and nuts. I had not eaten since dinner last night, although I had partaken of water when we had stopped at the posting inns to change horses and driver.

'I am going to miss Juliette's food.' André bit into his bread. 'She manages to make something small into something delicious.' He rubbed his stomach which rumbled in response. We both laughed.

'André, do you think Maman and Papa will be all right?'

'Where has that come from, ma soeur?'

'Maman said Papa was not well enough to manage the journey. And that cough. Do you think it might be serious?'

'Do not worry. I am sure he will be fine. I think it is much more likely that he did not wish to cross the sea.' André grinned.

'But Maman. She looked tired and there is something wrong with her back.'

'She has most likely been worried about you fulfilling this oath. Papa too.'

I pressed my lips together not convinced. 'Our parents are rather old, are they not?'

'That is true. Maman fifty-four and Papa close to sixty. Pourquoi?'

'I was just wondering how come they had us, particularly me, so late in life? Especially when I am only seventeen and expected to produce a child straight away. I do not understand.'

'Eat something else.' André passed me a fancy cake. 'Maman and Papa were not lucky with children. That is until they had me, and later, you of course. You know I had a twin brother?'

'Oui, Maman had told me that but nothing else. All I know is he did not live long.'

'He died before one-year. I was too young to remember him. But before they had me' – André coughed – 'Maman was unlucky with childbirth. She had babies who never reached more than a few months in her pregnancy and two boys born dead.'

'Why did Maman never tell me this?'

'Most likely she did not wish to discuss those things with her daughter.'

'But she discussed them with you?'

'Non, she did not. I overheard her talking one day when I was about fourteen. She had no idea I was in the house.' André squeezed my hand. 'Have something else to eat?'

I bit into a chunk of cheese. André was not the only one who would miss Juliette's food. She made a delightful *pique-nique* and my stomach was grateful as my nausea settled.

'Rest for a while.' André patted my hand.

Suppose my babies died. Would Charles still want me? Did he even want me anyway? I wondered if he would be gentle and kind like Papa. I was going to miss Maman and Papa but thank goodness I still had André.

*

André stroked my shoulder. 'It will not be long now. They said the crossing should not take longer than three hours. Let us go to the upper deck where the fresh air will help with your sickness.'

The wind had picked up and the rocking motion of the boat, along with closing my eyes for a short time, had brought back the nausea.

I followed André back up the steep stairs. Crowds huddled in different parts of the deck. I looked out at the sea. Waves rolled, splashing high against the side of the ship.

'Do not stand too close, ma soeur.' André pulled my cape closer to me as I shivered.

*

André pointed to the white cliffs. 'Look, Françoise, land. That must be Dover. See the chalk on the rocks?'

'Oui. It looks beautiful.' The sunrise reflected on the water. I took a deep breath to control the sickness in my stomach.

'Still nauseous?'

I nodded.

'You should eat something.' André unwrapped a muslin parcel and passed me a piece of bread from the hamper. 'Mange.'

I took a bite and did indeed feel a little better.

More people trundled up the steps. The deck was getting busier.

André took my arm. 'When the ship docks we must be ready to leave with speed in order to avoid these crowds.'

*

André raised his cane to alert a taxicab. The ship's baggage carriers packed our trunks on the vehicle while we boarded.

'To the station,' André said.

The horses trotted a short way until we pulled up outside a building marked Chatham.

André passed the coachman some coins.

A couple of porters took our trunks and showed us the way to the platform. The train was in ready and our trunks loaded. My brother and I stepped up to the *first-class* carriage where another couple of passengers were already sitting. One of the men smiled. His eyes sparkled. I smiled back and he doffed his top hat. André ushered me to the seat by the window.

The engine whistled before pulling out. We chugged past green fields and trees. After a while the locomotive pulled into a station and one of the gentlemen stood up. 'Good day to you, miss.' He smiled and stepped off the train.

Chapter 3

Tilly

It was still dark when I rolled out of bed, got dressed, and made my way downstairs to start the drawing room fire. I kneeled down on the stone hearth, pulled out the grate and emptied last night's ash into a tin bucket, creating clouds of dust, making me cough. I fanned the powder away.

Mrs Jarvis, the housekeeper, breezed in. 'Come along, young Tilly. We don't have all day. You've still got Mademoiselle Françoise's room to get ready.' She looked at her watch hung from her waist. 'Were you late in rising?'

'No, Mrs Jarvis.'

'Well hurry up, lass, and get that fire laid and then get yourself up to the new mademoiselle's room before breakfast. You'd best hurry because Cook needs you to help with the food for today's celebrations.' Mrs Jarvis tutted before shaking her head and leaving the room.

After finishing the dusting, I kneeled down at the grate. While scrunching up newspaper for the fire I daydreamed about my fellow, Archie. He was taking me to the servants' dance later this evening. I could hardly wait to marry him and be swept away from all this.

'Tilly, what are you doing? It's a good job it's me and not Mrs Jarvis. She sent me to see how you're doing and by the looks of it, not very well.' Cora got down by the hearth next to me and stacked the dry twigs around the newspaper. 'There.

Pass me something to clean this lot up.' She brushed loose mousy strands under her cap and got soot on her smooth round face. I tried not to giggle as I passed her the brush and shovel from the companion set.

Cora swept up the spilt ash and added it to the tin bucket. 'Now you get rid of that and I'll meet you upstairs in the new lady's room. And hurry, otherwise we'll miss out on breakfast.'

'Yes, Cora.' I picked up the bucket and made my way down the corridor and out into the yard. Who did she think she was bossing me about like that? Wait until my Archie took me away from here. That would show her. Frustrated old biddy, just because she didn't have a fellow. How old was she now? Twenty-three? She was going to be left on the shelf, that was for sure. No lad liked a woman with a sour tongue like hers.

*

'Come along you girls,' Cook said. 'You've nearly missed breakfast.'

Bacon and eggs crackled on the range. My stomach gurgled from the smell. What I'd give for a bacon butty but only Mr Hughes got one of them. The rest of us had to make do with the oats bubbling on the stove.

Cora and I sat down at opposite sides of the long wooden table and I chose the seat next to Archie. 'Morning Archie.' I fluttered my eyelashes.

Blond wisps hung slightly from behind his ears. 'Morning, treasure.' He kissed me on the cheek. His grey eyes glinted. He was so handsome.

'We shall have less of that, if you don't mind.' Mr Hughes, the butler, standing by the table, banged his fist down. 'This is a respectable household. Any more of that and you two can forget about the staff party tonight. And, Archie, aren't you supposed to be cleaning the silver?'

'Yes, Mr Hughes. Sorry, I'll go now.'

Cook passed Archie a muslin wrapped parcel. 'Take this with you, lad.'

'You spoil the boy.' Mr Hughes frowned.

I looked up at Archie as he left the room. He winked and blew me a kiss. I laughed under my breath.

Mr Hughes followed Archie out. I hoped Archie wasn't going to be in trouble.

'Here, get this down you.' Cook placed two bowls of steaming porridge on the table for me and Cora.

'Thanks, Cook.' I smiled. 'What do you think the French lady will look like?'

'Beautiful, I'm sure. Poor lass is only the same age as you.'

'What, seventeen?'

'So I'm led to understand. And having to come all the way from France. Imagine that?' Cook shook her head. 'Can't see it being easy for the lass being that far away from her ma.'

I'd have hated not seeing my ma and da, and my siblings too of course. It was hard enough only being allowed one Sunday afternoon a month but the thought of being all those miles away and in a different country. 'I heard it's an arranged marriage?'

'Aye, love, I think it is. Hurry up now and eat that porridge and come and start the washing up. We still have the food to prepare for this evening.'

Mr Hughes marched back into the kitchen. 'Stop this gossiping now. Cook, I'm surprised at you.'

'We were just saying that's all.' Cook flipped the bacon over in the frying pan. 'Got some bacon and eggs here for you, Mr Hughes.'

Mr Hughes rubbed his stomach. 'Thank you, Mrs Darby. Just what I need.' He sat down at the end of the table and picked up his knife and fork.

Cook set the plate of bacon and eggs down in front of him. I got up from the table, gathered up the dirty dishes and carried them over to the sink.

Chapter 4

Tilly

Elsie was taking in the sun as she stood outside rocking the perambulator. 'Are you ready?' she asked when I came down the steps.

'Aye.' I adjusted my straw hat. 'I can't wait to see what Mademoiselle Françoise is like. Cook says she's around my age.'

'Ugh. The baronet must be at least twenty-five.'

'I know. Are you enjoying your new position?' Elsie had been promoted from housemaid a couple of months ago to act as nanny for Catherine's baby girl. Catherine was the baronet's younger sister.

'I love it. Much better than getting down on my knees doing all that scrubbing.'

'I still don't know how you managed it?'

'They were desperate after Nanny left in a hurry and as I'd helped out as nursemaid, I was part trained so Lady Elizabeth's first choice. She's happy with my work so I think it will become permanent. It's strange having meals in my room though.'

'You're lucky. I could've done it. I've experience changing me siblings' napkins.'

'Can we change the subject please?'

'Do you think Bertha's dad will come back?'

Elsie shrugged her shoulders. 'No idea. I reckon it must have been too much for him after Miss Catherine dying. He never even looked at this sweet thing. I don't know how Lady Elizabeth coped so well but she adores this one.'

Cook and Mrs Jarvis joined us. 'I hope you two aren't gossiping.' Mrs Jarvis wagged her finger.

'No. We were just saying how excited we are. Weren't we, Elsie?'

'That's right.' Elsie rocked the perambulator to stop the baby crying.

I put my hand under the hood to stroke Bertha's face. 'Who's a lovely girl then?'

Mrs Jarvis slapped my hand away. 'Don't give the bairn your germs. Now come along otherwise we'll not get to the station in time.'

Bees buzzed over hawthorn hedgerow on either side of the dry mud footpath as we moseyed down. I sniffed. 'Don't you just love the smell?'

'It makes me sneeze.' Elsie put her hand over her nose.

'Can I push?' I asked.

'All right. But be careful.'

'I have pushed a perambulator before, you know.' I took over the handle and moved ahead to get away from Cook and Mrs Jarvis. 'I have a sweetheart,' I whispered to Elsie.

She put a hand over her mouth. 'Who?'

'Archie. But shh, it's a secret.'

'Archie? But he must be at least twenty-two.'

'So, what if he is? He's very handsome.'

'But, Tilly, you're only seventeen. What does your ma and pa say about it?'

'They don't know. No one knows except Daisy, and now you. Although Archie nearly let the cat out of the bag this morning when Mr Hughes caught him kissing me on the cheek. "None of that in this house if you don't mind." Archie moved out of the kitchen pretty sharpish, I can tell you.'

As we got closer to the station, red, blue and white banners hung across the road and a huge crowd waved flags.

'Oh no.' I turned around to Mrs Jarvis. 'We forgot to bring any bunting.'

'Don't worry. Mr Hughes has it in hand.'

'Good,' I said to Elsie, 'would've been awful if we couldn't have joined in with the crowd.'

Elsie turned up her nose. Feathery blonde hair stuck out from under her boater and her cheeks looked raw like she'd been scouring them. 'I think it's disgusting the baronet marrying her when he's so much older.'

'You think everything's disgusting.' She'd become so stuck up since her promotion. 'Have you got a sweetheart?'

'Not yet. Mr Right hasn't come along.'

'Archie's my Mr Right.'

'You haven't done anything with him, have you?'

'Not yet. But…' I knew I shouldn't be telling her but the words rolled off my tongue. If only Daisy were here but she had to finish off chores in the kitchen.

'What?'

'After the party, maybe.'

Don't, Tilly. You might end up with one of these.' Elsie signalled to the baby.

'My Archie says he won't let that happen and I trust him.'

Elsie glared at me but before she had a chance to say anything Mrs Jarvis came up close and put her hand on the handle of the perambulator. 'What are you girls gossiping about?'

'Nothing.' I grinned. 'We were just saying it's going to be fun dancing tonight. Will you dance at the party, Mrs Jarvis?'

'I might.'

'How about you, Cook?' I asked.

'Depends if I can find a young man to dance with. We'll need to push through this horde to get to the front. I wonder what Mademoiselle Françoise looks like. Poor sweet thing.'

Chapter 5

Françoise

'Faversham. This is our stop.' André took my hand and helped me off the train. A porter brought our trunks out of the station. André dipped his hand into his pocket and pulled out a coin and placed it in the porter's palm. The porter doffed his hat. 'Why thank you, sir.'

Masses of people bustled in top hats and boaters waving flags and calling out my name. Bunting in colours of the Union Jack shimmered in the summer sun. If only Maman and Papa could be here to see this. A grey-haired man dressed in a similar fashion to André with a long coat, vest, the same stiff collar and necklet, approached. He tipped his hat. 'Good afternoon, Mademoiselle and Monsieur Dubois. I am Mr Hughes the Dubois' butler and here to welcome you. Please.' He gestured to the English Landau.

'The baronet is not here himself?' André frowned.

'I'm afraid not, sir. Lady Elizabeth and the baronet are waiting for you at *Highwood Hall* ensuring everything is as it should be for the mademoiselle and yourself.'

I was disappointed Charles had not made the effort to meet me in person but hid my irritation with a smile to the people as I promenaded the red carpet to the carriage. Mr Hughes opened the Landau door and André helped me in. I raised my hand in a wave to the crowds forming a procession.

Our coachman pulled away and the horses galloped along until we came to Beckton where the road narrowed and the horses slowed their pace to a trot. Huge oaks and elms hung over the lane. As the horses jogged through the black iron gates of *Highwood Hall* a brass band played. Swags of pink blooms and yellow garlands draped across redwood greens. Crowds in hundreds waved *welcome* either side of the flowered arch but there was still no sign of the baronet.

'Are you all right, Françoise?' André took hold of my hand.

'I am nervous about meeting my intended but also confused. Why is he not here to greet me? All these people but not he.'

'It is certainly bad etiquette, my dear, but maybe what Mr Hughes said is correct. Perhaps he is getting things ready for you.'

The Landau stopped outside the mansion and the coachman disembarked. André stepped from the carriage first, went around my side, opened the door and helped me down. A cart had followed behind with our trunks. Two footmen rushed down the small flight of stone stairs from the house and relieved the boy of them.

A mature woman with good posture came down the steps. 'Mademoiselle Françoise.' She kissed me on the cheek and turned to my brother. 'Monsieur André.' She took his hand. 'Welcome to *Highwood Hall*. I'm Elizabeth. Please treat my home as your own.' Elizabeth was everything Maman was not. Tall, slim, elegant. The only thing similar was the silver-grey hair. Elizabeth's cobalt blue gown made my grey flannel dress look dreary.

Highwood Hall was a complete contrast to *Vue de Jardin* with its massive frontage, sand-coloured brickwork, and enormous columns that looked like they were holding the house in place.

We followed our host up the steps to a platform in front of the house.

'Please, sit down' – she pointed to the ivory wicker rockers – 'and allow our staff and villagers to welcome you properly.'

The band played *La Marseillaise*. I turned to André who smiled back at me. A maid brought out refreshments. I sipped the subtle tasting elderflower cordial and bit into a delicious piece of fruit cake. Both satisfying after our long journey.

A small child tottered up the steps and passed me a satin basket full of pinkish flowers. With a small curtsy, she said, 'Bienvenue, mademoiselle.'

'Merci. These are my favourite.' I sniffed the sweet peas inhaling their strong scent.

The girl turned to face André. 'Bienvenu, monsieur.'

'Merci.' He dipped into his pocket and handed her a coin. 'Here. This is for you. What is your name?'

'Hattie.' The child's eyes rounded as she held the penny. 'Why thank you, sir.'

Elizabeth nodded to Hattie to leave. The villagers and staff clapped as the child padded down the steps and back into the crowd as the butler came towards us.

'Mademoiselle and Monsieur Dubois, welcome to *Highwood Hall.*' Mr Hughes signalled with his hand for us to enter the house.

As we stood up, the crowd cheered. André and I waved before turning to step into *Highwood Hall.*

The mosaic tiled floor in the hallway gleamed. I ran my hand along the gold rimmed balustrades and looked up at the portraits hanging on the wall. I wondered who they all were.

'That one's Henri' – Elizabeth pointed – 'and this' – she pointed again – 'is Willeme. The Dubois brothers who made today possible.'

I acknowledged with a nod. *I wish they had not.* I could see a hint of André. The brothers looked identical, except one had a small dark mark on the side of his face. 'Papa said the brothers were twins.'

'They were indeed. It was quite a separation for Henri leaving Willeme behind. The brothers loved each other dearly – hence the oath. Henri kept a diary from the day he arrived here until just before he died. If you wish, you may read them. You'll find them in the library.' She turned to my brother. 'You too, Monsieur.'

'Merci.' He looked up at the two paintings. 'I think I would enjoy that.'

A woman with a round girth hurried towards us. 'Welcome, mademoiselle and monsieur.'

'This is our housekeeper'– Elizabeth gestured with her head – 'Mrs Jarvis. Anything you need she's the person. She keeps this house shipshape.'

'Thank you, madam. I do my best.'

'We know you do, Mrs Jarvis. Are Mademoiselle and Monsieur Dubois' rooms ready?'

'Yes, madam.' Mrs Jarvis raised her hand and two young girls shuffled towards us. 'Monsieur and Mademoiselle Dubois, this is Daisy and Tilly. They're very keen to meet you both.'

'Bonjour Monsieur and Mademoiselle.' The girls curtsied.

'They've been practising how to greet you all week.' Mrs Jarvis chuckled. 'Mademoiselle Françoise, Tilly will show you to your room, and a footman will be along shortly, Monsieur Dubois. I apologise for this delay.'

'No need to wait for the footman,' André said. 'I am perfectly happy for Daisy to show me if that is all right?'

'That's rather unorthodox,' Elizabeth said, 'but I don't see why not if Mrs Jarvis can spare Daisy.'

'Yes, of course, Lady Elizabeth. Girls, please show our guests to their rooms.'

'Mademoiselle,' Tilly said, 'this way, please.'

'If you'd like to follow me, Monsieur.' Daisy curtsied again.

Elizabeth smiled. 'I'll allow you to get settled but will see you shortly in the drawing room for tea.'

'Merci,' André answered.

We followed the maids upstairs. At the top Tilly turned right and Daisy left, taking André and me in opposite directions. I turned back to look at him. He mouthed, 'It will be all right.'

Tilly stopped along the corridor. 'This is your room, Mademoiselle Françoise.' She giggled. 'I've never spoken French before.'

I laughed with her. She seemed a nice girl, around my age, one that could be my friend if we were not maid and mistress.

'I'll turn back the bed for you.' She folded over the rich burgundy silk bedding.

I looked around the generous sized room and was drawn to the picture window with its velvet drapes matching the sheets. The view was beautiful. A massive lawn, but further in the distance a large lake I was impatient to explore. Maman was correct about it being grander here than home. I wondered when I would meet my intended. It was bad enough him not being at the station but unforgiveable that he was not at the house to greet us. Someone knocked on the door. I was disappointed when Tilly opened it to see two footmen. 'We have your trunk, mademoiselle.'

'Merci. Do please bring it in.' I turned back to glance out of the window until the door creaked shut letting me know they had gone.

'Shall I unpack, mademoiselle?'

'Merci.'

Tilly lifted the heavy lid of my chest and in silence took out several chemises, nightdresses, drawers, petticoats, camisoles and vests. She pulled out a silk scarlet dress and held it up. 'This is beautiful.'

'Merci. I am pleased you like it.' All of my attire was new, designed specifically for the trip to England.

One by one Tilly unpacked and hung my dresses in the wardrobe until she came to the wedding gown. 'Mademoiselle, this is wonderful.' She held up the white taffeta garment. 'You're going to be such a lovely bride.' She bit her lip. 'But…'

'What?'

'It needs something else. Would you allow me to add some little silk roses? Me mam always said I've a way with needle and thread.'

'Why, that would be lovely. Merci.'

Tilly grinned. 'We servants can't wait for the wedding.' She placed the gown on a hanger and hung it in the wardrobe along with the rest. 'The master's invited everyone and he's even put on a party afterwards especially for us.'

'That is kind of him. Is he a good employer?'

'Oh yes. Very much so. He's laid on a dance this evening for us servants with musicians. I love it at *Highwood Hall*.'

'How long have you been here, Tilly?'

'Hmm let me see. I'm seventeen. I was fourteen when I first arrived, so, three years. Lady Elizabeth even arranged for me to learn to read.'

After a tap on the door, the housekeeper entered. 'Excuse me, mademoiselle' – she turned to Tilly – 'what's keeping you, young lady?' – and then back to me – 'I hope she's not being too familiar, mademoiselle?'

'It is fine,' I answered, 'I am enjoying finding out about things.'

'She's a chatterbox for sure. I apologise. Get on with your job, Tilly.' Mrs Jarvis turned back to me. 'Tea has been served in the drawing room. Your brother's in there already.' Mrs Jarvis left the room leaving the door open.

Tilly giggled. 'Sorry, mademoiselle. I do get carried away. Me mam was always telling me off about that.'

'It is quite all right. Tell me, Tilly, do you miss your maman?'

'I did at first, but not so much now. Is this your first time away from home?'

'Oui.'

'Oui?'

'Oui means yes.'

'Ah. So now I've learnt more French.' Tilly giggled again. 'I'll come back here later and finish off. I should show you where to go for tea otherwise the old dragon will be after me. Oops.' She put her hand to her mouth.

I laughed again with her.

We meandered downstairs and along the hallway until she stopped at an open door. I heard voices, including André's.

As I strode into the brightly lit room, sun shone through the tall windows running across the far wall, reminding me of Maman and Papa's chambre. André was lighting up a cigar. He gave a small cough, unlike Papa's splutter, before placing the lighter down on a mahogany occasional table. 'Where is the baronet?' he asked Elizabeth.

'He'll be along shortly.' She turned to the clock, stood up and pulled on a lever, before noticing me. 'Mademoiselle Françoise. Good afternoon.'

'Bonjour, madame.'

André was at my side. 'Françoise, how is your room?'

'It has a beautiful view, mon frère, you must come and see.'

A maid I did not recognise hurried into the room over to Elizabeth. 'Yes, madam?'

'Cora, have you seen the baronet?'

'I believe he's on his way down.'

'Excellent. Please can you bring us some fresh tea? This has gone cold.'

'Certainly, madam.' The maid glanced in my direction and smiled before moving swiftly out of the room again.

Heavy footsteps drew me to the doorway. A young man with gleaming black hair in a side parting strolled in. I could see no resemblance to Henri and Willeme.

'Ah, finally. Charles, this is Mademoiselle Françoise and Monsieur André. Françoise, André, this is my son.'

'How do you do, monsieur?' I offered a slight curtsy. My heart beat fast. Maybe marriage to him would not be so bad after all. His build was similar to André's and grey-flecked trousers matching the waistcoat enhanced his slim physique.

'The pleasure is all mine, mademoiselle.' His near black eyes, like rich soil, sparkled. 'Please forgive me for my lateness.' He lifted my hand and brushed his lips against it.' His moustache tickled me. I was spellbound.

Daisy and Tilly entered with sandwiches, scones and cakes.

Elizabeth sighed. 'Finally, we can begin tea. These two people must be ravenous following their long journey. Will you pour, please, Tilly?'

'Yes, madam.' Tilly curtsied.

Although hungry my appetite had gone as butterflies consumed my stomach.

Chapter 6

Tilly

Couples linked arms and promenaded around the barn to the fiddlers' tune. I danced with Edward, the new footman, along with other men servants from the local houses. Edward was nice enough but he wasn't masculine like my Archie. Instead, his mousy hair framed a baby face emphasising buck teeth.

Archie had spent the whole evening dancing with other girls. On one occasion he winked at me but didn't come over. I felt sick. Daisy put her arms around me and told me to forget him as he wasn't worth it. My heart was breaking.

The musicians stopped playing to mark the end of the evening and Daisy and I left the barn. As we were ambling across the meadow back up to the Hall a hand touched my shoulder making me jolt.

'Hey, treasure. How come you didn't wait for me?'

'Come on.' Daisy pulled me along.

'What? So, you're not even going to speak to me then?'

I turned around. 'Tell me why I should when you ignored me all night?'

'I was trying to protect you. You know damn well we're not allowed relationships in the household. And Mr Hughes was already on to me.'

'He's right,' I said to Daisy. 'Give me a few minutes.'

'Are you sure? He could have had at least one dance with you. I'll wait.'

'No need,' Archie said, 'I'll walk her back.'

Daisy looked at me, eyebrows raised.

'I'll be all right.'

She shrugged her shoulders and sloped back up towards the house shaking her head.

'Now, treasure.' Archie took me in his arms. His lips pressed mine making my heart beat faster. 'Let's go somewhere quiet.'

'I'm not sure.'

'Don't be like that. I told you why I couldn't dance with you.' He grabbed my arm, pulling me back in the direction of the barn and further on until we came to another outbuilding where he steered me against the outside wall.

*

Daisy was tucked up in bed when I burst into the room.

She sat up quickly. 'What's happened?'

I sat on her bed, buried my face into her chest, and sobbed.

'Look at the state of you.'

I shook my head, still howling.

'Did he do this?'

I nodded.

'The sodding ratbag.'

'I kept telling him I didn't want to but he said I'd promised and wouldn't take *no* for an answer. Oh Daisy.'

She stroked my hair. 'You need to report him to the mistress.'

'I can't.'

'You can and you must.'

'I can't. It was me own fault. I'd promised him.'

'But you changed your mind.'

'That won't matter. I'll get the sack.' I rubbed down below. 'I'm so sore. I didn't know it was going to be like that.' I sobbed again.

'It shouldn't have been like that.'

'I've cramps in me belly so must be with child. What am I going to do? Me dad won't let me back home and I'll not be allowed to stay here. I'll end up in the workhouse.' I sniffled.

'Shh now. It's too soon to know that, and if you are then he'll have to wed you.'

'But what if he won't?'

'Don't think about that now. Get undressed. Come in my bed tonight. I'll look after you.'

I blew out the candle and threw my clothes into a pile on the floor. I never wanted to wear them again. I'd been so proud of my new linen blue skirt and white seersucker blouse that I'd made but now they were soiled. I threw my flannel nightdress over my head, climbed under the blankets and curled up next to Daisy.

My belly ached and I stung like I was on fire. *How could I have been so stupid?* After my tears were spent I lay in the dark going over and over what had happened. My heart beat faster as I recollected him ignoring my screams. Had it been my fault? I felt sick and dirty.

Chapter 7

Françoise

I walked into the noisy drawing room to find two young women laughing and chatting with Elizabeth. She had mentioned earlier how some of the local young ladies would be dropping around for afternoon tea. 'It will be a chance for you to meet some company of your own age.'

'Ah, Mademoiselle Françoise' – Elizabeth patted the mulberry velvet cushioning on the chaise longue – 'come and sit down next to me, dear.'

'Thank you, Lady Elizabeth.' I adjusted my gown before seating.

'Call me, Maman, please. I want you to feel at home. Now I'd like you to meet the Alcott sisters. This is Miss Grace' – she gestured to her right – 'and Miss Rebecca.' Elizabeth smiled at the girl next to Grace who looked a similar age to me. They did not look like sisters. Grace had dark brown hair and blue eyes but Rebecca's hair was like copper and gleamed. When she smiled her huge forest-green eyes shone. 'How do you do?' I said in perfectly spoken English. Papa had ensured that André and I were bilingual from a young age.

'You must be so excited, Miss Françoise?' Grace said. 'I can't wait to be wed.'

Elizabeth stood up. 'On that cue it's time for my departure. I'll leave you young ladies to talk freely. Cora will be in shortly with afternoon tea. Françoise' – Elizabeth rested her fingers on my arm – 'have a good time, my dear.'

'Thank you, Maman.'

No sooner had Elizabeth left the room when Rebecca asked me, 'How does it feel to be betrothed?' She clapped her hands. 'Do tell, please.'

'Terrifying, if I am truthful. Are you ladies married?'

Rebecca giggled. 'Goodness no. Our elder sister, Emily, will be first. She's twenty-three. Father keeps telling her she'll end up on the shelf if she doesn't find a husband soon. And then' – she tapped her sister's hand – 'it'll be Grace's turn.'

Rebecca would have no difficulty in finding a husband, I was sure. She was enchanting. 'Quel âge a t'elle, sorry, I mean, how old are you, both?'

'I'm twenty' – Grace fiddled with her fingers – 'and Rebecca's almost seventeen. You're lucky to be marrying Baronet Charles. He's so handsome.' Grace chuckled. 'I'd love to wed someone like him. Mother had hoped Emily and Charles would tie the knot but don't worry, we won't hold that against you. I hope we can be friends.' Grace gripped my hand.

'I hope so too.' I smiled.

Cora carried a tray of refreshments into the room. She placed the teapot and crockery down on the long occasional table.

'I will pour, Cora. That is your name, is it not?'

'Yes, mademoiselle.' Cora set the cake stand down next to the teapot and gave a little curtsy. 'Enjoy, mademoiselle.' She smiled at my guests.

I poured the tea into the floral-patterned china cups and passed them in turn to Grace and Rebecca. 'Do help yourselves to sandwiches.'

We nibbled wholewheat salad filled breads followed by freshly baked scones with jam and strawberries.

'What's your brother like? André, isn't it?' Rebecca's eyes widened.

'He is adorable and will make a wonderful husband.' I sipped my tea.

'I do hope we get to meet him.' Grace patted the white napkin across her mouth.

'I am sure that can be arranged.' I passed the bowl of fruit to my guests.

Grace waved the dish away. 'No thank you.'

'I've eaten more than enough.' Rebecca twisted round to the pianoforte. 'Do you play, Françoise?'

'Oui. I do. Do you?'

'Yes. We both do. I know, let's have a concert.' Rebecca beamed.

'That would be wonderful,' I said, 'but you go first.'

Rebecca stood up, ventured over to the instrument, sat down on the stool, stretched her back, held her hands in position over the keys and began to play.

After her final note, I said, 'Fantasia in D Minor. I adore Mozart.'

'Your turn,' the girls echoed.

'Very well.' I took to the tabouret. 'I hope you do not mind a little more Mozart.'

'Definitely not,' Grace answered, 'he's our favourite composer too.'

I closed my eyes before hitting the notes for *Sonata in C*.

As I finished the girls clapped so hard that it brought Charles into the room. 'Sorry to disturb you ladies but I just had to find out who was playing that delightful piece.'

'It was your lovely fiancée.' Grace clasped her fingers.

'I had no idea you played, Mademoiselle Françoise. Mother never said.'

'I have been playing since I was old enough to sit on the stool. It is a pleasure to discover this beautiful instrument but I do not recognise its shape. What is it called?'

'A Steinway grand. Please, you must play each day. It was Catherine's. I'm sure she'd have been happy that it's being used.' Charles moved towards me and kissed the back of my hand. 'I'll leave you ladies to continue. Until later, Mademoiselle Françoise. Miss Grace' – he nodded – 'and Miss Rebecca.'

As he left the room the girls giggled. 'Oh Françoise, you're so lucky to have a man who adores you so much.'

I smiled. 'Who is Catherine?'

Rebecca lowered her head. Grace stared at me. 'Has no one told you?'

'Told me what?'

She coughed. 'Catherine was Sir Charles's younger sister.'

'Was?'

'Yes, she died.'

'Oh. I wonder why no one has mentioned her. What happened?'

Grace looked up at the clock. 'It's time we were leaving, sister. We must not overstay our welcome.'

'No, we must not. Would it be all right if we visited you again, Mademoiselle Françoise?'

'Oui. Yes, please do.' I wondered what the mystery was behind Catherine's death but did not pursue it.

'I know,' Rebecca said, 'why don't we go for a picnic on Sunday? Bring Sir Charles and your brother. It is a shame we did not meet him today.'

'That sounds delightful,' I said.

'The men will be playing cricket down by the river. Don't you just adore watching them?' Rebecca continued.

'I do not know. I have never seen this game cricket.'

'Then we must do that' – Rebecca kissed my cheek – 'I'll arrange for our cook to make up a huge hamper. You don't need to worry about anything.'

'Until Sunday.' Grace brushed her lips against the side of my face.

'I will see you out.'

Elizabeth entered the room. 'I thought I heard you young ladies leaving.' She took my arm to gently pull me away from the door. 'I'll call Cora to escort you ladies out.' Elizabeth pulled a lever on the wall and Cora arrived in seconds.

Chapter 8

Tilly

I lay in bed wishing my monthly would hurry up and come. It had been four weeks since that awful night when Archie had done that thing to me.

'Tilly. Why are you crying?' Daisy leaned over and stroked my face.

'I keep thinking about that night. What am I going to do if I'm you know? And how am I ever going to avoid him once he gets back?' The master had sent Archie out of town to learn valet duties so he could replace old Joe, the existing valet, who was in poor health.

'He needs stringing up.' Daisy's face reddened. 'You should tell the mistress and he'll get the sack.'

'I can't. I told you. What will she think of me?'

'Just tell her before he does the same thing to someone else.'

'You should get yourself downstairs otherwise Cook's going to be after you.'

'You're right. Try not to worry and speak to Mademoiselle Françoise.'

After Daisy left, I rolled out of bed, pulled on my black tunic and piled my hair into a bun. As I tied my white apron around my flat stomach, I prayed it would stay that way. Daisy's voice echoed in my ear. *Try not to worry*. She was right. Mam always said if you worry it stops your visitor from coming. I tucked loose strands of reddish blonde hair under my mop hat and made my way to the kitchen.

'Good morning, young lady,' Cook said, 'what's with the long face?'

I shrugged my shoulders.

'Now that's hardly ladylike, is it? You'd best put a smile on that face before going upstairs.' Cook plonked a bowl of porridge in front of me. 'Get that down and then take the tray up to the mademoiselle. Daisy's getting it ready.' She turned to Daisy. 'Hurry up, lass. The mademoiselle will die of starvation if that's your fastest speed.'

Cook was harsh this morning. What had Daisy done to deserve that? And what had I done to be treated like a trollop by Archie? I spooned the lumpy porridge into my mouth forcing myself to eat something and drank down a cup of weak tea.

'Are you done here?' Cook asked me. 'If so, grab the tray and get yourself along to your duties.'

'Yes, Cook.'

Daisy looked at me. We rolled our eyes in turn.

'I saw that.' Cook slapped my hand. 'I shall be speaking to Mrs Jarvis about you pair if you don't pull your socks up.'

'Sorry, Cook,' we said in unison.

I grabbed the tray and made my way upstairs to Françoise's room. Although I'd been promoted to lady's maid, Mrs Jarvis had made it quite clear that I was still to help Daisy in the kitchen and house as required. I loved being Françoise's attendant and it had wiped that smirk off Elsie's face.

I was sauntering along the corridor when Archie came out from nowhere and grabbed me around my waist. He was back. I felt faint. He wasn't due back for at least another two days.

'Hello, treasure.' He smirked. 'Have you missed me? We'll catch up later.' He winked before marching off in the opposite direction and downstairs. Now that he was the master's valet it was going to be harder to avoid him when working on the same floor.

On reaching the mademoiselle's room, I knocked before entering. 'Good morning, mademoiselle.' My legs shook as I opened the door. 'Would you like me to draw the drapes?'

'Oui, Tilly, merci.' Françoise sat up in bed and I set the tray down in front of her before moving over to the window and pulling across the heavy velvet curtains. 'Would you like me to come back after you've eaten or is there something you'd like me to get ready?'

'Come back in half an hour. I am sure Mrs Jarvis has some errands she would like you to help with.'

*

I trudged over to the hen house to collect some eggs when someone seized me. I tried to scream but a hand was over my mouth. 'Shh, treasure, it's only me.' Archie pulled me around the side of the barn. 'I've missed you.' He was everywhere. How could I continue to work here?

'Well, I've not missed you. Leave me alone.'

'Don't be like that. You're my girl, you know that.' He put his hand on my breast.

'Get off me.'

'It'll be better next time.'

'There'll not be a next time. You treated me like a slut. You're an animal.'

He stroked my cheek. 'Don't say that. You know I love you and I was only trying to make it easier for you. Better to be quick and get it over with, you know, for your first time.'

'You hurt me and made me feel cheap. And suppose I'm with child?'

'You'll not be. Tonight then?' He started kissing me.

39

I slapped his face. 'Leave me alone.'

'Come on, my Tilly. Don't be angry with me.'

*

Mademoiselle Françoise was sitting at her dressing table brushing her hair when I arrived back upstairs.

'Sorry, mademoiselle, Mrs Jarvis sent me to fetch the eggs.'

'It is not a problem. Can you help me with my hair?'

I took the hairbrush from my lady and tried to steady my hand as I brushed her long dark hair and piled it up into a French knot like Anna, Lady Elizabeth's attendant, had shown me.

'Tilly, are you all right?' Françoise asked me. 'You appear upset.'

'Sorry, mademoiselle. Mrs Jarvis reprimanded me for taking too long fetching the eggs. It was my own fault. I shouldn't have messed around.' I moved to the wardrobe and selected an azure-blue gown. 'Will this do, mademoiselle?'

'Parfait.'

I frowned. 'Sorry, mademoiselle, I don't understand.'

'It means perfect.'

*

I charged into the kitchen and sat down next to Daisy at the refectory table.

'What's up?' Daisy picked up her spoon and sipped the pea soup.

'I've been trying to take your advice and not worry but…'

Archie and Edward paced into the kitchen. Archie winked at me when he thought no one was looking. Daisy squeezed my hand. 'He's back then? Just ignore him.'

'You chaps are late. Did you get caught up?' Cook asked.

'Yes' – Archie scraped the stool and flopped down opposite – 'the master needed me.'

'And I was called away to do an errand,' Edward said. 'I've only just got back from the blacksmiths. We're not too late, are we?'

'You're lucky that I kept some heated on the stove.' Cook got up, moved over to the pan, ladled a portion each into two dishes, and placed them down in front of the boys. She sliced a couple of thick chunks of bread. 'Here, you growing lads need to keep stocked up with energy.' The kitchen was loud with chatter as they all slurped their hot soup, dipping in bread, but I felt sick and struggled to eat mine.

Mrs Jarvis turned to me. 'Tilly, you're to help Daisy this afternoon. The drapes are to be taken down from the dining room and cleaned. You can work out the polishing and sweeping between you but Lady Elizabeth wants the room spotless. She's entertaining this evening.'

'Yes, Mrs Jarvis,' I said.

'After you've finished that you're both to help Cook in the kitchen as there's a lot of preparation required for this evening's meal. However' – the housekeeper wagged her finger at me – 'you must make sure you're back up with your mistress in time to help her get changed.'

'Yes, Mrs Jarvis,' I said again.

'Off you go then.'

Daisy and I picked up our dirty dishes and took them over to the sink.

'Leave them there' – Cook ushered us away – 'I'll sort that. You girls get a move on with the cleaning.'

Daisy and I rushed into the scullery to collect buckets, brooms and dusters. We trekked upstairs and along the corridor towards the drawing room. I was pleased we'd been asked to do the cleaning together as it was less likely I'd encounter Archie on my own again.

'I'll sweep and you polish.' Daisy swept the broom across the parquet floor.

'Let's get the drapes down first, otherwise they'll make more dust after we've cleaned.'

'Good thinking, Tilly. What was it you started to say earlier?'

I climbed up on the stepladder to undo the curtains. 'Shut the door first in case anyone hears.'

Daisy ran over to the doorway and closed the door. 'Go on then.'

'I was going to say he was back and…'

'Please tell me you've not let that ratbag near you again.'

'No. No, of course not, I…'

'What?' She caught the first drape in her hands.

I stepped down the ladder. 'He collared me when I went for the eggs and pushed me around the side of the barn. And when he started putting his grubby paws over me, I gave him what for I can tell you.'

'Good. Good. Thank goodness for that.'

'But…' I carried the stepladder to the other side of the window. 'He said that he'd behaved that way to be kind.'

'Kind. What?'

'He said it would hurt me less if he was quick.'

'From what you told me Tilly … he was nothing more than an animal.'

'Yes. You're right and that's what I told him.'

'Good for you.' Daisy beamed.

'But...'

'What?'

'He said next time would be better. I told him there wouldn't be a next time but…' I raised my shoulders. 'What if he forces himself on me again?'

Chapter 9

Françoise

André and I hurried down the hallway to the open front door.

Cook rushed behind us. 'Monsieur André.'

'Bonjour, Madame Darby.' André tipped his hat.

'Would you mind popping the picnic hamper into the carriage please as Edward's disappeared?'

'It will be my pleasure.' André took the wicker basket. 'Goodness, what have you got in here. It feels a weight.'

'Plenty of food to keep you all going and some bottles of my lemonade to quench you in the sun.' Cook rubbed her hands.

André licked his lips. 'I cannot wait.'

I followed André down the steps where Charles was waiting outside the Landau.

'Good morning, Mademoiselle Françoise.' Charles kissed my hand. 'Mother's inside.' He held the carriage door open and I slid in next to Elizabeth. Charles followed and sat opposite while André passed the hamper to the coachman before joining us. Arrangements had been made to meet Grace and Rebecca down at the river along with their elder sister, Emily, and Madam Alcott. Madam Alcott and Elizabeth were to act as chaperones.

The horses trotted along the dry mud path and I took in the scent of blackthorn and hawthorn blossom. My wedding was to be in August and now acquainted with Charles I was less anxious. As Grace and Rebecca kept mentioning, he was such a handsome man, and those big near-black eyes twinkled whenever he smiled at me. It was sad that Papa and Maman would not be here to see me walk down the aisle but I had my marvellous brother André. I hoped I would convince him to stay in England with me forever as I could not bear to be parted from him. The horses drew to a halt along the river where clusters of people were seated on the grass with picnics, and a group of men dressed in white were batting a ball and running up and down.

'Mademoiselle Françoise' – Grace and Rebecca ran towards me – 'you must come and meet Mother and Emily.' Rebecca took my hand. I looked back at Charles, Elizabeth and André, who signalled for me to go on.

I let Rebecca lead me. 'Bonjour, Madam Alcott,' I said on reaching her, 'begging your pardon I mean good afternoon.'

'That is all right, sweet girl,' Madam Alcott answered, 'I'm hoping you may teach my daughters some French.'

'I would be delighted.' I twisted to the river view. 'This is delightful. An idyllic picnic venue.'

'We knew you'd like it,' Rebecca said. Out of the three sisters, she was my favourite and I hoped we would become best friends. Elizabeth had been more than accommodating in ensuring I had friends of my own age and felt at home. I would write to Maman this evening and put her mind at rest. It had broke my heart when I left, but as she had said, 'there was no other way.' Would I do that to my child? I put my hand to my stomach imagining a baby inside.

'What is it, Mademoiselle Françoise?' Rebecca waved a hand in front of my face. 'Are you in pain?'

'Non, pourquoi?'

Rebecca frowned.

'I am sorry. It means why.'

Rebecca chuckled. 'You were holding your stomach.'

I laughed and whispered, 'I was imagining I were with child.'

She joined in the laughter too.

'What are you girls giggling at?' Madam Alcott asked.

'Nothing,' we said in unison as André, Charles and Elizabeth joined us.

André spread out a red and white checked sheet on the ground next to the Alcott's and Charles unpacked the hamper.

'You needn't have worried about bringing food, Sir Charles' – Grace fluttered her lashes – 'we have sufficient for us all.'

'Ah but we have brought Mrs Darby's lemonade.' Charles grinned, his dark eyes glinting.

Rebecca and I curled up on the grass next to Grace and Emily while Elizabeth and Madam Alcott stretched back in olive-green folding chairs. I wondered how old they both were. Madam Alcott seemed the senior and resembled Maman with her round girth and plump face.

After introductions were made to André, Madam Alcott said, 'Monsieur, allow me to introduce you to my daughter, Miss Emily Alcott.'

'How do you do, sir?' Emily smiled. Blonde ringlets peeked from her straw boater. With her thin face and pointed chin, unlike either of her sisters, she looked more mature than twenty-three.

Charles handed out a tin beaker of lemonade to me and an alcoholic beverage to Elizabeth and Madam Alcott.

'Mrs Darby's lemonade is my favourite.' Rebecca beamed.

'We have plenty to go around.' André winked.

Rebecca blushed like a ripe strawberry. Charles handed her a cup of lemonade and another to Grace while Elizabeth and Madam Alcott sipped brandy. Rebecca kept glancing at André and turning back to me red-faced and giggling. I thought it would be perfect if they were to fall in love and marry. My new best friend and my brother but it seemed Madam Alcott had designs on André as a good match for Emily.

Charles passed André a bottle of Cook's lemonade. 'Do you play?' He signalled to the men hitting a ball.

'Non, I have never played. And you?'

'I would normally but I don't have my whites with me today. To be truthful I felt it would be inappropriate to disappear on Mademoiselle Françoise's first social outing.'

'See that one there' – Rebecca pointed – 'that's our brother, Arthur.'

'The one with the fiery hair like yours?' I answered.

'Yes, that's him.' She touched a ringlet hanging from her bonnet. 'I hate this colour.'

'But it is beautiful. I have never encountered such enchanting hair.' I smiled.

Rebecca blushed again. 'I'm so glad we're friends.'

The sun was getting stronger so I put up the matching parasol to my deep purple gown and hat.

'Arthur will be over in a minute' – Madam Alcott fanned her face – 'looking for sustenance.' And no sooner had she said the words when Arthur sprinted over.

'Good afternoon, everyone.' He gazed at me. 'And this must be the infamous Mademoiselle Françoise my sisters have not stopped talking about.' He took my hand to his lips. 'They did not misjudge your beauty, mademoiselle.'

'Arthur.' Grace slapped his hand. 'Don't forget she's betrothed.'

'Ah yes. Please forgive me, mademoiselle.'

I was sure I was blushing like Rebecca had earlier so hid my face behind the parasol.

Chapter 10

Tilly

I dipped my elbow into the water to check the temperature before adding the folding bird-painted screen for Françoise's privacy. She was lovely to attend to, always had a smile for me and had made my last three months working as her lady's maid a pleasure. I removed her dressing gown, held a towel against her, and turned away.

'Merci.' Françoise took my hand to steady herself as she stepped into the bath making the water splash.

Once she was decent under the water, I asked, 'Would you like me to wash your back, mademoiselle?'

'Oui, merci. Why not call me Françoise when we are alone?'

'Thank you, mademoiselle, but I couldn't.' I dipped the sponge into the warm water and brushed it up and down against her back. 'You've such silky skin.' The words were out before I could stop them. 'I'm so sorry, mademoiselle. Please forgive me.'

'Do not worry, Tilly. I like it that you and I can be friends.'

I did too but that would change after today when she married the baronet and became Lady Françoise. The master would never allow me to be so familiar with his wife.

'Are you ready to come out now?' I asked.

'I think I had better. Tell me, how do you find Sir Charles?'

I placed a white towel around her and dabbed her soft skin. 'Like I've told you afore, he's a kind man and fair employer.' I wrapped the corset around Françoise and strapped the ribbons at the back. 'The master's a lucky man. To think in a few hours, you'll be mistress of the house.'

Françoise didn't answer but moved over to her dressing table and took a seat on the burgundy velvet covered stool. I combed her long thick hair and piled it up on top, leaving dark brown ringlets caressing her flushed cheeks.

'And now your dress.'

Françoise stood up away from the stool. I held the exquisite bridal gown in place as she stepped into it. Its silk-like fabric flowed to the ground. The bodice enhanced her slim waist and small bosom. I wished it were me getting wed today with Archie. And I wished he had cherished me the way the master adored my mistress. At least my monthly had arrived so my flat stomach and respectability were intact. The mademoiselle looked captivating. High cheek bones accentuated her beauty.

'You're a beautiful bride, mademoiselle. The master will be entranced. Have you a special choker you'd like to wear or should I choose one?'

'Indeed, I do' – Françoise pointed – 'in there.'

I reached into the drawer and lifted out a diamond necklace from the black jewellery case and gasped. 'This is beautiful.' I fixed it around her slender neck.

'The baronet bought it for me.' Her whole face radiated. She was obviously very much in love with him. 'It is my something new.'

'Do you have something old?'

'Mais oui. In that velvet pouch you will find a brooch. Please could you pin it on me?'

'Certainly, mademoiselle.' I picked up the silver-leaf pin and fastened it to the left-hand side of her gown. 'It's really pretty.'

'It was my grandmother's.'

'I looked around. 'What about your something borrowed?'

'Oh dear. I do not appear to have anything.'

'I can sort that. You must have something borrowed. Allow me a few minutes.' I hurried from the room leaving Françoise staring into the glass.

*

I rushed down the corridor back into the mademoiselle's room.

She turned around quickly? 'Did you manage to get something?'

I smiled and held out my hand. 'It belongs to Lady Elizabeth. I was on my way to see the mistress when I bumped into Anna who was coming to find me. Lady Elizabeth had realised you were unlikely to have something borrowed so sent this. I fastened the gold bangle around her tiny wrist. 'And look, it has a design matching your grandmother's brooch.' I grinned.

'Merci.' Françoise traced the leaf engraved design on the bracelet. 'And I have this' – she waved a small white handkerchief with a blue motif – 'something blue.'

'Just your veil now, mademoiselle.' I attached the long silk tulle veil to a small wreath of orange blossom and pinned it to her hair. She looked gorgeous. 'Your slippers.' I took one foot at a time and slipped her slim ankles into the white small-heeled shoes.

'I almost forgot,' Françoise said, 'the sixpence from Lady Elizabeth.'

Taking the silk purse from the drawer, I held it up. 'In here?'

'Oui. The sixpence must go under my foot. A strange custom you English people have.'

'Me mam says it's lucky.' I removed Françoise's left shoe, added the sixpence inside and re-inserted her delicate foot.

Françoise stood up, smoothed down the back of her gown and moved to the gilded framed full-length mirror. She fingered the silk roses bordering her neckline that I'd added. 'These are

49

parfait. Your maman was right about your skill with needle and thread.'

'You look like a princess, mademoiselle.' In a few hours she'd be a woman, the same way as me, but I hoped her first time would be better than mine.

Chapter 11

Françoise

I stared into the mirror. The full skirt in crisp smooth fabric flowed to the floor. I placed my hand on my stomach and wondered how long before my small waist disappeared once a baby started to grow inside me. How I wished Maman were here to tell me that tonight would be parfait.

'Tilly…'

'Yes, mademoiselle.'

'Nothing.' There was no way I could discuss that sort of thing with my maid yet I nearly had. What would Elizabeth say? It would be Tilly that would bear the punishment, not me; no doubt she would lose her job. Tilly adjusted the sleeves on the gown to puff them up just like Marie had that day at home. Dark curls brushed my forehead. Butterflies danced in my stomach. What would tonight be like receiving Charles' seed?

'Are you ready for your gloves, mademoiselle?'

'Oui. I am ready.'

'You must turn away from the glass as it's unlucky to see your reflection once these are added.'

I laughed before moving from the mirror as instructed and Tilly inserted my fingers into the soft white gloves.

*

Slowly I walked down the winding stairway. Tilly held my train to prevent me from tripping. André was standing at the bottom in a tailored jacket sitting snugly to his waist and grey striped cashmere trousers. A white brocade shirt and vest matched his pocket square. His top hat made him appear at least six inches taller.

'Ma belle sœur. Is it really you?' He took my gloved hand in his.

'You look très handsome, mon frère.' I inhaled the scent from the stephanotis sprig pinned to his left lapel above the pocket square.

'Your flowers, mademoiselle.' Tilly passed me a mixed spray of yellow roses, orchids and orange blossoms. I lifted the bouquet to my nose. 'Very pleasing.'

'Come, my dear.' André took my arm and led me outside, his patent leather boots squeaking.

As we reached the Victoria, crowds cheered and clapped. I was drawn to the grey horse, like Geneviève's, which made me think about her. I wondered whether I would ever see my best friend again. I had Rebecca now but Geneviève and I had been friends since kindergarten.

André lifted my train and took my bouquet as I stepped into the carriage. Once my veil was tucked in safely, he passed me back the flowers and the driver closed the door. André hurried around to the other side and climbed in beside me. My hand shook as I waved to the people. The driver flicked the reins and the horse slow trotted. A warm breeze touched my face.

André squeezed my fingers. 'Everything is going to be all right. Charles is a lucky man.'

'I just wish Maman and Papa were here.'

André took my hand to his lips. 'I am sure they are thinking about you right now. They would have liked to have been here too but you know that was not possible, ma sœur.'

'I understand.'

We drove in silence for a small distance with André and I offering small waves to the spectators standing along the lane.

I could not stop wondering what tonight would be like. Would it hurt? Would Charles find me attractive? Would I know what to do? Tilly had mentioned in passing that the baronet would keep his own room. This had come as a shock as Maman and Papa always shared the one chambre.

André clasped my hand. 'Are you all right?'

My heart raced. *Was I all right?* I was anything but all right. I wanted to be back home in our quaint house in France tending the plants in the garden or with my friend embroidering pillows.

André took out his handkerchief as we reached St John's Church, lifted my veil, and patted my eyes. 'Ma sœur. All will be well.'

My legs felt like they may collapse as André and I promenaded down the red carpet leading to the vestibule where the bridesmaids waited. Rebecca, Grace and Emily were in almost identical white dresses except they each had a different coloured sash, yellow, pink and orange, matching my flowers, around their waist. Yellow roses had been added in their piled-up hair and they each carried posies, similar to mine except smaller.

Two little identical boys peeped from behind Emily's skirt. These must be the Alcott twins. I had never encountered them before as they were always hidden away with their nanny. My baby would not have a nanny. Papa had said that my child would keep me busy.

'Hello,' I said in a soft voice to the brothers, both dressed the same in dainty light-grey velvet suits trimmed with white wide collars, but they quickly retreated behind their big sister. When they thought I was not looking they peeped in turn. Short blond fringes emphasised their cerulean blue eyes. I shivered at their uncanny likeness.

'Good afternoon, ladies' – André took off his hat and left it on the windowsill – 'little gentleman. Are you ready?'

The girls giggled and Emily flickered her eyelashes at my brother before turning to the children. 'Now you know what to do. You must hold Miss Françoise's train. Like this.' She placed the edge of my veil in each of their hands. 'Understand?'

They both nodded and I wondered if they could talk as they had not uttered a word.

André took my arm and led me down the geometric-patterned shiny aisle. The twins held my train and the Alcott sisters followed behind. The church was huge, almost like a cathedral. Arches along either side of the walls had picture scenes, and above the altar, stained glass windows. Organ pipes filled the area as the organist played Wagner's Bridal Chorus. I looked around for faces, recognising Tilly at the back. Rebecca's words echoed in my ears. 'Remember, look straight ahead.' We moved closer until we came to Elizabeth on the pew behind Charles. He was standing next to Arthur, his best man. Charles did not turn around but from his side profile he had a likeness of André, yet when I had seen the portrait of Henri and Willeme on my first day I had felt Charles bore no family resemblance at all. It must have been his dark eyes and black hair. I wondered whether he had Spanish ancestors as well as French. I clutched my posy tightly. My veil hid my eyes which was as well with tears threatening. Maman and Papa should have been here. It should have been Papa giving me away. André guided me closer to Charles and only then did my husband-to-be turn to look at me. He was dressed in matching clothes to my brother, as was Arthur, and they all had the same type of white boutonniere. Charles' hair gleamed and his near black eyes shone like coal. His dark moustache twitched when he smiled.

The vicar ushered Charles and I closer before speaking to the congregation beginning with, 'Dearly beloved, we are gathered together here in the sight of God…'

My mind wandered. Seventeen and to be married in a strange country and without my parents or friends. From a little girl I had dreamt of becoming a bride after falling in love with a handsome young man. Charles was indeed handsome and Elizabeth had promised me that he would be a good caring husband just as Frederick, her late husband, had been. She had not had an easy life with the death of Frederick and not long afterwards losing her daughter, although no one had told me what had actually happened.

My thoughts were broken when the congregation began to sing *O Perfect Love*. I opened my mouth to join in but my throat had tightened and no words would come.

The organ faded, the singing stopped and the vicar began, 'I require and charge you both, as ye will answer at the dreadful day of judgement…'

Although my English was fluent, I had no idea what he was talking about and wanted it to be over. The vicar continued and I caught, 'so long as you both shall live' and Charles answered, 'I will.'

I took a deep breath ready to begin my vows.

'Françoise Angélique wilt thou have this man to thy wedded husband, to live together after God's ordinance in the holy estate of Matrimony? Wilt thou obey him, and serve him, love, honour, and keep him, in sickness and in health; and, forsaking all other, keep thee only unto him, so long as ye both shall live?'

I looked ahead at the altar.

'Miss Françoise,' whispered the vicar.

I swallowed to clear my throat willing the words. 'I will.'

André came forward to give me away. This was Papa's job. The vicar continued to say the vows for us to repeat. I held on to Charles' words *to love and to cherish*.

Charles parted the slit in my glove and slid the ring on to my finger, saying, 'With this ring I thee wed, with my body I thee worship, and with all my worldly goods I thee endow…'

I looked down at the snakelike gold band set with rubies as the vicar continued with a prayer before joining our right hands. He said, 'Those whom God hath joined together let no man put asunder.' He continued speaking to the people.

I was now Lady Françoise Dubois and tonight my husband would visit my chambre before returning to his own. How I wanted a relationship like Maman and Papa, how even after years of marriage, they did not like to be apart. Maybe Tilly was wrong and Charles would not want to go back to his own bed but stay in mine.

The organist played and the congregation joined in and sang *Abide with Me*. Charles and I, along with André and Arthur, were led into the vestry where we were asked to sign the register before heading back down the aisle to Mendelsohn's *Wedding March*. I took care to look straight ahead and not at the guests as I had been told.

Chapter 12

Tilly

'Wasn't that a beautiful service?' I said to Daisy as we waited for the bride and groom to come out of the church. 'I'm so pleased the master allowed us to be part of their special day.'

'When I get married, I'm going to have a dress just like hers,' Daisy said.

'Me too.' I drifted in thought.

'Are you thinking about him?'

'Yes. I always thought he'd marry me, that is until he did what he did to me. And now he's seeing that girl from the village.' I sighed.

'I heard that's over. He most likely did the same to her as he did to you. Forget him. He's not worth it.'

I shrugged before nudging her. 'Look, here they come.'

Françoise came out on the master's arm. We watched as the wedding guests threw rice over the bridal couple.

'Look at those sweet little boys.' Daisy gushed.

'They're the Alcott twins. And the plain woman on Monsieur André's arm is their elder sister. She looks like she's set her cap at him.'

'You're not jealous, are you?'

'Don't be daft. I'd have no chance. Now come on we'd best go and finish off the chores so we have time to find something to wear for the party later.'

We meandered back to *Highwood*.

'You're so lucky being a lady's maid. I'm fed up scrubbing floors and washing dishes.'

'I have to do that too, don't forget, but I know what you mean. I love my job. Mademoiselle Françoise is so kind. Don't let me forget that I must get her room ready for tonight. I've already laid out her nightdress. It falls from the yoke and has long sleeves with matching lace around the collar and cuffs. I'd love one like that. So silky and soft. You should see it, Daisy.'

'Didn't you say you made it?'

'Anna helped me as part of my training but now I'm allowed to make everything on my own.'

'In that case you can make yourself a nightdress just like it. Can't you?'

'Aye, I suppose I can but it won't be made from posh silk material like the mademoiselle's. Mrs Jarvis says I've got to come in the kitchen later to help with the reception stuff.' I rubbed my hands. 'It's so exciting.'

Daisy nudged me. 'Here they come.'

I looked up as the carriage, led by its four white horses, past at a trotting speed.

*

Daisy linked my arm as we walked across the courtyard. 'Your hair looks so lovely like that.'

'Thank you. Yours does too.' I'd dressed both our hair in ringlets. Another skill Anna had taught me as part of my position.

'I wish mine was your shade.'

'The mademoiselle says it's like a strawberry blonde. Oh, I'd best stop calling her that. She's mistress now.' We both laughed.

As the light disappeared, a few men ventured down to the lake to set up the fireworks. The baronet, his new bride, and guests gathered at the bottom of the steps of the house.

Françoise had changed into an emerald taffeta tiered gown and wore a wide brim hat with a huge sash matching her dress.

'Look at that dress. I wish I could have one just like that.' Daisy said.

'That's my work.'

'What, you made it?'

'Well, I helped. But I shall make the next one unaided.' I grinned. 'Once I'm married, I'll have rich folk coming around to my house so I can design their gowns and I'll have a hoard of children running around my skirt. I can't wait to be a mam.'

'You're not, are you?'

I shook my head. 'No thank goodness. I don't want one out of wedlock. Need a husband first.'

'Phew.'

I looked up at Françoise and wondered what tonight would be like for her. I hoped the master would be really gentle not like Archie had been with me. She had a lace shawl around her shoulders but still shivered. André moved next to her, placed his arm around her shoulder and whispered something. He was handsome but not as handsome as Archie. Butterflies fluttered in my stomach as I thought about him.

Last month he'd come up behind me.

'Tilly.' He dropped his lower lip. 'I've really missed you. He put his hand out to stroke my shoulder but I'd yanked it away. 'I'm sorry about that night. You know I'm not that type of man. I was drunk. Forgive me?'

'I'm not interested. Just leave me alone.'

He sloped away and hadn't bothered me since. The next I heard was he'd got with some girl but now it seems he wasn't with her anymore.

Daisy tapped me on the shoulder. 'Penny for them.'

'Nothing much. Come on, let's get closer to the lake. It looks like the fireworks are starting.' We ran down the hill as the sky lit up like fire. A huge bang followed making me jump. I laughed.

We stood around the lake watching rockets shoot up to the sky and falling in a shower of sparks. Whizzing noises merged with echoes of *amazing* from the watchers. Catherine wheels pinned on tree trunks spun around creating blue, green and yellow flickers. One of the men passed around sparklers. Once lit, Daisy and I shook ours side to side keeping them at a distance. We laughed, scared at the same time in case we burnt ourselves.

An arm went around my shoulder startling me. I turned around expecting Archie but it was Edward. 'Hello, Tilly. You look pretty tonight. Will you spare a dance for me, later?'

I giggled. 'We'll see.' I rather hoped Archie would want to dance with me.

'You're not still hankering after him, are you?' Edward glared.

I felt my face burning like a light and hoped he couldn't see it in the dark. 'I'm not sure I know what you're talking about.'

'Good, because you deserve better than him.'

'You mean, someone like you?'

'That would be nice but either way, you don't want to have any more to do with him. I've heard things.' Edward shook his head. 'Don't trust him, sweetheart.' He patted me on the arm and walked off.

'What was that about?' Daisy asked.

'He was warning me off Archie. Who does he think he is?'

'Well, he's right. I'm worried about you. You know what Archie's like and just because he's a free man again doesn't mean…' Daisy sighed. 'Just stay away from him. I'll be watching you.'

'Are you sure you're not just a little bit jealous?'

'No, I'm not. You know I'm not.' Daisy pulled her shawl closer. 'I'm getting cold and they've started the music in the barn. Let's go up to the party. It looks like they've finished here now, anyway. Look' – she pointed – 'all the guests have gone back inside the house.'

I knew Daisy wasn't jealous but Edward was for sure. We trod back up the hill, lifting our skirts so as not to trip. As we reached the doorway to the barn, I spotted Archie inside. He was with Elsie and had his arm about her. He whispered something to her and they both laughed. So he'd moved on already or was he trying to make me jealous? Daisy and Edward were right. Archie was bad news. And I mustn't forget what he did to me. I stood watching them as they moved into the square.

'May I have the first dance, Tilly?' Edward had come up behind me. He had a habit of doing that.

'Go on then.'

He took my hand and we joined a set to make up the eight.

Chapter 13

Françoise

André kissed me on the cheek. 'Bon nuit, ma soeur. All will be fine.'

I went upstairs not knowing what to expect. When I arrived in my chambre a buxom woman was pulling down the bed. I remembered then that Tilly and the usual staff had been given the night off.

'Would you like me to help you undress, madam?' she asked without a smile.

'Yes, thank you.' I made a point of using all English as the girl may not understand, unlike Tilly who thrived on learning new French words.

The maid slipped the gown off my shoulders, unlaced the corset and held it in position while she placed a soft, silk nightdress over my head in order to protect my decency.

'Shall I draw the drapes, madam?'

'No, leave them, thank you.'

'Very well, madam. If there's nothing else.'

'Nothing else.'

The woman left the room without a goodbye or good night. I had not realised how much I had come to rely on Tilly's company with her little jokes and idle chatter. I was unsure what to do now. Should I get inside the sheets or wait on top of the bed for Charles? I decided to crawl under the covers and lay my head on the plump pillow, looking out towards the window where I could see a full moon illuminating the darkness. How long would Charles be? He had barely spoken to me today. Even when we had our first dance, he had stayed silent.

I waited and waited but he did not come. I got up, opened the window, and breathed in the warm night air. The moon and stars were romantic. Maman's voice echoed in my ear, 'It will be the most beautiful thing, Françoise, becoming a woman. It will hurt for a moment but be brave, my child.' I was being brave but where was my groom? I feared he was not coming. I left the window open, climbed back into bed and let the light breeze touch my face as I closed my eyes and sought solace in sleep.

Chapter 14

Tilly

I was already in bed when Daisy came to our room.

'Where did you get to?' I asked.

'Edward collared me. He's asked me to speak with you about him. He wants you to walk out with him,' Daisy said as she got undressed in the dark.

'What?'

'I know. He's really smitten. I hope you've not made any plans with a certain valet. I saw you talking to him.'

'Not yet,' I lied. 'I think I should though. He says he still loves me.'

She sighed. 'Don't fall for that one. Archie probably tells all the girls the same thing.'

'You don't think I'm special?'

'I do, yes. But I don't think he does and you're a fool to consider having anything to do with him. Have you forgotten what he did to you?'

'No, of course not, but he said he was sorry and I told you, he did that for my sake.'

'That's rubbish. You were lucky last time not being left with a child. Don't put yourself in that position again.' She climbed into her bed.

'I won't.' I lay looking at the moon shining through the open window.

*

Butterflies fluttered in my stomach as I headed towards the barn. Archie had promised things would be different this time and that I was his true love. I had waited until Daisy was asleep before creeping out.

Clusters of stars and a full moon stopped the sky being pitch black. As I reached the outbuilding someone grabbed me. I went to scream but a hand covered my mouth.

'Shh. It's only me.' Archie was carrying a lantern.

I looked up into his smiling face. 'Come on, treasure.' Archie led me inside the building and unlike last time, I went willingly. He lowered the wick until the flame was dim and placed the lamp just inside the entrance.

I sneezed.

'Shh,' he said again, 'someone will hear you.'

'Sorry.'

He tilted my chin, gently brushing his lips against mine, as he slipped my blouse off my shoulder and stroked my bare skin. My heart drummed. I gave a nervous laugh and allowed him to lower me onto the hay. As he kissed me, he shoved his tongue in my mouth, and his breathing got quicker. I let his hands wander up my skirt but then tightened as I remembered last time.

'It's all right, treasure. This time it'll be different.'

'But what if I end up with child?'

'You'll not and if it does happen, I'll wed you. You know I love you and if you loved me then you'll let me do this. Now relax and give yourself to me, there's a good girl.'

'I do love you, Archie.' I took a deep breath, closed my eyes, and let him fumble. After a sharp thrust the discomfort eased and it was all over in minutes. He slid off me and on to his back. I cuddled closer but he got up and put his trousers back on. 'Make yourself decent before someone finds us.' He moved over to the lamp and turned the wick springing the flame back to life. With the barn illuminated he fastened the buttons on his shirt.

As I stood up and fixed my blouse and skirt into position, I stared into his eyes seeking a glimmer of affection or kindness but there was nothing. I put my hand out to touch his face but he pushed it away.

'Not now. You go first. We mustn't be seen together otherwise we'll both get the sack.'

I waited for him to kiss me goodnight.

'What are you waiting for?' He frowned. 'On your way.' He opened the barn door and practically pushed me out.

How could I have been so stupid after Daisy had warned me? He didn't love me. Once I'd served my purpose, he couldn't wait to get rid of me. I stumbled back to the house in darkness feeling sick. Suppose he'd given me a baby. What then? Would he really be there for me? I didn't think so.

*

Daisy sat up in bed. 'Where've you been? I woke up and you weren't in your bed.'

'Nowhere.'

'You've been with him, haven't you? Don't even try and lie to me.'

I nodded. 'It wasn't what I was expecting.' I slumped down onto my bed.

'Was he rough again?'

'No. But afterwards he lost interest. He didn't even see me back or kiss me goodnight.'

'Tilly.' Daisy got out of bed and hugged me as I cried into her chest.

'How could I have been so stupid? And it wasn't even worth doing. It was all over in minutes.' I sniffled. 'What'll I do if I'm with child?'

Chapter 15

Françoise

I meandered through the garden admiring the tall sunflowers by the high wall and stopping to smell the strong fragrance from the pink cactus dahlias along the flower borders. Purple violas in a separate bed reminded me of the wood violet at home. I was deep in thought about *Vue de Jardin* and wondered how Maman and Papa were when André came up behind me.

'Good morning, ma sœur. How are you today?'

I burst out crying.

'Qu'est-ce que c'est, chérie?' He put his arms about me. 'Let us find a bench to talk.' I let him take my hand and lead me through the privet arch to a wooden seat on the other side.

'Sit down and tell your big brother what is wrong?'

I glanced around.

'It is all right. There is no one here except you and I. Is it Charles?'

I nodded.

'What has your husband done to cause such tears?'

'I cannot tell you.'

André frowned. 'Come along, ma sœur. We have always been able to talk to each other about everything.'

'It is…'

'You can tell me anything. I promise not to be shocked. Here.' He passed me his handkerchief.

'I do not understand' – I dabbed my eyes – 'I have left my home, come to this strange country, fulfilled the one-hundred-year-old oath and now…'

'But I thought you were happy. You have made friends. Lady Elizabeth has made us both more than welcome and you have a handsome husband.'

I sobbed again.

'What?'

I got up from the bench and paced up and down. André came next to me. He took my arm. 'Tell me.'

'Charles he is not…'

'Not what? Has he not been gentle? He promised…'

'He does not come to my chambre. I repulse him.'

'How could you repulse anyone? You are beauty itself with your porcelain skin and dark shining hair.' He rubbed his moustache. 'I do not understand. It has been more than two weeks since you were wed. Are you telling me he has never been to visit you at night?'

'Not once.' I cried into my hands.

'Leave this to me' – he patted my hand – 'I will find out what the problem is.'

'Please do not return to France, mon frère. Stay with me.' I buried my face in his chest and let the tears go.

'Now, now. I am not going anywhere. I will stay with you as long as you need me.' André wiped my eyes with his handkerchief. 'Let there be no more of this nonsense.' He tilted my chin. 'Take a deep breath, head up high, and be proud.' He took my arm. 'Come, let us walk.'

Chapter 16

Françoise

Tilly helped me into the magenta gown she had completed last night. It was a comfortable fit but still accentuated my small waist. The satin fabric flowed in tiers, brushing at my ankles. She certainly had a skill.

Charles was taking me out but I had no idea whether it would be just the two of us. All the note said, sent via a footman first thing, was I should be ready for a river trip by two o'clock. The sun was warm today so there was no need for a shawl. Tilly positioned my wide brim hat, adorned with a purple feather, on top of my soft curls.

As I was walking out of the door, Tilly called me. 'Madame' – she passed me a lilac silk parasol – 'have a lovely time.'

'Merci.' I took to the stairway and Charles approached as I reached the footwell.

'You look beautiful, my dear.' He kissed my hand. 'Ma chérie.' His dark eyes sparkled. What had André said to him? Charles had not been this attentive since before our wedding day over a fortnight ago.

'Come.' He took my arm and led me outside to the Brougham drawn by two silver-grey horses which I had named Arctic Steel and Ghost Star. Charles helped me up the step and onto the seat before sliding in next to me. I erected the parasol for protection against the sun.

The driver flicked the reins and we trotted down the mud lane. I wondered how old the boy was. He did not look fifteen. Charles took his watch from his pocket. 'We should arrive by noon. Mrs Darby has made us a picnic.'

'That sounds delightful. Will it be just the two of us or are the Alcotts, André and Maman joining us?'

'Just the two of us. I hope my company will not bore you. I thought it would give us time to get to know each other better. I fear I have neglected my bride since our wedding day. I'm sorry.'

I looked in his eyes and smiled with a nod. 'Do you have a favourite composer?'

'I'm not sure. Catherine was the musician of the family. I like to listen to music but I'm never quite sure who the composer is. How about you? Educate me.'

'That is a tricky question. I think my answer would have to be Mozart although I adore Beethoven, but then I also love Clementi.'

He chuckled. 'I do not know any of them. Play for me this evening. That's if you're not too tired after our jaunt today.'

'I would be delighted. I am quite sure I will not be fatigued.'

Charles rubbed his hands. 'Perfect. Our itinerary for today begins with a river trip and in the evening, I have arranged for you and I to dine alone. Afterwards you may entertain me with your musical skills.'

'It certainly is a beautiful pianoforte. You mentioned it belonged to Catherine.'

'That is so.'

'What happened to Catherine?'

'What has Mother told you?'

'She has not mentioned your sister at all.'

He stroked his chin making my heart beat faster. I longed for him to gather me up in his arms.

'Catherine.' He turned his face away from me momentarily before turning back. 'My sister, unfortunately, died in childbirth. The child survived. A girl. But perhaps the circumstances of Catherine's death is the reason I've not yet consummated our marriage.'

'I do not understand.'

'I am concerned in case the same thing happens to you.'

'But Charles, we cannot think like that. You have brought me across the channel to fulfill an oath but what is the point if we do not create an heir for the Dubois family name?'

'You're right of course. André made me realise that.'

'It must have been hard losing your sister. I cannot imagine life without my brother. How old was she when she died?'

'Nineteen. You must have seen her daughter, Bertha?'

'No, I have not but I have seen a nursemaid pushing a perambulator.'

'Ah yes. Mother employed a nanny to take care of Bertha. Her father, stricken with grief, went off the rails and no one knows where he is. He didn't even look at the child. Maybe one day he'll come back and claim his daughter. She's a delightful little girl.' He looked to the left. 'Ah, we have arrived. Take in that view.'

It was a beautiful sight. Willow reflected in the water. Couples picnicked on the bank while others rowed boats on the river. 'This is not the same place we visited with the Alcotts.'

'Same river but a different area. This part is quieter and there's no cricket. You must meet Bertha. She looks just like Catherine. Mother adores her. The child has kept a light in Mother's life, and you too of course. You're like a daughter to her.'

'She has been very kind. It must have been hard for her.'

'Anywhere here, Bert,' Charles said to the driver.

Bert pulled the Brougham over into the shade and Charles helped me down, took my hand and led me to the riverbank. 'What would you like to do first? Boating or picnic?'

'I think I'd like to go on the river. I have never been in a rowing boat before.'

'Let it be so. Come along, chérie.'

*

Charles' muscular arms twisted the oars. I looked around at the grove of oak and silver birch. Everything was going to turn out well. Charles was being attentive, just as I had expected my husband to be. A raft of ducks headed towards us, quacking, and a wedge of swans flew over, landing a little further up the river.

'Look at them,' I said, 'they are captivating.'

'Are you having a good time?'

'Indeed, I am. I love water fowl, particularly swans. The black one at *Highwood* is exquisite.'

'You've discovered our little piece of Heaven?'

'Yes. I find it peaceful and I have a wonderful view from my chambre window.'

'Perhaps we should have a stroll around there together.' He wiped his wet brow. 'How about over there for our picnic?'

'That looks like a delightful spot.'

He maneuvered the boat towards the bank and steered it under a weeping willow.

*

Tilly unlaced the ribbons on my corset. 'Did you have a good day, madame?'

'I did, Tilly. It was divine.' I placed the silk nightgown over my head.

72

'Would you like me to close the drapes?' Tilly asked as she pulled back the bed covers.

'Non. Leave them. I like to look at the stars.'

'Is there anything else I can get you, madame?'

'Non merci. You get yourself to bed. I will see you in the morning.'

'Thank you. Bonne nuit, madame.' She used the latest French words I had taught her.

'Bonne nuit.'

Tilly closed the door behind her. I was perched on the huge bed wondering if he would come when there was a tap on the door and it opened slowly. 'It's only me. Is it all right if I come in?'

'Of course, mon chéri.'

Charles joined me on the bed. He moved closer and unpinned my hair, letting it flow wild over my shoulders. His lips touched mine as he stroked my face, moving his kisses down my neck and back on my lips but this time pressing harder. He slipped my nightgown from my shoulders and rested my head down on the pillow. His kisses became urgent. I kissed him back, trying to keep in rhythm. This is what Maman had said married life would be like. Charles' hands moved lower caressing me, whispering incoherently. He moved his body on top of me and gently took me into womanhood. My tears embraced his face.

'Françoise' – he tilted my chin – 'ma chérie, I am sorry. I have hurt you.'

'Non, Charles. My weeping is for happiness.'

Chapter 17

Tilly

Tummy ache urged me to rush to the privy hoping my monthly had arrived. I sighed on discovering it still hadn't come. What was I going to do?

As I wandered back into the kitchen, Daisy looked up from the sink, tucking a loose blonde curl behind her ear. 'You look like you've seen a ghost. What's wrong?'

I shook my head.

'Still?'

I nodded, picking up the tea towel to dry the dishes as Daisy washed them.

'What are you going to do?' she whispered.

Cook marched back into the scullery. 'What are you girls chatting about?'

'Nothing,' I said setting the dry cups and saucers down on the large dresser.

'You both look guilty.' She chuckled, her plump cheeks glowing. 'I was young once too, you know?'

Daisy giggled. I didn't feel like laughing.

'Mrs Darby?' Mr Hughes called from outside.

Cook waddled out to the hallway to find him.

Daisy added hot water to the sink from a pan off the stove. 'You're going to have to speak to Archie.'

'I know. He promised to stand by me if this happened but as you know I haven't let him near me since.'

'Well, I hope he does, for your sake. You were lucky last time. I really don't know why you put yourself at risk again.'

I shrugged. 'Because I thought he loved me. He said I was his girl.'

Daisy rinsed the last plate. 'He'd better wed you, that's all I can say.'

'He's in the hallway. I'll catch him now.' I rushed from the kitchen. 'Archie' – I tapped his shoulder – 'can we meet later?'

His grey eyes narrowed. 'I'm busy.'

'It's important.'

He smirked. 'I see, so you've realised you can't do without me, eh?'

'Will you meet me or not?'

'To be sure, treasure.' He grinned. 'But first, I've something to fix.' He ran his fingers through his blond hair, adjusted his waistcoat, and straightened his dark tie. 'Half an hour then. By the barn.'

I watched him swagger down the corridor before I rejoined Daisy in the kitchen.

'Well?' she said, draining the dirty water.

'He was reluctant at first but agreed. I hope he'll be nice like the old Archie.'

'If you're in the family way then he'll have to do the decent thing.'

'I hope so.'

*

It was still daylight when I made my way across to the barn. Archie was standing outside smoking a cigar. I wondered whether he'd stolen it from the baronet. 'What kept you?' he said.

'Cook gave me extra chores. Shall we walk?'

'I'd rather go inside. This November wind's bitter.' He threw the butt to the ground and stomped it out with his shoe.

'All right,' I said, 'but only because it's warmer in there.'

'That's my girl.' He swaggered into the barn.

I followed him in and flopped down on a bale of hay. My heart pounded. What would he say? Would he keep his promise? I wrapped my cape tighter to stop me shivering but also to protect myself from him.

'So, treasure' – Archie dropped down next to me and fumbled my breast through my cloak – 'you couldn't do without me then?'

I pushed his hand off. 'We need to talk.'

'You should know by now that I don't do talking. I'm a doer. Come on.' He slipped his hand under my cloak and pressed his lips firmly on mine.

I slapped his hand and pushed him away. 'Get off. That's not why I asked you here. Seriously, you need to listen. I'm late.'

'I know you're late. So, let's make the most of the time we have.'

'No. I don't mean like that. I mean, you know... Late.'

He rubbed his chin for a moment before saying, 'Don't worry about it. You'll be fine.'

'But I'm really late. I've missed two, and I've been feeling sick. I think I'm… you know.'

He stood up and moved away from me. 'Fuck. What do you expect me to do about it?'

'Well, you promised to stand by me if it happened.'

'Well, it isn't mine. I was careful.'

'Archie' – I stood up next to him– 'you know there's only ever been you.'

He ran his tongue over his upper lip. 'So what are you expecting? That I'll marry ye?'

'Yes.' I slumped back down on the hay bale. 'That's what you said you'd do.'

'The bastard's not mine. Can't be. You haven't let me near you since. I bet you've been with loads of others. Edward for instance. You think I haven't noticed the glances between you and him?'

'How dare you?' I slapped his face.

He glared back at me holding his cheek. 'Just so you know.' He took a deep breath. 'Men don't marry girls like you. You're too easy. Men marry nice girls. Virgins, and I ain't marrying you, that's for sure.'

'But…'

'But nothing. Your mess. You sort it.' He adjusted his jacket and stormed out leaving me in tears, holding my stomach.

'Tilly.' Daisy crept into the barn and knelt down beside me. 'It didn't go well then?'

'Oh, Daisy.' I buried my head into her lap and bawled. 'Did you hear him? He reckons he'd been careful and it's not his.'

'Yes, I did. Shh now.' She stroked my hair.

'He said men don't marry girls like me.' I sniffled.

'What are you going to do?'

'I don't know. I won't be able to stay here, will I?'

'What about your family? Why not talk to your mam?'

'I could, couldn't I?' I sat up and blew my nose. 'Me da won't like it but maybe Mam can persuade him to let me stay.'

'It's worth a try.'

Chapter 18

Tilly

My legs trembled as I got closer to the one-storey cottage. The thought of coming back to live in this place with its three rooms made me feel sick. I lifted the latch and entered the dim parlour where only a small window offered light. The little ones ran up to me clinging the back of my knees. 'Tilly. Tilly. What have you brought us?'

'Get off me and I'll show you.' I put the wicker basket down on the wooden table. Cook always gave me a few treats to give to my three-year-old brother and sister. 'Here.' I dug in the hamper and passed a gingerbread man to each of them. 'Cook made these especially for you two.' The twins grabbed them.

I did not want to be like Mam and spend all my adult life having babies. She'd had ten in total and was getting on now, in her forties. I remembered how she'd screamed when those two were being born. I'd sent my younger sister to get Mrs Brown from down the road but it was me who ended up delivering them.

'What a nice surprise.' Mam waddled over to me and kissed my cheek. 'We hadn't expected you today.'

'I managed to get an extra afternoon off as I wanted to speak to you about something.'

Mam frowned. 'Now our Tilly, I hopes yous not been up to no good.'

'No. No. Mam. I've not.'

'Good. Nows help me set the cutlery for tea.' Mam shuffled over to the table. 'Did you manage to bring anything with yous?' She grinned her almost toothless smile.

'Yes, Mam. Cook gave me some corned beef. Look' – I pulled out the cold meat – 'and I've an apple and blackberry pie.'

The kids scrambled up on the stools as Da thumped through the door. 'Hello there, our Tilly.'

'Hello Da.' I passed him a plate of meat.

My elder brother, Frank, followed Da in and joined him at the table. Frank was tall and lanky just like Da. Mam said they had hollow legs. Our Frank was the image of Da, except Frank's hair was thick brown and Da's had thinned and turned grey. They both wore green plaid breeches and stripey waistcoats and from the back, when they wore hats, it was difficult to distinguish who was who. There was just the six of us around the table as my sisters were all in service now.

'You're looking rather bonny, our Tilly.' Frank pinched my cheek. 'Reckon they must be feeding you too well.'

I nudged Frank before chewing on a piece of meat. After we'd finished eating, I cleared the table to help Mam wash up.

'Here.' She passed me a tea towel.

As I was drying the plates I said, 'Please don't be angry with me but...'

'Oh Lord no' – she shot her hands to her face – 'tell me you're not.'

Da was behind me. 'What's going on?'

'She's got herself in the family way.'

I dropped the tea towel and clenched my fists. 'I might not be.'

'You dirty little slut.' Da picked up the birch cane from a bucket of water by the sink, and pushed my face towards the wall. 'Pull her skirt up,' he said to Mam.

'No, don't Da, please don't,' I begged.

'Arthur,' Mam said, 'please.'

'Shut your mouth unless you want some of this too… now pull up her skirt.'

'Frank, get the twins out of here,' Mam said, lifting my dress above my knees.

I tried wriggling free while Da waited for Frank to close the door behind him but I was unable to move. 'Please Mam, don't let him.' I winced. 'Da, please, no,' but he ignored me. Once the door had creaked closed, he thrashed the cane in the air and back down again, striking the back of my legs. 'One,' he counted.

I tried to escape but he held me firmly in place, lifting the rod and repeating his action, making me flinch with each strike until he finally yelled, 'Ten.' Shaking his head, he roared, 'To think that a daughter of mine…' Puffing and panting he dragged me screaming across the room. He opened the door and threw me to the hard ground. 'Don't bother coming back. Get yourself down to the workhouse. You're no daughter of ours.'

'Mam, please?' I groveled on my knees.

Mam bit her lip, squinted, and mimed, *I'm sorry, love.*

Chapter 19

Françoise

Charles came to my room twice a week following the night we consummated our marriage. He was always loving. Afterwards I would curl up next to him but his side of the bed was always empty when I woke up. I was falling deeply in love with my husband but feared he did not feel the same. His actions showed he loved me but he never spoke those words.

Six weeks later I began being sick each day confirming I was with child. Everyone in the household was ecstatic that I was to bear an heir for the Dubois name.

'You are very quiet, ma sœur.' André squeezed my hand as we sat in the back of the Landau. 'What are you thinking?'

'It is Charles.'

'What about him?'

'He has stopped coming to my chambre.'

'I would not take that to heart, ma chérie, it is most likely due to the child. He will not want to harm it. Once the baby has been born, I am sure he will return to your bed.'

What André said made sense but why did I doubt this?

As we rode through the country lane, I spotted a figure curled up by an oak tree. 'André, get the driver to stop. That looks like Tilly.'

André tapped the roof and pushed his head out of the window. 'Can you pull over, Bert?'

I opened the carriage door and rushed to the girl who had fallen in a heap. 'Tilly, is that you?'

Tilly lifted her head and pushed loose hair under her bonnet revealing tears on her flushed cheeks.

'Whatever has happened?'

'Me da, madame. He's disowned me.'

'André, come and help me.'

André was by my side.

'Help me get her to the carriage.'

He took one arm, while I took the other.

'Tilly,' I said, 'you are bleeding.'

'That'll be from me da thrashing me legs.'

Her skirt was covered in blood. It did not look like it had come from her legs. Between André and Bert, they managed to get her inside the carriage.

'I can't come back with you, madame.'

'Shh. We will talk about things once we get to *Highwood*.'

*

Tilly came out of the bathroom dressed in my dressing gown. The magenta silk robe was a perfect fit and complimented the red tones in her loose blonde hair. 'I really should not be using your bathroom, madame. If anyone should find out...' Her misty blue eyes glistened like aquamarine jewels.

'They will not find out. I have arranged for your friend Daisy to bring clean clothes for you. Now, why not tell me what happened?'

'I thought I was in the family way, madame. I tried to talk to me mam to see what she thought but she told Da and he went mad and thrashed me.' Tears fell to her pale cheek.

I sighed. Her father had left welts on the back of her legs. 'But you are not having a baby, Tilly. Or if you were, you are not now.'

'No, I suppose not. Me monthly must've come after he caned me or maybe I lost it. I dunno.' She held her tummy.

'Who was the father?'

'Archie, but he wasn't interested.'

'Archie?' I recognised that name.

'Yes, the master's valet.'

I shook with anger.

'I'm sorry, madame. Really I am.'

'I am not cross with you. It is the valet I am angry with.'

After a tap on the door, it opened slightly and Daisy peeped in. 'Madam, I have what you asked for.'

'Come in, Daisy.'

Daisy spotted Tilly and raised a hand to her mouth.

'Just leave the clothes on that chair. I am sure Tilly will explain later.'

'Yes, madam.' Daisy dropped the items as instructed and rushed from the room.

'Get dressed, Tilly,' I said.

Chapter 20

Tilly

Archie burst into the kitchen. 'You bitch.' He gritted his teeth, raising a fist at me.

'What's going on?' Cook hurried to stand between us.

'She's only gone and got me the sack.'

I opened my mouth to speak but closed it again. What was he talking about?

'And pray me, Archie Dobbs, how indeed did our Tilly here get you dismissed?' Cook glared at him.

'She told Lady Françoise I got her in the family way. But it wasn't me. More likely him over there.'

'Excuse me?' Edward jumped up away from the table. 'If it were me then I'd be gentleman enough to take her as my wife.' He threw me a look of sympathy.

Archie snarled. 'You're welcome to the little bitch.'

'I expect you got the sack because they've discovered what you're like.' Edward smirked.

Mrs Jarvis stormed in. 'What's all the shouting about?' She brushed her hands on her pinny. 'I can hear you lot upstairs. At this rate we'll have the master ringing down.'

'They've finally woken up to him.' Edward pointed at Archie.

'It was you.' Archie jabbed Edward. 'Wasn't it? It was you who got me sacked.'

'I never said a word but I can't say I'm not pleased.'

'Is this true?' Cook turned to me.' Have you been doing things you shouldn't have with Archie here?'

I put my hands to my face.

Mrs Jarvis moved towards me and squinted. 'You do know that's a sackable offence? I think you should be packing your bags too, young lady.'

'But where will I go? Me da won't let me back in the house.'

'You should have thought about that before being a bad girl. There's always the workhouse for your sort.'

Edward stretched his hand across the table and reached for mine. 'I'll marry you, Tilly.'

I closed my eyes. 'Thank you, Edward, but I'm sure my mistress won't allow me to go to the workhouse.'

'This is a respectable household and we don't want your sort bringing disrepute to it. You have until the end of the week,' Mrs Jarvis shouted.

Archie grinned at me. 'You didn't think you'd get off scot-free, did ya?'

Edward held his fist up ready to punch Archie.

'We'll have none of that fighting in my kitchen,' Cook said. 'Now if you've been dismissed, I suggest you pack your things and leave.' She tutted, shaking her head. 'How could you have preyed on such an innocent young lass.' She turned to me. 'Are you in the family way, dear?'

'No.' I whispered, 'I thought I was but I'm not.'

'Mrs Jarvis,' Cook said, 'it's clear this young girl fell fate to an older man's charm. Please reconsider your decision. She's a good worker and I for one wouldn't want to lose her and I'm quite sure Lady Françoise wouldn't want that either.'

'She doesn't' – I blew my nose – 'she told me not to worry.'

Mrs Jarvis glared at Archie and then turned to me. 'I'll reconsider but, in the meantime, Tilly and Daisy, get the dishes washed and this kitchen swept.'

I struggled to move from the table with my sore legs but managed to hobble over to Daisy. She'd already filled the sink with hot water from the stove.

Mrs Jarvis ushered Edward out with her hands. 'Out of here and on to your duties. And you, Archie Dobbs, can get out of this house.'

He stood with his hands on his hips. 'I think you'll find the master might have something to say about that.'

'Mrs Darby, I thought you said he'd been dismissed by Upstairs.'

'That's correct. He said so himself.'

'Upstairs but not the master. I think you'll find the baronet rather likes having me around.'

Edward lunged towards Archie.

Cook clapped her hands. 'Stop it now. Out of my kitchen both of you. I'll not have this kind of behaviour in here. Wait until Mr Hughes hears about these goings-on.'

Chapter 21

Françoise

March 1896

Cake stands with various sponges and scones were set up ready on two square tables covered in white linen. Elizabeth had invited the Alcott family but thankfully not the twins. There was something about their uncanny likeness that unnerved me.

André came into the room and joined me on the window seat. 'You do know that all this' – he waved his hand – 'is for my benefit?'

'I had a feeling it might be. What are you going to do?'

'I shall be civil but I have no intention of making a marriage proposal to Miss Allcott.'

'How about Miss Rebecca?'

He patted my hand. 'I am sorry, ma sœur, but I am not interested in any of the Alcott sisters.'

'Do you not think it is time you settled down?'

'You forget, Françoise, at some point I need to return home to France. I shall stay with you for a short time after the child is born but then…'

'But André…'

Elizabeth entered the room with our guests.

'Isn't Charles here?' She asked me.

'Non. He has not arrived yet.'

Elizabeth shook her head. Using the lever on the wall, she rang the bell. André helped me from the window seat and we moved to stand with the others. Rebecca placed her hand on my stomach and whispered, 'Not long now.'

'Rebecca, what are you doing?' Madam Alcott shouted. 'Take your hand off Madam Françoise, right now.'

'Sorry, Mother.' Rebecca dropped her hand.

I whispered to Rebecca, 'I feel enormous.'

'You look tiny.'

'That because my corset hides it.'

'Stop that whispering.' Madam Alcott shook her head. 'Whatever's got in to you today, Rebecca? You know it's rude to whisper.'

Rebecca and I hid our grins behind hand fans.

Mr Hughes entered the room with his arms behind his back. I was sure his grey hair had receded more since I'd arrived at *Highwood*. 'Yes, madam?' 'Ah, Mr Hughes.' Elizabeth smiled. 'Please can you ask Cora to bring in tea.'

'Yes, madam.' The butler's bushy moustache moved up and down as he spoke, making me want to laugh.

'And see if you can hunt down the baronet?' Elizabeth added.

'Of course, madam.' He bowed his head before shuffling from the room.

Emily fluttered her eyelashes at André, like she normally did, and Grace smiled at him. Poor André. He did not stand a chance. Rebecca appeared uninterested but maybe that was because she thought her two sisters had to wed first.

Cora carried sandwiches and tea on a tray. She appeared pale. I wondered if she was ill.

'Sit down, everyone please.' Elizabeth had positioned herself with Madam Alcott, Emily and André on one table, while on the other there was me, Charles, whenever he turned up, Arthur, Grace and Rebecca.

The maid moved around Elizabeth's table pouring tea. She was passing a cup to Madam Alcott when the crockery crashed to the floor.

'Stupid girl,' Madam Alcott shouted.

Cora burst out crying.

'No harm done,' André said to Madam Alcott. 'Here, have mine.' He passed her his untouched cup of tea.

Madam Alcott shook her head, tutting.

'Are you all right, child?' Elizabeth asked Cora.

'No, madam. I've got bellyache.'

'Send Tilly or Daisy to clean up and tell Mrs Jarvis I've said you're to take to your bed until you feel better.'

'Thank you, madam.' Cora curtsied and hurried from the room.

Madam Alcott sipped her tea. 'You know, Lady Elizabeth, you shouldn't allow the maid to get away with such behaviour.'

'Now, Agnes, remember this is my household.'

Madam Alcott grunted something under her breath.

Daisy entered the room with a dustpan and brush and swept up the broken china. Tilly followed her in. She placed a fresh cup and saucer in front of André and poured out his tea.

'Thank you.' He looked up at Tilly and smiled.

Tilly's cheeks pinked. I had a feeling she had become sweet on my brother. She picked up the cucumber sandwiches from the tray and was offering them to our guests when Charles strode in. 'Forgive my lateness. I was caught up with business.' He made his way to me and kissed my hand. 'My dear,' and then went over to Elizabeth's table and greeted Emily and Madam Alcott before returning to ours.

'Miss Grace' – he nodded – 'Miss Rebecca. Lovely to see you young ladies again. Arthur.' He shook hands with his friend before sitting down next to me and picking up his cup to take a sip.

My eyes were drawn to my brother who looked uncomfortable as he smiled, nodding at Emily's non-stop chatter. Poor André.

After tea was over, Charles suggested the gentlemen retire to the lounge for brandy leaving we ladies to move to more comfortable chairs in the drawing room for idle chit chat, mainly about babies. Did I have any names in mind? What did I think I would have?

Tilly poured sherry into crystal glasses for Elizabeth and Madame Alcott while Rebecca, Grace, Emily and I had more tea and nibbled at various sweets including jelly babies, bonbons and marshmallows.

Madam Alcott sipped her fortified wine. 'Lady Françoise, will your mother and father travel to England once the child is born?'

'No, I am afraid that is not possible. Their health would not stand up to the journey.'

'Oh dear. That is a shame. Well at least you have Lady Elizabeth. She will take care of you.'

I smiled.

'Françoise is like a daughter to me.' Elizabeth got up from the chaise longue, smoothing down her azure blue gown. 'Agnes, why don't I show you the nursery and allow these young ladies to chat amongst themselves?'

'That would be delightful.' Madam Alcott popped another marshmallow into her mouth as she struggled to get out of the armchair. I was sure she had gained more weight than me in the last few months. I suddenly realised that it had been at least one month since I had received a letter from Maman and Papa. That was most unusual. I made a point to ask André if he had heard anything. I hoped nothing was wrong but agitation stirred inside me, alerting that all may not be well.

Chapter 22

Tilly

Cook took the large bird from the oven and set it down on an oval platter. 'Edward, take this up. Girls, get the roast potatoes and vegetables on the tray.'

'Yes Cook.' Edward picked up the goose.

'That smells delicious,' I said, helping Daisy load the silverware containers of carrots, leaks, cabbage and turnips. Upstairs needed to be served first and Edward would bring the remains of the bird back down for us. Cook had made sure there was plenty of vegetables. I was starving and couldn't wait until it was our turn to eat. Poor Cora was still in bed with belly ache. I'd heard Mrs Jarvis and Mr Hughes yesterday saying if she wasn't better by today that the doctor would have to be sent for. She did look proper poorly. I hoped it was nothing serious.

Daisy and I carried laden trays out of the kitchen. Cook shouted, 'Daisy, you've forgotten this.'

'Sorry.' She charged back and picked up the silver-plated gravy boat, adding it to her already loaded tray.

'The sooner Cora's back in here the better.' Cook tutted.

When we arrived upstairs, Edward had already placed the goose in front of the baronet who had the carving knife and fork in his hand. I licked my lips. I could almost taste the meat. As we moved around the table serving food, I glanced at André sitting next to the eldest Alcott girl. I gritted my teeth. Françoise had told me Lady Elizabeth and Mrs Alcott were trying to strike up a marriage union between André and Emily and this is what the special dinner was for. There was no point me being jealous when I had no hope, he the brother of a lady, and me a maid, but he'd been so kind since that day he and Françoise had rescued me.

I placed carrots, cabbage and leeks on his plate.

He turned around and smiled. 'Merci, Tilly.'

Butterflies fluttered in my belly. I felt someone standing close and turned around. Archie nudged me as he leaned over to pour red wine into André's glass. My butterflies of excitement turned to nerves. He was always there. No one knew how he'd managed to convince the master not to sack him. I weaved by him to finish serving the guests and then stood aside until Lady Elizabeth dismissed us.

Once out of the room, I charged downstairs.

'Slow down' – Daisy grabbed my arm – 'what's the matter?'

'It's him. He's always taunting me.'

'Don't let him get to you. Come on.'

*

I was letting out the seams of Françoise's nightdress to accommodate her growth when she came into her room, fanning her face.

'Help me out of this please, Tilly. I can't breathe.'

I undid the laces of her corset.

'That's better.' She put the palm of her hand across her large belly. I was sure she was bigger than Mam had been when she had the twins. 'Tilly, are you all right? You looked upset when serving dinner. Is he bothering you again?'

'He's still tormenting me but I make sure I'm never alone with him.' I placed the adjusted nightdress over Françoise's head.

'Good.' She sat at her dressing table. 'I cannot believe those Alcott women. All over poor André. Madam Alcott is insistent that he takes one of the girls off her hands. I would be happy if it were Rebecca but not the other two.'

Since that day Françoise rescued me, we'd developed a closer relationship, so much so, I had become her confidante. I released the pins from her hair and stroked the brush through her thick locks. 'I thought you liked Grace.'

'She is all right but if André must marry any of them, I would prefer it to be Rebecca. Of course, Madam Alcott would not allow that.' Françoise sighed. 'André is not interested in any of them. He is talking about returning to France shortly after the baby is born.'

'Have you heard from your parents yet?' I pulled the bedcovers down.

'Non. Neither has André. Something must be wrong.'

Chapter 23

Françoise

The sun shone causing me to squint as I sauntered across to the wild garden. Placing a hand in my back, I leaned over to sniff the fragrance of the bluebells which brought a tear to my eye. Maman's favourite. I missed her and Papa so much. André was booking passage to France to ensure all was well as neither of us had heard from our parents for weeks. I wished I could go with him but that would not be possible even if I were not with child.

Footsteps on the cobble footpath alerted me to look up.

André headed my way. 'I thought I might find you here,' he said. 'Let us sit down.' He guided me to a seat next to forsythia shrubs with bright yellow blooms. A hint of violet made me sneeze as I eased myself down on the bench. André passed me his handkerchief.

I dabbed my nose. 'Do you have to leave?'

'You know I do, ma sœur. We need to know what is going on.'

'When must you go?'

'Tomorrow. I leave at sunrise.'

'Will you take a letter to Geneviève?'

'Absolutely, and I am certain I shall be bringing one home for you.' He squeezed my fingers. 'I will not be gone long. You have two months before the child is due and I promise to be back before then.'

I rested my hand across my stomach. I wished Maman were here.

*

Highwood Hall
Beckton
Kent
England
12th April, 1896

My dear friend, Geneviève,

How are you?

I miss you arriving at Vue de Jardin unannounced and I miss riding together in your Phaeton, or simply sitting together embroidering cushions. But mostly, I miss being able to talk to you. I have made a pleasant friend but I cannot confide in her like I could you.

Regarding my husband, I love him, but I am unsure of his reciprocation as he stopped coming to my bed once I became with child. André said I should not worry, that Charles, most likely, does not wish to hurt our unborn but I wonder if it is more than that. Perhaps he finds my size repulsive. Papa would never have contemplated sleeping in a separate chambre to Maman. Not for any reason.

André and I are worried about Maman and Papa, hence why André must travel home to France to check on their health. I am going to feel so alone while he is gone. I wish you were here with me.

Please write back and André will bring your letter.

Affectionately yours always
Françoise

*

Charles, Elizabeth, André and I sat around the table for supper. I nibbled at cold meat, cheese and bacon, but had no appetite. My stomach pulled at the thought of André leaving me here at *Highwood*. I had never known a time in my life when he was not around.

'You look distressed, dear.' Elizabeth rested her hand on top of mine. Her slim fingers were a complete contrast to Maman's chubby ones. 'Are you concerned about your brother's trip? You know that Charles and I will take care of you.'

'I know. Merci.' I forced myself to smile. Elizabeth did not seem the maternal type. She always appeared immaculate. Even this evening she was dressed in a maroon taffeta gown with a high collared neckline suitable for the ballet or opera.

'I have told Françoise' – André patted a napkin across his dark moustache – 'I will be back before the child is born.'

I smiled but wanted to cry.

'Did you write your letter to Mademoiselle Geneviève?' André asked me.

'Yes.' I passed him the rose-coloured envelope addressed to my friend and he popped the letter into his flap pocket. 'I will get it to her as soon as I am able.'

'Merci, mon frère. If you do not mind, I will say my goodbyes now. I fear I am under the weather and must rest.' I stood up away from the table. 'Maman. Charles. Goodnight.'

Chapter 24

Françoise

I awoke in the middle of the night to the baby pounding at my stomach. Was it a foot? An arm? After wrestling in bed for over an hour I decided to seek solace with my husband. I climbed out of bed, slipped on my dressing gown, crept from my chambre and down the corridor. As I turned the corner to Charles' room, his door creaked open. Was he coming to find me? I held back, hiding behind the wall and watched. However, it was not Charles who appeared but Anna, Elizabeth's lady's maid. She whispered something to him before the door closed. Why was she in Charles' room? Was he ill? Was Elizabeth ill? There must be an explanation. Not wanting to be discovered creeping around in the middle of the night, I tiptoed back to bed and waited for news, but no one came. Eventually I must have fallen asleep.

*

The sound of drapes being drawn and the room brightening forced me to open my eyes.

'Good morning, madame.' Tilly beamed. 'Did you have a good night?'

'Not really. I was rather restless.'

'Bless you, madame,' she said softly, 'I remember me mam getting like that as she got further on.' She came towards me as I flipped back the sheet and rested on the edge of the bed.

'Has there been any news from Monsieur André?' I asked.

'Not yet, madame.' Tilly put my dressing gown around my shoulders.

'Is Lady Elizabeth ill?'

'I've not heard that she is, madame.'

'The baronet?'

'No. The baronet's fine. He's gone out for the day on business. What makes you ask?'

'Just a feeling.' Why then was Anna coming from Charles' bedroom? Had I dreamt the whole thing?

*

Restless at bedtime, I got up, made myself decent, and headed out of my chambre.

Moonlight from the high dome window broke the darkness. I tiptoed along the passageway, stopped before turning the corner, peeped out and waited.

The door opened and Anna appeared with Charles. He whispered something, before pulling her closer and kissing her full on the lips. He was sharing his bed with her.

I felt sick. There was no other explanation. How could he do this to me? I placed my hand under my heavy stomach and shuffled back to my room.

Once there, I hurried into the bathroom and retched over the basin. Afterwards I flopped on the bed and sobbed into the pillow. My tears spent, I moved to the dressing table and took out a sheet of notepaper from the drawer and dipped a pen into the inkwell.

Highwood Hall
Beckton
Kent
England
2ⁿᵈ May, 1896

Dear André,

Charles has betrayed me. You must book passage for me to France. I am unable to stay here any longer. My baby will be born at Vue de Jardin and we will remain there with Maman, Papa and you. Charles does not deserve this child. I will explain all when I am home.

Affectionally yours
Françoise

After writing the letter I screwed it up and threw it into the wooden receptacle. I knew it could not be sent. Maman would be disappointed in me and Papa cross. He would say I had responsibilities and I was no longer a girl. I must keep my promise, bound by the oath. That absurd oath had destroyed my life. I screamed, climbed back into bed and sobbed some more.

*

I was already awake when Tilly entered my chambre and drew back the curtains.

'It's a lovely morning, madame,' she said. 'Perhaps you'd like a stroll around the garden today?' She went to my wardrobe and held up a pink-striped day gown. 'How about this one?'

'I think I shall stay upstairs today, Tilly, as I am feeling under the weather.'

I had no wish to make conversation with Elizabeth or Charles and wanted to be on my own.

'Should I send for the doctor?' Her blue eyes twinkled when she smiled.

'Non. That is not necessary.'

'Very well, madame. I shall bring your breakfast on a tray.' Tilly opened the door as Charles entered.

'Wait outside, Tilly.' He gripped a buff envelope in his fingers.

'Non,' I said. 'I do not wish her to go. What is it that you want?'

'Françoise.' Charles eased himself down on the edge of the bed next to me and took my hand. 'I have news. Tilly, leave us, please.'

'Yes, sir.' She closed the door behind her.

Charles continued to clutch the letter. 'Dearest, there's no easy way...'

'What? What does the letter say? Let me see.'

He brushed his fingertips across my cheek. 'I'm sorry, my dearest, but your papa has passed on. Unfortunately, he succumbed to consumption. Your maman was with him till the end.'

'I do not believe you.' I punched his chest with my fists. 'Papa cannot be gone.'

He held my hands in his grasp. 'I'm sorry, dearest.'

'Get out. I do not wish you near me.' I managed to escape from his grip and pushed him away. 'Go.'

Charles wiped his handkerchief across my face, soaking up my tears, before standing up and leaving. As he opened the door, he whispered something to Tilly I could not hear before saying, 'Look after your mistress.'

'Yes, sir.' She came back in and hovered over me. 'I'm so sorry, madame.'

'It cannot be true.' I cried into my hands. Before long the door squeaked forcing me to glance up.

'Leave us, Tilly,' Elizabeth said.

'Yes, madam.' Tilly left the room.

'Françoise, child, I'm sorry for your loss.' Elizabeth pulled up the rose-cushioned chair. 'But dear, why did you push your husband away when he came to support you?'

I turned away from her questioning eyes.

'Françoise, you can't allow yourself to wallow like this. It isn't good for the baby.' She took a deep breath. 'It was a blessing your papa passed when he did.'

'How dare you?' I stared into her cold grey eyes.

'I apologise, dear. I did not mean to sound callous. What I meant was: would you have wanted him to suffer? André stated in his letter that your father was a fraction of the man you remember. Your maman, bless her, stayed by his bedside to the end. Take comfort in that, my dear.' She patted my upper arm. 'Now shall I send Charles back up to take care of you?'

I sat upright. 'Non. I do not wish him near me.'

'What is with this nonsense, child?'

'Charles has betrayed me. He has been sleeping with your lady's maid while my papa was dying. How could he do that to me?'

Elizabeth took my hand in hers. 'Men, my dear, have needs, and it's not unusual for a husband to take a mistress when his wife is incapacitated so to speak.'

'Pardon?'

'Certainly, my own husband, Frederick, sought solace in the arms of other women on more than one occasion. It did not mean he no longer loved me, just like Charles still loves you, and he wants to be here with you now, taking care of you.'

'Papa would never have been unfaithful to Maman. Charles has betrayed me. He promised to be true while all the time he has given his heart to another.'

Elizabeth tittered. 'Nonsense, dear, his heart is yours. I agree, him seeking his requirements with Anna was too close to home. I shall rectify that immediately. I shall dismiss her, although it may be a few weeks before I can let her go as I will need a replacement.'

'Thank you.' I sniffled.

Elizabeth rose from my bed. 'I'll tell Charles you're ready to see him now.'

'Non, do not. I do not wish to see him. I will stay upstairs today. Send up André's letter, please, so I may read for myself what he said.'

'Certainly, my dear. Rest now.'

Chapter 25

Tilly

Propped up with pillows in bed, Françoise was moving cold meat and eggs around on her plate, her normally glowing cheeks now paled. Someone tapped the door. I opened it to find Edward holding out a silver tray with a buff envelope on it. 'Her ladyship sent me up with this.'

'Thank you, Edward.' I picked up the letter.

He winked before turning away and sauntering down the corridor. Poor Edward, he never gave up.

'What is it, Tilly?' Françoise asked.

'It's the letter, madame.'

Françoise took the envelope from me and I relieved her of the breakfast tray. She whimpered as her eyes darted across the page. Her lips trembled as the note shook in her fingers and dropped to the floor. She screamed, 'It cannot be true. Papa. Papa.'

I eased myself down onto her bed, put my hand around her shoulder, and let her head sink into my lap as she wept.

After more than half an hour my back and arms ached. Although Françoise had stopped crying, she wouldn't let me leave.

'Let me fetch the baronet or Lady Elizabeth,' I asked.

Françoise shook her head. 'Non, I do not wish to see anyone.' Her eyes widened. 'Tilly.'

'Yes, madame, I'm here.'

She pulled back the sheet revealing a wet patch.

I dropped formality. 'It's all right, Françoise. It looks like your baby's making an early arrival. You must allow me to speak to Lady Elizabeth. A midwife will need to be called. I'll be right back.'

She squeezed my hand. 'Hurry, please. I do not wish to be alone.'

I rushed through the doorway, stopping to turn back and check on my mistress. Her complexion had paled and her eyes were wide open with fear. I charged downstairs, knocked on the drawing room door and didn't wait for an answer. 'Forgive the intrusion, madam, but it's Lady Françoise, her labour's begun. Shall I send Daisy for the midwife?'

'No. You get back upstairs and stay with your mistress. I'll arrange for Mrs Jarvis to organise the nurse and Dr Morris. I don't want to take any chances.'

'Yes, madam.' As I left the room, Elizabeth pressed the lever to ring the bell. I made my way back upstairs.

I found my mistress groaning, kneeling on the bed. I rubbed her back. 'Everything's going to be all right, Françoise.'

She didn't answer but wailed, rocking backwards and forwards.

'Lady Elizabeth has sent for the midwife and doctor. They'll be here shortly.'

'It is too soon,' Françoise whimpered, 'it is too soon.'

'Shh.'

*

Where was the doctor and midwife? It had been hours. Françoise's pains were getting stronger.

'The baby is coming,' she said.

'Don't worry, Madame Françoise, I know what I'm doing. I delivered my twin brother and sister.'

Françoise groaned, moving from the bed to the window and back again, writhing in agony. Beads of sweat covered her brow. I bathed her forehead with a tepid flannel to try and cool her down.

'It hurts,' she said repeatedly. 'How much longer?'

I wasn't sure what was going on. It hadn't been like this when Mam had the twins. Where was the doctor? Something wasn't right. Françoise's pallor had turned grey.

Dr Morris finally arrived at half past five in the morning. He glared at Françoise and shook his head. 'How long has she been like this?'

'Too long,' I whispered. 'What kept you?'

'A complicated labour for Lady Morgan in the mansion down the road and the midwife was delivering twins to a woman in the village. We're here now though. Get downstairs, girl, and tell the nurse to hurry. She was coming up the driveway as I arrived. Tell her it's a matter of urgency.'

Françoise's face contorted as she screamed again.

'Hurry now,' the doctor ordered, 'we need to try and save your mistress.'

*

I rushed into the kitchen. The midwife was laughing and joking while sipping a cup of tea.

'The doctor needs you upstairs now.'

'All right,' she said, 'I'm just having a quick cuppa.'

'You don't have time. He said it's urgent. Go now.'

She slammed her cup down onto the saucer, picked up her bag and stormed out.

'What's with the long face?' Cook asked.

'The mistress is having complications.'

Cook stirred the pan of broth. 'Complications? What do you know about complications?'

'She's been in labour for almost twenty-four hours. But it weren't right. It weren't like when me mam had the twins. Something's not right and the look on the doctor's face when he came in confirmed it. I hope Lady Françoise and the baby are going to be all right.'

Cook moved away from the stove and hugged me. 'Now our Tilly, don't you go worrying yourself. The mistress will be fine. She's young and healthy.'

'I hope so.' I yawned.

'You need to take yourself off to bed for a while if you've been up all night, otherwise you'll be no good to your mistress later when she needs you.'

'Thanks, Cook.' I headed off to my room but knew that I'd be unable to sleep. I kneeled on the floor and put my hands together in prayer. 'Please God, please let Françoise and her baby live.'

Chapter 26

Tilly

Françoise was lying facing the window when I entered her room. I put the tray down on her dressing table and quietly approached, placing her arm under the crisp cotton sheet.

'Tilly?'

'Yes, madame, it's me. I've brought you some soup to help build you up as you've had such a rough time.'

'I am not hungry.'

'Please, Françoise.' I dropped formality. 'Please try. Lady Elizabeth's organising a wet nurse and I know how much you wanted to feed the baby yourself.'

'He may not live. The doctor said his lungs are undeveloped.'

'All the more reason you should feed him yourself then. Come on, sit up.' I propped up her pillows and picked up the bowl. 'Come, try.' I spooned the warm broth into her mouth.

She sipped a couple of spoonfuls before pushing the spoon away. 'I do not wish to eat.'

'Please.' I managed to coax her to sup half of the contents of the dish before she pushed me away again.

'Where is my baby?'

'He's in the nursery. Would you like me to bring him?'

'Oui.'

I patted her hand. 'I'll be right back.'

I rushed upstairs and pushed open the door on the left.

Elsie was rocking a walnut cradle. 'Hello Tilly, what are you doing here?'

'I've come to get the baby.' I picked up the tiny infant swaddled in a blue blanket. He had a head of thick jet-black hair just like the baronet.

Elsie held out her hands to stop me. 'I don't think you should take him.'

'My mistress has asked for him, and as he's her baby, I think that's what counts. Don't you?'

Elsie shrugged her shoulders. 'I suppose so. You'd best not get me into trouble though.'

I hurried from the nursery taking care on the stairs. When I got back into Françoise's room she was staring into space. 'Here. Take him.' I laid the baby in her arms.

She gazed back into the newborn's dark eyes, colour slowly returning to her cheeks. 'Oliver,' she whispered, 'that will be your name.'

'That's a wonderful name, madame,' I said. 'Would you like to try and feed him?'

'I am not sure. I am rather tired.'

'Françoise, if you don't feed Oliver then he'll have a wet nurse. Is that what you want?'

'Non.'

I adjusted her nightgown and put Oliver to her breast in the way I'd seen Mam do when feeding my twin siblings. It took me a few adjustments to get him latched on and then he began to suckle. 'See,' I said, 'he knows what to do. He's a clever little thing.'

Françoise relaxed the blanket from him and stroked his small cheeks as she shed silent tears. She'd finished feeding and was presentable when there was a knock on the door. The baronet entered without waiting to be invited.

'I see you're getting acquainted with our son.' He glanced at me and said, 'Why don't you go and get some sustenance, and I'm sure you are in need of a rest.'

'Yes, sir. Thank you, sir. I'll be back later, madame.'

Chapter 27

Françoise

'May I?' Charles signaled to the baby. I allowed him to take Oliver from my arms although I wanted to keep hold of him. The doctor's words kept going over in my head. He's a good weight but still too early. We must keep him warm. Oliver made a small whimper so Charles rocked him.

'You have done well, my darling. He's a wonderful little boy. We must give him a name.'

'His name is Oliver.' I looked up at Charles. 'I hope you do not mind.'

'Oliver. Oliver,' he repeated. 'I like it. Oliver it shall be. Oliver Louis Charles Frederick Dubois. What do you think?'

'Parfait. Perfect.' I thought it was thoughtful he'd chosen Louis after Papa.

Footsteps came along the corridor and Charles opened the door to a footman carrying a cradle. 'Where would you like it, sir?'

'Just down here next to my wife please, Edward.'

Edward placed the cradle down. 'Is there anything else, sir?'

'No, that will be all. You can go now.'

'Thank you, sir.' Edward bowed his head before leaving.

'I thought you would like Oliver in here with you until you're feeling better. Plenty of time for the nursery after that.' Charles' dark eyes sparkled causing my pulse to quicken.

'Thank you.' I smiled.

Oliver didn't stir when lowered into the cot by Charles. He was being so kind and thoughtful but could I trust him again?

He took a pew on the edge of my bed and lifted my hand to his lips. 'I'm so sorry about your papa, dearest. It must have been a dreadful shock.'

'It was. Is. I still cannot believe it.'

'I promise to take care of you. Mother told me about your conversation about... I'm sorry you had to find out but I vow to be true to you from now on.'

'But why?'

'Because I am weak. I am sorry and promise it will never happen again. You and Oliver are all that I need. Please, Françoise, say you'll forgive me.'

'I must have time to think.'

'Of course. Take all the time you need.'

I allowed Charles to rock me in his arms as I sobbed for Papa.

*

Elizabeth gazed into the cradle. 'He's a bonny little boy, isn't he? Let's just hope he's strong enough to survive.'

Oliver whimpered.

'Can you pass him please, Maman Elizabeth, so I can feed him?'

'You don't want to be doing that. I've hired a wet nurse.'

'I do not wish to have a wet nurse. I shall feed Oliver myself. Pass him, please.'

Elizabeth lifted Oliver from his bed, swaying him in her arms for a few moments before placing him in mine. 'I'll come back later.'

I had just put Oliver to my breast when I heard voices coming upstairs and Elizabeth re-entered. 'Françoise, make yourself decent, you have a surprise visitor.' She turned to the doorway as André came rushing in.

'Françoise, comment vas-tu, ma soeur?' He kissed the side of my face and stroked Oliver's brow. 'Bonjour, jeune homme. I am your uncle.' André looked up at me. 'There is someone else to see you.'

I turned to the door but no one came through though the stairs creaked as soft steps treaded up them. The door opened wider.

'Maman.'

Maman was by my side. She took Oliver from me and passed him to André. 'Ma chère enfant.' She wrapped me in her fold.

'How come… I do not understand?' I glanced from Maman to André for an answer.

'There was nothing left in France for Maman so I managed to convince her to come to England.' André rocked Oliver.

Warm tears fell to my cheeks.

'There now, ma fille.' Maman hugged me tightly.

Chapter 28

Françoise

Charles entered my chambre as the physician departed.

'Good day, Françoise. How are you this morning?'

'Dr Morris said I will be able to get up tomorrow.'

He tucked a strand of my hair behind my ear. 'That is good news, my darling. We have missed you downstairs. I have brought you a gift.' He passed me a small package.

'Merci. Do you think you could draw the drapes back, please?'

'Certainly, my darling, if the doctor said that was permissible.'

'He did.' I fumbled the package in my hands.

Charles moved over to the window and pulled open the curtains. I put my hand to my eyes as the sun was blinding. 'It looks a lovely day.'

'It is.' He came back over and perched on the edge of the bed. 'Are you going to open your gift?'

'Oui.' I unwrapped the white tissue revealing a red cloth book with gilt lettering to the spine. '*Pride and Prejudice.*'

'I am under excellent authority that the ladies love this book. Have you heard of Jane Austen?'

'Oui, but I have never read her books. I will enjoy this I am quite sure.'

'I will leave you to rest, ma chérie, and I look forward to hearing what you think about the author's writing.'

'Merci.' I flipped through the cloth pages and was admiring the wonderful illustrations when I heard Oliver cry from outside my room. I put the book down on the cabinet and held my arms out in anticipation when Tilly came in and passed my son to me. 'Merci, Tilly.' I put Oliver to my face. 'He smells so good.'

'He's just been bathed and fed.'

I touched my breasts. 'I so longed to feed him myself.'

'I know, madame, but the doctor said you were too poorly and needed to be left alone.'

I had failed my son and Elizabeth had got her way about employing a wet nurse. I cradled Oliver in my arms. 'The doctor said I may get up tomorrow. I am excited. It has been dull spending time here, especially when the room had to be darkened and I was unable to read. I cannot wait to push Oliver around the garden. It must look beautiful out there now. I imagine the magnolia must be blooming.'

'It is, madame.' Tilly picked up the book. *Pride and Prejudice.*'

'Oui.' I switched Oliver to my other side as my arm ached. 'The baronet gave it to me earlier. Have you read it?'

'No, but I know of it. From what I gather it's about a Mr Darcy. I overheard some ladies chatting about it one day in the park. They were quite excitable.'

I gave a small laugh. 'Intriguing. You are welcome to read it after me.'

'Why, thank you.' Tilly clasped her hands together as she looked closely at me. 'You look tired, madame. Shall I take him?'

'Oui. I must say I do feel fatigued.' I passed Oliver to Tilly. 'Call me Françoise, remember. We are friends. We have been through so much together.'

'I will try. Rest now and I shall return Oliver to the nursery.'

'Merci.' I picked up the book and began reading. *It is a truth universally acknowledged…*

*

I was already awake when Tilly pulled the curtains back and the sun shone across the bed.

'It looks like a glorious day.'

'It is, madame.' Tilly went to the wardrobe and pulled out my emerald taffeta gown and helped me wash and dress. As I stood up my legs became unsteady. Tilly grabbed my arm. 'It is to be expected, madame. I will help you,' she said as Charles entered.

'You look enchanting, my dear. Tilly, you may leave. I will assist my wife.'

'Yes, sir.' Tilly smiled at me.

'Come, dearest.' Charles took my arm and led me out of the room and downstairs into the dining room.

Elizabeth was already at the table but got up and rushed to my side. 'You're looking well, my dear. Come, sit down and have breakfast.'

As I took a seat next to Elizabeth, Maman and André came in and joined us.

'Ma sœur.' André kissed my cheek. 'We have missed you, have we not, Maman?'

'Comment vas-tu mon enfant?' Maman touched my shoulder. 'You have had a rough time.' Maman had been my only visitor this past week. The doctor said I was to be left alone but she had insisted on seeing me each day.

'I am well, Maman. Charles and I are going to take Oliver for a meander around the garden after breakfast.'

'Do not try and do too much.' Maman pulled a chair away from the table, perching herself next to me. 'Charles, you must take care of my daughter.'

'I will, Maman' – he stretched over and squeezed her hand – 'do not worry.' Charles strode over to the sideboard and served bacon and eggs on to a plate, returning to the table and placing the breakfast in front of me. 'Eat. You need your strength if we are to take our son for a walk.'

I hoped I would be able to eat. Everyone sat around the table chattering as knives and forks scraped across the dishes.

*

Tilly pushed Oliver into the sunroom.

'Thank you, Tilly. You may go. I will ring if we need you.' Charles put his arm around my waist. 'Are you ready, chérie?'

'Oui.' I gripped the perambulator handlebar to help steady my legs as I pushed Oliver out of the door into the sunlight, stopping to allow Charles to peep under the hood. I followed suit. Oliver was tiny. He appeared lost in the huge space.

'Thank you, Françoise, for giving me such a wonderful son.' Charles leaned his forehead to me before brushing his lips on mine.

I glanced up into his dark eyes. My husband was being attentive, more like Papa had been to Maman, but could I trust him?

'Are you ready?' he asked. 'We shan't walk for long and we'll take regular rests.'

'I am ready.' I gripped the handlebar and pushed the heavy carriage along the footpath, not stopping until we reached a bench under the magnolia in bloom at the east part of the garden.

Charles put the brake on before leading me to sit down. He put his arm around my shoulder. 'It's a warm day.'

'Oui. It is wonderful to be out in the fresh air.'

'Have you managed to read the book yet?'

'I have started but not yet finished. It is a wonderful gift, thank you. So thoughtful.'

'Anything for my dear wife.'

'Please, pass me Oliver. I would like to cradle him.'

'Of course, my dear.' Charles reached under the hood and scooped Oliver up in his shawl, placing him in my arms.

We both stared down at our son.

'He looks like you,' I said. 'Look at those dark eyes and hair.'

Charles stroked our baby's cheek. Oliver's mouth mimicked a smile.

'Wind,' I said.

We both laughed.

'The doctor said his lungs are not yet fully developed. We need to take care.' I held my son's tiny hand. 'He suggested no outside visitors for at least four weeks.'

'And so it shall be, my dearest.'

Chapter 29

Françoise

'Cook has made you a picnic hamper' – Tilly swung the basket – 'and said to tell the baronet that she's included her homemade lemonade.'

'Thank you, Tilly. Could you get Oliver ready for me, please?'

Elizabeth wandered into the hallway. 'Did I hear you mention Oliver, dear?'

'Oui, Maman Elizabeth. Charles and I are taking him to the river with us this morning.'

Elizabeth ushered me into the drawing room where Maman was reading a book in an armchair by the window.

'What appears to be the problem?' I asked Elizabeth.

'It's not a good idea to take the child out. He's too vulnerable. It's one thing taking him for a stroll around the garden but another to take him out to a public place. He's not five weeks yet. We need to protect him?'

Maman put her book down and came over. She rested her hand on my upper arm. 'I am inclined to agree with Elizabeth.'

'But I do not wish to go without Oliver. We will picnic in the garden then.'

Elizabeth frowned. 'You should spend some time with your husband. Remember you're a wife as well as a mother.'

'It will do you good to have time with Charles,' Maman said, 'and you need not concern yourself about Oliver as I shall spend time with him while you are gone.'

Heavy footsteps echoed along the hallway. I glanced up as Charles entered. 'Are you ready, ma chérie?' He gazed around the room. 'Where's Oliver? Hasn't Tilly brought him down yet?'

Elizabeth moved closer to Charles. 'You and Françoise are to go on your own. It's not safe for the child to go out in a public place yet. He's too small. Remember what Dr Morris said. We must take care to protect him. You young people have some time together. It's a lovely day. Go and enjoy.'

I looked to Maman and she nodded in agreement.

'Very well, my dearest wife. Let us go and have some fun. I see you have a picnic?'

'Oui,' I said as he took my arm and led me outside to the Phaeton.

*

Charles spread a red and white checked sheet under an overhanging willow. I adjusted my gown whilst lowering myself to the ground. The area was deserted other than ducks gliding on the water. We watched and laughed as they bobbed their heads creating ripples.

'Let's have some of Cook's lemonade.' Charles rooted through the hamper and pulled out a bottle. Removing the lid, he poured the liquid into tumblers and passed one to me. He clinked his cup with mine. 'To my beautiful wife.'

'Merci.'

'Are you happy, Françoise?'

'Oui.' I sipped the cool lemonade. 'I have a lovely son. How could I not be happy?'

'You must miss your papa?'

'Oui, I do, but I have Maman here and she would still be in France had Papa not died. I miss my friend, Geneviève. I was thinking that maybe you could ask Arthur Alcott if he would write to her. She would like that. Jokingly, I know, but she suggested I find her an English beau so she could come to England and join me. Would it not be wonderful if Arthur were to marry Geneviève?'

Charles chuckled. 'Françoise, you're a wonderful romantic. I'm sure that isn't going to happen but I will pass your friend's details on to Arthur. Now let's eat.' He rubbed his stomach.

I unwrapped a package and passed him a slice of pie.

'Doesn't Mrs Derby make the best pork pies?'

'She does indeed.' I laughed.

After we had finished picnicking, Charles moved closer, removed my hat and unclipped my hair, allowing it to run wild on my shoulders.

'Charles, not here.' I tried to clip my hair back up. 'What will people think?'

'Look around you, Françoise, there's no one else here except you and I. Now shh.' He lowered me to the ground, caressing my face and neck. 'I am indebted to you, my dearest. You've given me the most treasured gift possible. Not only a child, but a son, an heir to *Highwood*. We have fulfilled the oath and it's made us happy too. Has it not?'

'Oui.' I kissed Charles back as his lips touched mine. Could I forgive him?

*

On arriving back to *Highwood*, I went straight upstairs to the nursery. Oliver was sleeping. 'Hello, little one.' I brushed his cheek with my fingertips. His breathing was a gentle purr. 'Demain, ma pupuce, you will get to meet my friend Rebecca and her sister Grace. They are going to love you as much as I do.'

'Françoise.' Charles put his hand around my waist.

I looked up from the crib. 'What is it?'

'Dinner's being served in the dining room and everyone's waiting.'

'We had best go then.' I leaned over the cot. 'Bonne nuit, my little one.'

*

'Ah, there you both are.' Elizabeth took a bread roll from the plate in the centre of the table 'We thought we were going to have to send out a search party.'

I took a seat next to Maman. 'I was with my son after being away from him for hours. How has he been?'

'He has been a delight. Come, my child, eat.' Maman served me a bowl of chicken soup.

'Merci.' I supped the warm liquid.

'We had a wonderful day, didn't we, my love?' Charles touched my shoulder before making his way to the head of the table.

'We did. It was a lovely day. Merci.'

'It is important you have more days like that together as a couple.' Elizabeth picked up a glass and took a sip of water.

'Tomorrow my friends are coming to meet Oliver. Will you be here too, Charles?'

'I would not miss it. I've heard Mother's organised an excellent spread.'

Chapter 30

Tilly

Cook took a chocolate sponge from the oven and put in two more sponges, one pink and one yellow, for the Battenburg. A range of iced and decorated tiny cakes sat on the cooling rack. Daisy and I had to try and keep up with washing the baking dishes in order that Cook could reuse them to make more treats.

'Come on, Tilly, get a move on, lass,' Cook said, 'I need to make a Victoria sponge.'

I rinsed the last baking tin and Daisy dried it before passing it to Cook.

The Alcott sisters were coming to meet little Oliver, and Lady Elizabeth had insisted on a tantalising afternoon tea, including pralines, almond sweets and a large quantity of mixed sweets.

The bell on the front door chimed. Cook wiped her hands on her pinny. 'That'll be them. You lassies get this lot upstairs. Edward,' she called, 'can you come and help?'

'Yes, Cook.' Edward winked at me. His hazel eyes sparkled.

'He's still sweet on you,' Daisy whispered. We both laughed, venturing upstairs armed with silver trays crammed with sandwiches, cakes and treats.

Edward came up behind us. 'Ladies, let me.' He knocked on the drawing room door.

When Lady Elizabeth called, 'Come,' we entered and set the food down on the table. Daisy made her way over to Françoise and peeped at Oliver in his cradle. 'He's so tiny.'

'Yes, he is,' Lady Elizabeth said, 'but come away now, Daisy, we don't want you breathing germs over him.'

'Sorry, madam.

'Tilly,' Françoise said, 'can you stay please? You can pour tea for our guests and help me with Oliver.'

'Yes, madame.' I caught Lady Elizabeth flash an angry look at my mistress. I loved how Françoise and I had become closer since her long labour.

'The child should have a nanny.' Elizabeth frowned. 'Not your maid looking after him.'

'I don't mind,' I said.

'It isn't up to you, Tilly.' Lady Elizabeth huffed. 'Oliver needs someone qualified.'

Françoise stood up. 'I am sorry, Maman Elizabeth, but Oliver is my son and I am happy with Tilly caring for him. I do not wish to have a nanny so there is nothing else to say. It is my decision.'

'We'll see what Charles has to say about that, but for now, sit back down. Your guests will arrive shortly.'

Françoise rocked Oliver's cradle, muttering something as Rebecca bustled in. 'Where is he?' Rebecca charged over to Françoise and leaned in to look at Oliver. 'He's beautiful, Françoise. He looks just like Sir Charles. How are you, my dear friend? I hear things have not been easy for you.'

'I am doing fine now and enjoying being a maman.'

Rebecca perched on a seat next to Françoise and they were chatting as Grace Alcott stormed in. 'Where is he?' She coughed. 'Let me see.' Grace coughed again as she pushed past her sister.

Lady Elizabeth jumped up from the couch. 'That sounds like the one-hundred-day cough. You must go now. Both of you. Oliver will not stand a chance if he contracts that.'

'I don't think it is. Although' – Grace put her hand to her mouth as she coughed again – 'the twins have been coughing a lot. Oh dear… I'm sorry, I didn't mean to bring infection to your home. We'll leave now. Sister, come quickly.'

Rebecca gave a long look to Françoise before joining her sister and leaving.

'I think I should take Oliver upstairs.' Françoise picked up the baby as her maman entered. 'What is happening? Where have your guests gone?' she asked.

'I sent them away,' Lady Elizabeth said, 'I'm concerned the elder sister was suffering from chincough.'

Françoise's maman shook her head. 'Non. Non. Not coqueluche. That cannot be. We cannot lose the baby too.'

*

Plates of assorted cakes were laid on the refectory table for the staff to eat after supper but I had no appetite. I was concerned about Oliver. How could that Alcott girl have come to *Highwood* knowing she had a cough? Even if it wasn't the dreaded hundred-day one, she should've stayed away from a new baby. I hoped Oliver was going to be all right. It was worrying as Dr Morris had already said he risked mortality being small and under-developed. I knew from when Mam had lost my brother at six months that this bronchial disease was particularly fatal for babies. I prayed Oliver wouldn't get ill.

Chapter 31

Françoise

The front doorbell chimed and within minutes Dr Morris marched into the drawing room. 'Where's the child?'

'He is here.' I steadied the cradle.

The doctor placed his black bag down on the chair and put his palm across my baby's forehead. 'He has a fever.'

Oliver coughed, almost gasping for breath.

The doctor shook his head. 'I'm sorry your ladyship but there's no doubt the child has chincough. My advice is to keep him cool and hydrated' – he shook his head – 'however, I fear it's only a matter of time as the infant's lungs are too weak.'

'No,' I screamed.

Charles put his arm around me. 'We will pray, my dear. Come to chapel with me.'

'Non. Non. I am not leaving my baby.'

Maman stroked Oliver's tiny cheek. 'I will get something to cool him down.' She hurried from the room.

Doctor Morris picked up his bag. 'Let the fever run its course and do as your husband suggests and pray. There's nothing else to be done. Good day. I regret I can't offer better news.' He left the room tutting and shaking his head.

Maman returned with a bowl and sponge. She dabbed Oliver's forehead. 'Tilly is making sure that the wet nurse is on hand.'

Charles placed his hand on mine. 'Come to chapel. We'll pray together.'

'Non. I am staying here.' I lifted my baby from the cradle and rocked him in my arms.

Maman loosened Oliver's clothes. 'Charles, I will come to pray with you. Françoise, Oliver will be cooler in the cradle and keep bathing him. Not just his forehead but his chest and the back of his neck too. Charles and I will go to chapel and pray. We must not give up.' Maman turned to André. 'Will you come too, son?'

'Non. You two go' – André rested on the couch next to me – 'I will stay with Françoise.' Once they had gone, he said, 'Are you going to put him in the cradle as Maman suggested?'

'Non. I am going to hold him every minute I can. I never want to let him go.' I stared into my baby's closed eyes while mopping his brow.

Tilly entered. Her eyes appeared red and puffy like she had been crying. 'The wet nurse is waiting, madame. Shall I take Oliver?'

'Non. Not yet.' I held him to my chest. 'Why was I not able to feed my own baby? Maybe if I had he would not have taken ill.'

'That is not so, ma sœur. It would not have made any difference. But now you must allow Tilly to take Oliver so he may be fed to keep him hydrated.'

Tilly held her arms out. 'Madame?'

André squeezed my hand. 'Remember what the doctor said, ma sœur. You must keep him hydrated.'

'But I do not want to leave him.'

'I know, but you must. It will not be for long. Tilly will bring him straight back.'

'I will, madame. It shan't take long for him to be fed.'

'Françoise?' André held out his arms to take Oliver.

'Non.' I shook my head and hugged my baby tighter.

'You need to let him go.' André prised Oliver from my arms and passed him to Tilly.

'I will hurry back, Lady Françoise.' Tilly's eyes glazed as she shared my pain.

The room appeared suddenly silent without Oliver. My stomach bore tight knots. I got up and shuffled over to the window. Looking out, I remembered our strolls. The first time I had ventured into the garden with him. He had looked so tiny in the giant perambulator and now he may never grow to fill it. *Please God do not take my baby.*

André came up behind me and put his arm about me.

'He cannot die.' I put my hand to my mouth. 'I have only had him for five weeks. It is not right. It cannot be right.'

'I know, ma sœur.' André held me in his arms and let me weep. 'I know, but we must not give up hope.' He patted my back.

Chapter 32

Tilly

On June 6, 1896 the clocks at *Highwood* were stopped at three o'clock, marking the time when baby Oliver departed from this world. The curtains had all been drawn, photograph frames turned face down and mirrors covered in crepe to stop Oliver's spirit becoming trapped in the glass. A wreath of laurel and yew had been hung on the front door to alert neighbours and visitors that a death had occurred. The bell knob was draped with black crepe and tied with white ribbon.

I squeezed my eyes to prevent tears falling but one escaped and fell to Oliver's ice-cold face as I washed and dressed him in a blue gown with a lace frilled collar. It was Françoise's favourite.

I knew what to do as I'd watched Mam prepare my baby brother. Simon was his name. Another tear fell. Was it for Oliver or Simon? Or both? I'd been eleven or twelve at the time. Da told me to help Mam, but once the parlour door was closed she said to sit on the chair and not say a word. Was it me who'd killed our Simon? I'd had the cough but then so had my siblings. I shook my head. No. No, it wasn't my fault, no more than it had been Grace Alcott's that Oliver had died.

Mam had cried in bed at night when she thought no one could hear her. Next thing she was expecting and later gave birth to the twins. Da had said no one was to mention Simon's name again. He'd been a bonny little thing. I used to be like a little mam to him. Bathed and changed him. Rocked him in my arms. I hadn't thought about him for years but now getting Oliver prepared, Simon wouldn't leave my mind. I slapped the side of my head.

Oliver was ready. I laid his tiny body in the cradle and he looked like a doll, just as Simon had.

Françoise had been so distraught since Oliver's passing that her maman insisted she take to her bed for recovery. I hoped her mind would not go. Mam didn't have time to grieve with a hoard of kids and a husband. She'd get up at five to cook Da's breakfast before he went to work and by six o'clock she'd be scrubbing the kitchen floor but she never complained. It was her lot, she'd say.

There was a knock on the door. A middle-aged man tiptoed into the room, his head bent, and his dark suit loose on his narrow shoulders. He carried a black box and frame. 'I'm here to photograph the young deceased.'

I stepped away to the side of the room as he took off his hat and began assembling the tripod and camera.

He moved the lens forwards and back, focusing on baby Oliver. Afterwards he took the glass plate, added a substance, and slipped it back into the camera. He checked and examined the glass to see how it was doing and then repeated the process three times.

'I am finished. The developed image will be delivered to Sir Charles.' The photographer gathered up his equipment, picked up his hat, took one last peep at Oliver before tipping his hat and saying to me, 'Good day, miss,' and leaving the room.

After snipping a lock of Oliver's dark hair, as instructed by the baronet, I placed it into an oval, gold-plated locket he'd given to me earlier. I lifted Oliver from the cradle and gently laid him in the small white coffin on the cooling board, which took pride of place in the parlour, and I scattered flowers on his porcelain face and around him.

Chapter 33

Françoise

It had been four days since my dearest Oliver had closed his eyes for the final time. Today we had to say goodbye to him forever. Mr Hughes had sent out invitations to the Dubois' friends and acquaintances to attend Oliver's funeral. Elizabeth had been adamant that the Alcotts stayed away and I was at a mind not to care either way. Lots of chairs had been assembled in the drawing room.

Tilly helped me into a black crepe gown. I do not know how I would have managed without her. She had insisted on getting Oliver ready and had become much more than a maid, she was a true friend.

My tears had dried up after days of weeping. Charles had been fairly attentive but it was Maman, André, and Tilly who were my support.

'Madame, are you ready?' Tilly asked.

'Oui.' I adjusted my gown. I knew I would never be ready. André and Maman were on the landing as I came out of my chambre and we went downstairs together. We joined Charles and his mother in the parlour to say our goodbyes to Oliver where candle and flower fragrances merged.

Tears I thought had evaporated returned. Charles passed me his handkerchief and I dabbed my eyes. Maman groaned. Elizabeth who normally showed no emotion broke down and cried. André squeezed her hand and led her away from the coffin. Maman went with them. Charles and I leaned over the casket and as I caressed Oliver's flawless face Charles kept his arm about me.

'I have something for you' – he took a gold necklace from his pocket – 'look.' He opened the locket. The oval frame on the left-hand side had a picture of Oliver. His near black eyes glared back at me. A lock of his black hair was inserted in the right. Charles placed the necklace around my neck and fastened the clasp at the back.

I stroked the gold floral motif. 'Thank you, Charles. It is beautiful. I shall treasure it for evermore.'

'It's time,' he said, 'our mourners are waiting.' He wiped my eyes before leading me out of the parlour and along the corridor to the drawing room. There I took my seat beside Charles at the head of the line. Elizabeth sat on the other side of him and André was next to me with Maman on his right. The room was crammed with ladies and gentlemen. Most of them I did not recognise.

*

André lifted Oliver, in his casket, feet first from the house. He was taken out this way so he was unable to look back and beckon someone else to go with him but how I longed to be taken with him. André slid Oliver into the domed, white-framed, glass hearse and surrounded him with flowers. Ostrich plumes decorated the carriage and ponies.

André and the clergy headed the procession on foot. Oliver's carriage was next, followed by Charles, me and both our mamans. The rest of the mourners walked behind us.

Charles took my arm to steady me as we slowly shuffled along. How could this be happening? First Papa and now Oliver. How could God be so cruel? I had fallen in love with my child and now he was gone. Maman said I would learn to cope with Charles at my side, as she had done with her lost babies, but Charles was not Papa. Charles did not love me like Papa had loved Maman.

We arrived at the graveyard where gravediggers stood beside the hole waiting. The plot for Oliver was next to Charles' sister Catherine, and his father Frederick. Now my little boy was to be alone until Charles and I joined him.

We stood around while the tiny coffin was lowered by the gravediggers using long braids. I reached for my locket and brushed my fingers against the engraved flower, crying silent tears. Once Oliver was interred the priest and his clerks approached the graveside. Charles gripped my arm as the priest said, *Lord have mercy upon us* and followed with the *Lord's Prayer.*

Earth to earth, ashes to ashes, dust to dust. The priest took a handful of earth and sprinkled it on Oliver's coffin. Charles passed me his handkerchief and I let my tears flow free.

A clap of thunder roared. The mourners looked up at the darkened sky.

Elizabeth gripped my hand and smiled. 'Oliver has reached Heaven,' she said as torrential rain poured.

Chapter 34

Tilly

Daisy and I watched out of the window as Cora climbed into a cart with her da. Her rosy cheeks had gone and were replaced with a ghostlike look. I hoped she wasn't going to die too although she can't have had the one-hundred-day cough like Oliver as she hadn't been coughing. It was her sickness and bellyache that were the problem. The doctor had visited yesterday after Mr Hughes and Mrs Jarvis felt she should be checked out.

Once the cart had gone, Daisy ushered me outside. 'It seems our Cora is in the family way.'

'How do you know?'

'I heard Cook and Mrs Jarvis talking about half an hour ago.'

'But who? When?'

Daisy shrugged her shoulders.

'But she wasn't courting and she never goes anywhere except home to her mam and dad.'

'I know. And that's why I've been thinking. I reckon it was Archie.'

'What?'

'It's the only explanation. I think he must've done to her what he did to you.'

'That does seem likely as there's no way Cora would've given herself willingly to him. She wasn't that kind of girl.'

'You need to tell Lady Françoise.'

'I can't do that. She's in no state. She's only just buried her son.'

'Then leave this house before he does it to you again. I'm going to get myself out of here. I don't trust him.'

'What are you girls up to out there?' Cook called.

'Nothing,' I said, 'we're just taking a quick break.'

'Be back in five minutes. I need Daisy in here, to peel the potatoes, and you need to be with your mistress.'

'Yes, Cook,' we answered together.

'Listen, Tilly,' Daisy continued, 'there's a new household moved into the big house up the road at Cooper's Lodge. The Martins. I've heard they're looking for staff. Come with me. I reckon we'd both get fixed up.'

'I can't, Daisy. I can't leave Françoise. Not now. She needs me.'

'Daisy,' Cook shouted.

'I'm coming.' Daisy headed towards the door but turned back when a carriage pulled up outside at the side of the house. We both glared as Anna, Lady Elizabeth's lady's maid, made her way towards the Landau while a boy loaded up her trunk. Scowling, she glanced back at the house before stepping into the carriage. The driver flicked the reins as the horses trotted down the drive.

'First Cora and now Anna. What's going on?' I asked.

We rushed inside to Cook, and Daisy said, 'You're never going to believe this but Anna's just left.'

'You're not telling those tall tales again, are you, Daisy?'

'No, she isn't,' I said. 'I was there too. The driver loaded her trunk onto the carriage and she got inside.'

Cook looked up from the saucepan. 'Well, I never. I'll speak to Mrs Jarvis later.'

Chapter 35

Françoise

July 1896

I rose from my seat and moved towards the window. 'I cannot believe what you are saying.'

'I know, ma soeur, it is hard to digest, but you understand, I could not keep this information from you?' André flicked hair away from his forehead.

I grabbed the back of the armchair to steady myself.

André was at my side. 'Come, sit back down.' He lowered me onto the chaise longue and sat next to me.

I pressed my fingers into my brow. 'Surely Charles would not do that to me?'

'I did not think so either but the facts speak for themselves.'

Heavy footsteps echoed along the hallway. Charles pushed open the door. 'What's the urgency?' he asked. 'Françoise, dearest, is there a problem?'

André shot up. His face radiated red. 'Yes, monsieur, there is a problem and that problem I am saddened to say is you. The way you have treated my sister, your child bride, and abandoned her while she's mourning.'

Charles blinked. 'I don't understand.' He glanced across at me. 'Françoise, do you know what this is about?'

I got as far as, 'Unfortunately…'

'Françoise, I will deal with this.' André glared at Charles. 'It has come to my attention that you are still visiting the trollop's bed.'

Charles frowned. 'I don't know what you're talking about.'

'I think you do.' André raised his voice. 'You have been down in the village when your place was here consoling my sister after the loss of Oliver.'

Charles glanced across at me. His coal-like eyes glazed. 'I'm in mourning too.'

'It is true, mon frère,' I said, 'he is grieving too.'

'That may be so, Françoise.' André's voice softened. 'But the difference is you have been here to support him whereas he…' He raised his voice again. 'He has sought solace with his strumpet. And please do not try and deny this, monsieur. You have been seen.'

Charles put a hand to his face. 'Please accept my apologies, Françoise. I did not set out to deceive you.'

'Then why?' I got up and moved over to the fireplace next to Charles.

He drummed his fingers on the mantelpiece. 'It's complicated.'

'Complicated?' André stomped towards Charles. 'Complicated.' He threw his arms to the side. 'You are lucky, Monsieur Dubois, that I am not casting my glove at your adulterous face.'

'André, please do not.' I covered my eyes. 'Charles,' I asked, 'is it true? Is she carrying your child?'

'She means nothing to me, dearest. It is you I love, but yes, I'm afraid the child is mine.'

'Then I can no longer stay here.' I turned to André. 'Mon frère, please find a new family home for us far away from *Highwood*, and discuss a settlement figure with Charles on my behalf.'

'Françoise, please, no' – Charles drew me back – 'I beg you not to leave me. She means nothing.'

I pushed him at arm's length. 'But the child does.' I took a deep breath. 'I am sorry, Charles, but you cannot expect me to stay here when I have lost my child and you will have a new son or daughter in close proximity.' I headed for the door and once behind it, covered my eyes and sobbed.

*

Elizabeth paced the room. 'I don't believe I'm hearing this. I've already dismissed Anna and must put up with that surly maid who never has a smile, and now…'

'It is true, Maman Elizabeth. He admitted it to me.' I blinked to stop myself breaking down in tears.

Maman leaned forward on the armchair and said to Elizabeth, 'My husband and I trusted you to take care of our daughter.'

'And I have.' Elizabeth picked up the teapot. 'Madam Antoinette,' she said to Maman, 'join me in tea and we'll discuss the situation.'

'Non. I do not wish for tea. What is there to discuss? André is seeking an alternative family home for us.' Maman clasped her hands.

'That's far too drastic.' Elizabeth placed a cup of tea on the occasional table towards Maman and passed a cup to me. 'Françoise, please don't go. I have already lost a daughter and my grandson; I can't lose you too.'

'But, Maman Elizabeth, you still have Bertha, and soon you will have another grandchild, possibly a grandson, who will live in close proximity. I cannot stay here with he or she so close knowing what has happened to my baby boy and it is unfair of you to expect me to. Charles is still visiting Anna's bed, and

138

once the child is born, he will see the child every day. He or she may be illegitimate, but they will be your blood.'

Elizabeth took a sip from her beverage. 'Please, Françoise, please reconsider. Let me speak to my son.'

Maman pushed away the cup and saucer. 'Elizabeth, you cannot expect ma fille to stay here while Charles flaunts his expectant mistress.'

'No, of course not, but suppose I guarantee he will no longer see her?'

I took Elizabeth's hand. 'You cannot make that promise. Once we leave, I will stay in touch, but please, I do not wish Charles to know our whereabouts.'

'Very well, dear. I understand.' Elizabeth poured more tea.

Chapter 36

Tilly

It wasn't the same at *Highwood* after Daisy had left two days ago. The new maids, Ethel and Ada, had arrived together from the same household. Last night they'd excluded me from their conversation as they giggled in the corner of the kitchen when Cook and Mrs Jarvis weren't around. I even missed Cora and Anna. Anna's replacement was a strait-laced spinster. Why Lady Elizabeth had chosen someone like that I was unable to comprehend.

Françoise had asked to see me in the drawing room. As I made my way there someone grabbed me from behind. 'Hello, treasure.' Archie smirked. 'I imagine you and I will be seeing more of each other now Daisy's out of the way.' He winked before leaving me with my heart racing. How was I going to avoid being on my own now that Daisy had gone?

I tapped on the door. When Françoise called, 'Come in, Tilly,' I entered. She was on the chaise longue pouring tea into flowery patterned china.

'Sit down, Tilly.'

I looked around the room unsure what to do.

'It is all right. There is no one else here. Come. I need to speak to you.'

With trepidation, I approached the chair opposite her, my legs trembling as I eased myself down. 'Yes, Lady Françoise.' I made a point of keeping to formality in the event the baronet or Lady Elizabeth wandered in.

'Relax, Tilly. We are alone and will not be disturbed.' She passed me a cup of tea. 'Help yourself to a teacake or biscuit.'

'Thank you, madame.' I reached across and chose a digestive from the plate.

'It's Françoise, remember. We are friends.'

I smiled feeling far too nervous to say her first name out loud. I took a bite of the biscuit and wondered what Daisy would make of this. Perhaps Françoise was going to dismiss me. Crumbs got caught in my throat causing me to cough. I sipped the tea to clear it.

'How are things now with you and the baronet's valet? Is he leaving you alone?'

I chewed my lip. Her eyes were puffy from crying. I didn't want to add my burden to her worries.

'Tilly?' She stared straight at me. 'What's going on?'

I coughed. 'Now that Daisy's left…' I turned away.

'Tilly, tell me.'

'Now that Daisy's gone, I can't be sure of staying safe.'

'Pourquoi? Has something happened?'

'He grabbed me just now as I was coming in here.'

She sighed, shaking her head. 'Then what I have to say may suit.'

My pulse quickened. 'Are you dismissing me?'

Françoise gave a small laugh. 'On the contrary, my dear friend. I have plans and you fit in to them nicely.' She got up, strolled across to the windowsill and sniffed the soft-pink sweet peas in the vase. 'Such a strong scent, don't you think, Tilly?'

'Yes, madame. They look and smell beautiful. But please, tell me more about these plans.'

'That was wrong of me to keep you in suspense. I get that from mon frère, he is always tormenting me that way.' She laughed before making her way back to the chaise longue. 'Now, what I am about to confide in you must not leave this room. Understand?'

'I understand. I don't have anyone to talk to now that Daisy and Cora have gone. Elsie doesn't bother with me now she's made friends with the nannies of surrounding households. It's all changed at *Highwood*. No longer the happy place it was. I know why Daisy and Cora left but no idea why Anna did.' I popped the last bite of biscuit into my mouth.

'Anna was dismissed.'

'Dismissed?'

'Oui. At my request.'

'But why?'

'I discovered she had been sharing a bed with my husband. I am sure there must have been gossip downstairs.'

'No. I hadn't heard anything.'

'Well, the valet knew. And that I understand is why the baronet refused to dismiss him. I fear he was blackmailing my husband.'

'I had no idea.'

'I will not go into it all now but I discovered recently that Anna is with child sired by the baronet.'

I put my hand to my mouth. 'Françoise, I'm so sorry.'

'I do not need pity, Tilly. What is done is done. However, I can no longer stay at *Highwood*.' Françoise got up and moved back to the window but this time looked out at the garden. 'I shall be sorry to leave here as I love it, but you understand how I cannot stay?' She turned back to face me.

'Yes, of course. But where do I fit in?'

'André is seeking a new family home near Oxford and I would like you to join us. You have a wonderful way with needle and thread. What you do not know is that prior to coming to *Highwood* I used to make a lot of my gowns. Not to the same standard as you but good enough to wear for scrambling through the woods and up trees.'

I chuckled. 'Really? Your father allowed you to do that?'

'Oui. He did. Although he had insisted I learned to sew. Even with funds from England, there was insufficient money to keep up with my wardrobe when I constantly had mishaps. André and I were always getting up to mischief. It was therefore rather a shock when Papa announced on my seventeenth birthday that I was to come to England and marry. "Time to grow up," he told me. I cried that night knowing I would never again be able to run wild.'

I took a sip of tea. 'I've never done that. Before I came here, I had to help Mam care for my younger siblings and then once here…' I took another sip of tea but mainly to hide my moist eyes.

'I understand. You have not had an easy life. Anyway, I am digressing. I would like you to help improve my sewing skills in order that we may set up a small dressmaking business. I shall portray myself as a widow. I am still in mourning for Oliver so my gowns will reflect bereavement anyway, and you, my dear friend, will be introduced as my companion. What do you think?'

I mulled everything around in my head, unsure of what to say. What did I have left here apart from Daisy and she was in another household? At best we'd only see each other one afternoon a week. I had no family since Da had disowned me and I desperately wanted to get away from Archie.

'Do you need time to think about it?'

I thought about Mam. 'Perhaps I do need a little time. I would like to speak to me mam first.'

'Are you sure about that, Tilly? What about your papa?'

'I shall be careful. It's my half day off tomorrow. I will visit then and give you my answer later. Will that be all right?'

'Oui. Of course. But please, be careful.'

'I will, and there's something you should know about Archie.'

'What is it?'

'I think he may have done the same to Cora as he did to me. Daisy left because she was too frightened to stay for fear he'd do it to her too.'

'I shall speak to the baronet and Lady Elizabeth. Sir Charles has nothing to fear from the valet now. He will be dismissed with immediate effect.'

Chapter 37

Tilly

My heart beat faster as I approached the cottage and heard the front door creak open. I rushed to hide behind an ancient yew. Da came out first and Frank followed. Frank hadn't changed at all, still tall and lanky, with that thick head of brown hair. I missed his teasing.

'Wait for us,' squealed the twins as they raced across the field after Da and Frank.

Once they were out of sight, I made my way to the back door, tapping it before opening. 'Mam.'

She turned around from the scullery sink. For a moment her eyes lit up at seeing me but her almost toothless smile soon dropped. Her face paled to almost white. 'Tilly. God in heaven, girl, what yous doing here?'

'I need to speak to you.'

Shaking, she ushered me in. 'Quick. And shuts the door behind yous. Yous can't stay long as your da will be back soon and if he catches yous…'

'I know but I had to see you.'

Mam picked up a pan of boiling water and poured water into the teapot. 'Sit yaself down and have a cup of char but then yous must go.' Harsh lines protruded on her forehead that weren't visible last time I was here and she'd lost a lot of weight. I hoped she wasn't ill.

Mam passed me a chipped mug. 'Here. Now tell me why yous here.'

I sipped the weak tea. 'Are you ill, Mam?'

'That's not why yous come here, girl, and we haven't much time so yous best get on with it.'

'My mistress is moving and wants me to go with her.'

'I see. And your babby?'

'I never had one.'

'False alarm then.' She sighed. 'All that bother for nothin.'

'It seems so.' I wasn't going to tell her I'd miscarried after what Da had done to me.

'So, where's yous going?' Mam dug a hand into her back as she sat down at the table with me.

'Near Oxford.'

'Where's that?'

'Somewhere northwards, I think.' I took a deep breath and almost whispered, 'I wanted to talk to you about something.'

'Go on.' She fidgeted with her fingers.

'My mistress's baby died recently.'

'Poor lady. I'm sure she'll be blessed with another one soon.'

'Maybe. Look, Mam, I know we were never allowed to mention but...'

'What?'

'It brought back memories of our Simon.'

Mam put her hand to her face. 'Don't, our Tilly.'

'We never talked about him. It was like he hadn't existed.'

'And I don't wants to talk about him now. I think yous should go.'

'Sorry, Mam. I didn't mean to upset you but I need to know. Was it my fault Simon died?'

'Of course not, yous stupid girl. Now don't start dragging things up that are best forgotten.'

'But, Mam, he was...'

'I knows quite well what he was and I don't need yous comin here and upsettin me. Go. Hurry before your da gets back and we boths get a thrashin.'

'Do you think he'll ever allow me home to visit? I miss everyone. The twins look like they're growing up.'

'Aye they are. And no, our Tilly. Yous dead to your father and if he catches yous here he'll give yous a beating and mees too for lettin yous in. Go with yous mistress and have a good life.'

'You think I should go to Oxford?'

'Yes, I does. Make a good life for yous.' She stood up. 'Yous must go. Hurry.'

I got up and put my mug by the sink.

She followed and just for a moment hugged me. 'I does love yous.'

I opened the back door. 'I love you too, Mam.' I rushed away from the cottage as Mam closed the door behind me. When I looked back, she was gone. I heard the twins squealing so I quickly hid behind the enormous yew and watched.

'I'm coming for yous,' shouted Frank, picking them up, one by one, and swinging them around.

I hated Da for depriving me of my family.

PART II

Chapter 1

Françoise

March 1897

The Landau pulled into the drive of our new home. André had not been exaggerating about its beauty. I adored the whitewashed walls and Georgian windows. It was larger than *Vue de Jardin* but smaller than *Highwood* although it still had plenty of surrounding greenery. I touched my flat stomach. It seemed so long ago when Oliver was inside me, and nine months since we had buried him, leaving me hollow. My last memory was of him lying in the white casket robed in his beautiful blue dress looking like he was sleeping. I had prayed for his black sapphire eyes to open. That it was all a bad dream. But he had not opened his eyes because it was not a bad dream, it was real. My beautiful boy had gone. It broke my heart all over again when I visited his graveside before leaving *Highwood* to say my final goodbye. Charles now had his illegitimate son so I was pleased to have finally made this move.

André opened the carriage door, took my hand and helped me out before assisting Maman. 'What do you think?' he asked.

'It is beautiful,' I answered, 'we shall name it *Sunbury Manor.*'

Maman put her arm about me. 'You will be happy here, ma fille.'

Tilly stood behind André as he passed a few coins to the coachman. 'Merci, monsieur.'

The driver tipped his hat before flicking the reins and the horses trotted back down the drive as I ambled towards the house. Pink camellias bloomed in the borders. I moved closer to take in their strong jasmine scent. 'I will never forget you, Oliver,' I said aloud.

'None of us will.' André sniffed the flowers. 'They are delightful. Now come. All of you. I am excited for you to see.' He unlocked the arched framed black front door and led us into the reception area. André had sent a wagon ahead with our belongings and appointed workers from the village to unpack and complete various tasks, which must have included polishing the floor as it shone in the wide hallway.

We followed him through another arched doorway. 'This is the drawing room,' he said.

I surveyed the large area. Elm floorboards bordered a scarlet floral carpet. A seating area consisted of two silver-grey, three-seater couches, and an upright dusty pink velvet armchair, perfect for Maman.

'Tilly,' Maman said, 'come and help me make tea while André finishes giving Françoise a tour of the house.'

'Non, Maman,' I said. 'Tilly is to finish the tour too. She is not here as our maid.'

Maman shook her head. 'Do not talk nonsense, child. What is this world coming to when gentry mix with servants?'

'Times change, Maman. We are almost in the twentieth century and Tilly is my friend. I do not know how I would have got through this last year without her.'

Tilly turned to go to the kitchen. 'I should go and make tea, madame.'

André pulled her back. 'No, Tilly. You need to see the house.'

'I suppose I had better make the tea then.' Maman tutted. 'Goodness knows what your papa would make of this.' She waddled along the corridor.

Tilly's face reddened. 'I don't wish to cause a problem.'

'You are not. It is Maman's old-fashioned views that are causing a problem. I told her before we came that you were not coming with us as a servant. I meant what I said. You are my friend.'

'But if I'm your companion, surely that still makes me a servant.'

'Non. You will be introduced as my assistant. I will not have you as a servant no matter what Maman or anyone else says. You are my friend.'

'Shall we continue with this tour?' André interrupted.

We followed him down the hallway until he stopped at a door entrance and smiled. 'And this is your workroom.'

Tilly and I, open-mouthed, moved around the room, checking the three mannequins, a sewing machine and a cabinet consisting of various fabrics and thread. Sunlight from the huge windows was perfect. 'You've thought of everything,' I said.

'This room is due to Tilly,' André said. 'She provided me with a full inventory of your work requirements. Let us return to the drawing room for a while and have tea. We will make a list of what to do next.'

We strolled along the corridor and into the drawing room. A rattling of china echoed in the wide space as Maman pushed in a trolley of refreshments, still muttering under her breath. She poured tea into the cups.

'We need to think about staff.' André nibbled a chicken and ham sandwich.

'Well, we would not need to worry if you let Tilly do her job.' Maman passed around a plate of breads.

'Maman, both Françoise and I have told you that Tilly is not here as a maid. She is here as Françoise's assistant with the new business. I will employ a couple of local girls. Now, you must sit down and not do anything else strenuous today. You are too old to be waiting on us all like this. We are all fatigued, but particularly you.'

'Merci, mon fils.' Maman flopped into the armchair. 'This is perfect.'

'André is right, Maman. You look exhausted. Tilly and I will fix a meal this evening.'

'Talking of Tilly.' André beamed. 'Have you always been Tilly, or has your name been shortened?'

'My birth name is Matilda but I've only ever been called Tilly.'

'Matilda. Matilda,' André repeated. 'Yes, I like it. I think you should be known as Matilda. Would you object to that?'

'Not at all. I love it.' Tilly's blue eyes sparkled.

Maman muttered under her breath and glared at Tilly.

Chapter 2

Tilly

Dear Daisy,

We have finally arrived. The house is lovely although not as grand as Highwood. Oxhaven appears to be a nice village. It took three days to get here. On the trip up we had to stop overnight twice and stay in an inn but Monsieur André would not allow Lady Françoise, Maman Antoinette or me near the saloon. We were ushered straight upstairs to our rooms.

I'm sorry that we didn't get together before I left. I miss you. It's been so long since I last saw you. It must be three months or more. They seem to work you very hard at Coopers Lodge but I hope you're happy there. I hope that one day you'll be able to visit me here.

Lady Françoise and I are to set up a business as dressmakers with wealthy women from the village as our clients. Maman Antoinette hates me. I think she sees me as an upstart and would prefer to have me in the kitchen scrubbing floors. I fear it will take some time to win her over but I shan't give up. Lady Françoise has been giving me elocution lessons to ensure I speak proper, I mean properly.

I have a bedroom of my own. Can you believe that? A lovely room it is too.

Monsieur André's so handsome. I think I may just be a little in love with him although I can't imagine he'd ever be interested in someone like me and his maman would never allow it. My heart has long forgotten Archie. I wonder why he's still hanging around Beckton. I can't see him getting another position locally after the baronet refused to give him a reference. I was so pleased to finally get away from him.

I have made bread and broth for luncheon although Monsieur André likes his bread with cheese.

I miss Mam and my siblings. Maybe one day Da will forgive me.

Monsieur André's calling. I'd better go.

Write soon.

I love and miss you.

Forever your friend
Tilly

p.s. Monsieur André calls me Matilda. How posh is that?

Chapter 3

Françoise

'Mrs Taylor at the village retail establishment has kindly offered to speak to her clients about our dressmaking.' I placed the shopping basket on the scullery counter and turned to Tilly. 'She believes we will be busy in no time at all.'

'Our new venture is exciting. I've just come in here after checking the stitching on the gown you finished last night.'

'And?'

'Perfection. You'll be teaching me shortly.' Tilly filled the kettle for tea as André entered the scullery with his hands behind his back.

'How did you get on?' he asked.

'I was telling Tilly that Mrs Taylor predicts sending us lots of clients. And Tilly here was just saying how proficient I am in my new skill.'

'You will need a diary to book appointments.' André grinned.

'Oui. You are quite right, mon frère. We must purchase one. I will add it to the list.'

André beamed as he passed me a large book from behind his back.

'Parfait.' I took the diary and placed it on the table. 'Mmm. What is that lovely smell?'

Tilly hurried to the oven, opened the door, and pulled out a cob loaf. 'I've made bread.'

André sniffed the bread. 'Smells wonderful.' He rubbed his stomach. 'We should have that with fromage. You did manage to pick up some Brie de Meaux, ma sœur?'

I smiled. 'Bien sûr. I know it is your favourite and I also managed to purchase a cheddar wheel.'

André's eyes glinted.

*

I followed Tilly into the work dressing room. Finished gowns hung on a rail by the window. Emerald, Prussian blue, gold with a pink floral pattern, violet and magenta. I ran my fingers across the silk and satin fabrics. Each gown had been completed with a surplus of eight inches that could be let out, and they could all be taken in.

The mannequins displayed unfinished dresses with a close-fitting bodice, the skirt tightening in at the waist and falling naturally to the ankles. Maman had booked in our first appointment for today with two spinster sisters.

'It is almost four o'clock. Are you ready?' I asked.

'I think so.' Tilly smoothed down her purple dress, a tight bodice showed off her small waist. Her strawberry blonde hair was pinned away from her face and fell in ringlets down her back. She was beautiful and showed no sign of being a former maid but appeared like she had come from a well-bred family. I had noticed the way André looked at her too.

The knocker on the heavy front door echoed throughout the house and footsteps clip-clopped down the hallway. Maman entered. 'The Livingston sisters, Françoise.'

'Good afternoon. Do come in.' I ushered in the ladies. 'This is Mademoiselle Matilda, my assistant. What can we do for you today?'

'We are hoping to each order a gown,' the elder one said. 'Forgive me' – she held out her hand – 'I'm Miss Blanche

156

Livingston and this is my sister Miss Caroline.' Blanche smiled exaggerating her thin lip. Her mouse-colour hair piled high and brushed back accentuated her broad forehead.

'How do you do.' I released my hand. 'Miss Livingston, I shall look after you today, and Mademoiselle Matilda will take care of Miss Caroline.'

Caroline giggled like a giddy young girl. Unlike Blanche, Caroline's hair was tied loosely at the back and held in place by a rhinestone comb.

Matilda and I fitted our first clients.

*

'How did it go?' André popped a wedge of brie into his mouth.

'Very well,' I answered. 'They each ordered a gown.'

'What were the ladies like?' André grinned.

I laughed. 'I fear they would be of no interest to you mon frère. The elder one, Blanche, must be thirty and the younger one, Caroline, is attractive but had an annoying frivolous giggle.'

'Du matin,' Maman interrupted, 'we have two maids starting for cuisine and household chores.'

André broke a chunk from his bread. 'Bonne. That will make things easier for us all. We are slowly getting this household into shape.' André waited for Maman to leave the room before turning to Tilly. 'Matilda, would you do me the honour of escorting me down to the river after supper? I hear it is lovely this time of the year.'

'Thank you, André. I would like that. By the way, Françoise, I forgot to mention you have a letter.' He passed the envelope to me and I ripped it open.

Highwood
Becton
Nr Faversham
Kent
6th May, 1897

Dear Françoise,

    I hope you have settled into your new home. What I have to tell you will come as a big surprise but Charles is no longer with Anna and he is desperately missing you. I know you swore me to secrecy regarding your new abode but please, please, allow me to pass on your details so he can write to you.

    Highwood isn't the same without you. We have new staff and it's no longer the happy place it once was. I wish you'd reconsider and return home where you belong.

    Yours truly
    Elizabeth

I screwed up the letter and threw it into the grate to burn once the fire was lit.

Chapter 4

Tilly

André burst into the workroom forcing Françoise and I to glance up.

'I've been speaking to some of the villagers,' he said, 'and it seems the nation is to have a day off to celebrate Queen Victoria's Diamond Jubilee.'

'That's generous.' Françoise carried on pinning a dart in a ruby silk gown for one of our new clients.

'You know what this means?' He paced up and down the room.

Françoise looked up from the garment. 'No, what?'

'We must be patriotic now that England is our home. I thought we should have a garden party but not just any garden party, one with dancing. A real celebration. It will also offer potential to gain additional customers both for you ladies and myself. What do you think?' he asked with a broad grin, his bright blue eyes sparkling.

I hung the almost finished emerald robe on the rail and turned to face Françoise. 'He's right. We should.' I was falling in love with André more each day. Today he looked even more handsome than usual with his glowing tanned skin from working outside. He worked so hard. If he wasn't working on his clients' books, he was in the garden pottering. And only last week he'd turned up with half a dozen chickens and spent until dark building them a coop.

'I have spoken to Maman who is happy to write invitations and I will order the food.' André rubbed his hands together. 'We shall invite all the villagers.'

'All right,' Françoise said, 'it cannot hurt to get to know our neighbours better and as you say, England is our home now so we should be patriotic.'

'I will let Maman know immediately and then get on to the food suppliers. We only have three weeks to be ready. I do enjoy a party. Do you remember the parties we had at home, Françoise?'

'Yes, I do. You are so like Papa. He always got excited organising parties.' She dabbed her eyes with a handkerchief. 'Excuse me. I need a glass of water.'

André followed her out. 'Ma sœur,' I heard him say before his voice tailed off.

I took the emerald gown from the rail, perched back on the stool, and removed the tacking from the garment. There. It was finished. I was proud of this gown which was a surprise for Françoise. She thought I was making it for a client but the colour was perfect for her and now we were to have a party she'd have a chance to wear it.

I hadn't gone to many parties and I'd never been part of organising one. André was right. This was exciting. Exactly what we all needed.

My stomach rumbled. It must be time for tea. I re-hung the gown and made my way to the kitchen.

Chapter 5

Françoise

Over the last couple of weeks André had been cutting up white cotton sheets and painting Union Jacks on them. Tilly and I had helped him make blue and white bunting and today we had hung it across oak and sycamore trees ready for the party.

André bustled into the drawing room. 'Another letter for you from *Highwood*, ma sœur.' He placed it on the mahogany occasional table in the middle of the room. 'The musicians are to arrive at six this evening and the food is ready. Maman has received around one hundred RSVPs so it looks like we are going to be busy.' When I didn't answer, he said, 'Françoise?'

'Sorry. I was wondering what is in the letter this time. Whether it is worth reading before it ends up on the fire.'

'It may contain something important. Elizabeth could be unwell.'

'You are right. Naturally, I will read it.'

André turned to the black-slated mantel clock above the fireplace. 'Hurry though as you need to get dressed. And I must do so too. We have two hours before our guests arrive.'

André rushed from the room and I picked up the buff-coloured envelope and ripped it open.

Highwood Hall
Beckton
Faversham
13th June, 1897

My dearest Françoise,

    Do not be cross with Mother. I wouldn't leave her alone until she finally agreed to post this letter on my behalf as she refused to give me your address. I fear I made a dreadful mistake. It was only once you'd gone from my life that I realised just how much I missed you. I promise to break all ties with Anna. Please come back home, my love. I need you.

    Yours forever
    Charles

I scrunched the paper up and threw it into the grate.

*

André and Tilly's eyes were fixed on me from the foot of the stairs as I strolled down.

'Ma sœur.' André's eyes widened. 'You look enchanting.'

Tilly adjusted my gown after I'd taken the last step. 'You look beautiful.'

'Thank you, Tilly. I adore it. I cannot believe you tricked me into thinking this was for someone else.' The emerald taffeta rustled as I moved.

'Tilly looks divine too, do you not think, Françoise?' André could not take his eyes off her.

'Indeed, she does.' I touched Tilly's gown. 'The rose-coloured silk enhances your strawberry blonde hair.'

Tilly blushed. She really did look adorable. The high-necked bodice heightened her tiny waist and her hair hung down in ringlets from the gold-coloured hat topped with a pink feather. They made a handsome couple, she and André. He certainly appeared mesmerised by her. I did not think either of them would notice if I disappeared. André fitted well as Lord of the Manor in his long jacket and top hat.

'Goodness me, mes enfants. You look so…' Maman hugged me.

'You too look alluring, Maman.' I released myself from her hold. 'The indigo satin matches your eyes.'

Maman gave a small chuckle. 'Merci, ma fille. I know you are trying to be kind but my alluring years are bygone.'

'Shall we?' André linked arms with Maman and I.

*

Crowds were filling the grounds of *Sunbury Manor*. I put up my parasol as did Maman and Tilly. It was certainly a warm and sunny day for the celebrations. Union Jacks hung from the trees along with blue and white bunting. Marquees had been erected around the sides to provide shade as well as refreshments.

The Livingston sisters made their way towards us.

'Madam Françoise, it's a wonderful day for a garden party. No sign of rain at all. We're going to have such a lovely time.' Caroline did a twirl. 'And as you see I'm wearing my new gown.'

'The powder blue suits you,' I said, 'and I adore the hat.' Her hair hung in ringlets like Tilly's. I was thinking how attractive Caroline looked but then she spoiled it with that frivolous laugh.

'Why, thank you. I really like how it imitates the gentleman's top hat but smaller and I am so fond of the white feather and small roses.' She waved her hands out in front. 'Which of course, match my gloves.' She giggled again.

'Caroline, we must let these good people greet all their guests.' Blanche pulled her sister away.

André chuckled. 'I see what you mean about her not being spouse material for me.'

'Now, mon fils' – Maman prodded André's shoulder – 'I did not bring you up to be unkind. I am sure Miss Caroline is a very nice lady.'

'I am sure too, Maman' – André put a gloved hand to his mouth – 'but have you ever in your life though seen two sisters so unalike?'

'That is enough now. Come. You have guests to attend to.' Maman tugged hold of André's arm. 'Did you set up a table with the diary for me?'

'Yes, Maman. I have positioned one under the oak to protect you from the sun.' André gave that sheepish grin reminding me of Papa.

*

Maman was in her element booking appointments. The ladies just kept coming.

'Comment vous-appelez vous?' she asked the lady in olive green.

'I'm sorry.' The lady frowned. 'I do not understand.'

'Please accept our apologies,' I said to the woman. 'Maman, you must speak English. Remember we are in England.'

'Forgive me.' Maman touched her head. 'My age makes me forgetful at times. Please, madame, what is your name?'

The lady smiled. 'I understand. It must have been difficult for you to leave your country.'

'Oui. I mean yes, it was, but my family are here and we love England and wish to be patriotic. What did you say your name was?'

'Now I'm the one to be sorry. I did not say. Lady Astley' – she stretched out her white-gloved hand for Maman to shake' – I live the other side of the village at *Hargreaves Hall*.' She glanced at me. 'And you must be Françoise Dubois, the widow I've heard so much about?'

'Yes, that is me' – I extended my hand – 'I am pleased to meet you, Lady Astley.'

Maman flipped the page over in the diary 'We are able to offer a consultation and fitting next Wednesday at two o'clock. Does that time suit, Lady Astley?'

'That will be perfect. Merci.' Lady Astley smiled and Maman offered a small giggle in return.

*

The musicians set themselves up on the makeshift stage. André had employed a string quartet consisting of a cellist, viola player and two violinists. The first violinist stroked his bow against the strings and music rang out.

'Matilda, may I have the pleasure of this dance?' André held out his hand to Tilly.

'Thank you. I'd like that.' Tilly took André's hand and he led her to the area of the grass marked for dancing.

I felt like a wallflower watching André and Tilly. His eyes never left hers. They were like a couple in love. I remembered looking at Charles that way. I sauntered across the lawn to find Maman to ensure she stayed away from the dance area but need not have worried as she was busy chatting to a middle-aged woman.

'Françoise.' Maman took my hand. 'Miss Brown, this is my daughter. Françoise, Miss Brown is a governess from one of the big houses in the village.'

'How do you do?' I said, shaking her hand as I studied her thin face, pointed chin and round glasses.

Someone touched my arm. I turned to face André.

'There you are. We wondered where you had gone. Come dance with me.'

'Matilda,' Maman said, 'please fetch a lemonade for Miss…' That was all I heard before André whisked me away.

As we twirled around with the other couples, I said, 'You and Tilly are getting on well.'

'I like her, Françoise. I like her a lot. In fact, I think I am falling in love with her. Would that be a problem?'

'Not for me. I would adore that. Maman however, is another matter.'

'I believe part of me fell in love with her on that day we found her huddled up by that tree. She seemed so vulnerable and I wanted to protect her.'

Before I could respond to his statement, we had to swap dance partners but once back in the arms of André, I said, 'You should tell her.'

He led me away from the dance area and over towards the old yew. 'Do you think she could love me?'

'Without a doubt, mon frère. I would say she already does.'

'If I were to ask her to marry me, how do you think Maman would react?'

'I think you know the answer to that question, but if you love her as you say, do not let anything or anyone get in the way of your happiness.'

André rubbed his hands and spoke quickly. 'I never thought something like this could happen to me. No other mademoiselle has ever made my heart beat like this.'

'I am happy for you, mon frère. Really, I am.'

*

As the musicians began their final piece for the evening, fireworks sparked and the crowd meandered towards the river. Reds and yellows exploded in the sky reflecting in the water. Men and women gasped at the wonder of it all. André took

Tilly's arm. If two people were ever meant to be together it had to be those two.

'Is there something I should know,' Maman asked me.

'I am sure André will speak to you. But if there is, how would you feel?'

'I will not allow it. The girl is nothing but an upstart. I shall speak to Lady Astley about finding a decent young lady as a wife for my son.'

'It is not up to you, Maman. Please do not meddle.'

'I fear your papa would be ashamed of you both. Did we not bring you up to know what is right and wrong?'

'He loves her, Maman. Do not interfere.'

Chapter 6

Tilly

André, Françoise and I dawdled out of *Sunbury Manor's* iron gates. I was happy to be alone with André but his mother insisted Françoise act as a chaperone.

As we wandered down to the riverside, the smell of white clusters of winter garlic travelled to my nose and the sun shone on the river. I adored watching a purple bodied dragonfly with iridescence wings hover over the golden reeds. It felt good to be alive. My life had changed so much this last year. Françoise had not only provided me with elocution lessons but had ensured I was well-read. I was even attempting to write a poem after being inspired by William Wordsworth's *I Wandered Lonely as a Cloud*. Who'd have thought Da disowning me would be a blessing?

André stopped and turned to me. 'Are you all right, Matilda?' His bright blue eyes sparkled.

'Yes, thank you. I'm just taking in this wonderful view.'

'It is rather beautiful.' André moved closer to me. 'As are you,' he whispered.

Françoise coughed. 'I am going to meander over to that lovely old oak and watch the sunset while you two people have a little lone time together.' She strolled over to the tree.

André lifted my hand, brought it to his lips and kissed it. 'You must know, Matilda, that you have stolen my heart.'

My pulse quickened. 'No. I didn't know.'

'I think I started to fall in love with you that day Françoise and I rescued you and I have not stopped thinking about you since.' He bent down on one knee. 'I know this may seem sudden but I believe we were brought together that day for a reason. Matilda, ma chérie, will you marry me?'

I put a hand to my mouth. 'But what will your mother say? And Françoise?'

'Françoise loves you as I do. And as for Maman, we will have a fight on our hands but please say oui.'

I sighed. 'She'll hate me even more.'

'And my love for you will compensate. Say oui.'

'But your mother will never allow it.'

'It is not up to her who I choose to marry.'

My heart banged like a drum, partly because of André's declaration of love but partly because I wasn't sure whether I was up to standing against his mother.

'Tilly?'

'Oui, mon chéri. Yes. I will.'

André picked me up at the waist and swung me around. Françoise made her way back towards us with a wide grin. 'She has said oui?'

'She has. We must set a date. I do not wish to wait. We shall wed in September. Oui?'

'Oui.' I said feeling like my heart would burst. 'But first we need to convince your mother.'

Françoise linked her arm in mine as we wandered back to the house. 'Soon my dearest friend we shall be sisters. Maman will have to accept it.'

Maman Antoinette was hovering outside the house as we wandered up to the front entrance. She glared at me, shaking her head, before heading inside.

'Maman.' André let go of my arm and chased after his mother.

*

Sunbury Manor
Oxhaven
Oxford
Oxfordshire
29th June, 1897

Dear Daisy,

You're never going to believe this but Monsieur André loves me too and he's asked me to marry him. We will wed in September. I can't believe how lucky I am. Unfortunately, his mother still hates me and thinks I'm an upstart. André has told me not to worry, that we'll manage to win her around. Either way he said he's marrying me and no one or nothing will get in his way.

I wish you could come to the wedding. Maybe it can be arranged? Lady Françoise is to make my wedding gown. I've taught her to dressmake and she's become quite adept. I believe she'll be teaching me before long. Monsieur André says we'll have a photographer which means I can send you a photograph if you're unable to attend. I'm so happy. This definitely was the change for the better. I miss my mam; do you ever see her? I miss my siblings too, but not Da. I never want to see him again after he was so wicked towards me. André says he'll never hurt me like Da did. I still have the scars on my legs.

I must sign off as I can hear André calling me.
Write back soon.

My fondest love
Tilly
xxx

After placing the letter in the envelope, I wrote down the address, licked the envelope shut, and stuck on the penny stamp. 'Coming,' I called and ventured downstairs.

'There you are, my dearest. I believe Françoise was looking for you to do a fitting. May I have a sneaky peep?'

'Definitely not. It's unlucky for the groom to see the bride's gown before the day.' I held up the envelope. 'I was hoping for a stroll down the lane to post my letter. Would you like to join me?'

André turned towards the window. 'The sun is shining so I believe a saunter would be a delight. You had better check with Françoise though if she is waiting for you.'

'I will.' I kissed him on the cheek. André was such a gentleman. He had not tried to touch me improperly at all. 'I can wait,' he'd say, stroking my arm. I kept questioning myself whether it was real.

I peeped into the dressing room where Françoise was waiting with my gown on the mannequin. 'Good morning, Tilly, how are you today?'

'I'm well, thank you, Françoise. I was about to pop out and post my letter. Would you like to join André and I?'

'Merci, mais non, I must decline. You and André go. Perhaps you can pick up the eggs from the hens on your way back in.'

'Yes, of course. And we can do the fitting when I get back?'

'That will be fine. I shall continue with Mrs Taylor's gown as she is sending her horseman to collect it this evening.'

André and I left the house and meandered down the lane hand in hand.

Chapter 7

Françoise

Tilly and André looked so in love. I was happy for them but I could not help feel a slight twinge seeing what they had while I had nothing. I thought I had love with Charles before discovering his affair with Elizabeth's lady's maid. Then came the realisation that she was with child after we had lost our dear little Oliver. Life was so unfair. It had not only stolen my child but my husband too.

Maman had refused to come out of her room for more than two weeks. I think she thought her protest would make André change his mind but that was never going to happen. He was far too much in love. Why could Maman not see Tilly as the wonderful caring person she was instead of seeing her as a servant?

I slumped down into the chair and imagined Charles stroking my shoulders and kissing me from the neck down. His lovemaking had been so gentle and loving. How could he have faked that? It seemed so real. I dabbed my eyes with a lace handkerchief. *This is no good Françoise Dubois, pull yourself together.* I slapped my hands into my lap, got up and started back on Mrs Jennings' gown. There had been a lot of work in this one as she was a large woman. The dark blue satin fabric cut in layers with a high bodice would hopefully conceal a lot of her flaws. I sighed. It was no good, my heart was not in it. I checked the clock on the wall. Time for luncheon. I dawdled down to the kitchen where Sally, our new maid, was taking bread out of the oven.

'That smells delicious,' I said.

*

'Ah, there you are, ma fille.' Maman appeared at the sunroom door. 'What is it you are reading?'

'*Pride and Prejudice*' – I held up the book – 'Charles bought it for me as a gift just after Oliver was born. With everything that happened… Look' – I patted the bamboo seat – 'why not come and join me? The garden is blooming with marigolds, phlox, roses and not forgetting my favourite, sweet peas.'

Maman adjusted her skirt before sitting down and looking out the window.

'I am pleased to see you have come out from your room?'

'I could not stay there forever. There is far too much work to be done. I am sure it has been difficult for you managing without me.'

'Oui, Maman.' I put the book down onto the windowsill. 'How would you like a stroll around the garden?'

'I will get my hat and shawl.'

*

I linked my arm with Maman as we meandered around the garden path. 'Do you have a favourite flower beside the bluebell?' I asked her.

'Oui.' She leaned over to the scarlet rosebush and sniffed. 'This one. It reminds me of your papa. He always brought me a red rose for special occasions or…'

'Or what?'

Maman held a hand in her back. 'When he wanted to apologise.'

'Are you in pain?'

'Just the normal problem with my lumbago.' She stretched upright.

'Come. We shall sit down.' I led her over to the bench a few feet away.

Once we were both seated, she asked, 'Is he with her?'

A bike of bees hovered over lavender. 'If you mean Tilly. Yes.'

She shook her head. 'Your papa would be ashamed.'

'He loves her, Maman. Why not try and get to know her?'

'She is a servant.' Maman brushed a swarm of gnats away from her face.

'Not anymore. Tilly is a skilled dressmaker. She is kind and has been a true friend to me.'

'Dressmaker? You are the one creating the gowns. She is your assistant, whatever that means.'

'Non, Maman.' I raised my voice. 'Tilly is talented. It was she who created that wonderful cerulean blue satin gown for you to wear at the party. She picked out the fabric purposely to match your eyes. And it was she who spent hours hand-stitching the pearls on the bodice to get everything perfect for you.'

Maman's mouth dropped. 'It was not you?'

'Non. Look, Maman, all I ask is that you give her a chance. Get to know her.'

'I am not making any promises.' She shivered. 'I think I would like to go back inside.'

Chapter 8

Tilly

I was enjoying reading about Elizabeth Bennet and Mr Fitzwilliam Darcy in Françoise's copy of *Pride and Prejudice*. 'It will be interesting for us to discuss it afterwards,' she'd said.

The door creaked open making me glance up as André's mother waddled into the sunroom. 'Bonjour, Mademoiselle Matilda. May I join you?' she asked sinking down into the deep-cushioned sofa.

'Of course.' I put the opened book down on the windowsill. 'What can I help you with, Maman Antoinette.'

She licked her upper lip. 'How can I put this? Hmm. You are a lovely girl. Talented and kind as my daughter consistently tells me but you must see that nothing can come of this union with you and my son.'

'Why is that?'

'Because you must agree with me that he needs an upstanding wife. A lady.'

'But André has chosen me. We love each other.'

She patted my hand. 'I know, dear, but love is not always enough. André's papa would turn in his grave if he knew.'

'I'm sorry, Maman, but I won't give André up. If he wants to back out of our engagement then I'll honour his decision but otherwise I shall marry him next month as agreed.'

'My dear, I fear you are not listening to me. I am not asking but telling. Look, I have some funds from my late husband's estate. It should have course all gone to André but being the good son he is, he insisted I should get a share. I am happy to provide you with a settlement.'

'I'm not interested in your money, Madam Dubois' – I picked the book up from the windowsill – 'this discussion has ended.' I stormed out, hurried upstairs to my room, threw myself onto the bed and sobbed. She was never going to accept me. Only last night Françoise had said she'd spoken to her mother who'd agreed to try and get to know me better.

A knock came on my door. I slid off the bed and opened the door to Françoise.

'Tilly, how are you?' She pressed my upper arm. 'I was worried when you charged upstairs.'

'She hates me. She tried to buy me off.'

'Who did? What happened?'

'Your maman. She doesn't want me to marry André. She said she'll give me money if I don't.'

'She did what?'

'I know. I couldn't believe it either. She thinks I'm an upstart, doesn't she? Am I?'

'Non, non' – Françoise put her arms around me – 'you are anything but. As I told Maman you are a talented, kind woman and your friendship means everything to me. Do not let my maman spoil things? We should tell André.'

'No, I don't want him to know. The last thing I want is to turn him against his mother. I need to win her over.'

'We will win her over, my dear friend.' Françoise picked up the copy of *Pride and Prejudice*. 'As Jane Austin proved in this book, love can conquer all.'

Would André and I be able to conquer Madam Dubois' prejudice. I hoped so.

Chapter 9

Françoise

I stitched the final piece of lace to the gown.

'Is your lumbago playing up?' I asked Maman as she hobbled into the workroom.

'It is, ma fille.' She held her back as she bent forward.

'Come. Take a seat.' I got up and pulled across one of the armchairs used for clientele.

'Merci.' She groaned as she sank into the seat. 'That is a beautiful gown. Is it for Lady Astley's niece? I heard she was to be wed this autumn?'

'Non, Maman. It is for Tilly.'

Maman tutted. 'The wedding is still going ahead?'

'Yes, despite you trying to buy Tilly off.' I placed the gown on a hanger and hung it on the rail. 'Parfait.'

'It really is.' Maman dabbed her eyes. 'I wished Papa and I could have seen you walk down the aisle.'

'I wish you could have been there too.' As I removed Mrs Taylor's garment from one of the mannequins, my mind strayed to yet another letter I had received this morning from Charles, begging me for my love. I gave him my love and he threw it back at me.

'Did she tell him?'

'Who? What?'

'Matilda. Has she told André what I said?'

'No, Maman. She has not.' I added a neck fastening on the gown. The cobalt blue brought out the colour in the shop owner's eyes.

'That was good of her.' Maman chewed her bottom lip. 'I thought she would.'

'No, Maman.' I raised my voice. 'No, she did not. And that is because she did not wish André to know what his maman was capable of.' I shook my head. 'Really, Maman, I could not believe you would do something so despicable.'

'I had to do something. I was desperate.'

I moved over to Maman and knelt down next to her. 'Listen, Maman, Tilly and André will marry no matter what you say. You have no power over this so if I were you, I would start treating her like a daughter. Otherwise, you could find yourself excluded once they are wed.'

'André would not do that.'

'Really? I would be cautious, Maman, because if you continue to behave this way then there is nothing to stop André taking Tilly and purchasing a home of their own. He has the means. And I am telling you now that he has never felt this way about any other woman. He really loves her. Do not stand in their way.'

Maman's eyes widened.

I took her hand. 'Please, Maman, for André and for me, please try and get to know Tilly. I promise you will learn to love her as André and I do. She is a kind, gentle, wonderful, talented woman and mon frère is lucky to have her as his bride. Now please, let them be happy.'

'Yes, ma fille. I will try.' She leaned forward in the seat.

'Let me.' I took her arm.

Her knees creaked as she stood up and shuffled over to Tilly's wedding gown. 'It is a masterpiece. The lace is exquisite and the silk perfect. You have learned well, ma fille.'

'It was Tilly who taught me. All I could do beforehand was put together my play gowns at home.'

'She is a good teacher although I always saw your talent in needlecraft.' She touched the fabric. 'I am sure Matilda will make a wonderful bride. I will try to hold my tongue. Now, I must retire to my bed and leave you to finish.' She hobbled out of the room without saying another word.

*

The front door slammed. Tilly entered the workroom. 'Françoise, what are you doing still working at this time? It has gone nine o'clock. André and I could not believe it when we saw the light on in here as we came back in.'

'I wanted to get Mrs Taylor's gown sorted.' I held it up. 'What do you think?'

'It's lovely. The blue satin will be flattering on her figure.'

Mrs Taylor had been our best customer these past couple of months. 'Do you think she has a new husband in mind? She has been a widow for a few years now and she has ordered a lot of new gowns.'

'Wouldn't that be nice? I do hope so. She is such a special lady. It would be wonderful for her to find some happiness with a new man.'

'That is what I thought.' I smiled. 'Would you like to see your gown? I have finished it.'

'You've finished it? Yes please. Where is it?'

'On that rail behind you. Maman was admiring it. She said you would make a wonderful bride.'

Tilly grinned. 'She said that?'

'Oui. Now come.' I placed Mrs Taylor's gown on the mannequin and lifted Tilly's off the rail and offered it up against her.

'Françoise.' She put her hand to her chest as her blue eyes became moist. 'I am going to look like a princess. Is it too late to try it on?'

'Tilly, Françoise, what is going on?'

'Quick. André is coming.' I took the gown from Tilly and hung it in the dressing room.

André tapped on the door. I opened it slightly. 'You cannot come in. Tilly is trying on her wedding gown.'

'Please, ma sœur, may I have a little peep?'

'Non. Go and make us some drinking chocolate. We shall be with you in the drawing room soon.'

'All right, if I must.'

'You must. Now go. Your betrothed is waiting for me.' I closed the door behind him.

'Has he gone?'

'Oui.' I drew back the curtain.

A few minutes later, Tilly was looking like a princess in her bridal gown. The silver brocade bodice emphasised her small waist, and the high collar flattered her slender neck.

Tilly picked up the skirt. 'Françoise, these pearls embroidered on the lace are beautiful. It must have taken you hours to do this.'

I smiled. 'It did but it was worth it. Do you not agree?'

'I do.' Her face reddened. 'I never ever thought I'd wear a gown like this. I said you'd be teaching me before long. Didn't I?'

'I am proud of it. I thought I would embroider pearls on the veil too.'

Tilly shook her head. 'I feel quite overwhelmed. I need to sit down.'

'Come, my almost sister, let us get you out of this gown and go and find André.'

Chapter 10

Tilly

I knocked on the study door before opening it.

André glanced up from a ledger. 'Matilda, my dear, thank you for joining me.' He pushed away the journal and placed his pen in the inkwell.

'Is that Mrs Taylor's books?' I asked.

'Oui. I have almost finished. But the reason I asked you here is to discuss something important.'

'Oh?' I adjusted my frock as I sat down on a straight chair the other side of the mahogany desk.

'As you are under twenty-one, your father's permission was required in order for us to wed.'

'I didn't know that. Does that mean we can't marry?'

André smiled. 'Non, ma chérie.' He picked up a buff envelope and took out a letter. 'I knew that to be the case and took the relevant action. Here' – he waved the piece of paper – 'Your papa has given his permission for me to marry you.' André took a deep breath. 'Although, I am afraid, there are terms.'

'Terms?'

'Read for yourself.'

I took the note.

Dear Monsieur Dubois,

I grant permission for you to marry my daughter, Matilda Ann Greenwood, providing I receive payment of five pounds by return.

Arthur Greenwood
Signed … X

'How dare he?' I pushed the note across the desk. 'I wonder who he got to write that as he can't even read or write.'

'I have no idea but he has marked an 'X' as his signature. Fret not, chérie, for I will pay his due. A small price to spend the rest of my life with you. I have instructed my contact in Beckton to organise the settlement with your papa and ensure he provides a receipt. We will wed next month as arranged. Do not fear.'

'I'm the luckiest girl in the world.' I stretched across the desk and gripped André's hand.

'I am the lucky one.'

'I'm so angry though' – I sat back and clenched my fists – 'he didn't even ask after me. All he wants is money.' I took a deep breath. 'Do you think you could ask your friend to check on my mother and siblings?'

'Of course, my sweetness. That can be arranged.' André got up from behind the desk. 'Come now, let us eat luncheon.' His stomach rumbled.

'You know my mother won't see any of that money,' I said as we made our way to the kitchen. 'It'll be one of his drinking cronies put him up to it. He wouldn't have the brains to come up with it on his own.'

'Never mind that now.' André laughed.

'What?'

'I was just thinking how far you had come since your elocution lessons with Françoise. Not so long ago you would have said me mam.'

I laughed with him. 'You're right. I'm a different person now.' My smile changed to a frown. 'But, André, what happens if we don't hear back in time? The bans are due to be read next week?'

'Trust me, ma chérie. I have it all in hand. Now come, let us eat.'

*

I cleared up the dishes from luncheon. Sally only worked part time so Françoise, Maman Antoinette and I all mucked in, although if Maman Antoinette had her way it would be me doing it all. Françoise had chastised her mother on more than one occasion. 'Tilly isn't here as our maid, Maman.'

André coughed, breaking my thoughts. 'Matilda, there is someone I'd like you to meet this afternoon?'

I turned away from the sink. 'Me?'

'Oui, you. Do not sound so surprised, you are my betrothed after all.'

'That sounds intriguing, mon frère.' Françoise picked up a tea towel and began drying the pots.

'You too are invited, ma sœur. We are to meet my mystery person at the new tearooms in the village.'

'Oh, do come, Françoise.' I rinsed the last bowl.

André's mother padded back into the kitchen. 'Come where?'

'We are off to the village to the new tearoom to meet an acquaintance of mine and I hope you will join us?'

'Bien sûr. Naturally. I shall go and get ready.'

'We are leaving at two o'clock, Maman. Do not be late.'

'Do not worry, mon fils, I will be ready.'

183

I turned towards the sink to hide my feelings. Another day no doubt that André's mother would spoil for me.

*

André pulled up the Landau outside a picturesque building with a sign above saying *Bridge Tearooms*.

He stepped down from the carriage and took our hands in turn starting with his mother. 'Come along, ladies.' He headed to the entrance where we were greeted by a waitress dressed in a similar uniform to what I'd worn at *Highwood*.

'Monsieur Dubois, welcome. Please, come this way. My name's Ivy and I shall be looking after your party today.'

André followed the girl down the parquet-floored aisle. We stayed close behind. Ivy stopped at a round table by a window with six rose-velvet chairs. 'I hope this is suitable.'

'It is perfect. Merci, Ivy.' André pulled out a chair. 'Maman, you sit here and Matilda, dearest, you will be next to me.'

'Thank you.' I eased myself down, taking in the garden view as Ivy passed the menus and left spare ones on the vacant seats.

'Our mystery guests will be here shortly. Françoise, you are here.' André pulled back one of the chairs as Lady Astley made her way over to our table with a younger man. I thought she was a widow. Maybe that's why André brought us here so he could introduce us to Lady Astley's intended.

André's mother's face beamed. 'Lady Suzanna, what a wonderful surprise.' Maman Antoinette had become good friends with Lady Astley.

André, still not seated, held out his hand to the gentleman. 'Matthew, delighted you could make it. Lady Astley.' He bowed his head. 'Please.' He pulled back the chair next to his mother. 'Do sit down.'

184

After the kerfuffle of scraping chairs André took the seat next to me. 'Ladies, please let me introduce you to Monsieur Matthew Astley, Lady Astley's nephew.'

I smiled with relief. The thought of him as Lady Astley's betrothed was too much. Matthew was handsome. Mid-twenties, tall, blond curls falling across his brow, and he had a trim moustache. What was André up to? Was he matchmaking for his sister?

Ivy headed our way. 'Are you ready to order, sir?'

'Oui' – André glanced across to his friend sitting in-between Françoise and me – 'afternoon tea for all?'

Matthew looked to Lady Astley before answering, 'Perfect.'

Ivy gathered up the menus before disappearing into the back of the tearoom.

André's mother faced her neighbour. 'Lady Suzanna. This is a delightful surprise,' she repeated.

'You'd no idea?' Lady Astley smiled.

'None at all.'

'André loves surprises.' Françoise chuckled.

The waitress pushed a trolley over and placed tiered plates of small triangular sandwiches, scones and cakes. It took me back to *Highwood* where it would've been me serving the refreshments and if André's mother had her way I'd be doing it now. She caught me unawares when she smiled at me. What was she up to?

Everyone chatted small talk while we nibbled on breads and sipped tea from the blue-flowered china cups. Ivy returned with a silver ice bucket containing a champenoise of champagne and poured the sparkling liquid into each of our goblets set on the table.

'Merci.' André gestured to the waitress she could leave.

'Thank you, sir.' She hurried across to a table by the door to clear away the dishes.

André picked up his drink. 'Please raise your glasses to my wonderful fiancée, Mademoiselle Matilda.'

Everyone raised their goblets. 'Mademoiselle Matilda,' they echoed, including Maman Antoinette.

I felt my cheeks burning so hid my face behind the glass and sipped the sparkling wine.

'Now, mon frère, delightful as this is to meet Monsieur Astley' – Françoise's emerald eyes sparkled – 'I believe there is a specific reason for us being here today.'

'My sister knows me too well. Françoise, you are exactly right. I have asked Matthew to be my groomsman and he has agreed.'

'It will be an honour.' Matthew took Françoise's hand. 'And perhaps, madam, I may escort you on the day?'

Françoise picked up her glass to drink but not before I noticed it was her turn to blush. 'I am not sure, monsieur.'

Chapter 11

Françoise

I hung up Lady Astley's gown on the rail. She was due any moment for a final fitting. The olive-green velvet would enhance her eyes. It was a shame she had never remarried. In many ways she reminded me of Elizabeth with her tall slender figure but Lady Astley's hair was snow-white rather than greying and she dressed it in a bun of tight curls.

Tilly wandered in. 'You've finished?'

'Oui. What do you think?'

'Perfect for an elegant woman like Lady Astley. What did you think of Mr Astley?'

I tidied up my needle box and put it away on the side. 'He seems a nice gentleman.'

'He's sweet on you.' She beamed.

I felt my face flush. 'Do not be foolish, Tilly. Have you forgotten I am portraying myself as recently widowed?'

'And that matters because…'

'Stop that nonsense now,' I said as high heels click clacked along the hallway. Maman pushed open the door. 'Lady Astley for you, Françoise.'

'Do come in, Lady Astley.' I led her to one of the gold-floral high back armchairs we used for clients.

'Bonjour, Madame Françoise. Miss Matilda.' Lady Astley often liked to drop in a couple of French words.

Tilly moved over to the clothes rail and brought the gown to our client.

'You have done a wonderful job, my dear,' Lady Astley said to me. 'I do hope I can still fasten that bodice after all those scones and cake we ate last week.'

Tilly and I laughed.

'I will leave you to it, Lady Suzanna,' Maman said. 'I am going to ensure Sally has our afternoon tea ready for when you are finished in here.' She chuckled. 'I must inform you though, that means eating more scones and cake.' Maman padded back down the hallway.

Tilly and I fitted Lady Astley into her gown. She looked at her image in the Cheval mirror, swaying. 'My goodness. I swear this garment has knocked ten years off my age.'

'You look divine,' I said and Tilly agreed. 'The gown fits you perfectly. Would you like to take it with you today?'

'If that is convenient.'

'It is.' Tilly smiled. 'I shall wrap it while you and Maman Antoinette enjoy tea together.'

'I don't suppose I could have a preview of the bride's wedding gown?'

'Now, Lady Astley, you know we can't let you see it.' Tilly chuckled. 'Madame Françoise wishes to unveil her masterpiece when I wear it on my wedding day.'

*

Tilly and I linked arms as we strolled around the garden. We put up our parasols as although it was nearing six o'clock in the evening the August sun was still strong. Red Admiral butterflies fluttered around the buddleia. They were more than happy to share one lilac flower between three or four of them. We meandered along the winding footpath until reaching the rose bed where reds, pinks and yellows bloomed.

'What do you think about Mr Astley,' Tilly asked as we continued walking.

'Like I said earlier, he seems a nice enough gentleman. Tilly, has André put you up to this?'

'No, but I've noticed that longing look you sometimes have when André and I are together.'

'I am sure I have no idea what you are talking about.'

'Come on, Françoise, admit it. You miss Charles.'

'Oui, I do. I do not believe I have ever denied that but where does Monsieur Astley come into this?'

'Because he's an eligible bachelor.'

'Have you forgotten, Tilly, that I am still legally married?'

She covered her mouth. 'Oh yes. I think I had.'

'Well let us not have any further talk about matchmaking.' I stopped at the sunflowers where a dozen or more had grown six foot tall against the wall. 'Sunflowers always make me smile and it is like their faces smile back at me.' I laughed.

Tilly strolled on and stopped at another flower bed. 'These purple ones are lovely.'

'They are dahlias.'

'How did you learn all the flower names?'

'My papa taught me. We should make our way back inside. I imagine Lady Astley will be wanting to leave.'

'Yes of course.' Tilly took my arm and we sauntered back to the house.

Chapter 12

Tilly

We were in the workroom when André's mother hurried in. 'Come quickly. Viens vite. There is a carriage coming up to the house but it has no horse pulling it. Vite.'

Françoise and I glanced at each other. She shook her head.

'I am not insane. André is out there now. Viens vite.'

'We should go and see,' I said to Françoise. I hung Françoise's gown, the one she was to wear for my wedding, on a mannequin, and Françoise carefully arranged my veil over another.

Maman Antoinette waddled out of the room and we followed her to the outside steps.

What was this vehicle? It looked like a Brougham carriage but without a horse. Was it magic? 'André's speaking to the driver,' I said. 'I wonder who he is.'

'It is exciting.' Françoise pulled her shawl closer. 'Let us go and see.'

As we made our way nearer, she held back. 'It is Charles. What is he doing here? How did he know how to find me? Elizabeth promised.' Françoise turned to go back to the house.

'Why are you going back inside, Françoise?' Maman Antoinette asked as she caught us up.

'It is Charles. I do not wish to see him.' Françoise's face paled. She looked like she may faint.

'You need to rest for a while.' I led her to a bench.

'Do not let him see me.'

'Don't worry, I won't.'

'Sir Charles?' Maman Antoinette's mouth dropped. 'How?'

'Je ne sais pas. I do not know,' Françoise answered, her voice shaking.

'Stay here.' I squeezed her hand. 'I'll send him away.' I marched down the drive to the carriage.

'I'm the bearer of news,' Charles said to André as I reached them, 'news that wasn't appropriate to include in a letter. Please. It's Tilly I need to speak to, although I can't help hoping that Françoise will allow me a hearing too.'

'Me?' I asked.

'I'm afraid so, Tilly, but it would be better if we were to go inside?'

André sighed. 'You had better come in then.'

'But André, I promised Françoise I'd send him away.' I tightened my cloak. September had arrived with a vengeance.

Charles tilted his head. 'It really would be better if we went inside, Tilly.'

André took my arm and gently pulled me away. 'Go up to the house and send my sister inside. We will take Sir Charles into the kitchen.' He strode back to Charles and I ran up the drive to Françoise and Maman Antoinette.

'Is he leaving?' Françoise asked.

'Not yet.' I leaned towards her.

'But you promised to send him away.'

'I know, and we will, but first he has news for me. News it seems that couldn't be put in a letter.' I took her hand. 'I need to hear him out. You do understand?'

'It will be a ploy. What news could he have?'

'I don't know, Françoise, maybe he has information about my family?'

'Then you should hear him out but I don't want to see him.' She let go of my hand, got up from the bench and staggered into the house.

'What did you say to her?' André's mother asked.

'Sir Charles has brought news for me and André's invited him into the kitchen. You should go inside with Françoise.'

Maman Antoinette glared at Charles and André as they ambled up the drive. André walked up to the bench. 'Go inside, Maman, and take care of Françoise. It is Tilly who he has come to see. Maybe you can persuade ma sœur to allow him a hearing before he leaves. It might help her. We can all see how much she misses him. André took his mother's arm to assist her. She shuffled back into the house waving her hands and muttering.

Chapter 13

Françoise

I shouted at André as he entered the drawing room. 'How could you? How could you bring the man who betrayed me into my new home?'

'Françoise, I am sorry, but he brings news for Matilda. Although, ma sœur, I have invited him to stay this evening as it is too far for him to travel back to *Highwood*. He needs rest and refreshment.'

'Well keep him away from me.'

'I think you should at least give him a hearing. Who knows, it might stop the letters if you were to have a final conversation.'

I shot up from the couch and moved to the front window to look out on the drive. What was that strange vehicle? My heart paced at the thought of Charles being close to me but I could not allow my heart to rule my head. He had deceived me twice, what was stopping him from doing it again?'

André came up behind me and rested his hand on my shoulder. 'I have seen that sad look in your eye. It has to be worth a meeting with him, surely?' André sloped over to the fireplace and picked up a letter from the mantelpiece. 'By the way, have you seen this? It is from Mademoiselle Geneviève?'

'Non, I have not.' I hurried over and took the light blue envelope from his hands. I sank into the chaise longue and took comfort in my friend's stylish handwriting before breaking the red seal on the back. I scanned the neat handwriting.

André lowered himself down next to me. 'What does the lovely mademoiselle have to say?'

'She is getting married.'

'Married? To whom?'

'Do you remember Jacques Blanchet?'

'Bien sûr, he must be close to thirty.'

'Oui. Un bel homme.'

'I seem to recollect he has a look of your husband.'

'Oui, he does have a resemblance to Charles' looks but hopefully that is all he has.' I scanned the letter again. 'She regrets being unable to marry Arthur Alcott as she enjoyed corresponding with him.' I glanced at André. 'I had so hoped she would marry an English gentleman and come to live here.'

'That was a fairy tale, ma sœur.'

'I know, but you cannot blame me for dreaming.' I read further down the page. 'But wait, she said that once they are married Jacques has promised they can come to England and visit me.' I looked up at André. 'She has asked if they will be welcome to stay with us?'

'When are they getting wed?'

'Not until March. How exciting. I shall get to see my cherished friend again. I do hope her married life works out better than mine.' And then I remembered Charles in our kitchen talking to Tilly. I put the letter back into its envelope. I would answer it later. I got up and went back to the window and looked out at his horseless carriage parked down the drive.

André tapped my arm. 'Worry not, ma sœur. I will arrange for Sally to make up a room for him.'

Chapter 14

Tilly

Charles sat at the table while I poured the tea. 'This must be hard for you, Sir Charles.' I placed a mug down in front of him and took a chair opposite.

'Sorry, Tilly, in what way?'

'Tea in the kitchen.'

'It's not a problem.'

'Really?' I added a sugar cube to my drink and stirred it. 'You said you had news?'

'I do.' He took my hand.

'What is it?'

'Tilly, I'm afraid… I'm afraid your mother passed away earlier in the year. From what I can gather…'

I could see Charles' mouth still moving but I'd switched off listening. Mam was dead. How? I released my hand from his, rushed to the bathroom and leaned over the lavatory to be sick. When I came back out, Charles was waiting.

'Are you all right, Tilly?' he asked. 'I'm sorry to be the bearer of such bad news and I'm sorry you're only just finding out. I wrote to Françoise as soon as I heard, asking permission to visit but she never replied. My mother eventually passed on your address in order that I may come and break the news.'

'Mam dead. I can't believe she's dead.'

He took my arm. 'Why don't we go for a walk outside and I'll tell you everything I know?'

I grabbed my bonnet and cape and let him lead me to the garden. It was a gloomy day, not a hint of sunshine, exactly how I was feeling right now.

'I believe it was quick,' he said, as we wandered by the rose bed.

'What did she die from?'

'Dropsy,' I'm told.

'Dropsy. What does that even mean?'

'Her heart maybe.'

Her heart. Was it me? Or was it Da and the beatings he gave her. Or having all those babies? Working so hard even as she got older? Would I ever know? 'I can't believe it. Mam can't be dead.' I sobbed.

'Here.' Charles dug into his pocket and passed me a handkerchief. 'I'm really sorry.' He squeezed my hand. 'There's more.'

'More?'

'Would you rather I allowed you time to digest the news of your mother?'

'No. I need to know everything.'

'As long as you're sure.'

I nodded.

'It seems your father became a wreck after your mother passed and he started drinking heavily.'

'Started? He was always drinking.'

'Hmm. I see. Well, it seems one night he didn't come home, and the next day he turned up with his new wife.'

I put my hands to my face. 'A new wife?' How could he replace Mam so quickly? Hadn't he loved her at all?

'He told your brother, Frank, the twins needed a mother.'

'Who is she?'

'All I know is she's around twenty and her father was desperate for someone to take her off his hands.'

'And is she a good mother to the twins?'

Charles turned away.

'Is she? Tell me.'

'I'm afraid not.'

I bit my lip. 'I will speak to André and ask him if the twins may come here.'

'There's no need.' Charles smiled. 'Some good news for you at least. Your brother Frank's going to take them. He's to wed a nice girl. Ada. Twenty-two. You may remember her from the Benson household.'

'No. I don't.'

'The wedding is in two weeks. Your father has expressed no objection to the twins living with Frank, and Ada's more than happy to be a good mother to them.'

'At least the twins will be safe.' I sighed.

Charles stopped at a bench under the old oak. 'Let us rest for a while.'

I eased down onto the cold metal.

Charles took my hand and smiled. 'I've offered Frank a smallholding on *Highwood* with a tied cottage.'

'At *Highwood*?'

'Yes, the dwelling is empty after an elderly tenant died. The land is overgrown so it needs a lot of work but your brother is a hard worker and wasn't put off.'

'No, Frank wouldn't be.'

'He has accepted the offer, and he and the twins will move in next week, with his wife joining them after the wedding.' He patted my shoulder. 'So you need not worry. The twins will be in safe hands.'

'Yes. Thank you.'

'If Françoise and you were to return to *Highwood* then you'd be able to see Frank and the twins often.'

I didn't want to return to *Highwood*. I didn't want to go back to being a lady's maid. I loved my life at *Sunbury*. It was all too much to take in. Mam dead. Da remarried to a woman around my age. Frank getting wed and going to live at *Highwood*. Charles expecting me to return to my old life. I pressed my fingers into my temples. It was too much. I needed to be on my own. 'Thank you, Sir Charles. If you'll excuse me I must…' I hurried down the footpath and did not stop until I came to a seat under a silver birch. I crumpled up on the bench and let myself sob.

Chapter 15

Françoise

I made my way to Tilly's chambre. Her sobs echoed from behind the door. I knocked. 'Tilly, it is me. Please may I come in?'

Sniffling, Tilly opened the door. She blew her nose. 'I'm sorry I didn't manage work today. I couldn't face it.' She started sobbing again.

'Tilly, that is not why I am here. I heard about your maman and knew you would be upset.' I led her to the bed and perched on the edge next to her. 'André wanted to come and find you but I asked him to let me. I hope that was all right?'

Tilly nodded, bent her head into my lap and sobbed. I brushed hair away from her eyes and stroked her face. She glanced up. 'Do you think it was my fault?'

'Pourquoi? I do not understand. Why would it be your fault?'

'Because of that day, you know? That day you found me?'

'Non. Definitely not. It could have been anything, Tilly. You must not blame yourself.' I patted her hand. 'André mentioned your brother is getting wed and plans to take up a tenancy at *Highwood* and your twin siblings will go with him. That must be good news?'

Tilly glanced up at me. 'I'm so selfish, Françoise.'

'How could you ever be selfish?'

'Because I don't want to go back to my old life. I love it here. I love André. I don't want to go back to being a lady's maid or a kitchen maid.' She sobbed again.

'What has brought this on? You will never go back to being a lady's maid or any other maid. What makes you think that?'

'Charles. If you go back to him. And that makes me even more selfish because I know how much you love and miss him but…'

I held her face. 'Now listen, Tilly. Whatever happens between Charles and I will not affect our relationship. You are family. And what is more, have you forgotten you are to marry André?'

She shook her head. 'All I know is I should be crying for Mam and not for myself.'

'Shh.' I rocked her in my arms. 'Listen, you should eat something. Why not wash your face and come down for supper? Crying up here on your own is not going to help.'

'All right.' She slid off the bed.

*

Tilly and I entered the dining room together. Maman, Charles and André were seated at the table but all three stood up on our arrival.

André came over and took Tilly's arm. 'I am so sorry for your loss, ma chérie. It must have been awful for you to find out that way. I cannot believe your family never tried to make contact. Come. Let us sit.' He led Tilly to the table.

Maman got up and served a bowl of chicken soup and placed it in front of Tilly. She took her hand. 'I know things have not been easy between us but I promise to try harder. You must call me, Maman. No more Maman Antoinette.'

*

Maman, André and Tilly left the dining room. Charles rose to leave.

I rose from my seat. 'Charles, do not leave yet. I have something to say to you.'

'Of course, my dearest.' He lowered himself down on the high back chair, smiling with those coal-like eyes but I would not let them sway me from what I was about to say.

'How dare you?'

Charles sat upright. 'Pardon?'

'You manipulated Tilly to coerce me into returning to *Highwood* – I threw my hands into the air – 'and in the same breath as telling her about her maman passing away.' I shook my head. 'I am not certain I know who you are at all anymore.'

'Françoise, dearest, please calm down, it was never...'

'Do not tell me to calm down.'

'It was never my intent to manipulate Tilly, as you put it.'

'You made her think she had to go back to her old life at Beckton as a maid. She is much more than that. She is a well-educated woman. Talented. And somewhere you have forgotten she is about to become my brother's wife.' I took a drink of water and tried to calm my pounding pulse.

'Françoise, if you ever let me get a word, I will try and explain.' He smiled, twinkling those dark eyes at me. 'I most certainly had not forgotten that Tilly was to become André's wife.'

I chewed my bottom lip. 'But you did try to entice her back to *Highwood* with the view that she would encourage me to return, did you not?'

'Yes, for that I am guilty, but only because I'm desperate, my love, to have you back home with me. However, at no time had I considered Tilly would return in her previous role but as your brother's wife.'

It seemed I had been rather impetuous. Papa was always accusing me of that. Listen to reasonability before racing in, he would often say. I wanted to hide my face as I was sure it had turned ruby red. 'Even so,' I said, 'we cannot get away from the fact, you thought by convincing my friend *Highwood* was the right thing, she would encourage me to return.'

'Yes' – he put his hands up – 'I've already admitted to that. I'm sorry but I miss you.'

'But can you not see that was wrong? I am my own person and will not be led by anyone. And you must apologise to Tilly.'

'I see that now' – he slapped his arm – 'and I will make my apologies to Tilly.' He stretched his hand across the table and held mine. His almost black eyes glistened. 'Please will you spend some time with me as I've driven up all this way?'

I thought back to his lips brushing against mine. Butterflies flapped in my stomach. I glanced up at the clock. 'It is getting late.'

'The night is still young.' He stroked his fingers against my wedding ring reminding me we were man and wife.

What was he suggesting? My body yearned for him but if he thought I would allow him back into my bed... I released my hand from his hold and got up from the table. 'It is half past nine. I have work to complete before retiring to bed and I imagine you will need to make an early start in the morning for your journey back to *Highwood*. Good night, Charles.'

Chapter 16

Françoise

Laughter and chatter came from the kitchen. On entering, I glared across the room at Charles who was at the table laughing and pouring a cup of tea. My stomach somersaulted. 'I thought you would be gone by now?'

'Not before you and I had spoken.'

Maman patted the chair next to her. 'Come and sit down, ma filles, and allow this young gentleman an hour of your time. Please listen to what he has to say.'

'There is nothing to say.' I pulled out the chair to sit down.

André adjusted his jacket. 'Now, Françoise, why not give Sir Charles a chance? He is here to try and make amends.'

'Have you all forgotten how he treated me?'

'No, of course not.' Tilly smiled. 'But it can't hurt to at least listen, surely?'

Charles smiled, his dark eyes pleading. 'Please, Françoise.'

They were spellbound; one by one, Maman, Tilly and André beseeched me. How had Charles managed this? I supposed there was no harm in hearing what he had to say. 'All right, I will listen.'

My family got up from their seats in turn and proceeded towards the kitchen door. André stopped. 'Would you like me to stay, ma sœur?'

I shook my head. 'Non, you go.'

Once Charles and I were alone he moved to the chair across the table from me. 'Cup of tea?'

'Oui, s'il vous plait.'

He poured from the teapot and slid a cup across the table. 'Merci.'

'Thank you for granting me a hearing.'

'I cannot promise what you have to say will make any difference.'

'I understand.'

'Well?' I asked.

He took a deep breath. 'Firstly, I'd like to say how sorry I am, Françoise. Not just for my deceitful behaviour but for not choosing you at the time.' He ran his fingers through his gleaming black hair. 'I'm no longer with Anna. I've broken all ties. In fact, I've not seen her since shortly after you left. It was only after you were gone, I realised I could not be without you. A child could not make up for the loss of your love in my heart.'

'And what about your illegitimate son?'

He looked directly at me. 'The child's not mine.'

I added two sugar cubes to my cup and stirred with a spoon. 'I see.'

'What does that mean?'

'It means that once you found out the child was not yours you realised you wanted me.'

'No' – he stretched his arm across the table and rested his hand on mine – 'it wasn't like that. It was only after I told Anna I could not stay or see the child again that she roared at me the boy wasn't even mine.' He took a sip of tea. 'You're not going to believe this but the father is my valet. It seems he and Anna had plotted together. The plan all along was to seduce me and then say the child was mine in order that they both benefited financially. That's how he knew about the affair. Françoise, we've both been victims in this. I was weak after our lovely Oliver departed and Anna took advantage.'

I moved my hand away from his. 'Are you suggesting you have been a victim as much as me? I do not remember being unfaithful to you. I was there in my chambre every night waiting for you to come to me in order we may comfort each other but you…' I stood up and paced the room. 'You were sharing your bed and impregnating another with your seed. And although now you are saying it was not your seed… Does that really make any difference? I cannot see how you expect me to forgive you, Charles.' I dabbed my eyes. 'I need time.'

*

I slip-stitched the neckline on the maroon velvet gown. 'Can you believe the man?'

Tilly broke the thread with her teeth after sewing the last pearl on Maman's wedding outfit. 'But if the child isn't his?'

'I gave him my heart and he broke it.' I held the finished gown up. 'What do you think?'

'Mrs Roberts will be pleased.' Tilly draped Maman's sapphire blue gown on the mannequin.

'It is stunning. You have gone to so much trouble for Maman.'

Tilly shrugged her shoulders. 'Maybe it will make her like me better.'

'Maman said she'll try harder, remember. She even wants you to call her Maman.'

'But she's not my mother, is she? I'm never going to see my mam ever again.' Tilly cried into a handkerchief.

I got up from the stool and went over to my friend and put my arms around her. She sank her head into my chest and wept.

'Life has cheated you, mon amie. It is hard to accept your maman has gone but let me help you, like you helped me, when my papa died.'

'I'll try.' Tilly dried her tear-stained cheeks. She sniffled. 'What are you going to do about Charles?'

'What about him?'

'André's asked him to stay on for a while. To give you a chance to sort things out.'

'That is not going to transpire.'

'But how would you feel if something happened to him?'

I turned away from her. 'I do not know.'

She turned me back to face her. 'I think you do know, Françoise. You love him.'

'I have never denied that.' I looked up at the clock. 'It is almost time for dinner.'

'I'm not hungry.'

'You need to eat. Come.'

'Only if you agree to spend some time with Charles.'

'Tilly!'

'Please. Go for a picnic like you used to.'

'A picnic in this weather.'

'It might warm up again. If not, something else. A candlelit dinner or a picnic in the barn.'

'I will think about it.' I passed her my hand. 'Come.'

Chapter 17

Françoise

'It looks wonderful,' I said after Tilly finished styling my hair. She had piled it loosely on my head. Soft chestnut brown curls caressed my forehead and cheeks.

'You look beautiful, Françoise. Charles will be unable to resist you.' Tilly headed to my wardrobe and took out a day frock. 'I've chosen this one to match your eyes.'

I slipped off my dressing robe and stepped into the emerald velvet gown.

She laced up the bodice from behind. 'I'm pleased you decided to give Charles another chance.'

I smoothed my hands down the soft fabric and glanced in the Cheval mirror. Puffed sleeves broadened my shoulders and the tight bodice showed off my small waist. 'I am not making any promises, Tilly. What is there to stop him betraying me again?'

'He does appear remorseful.'

'That is what he says.'

'And now that business with him not expecting me to return as a maid is cleared up… although I'm sure your maman would prefer that.'

'I thought Maman had been better towards you since the news of your mother passing.'

'She has, but I can't help wondering for how long.' Tilly took out the diamond choker from my jewellery box and held it up. 'Why not wear this?'

'I do not wish to give him the wrong impression.'

'It seems a shame to keep it locked up in a box.'

'That is true. All right then.'

Tilly stood behind me and fastened the necklace around my neck. 'There. You look gorgeous.'

I ran my fingers across the diamond, thinking back to when I had worn the pendant on my wedding day. My pulse quickened. Could things work for us?

'Would you not like the chance to have another baby?'

'I cannot replace Oliver. I do not wish to.'

Tilly gently squeezed my fingers. 'I know that, Françoise. Oliver can never be replaced but wouldn't it be wonderful to hold another child in your arms?'

I closed my eyes. Would Charles and I have parted had we not lost our dear son? Had I been too hard on him when he had sought comfort with another after our loss. Maybe with her he could forget what had happened? I re-opened my eyes and turned to my friend. 'Very well, I will try today and see what happens but I am still not making any promises.'

Tilly kissed my cheek. 'That is all anyone can ask, my friend.'

*

Charles swayed the hamper basket as we strolled down to the river. It was a lovely day for a picnic as the weather had become milder. Two weeks earlier it had chilled my bones. 'Let us sit under here.' Charles ambled over to the willow. He unpacked a red and white sheet from the basket and laid it on the grass.

I joined him on the ground and looked out at the sun glistening on the water. The velvet fabric was a little warm.

'You look flushed, my dear. Why not remove your shawl?'

I glanced around at the deserted area.

'There is no one else here.' Charles gently removed the shawl from my shoulders. 'Now, are you hungry?' He rummaged through the hamper.

I held my stomach as it rumbled.

Charles chuckled. 'I think that answers my question. Here.' He passed me a chunk of bread filled with cheese and poured me a beaker of lemonade.

I sipped the drink as he poured a glass for himself.

'Do you not miss Mrs Derby's lemonade?' he asked.

I shrugged my shoulders. 'Sally copes well enough.'

'Indeed, she does, but no one can make lemonade quite like our cook at *Highwood*. She misses you.'

'Really?'

'Yes. We all do. And Mother…'

'Oui. Lady Elizabeth writes often but I have a new life now, here with Tilly, André and Maman.'

He took my hand and gripped my fingers. 'Does that mean there's no chance for you and me?'

My heart banged. 'I did not say that but…' I pulled my arm away. 'I do not know. It is hard to forget what you did.'

'I understand' – he moved closer and took my hand again in his – 'I was weak but I'm stronger now. And I now know that it is you who holds my heart.' He lifted my fingers to his lips and smothered them in kisses.

'I gave you my heart and you shattered it into tiny bits. My heart was already breaking when our beautiful Oliver slipped away and I needed you.'

'I know.' Charles kept hold of my hand. 'I should have been there for you and I wasn't and for that I regret every single moment. Please, my darling, I am trying to make amends. You're my wife and I'm not whole without you. Will you at least try to forgive me?' He moved closer and just for a brief moment his lips brushed against mine.

My pulse pounded. How could I conceal my feelings? I wanted him to kiss me and I wanted to be a wife in whole to him again but my head reminded me of the misery he had caused. I sat upright. 'Let us eat and then maybe we can have a meander along the river.'

A trio of ducks waddled our way. I threw out some breadcrumbs and we laughed together as the two mallard and a drake scrambled for the bits of bread. Charles saw this as an invitation to move closer to me. He stroked my face and brushed his lips against mine. For an instant I let them linger. I pushed him away. 'Please, Charles, non. Come, gather up the picnic and we will take a wander along the bank.'

Charles folded the cloth and placed it into the basket along with empty beakers and food parcels. He stood up and stretched out his hand to help me. Afterwards he placed the shawl around my shoulders. 'May I at least hold your hand?'

I glanced about to make sure there was still no one else around before saying, 'Oui. You may do that.'

We trampled hand in hand across twigs and bronze leaves with the three ducks following. As we reached the bank the waterfowl waded into the river and fluttered their wings before settling down to paddle.

Charles turned me to face him. 'I'm sorry, Françoise. I didn't mean to rush you.'

'I accept your apology. I imagine you will be leaving shortly as it is the wedding next week?'

'I was hoping you would allow me to stay for the wedding.'

'But Lady Elizabeth will be expecting you home.'

'My dear mother has informed me that I must not return to *Highwood* without my wife.'

'But supposing I never want to leave *Sunbury*. I like it here. I am happy.'

'Then it looks like I may never leave either.'

I started walking again. 'I am not sure how that will work. Who is running the estate while you are away?'

'I have a trusted right-hand man. Please, Françoise, may I stay for the wedding?'

'I will think about it.'

The trees rustled from a rush of wind. I shivered. 'It is turning cold. I looked up at a huge black cloud. 'I think it is going to rain.' Before my words were out there was a bolt of thunder and torrential rain belted down causing ripples on the water.

'Quick' – Charles led me over to an old yew tree – 'we will shelter here until it stops.'

I did not argue as my clothing would be ruined if it got wet.

Charles put his arm about me to help stop my shivering but no sooner had the downpour started it stopped and the sun was shining again. Charles pointed upwards to a perfectly formed rainbow over the river. 'God has sent a sign, my dearest. A sign of hope. You see, there is hope for you and me.'

Chapter 18

Tilly

Françoise hung up the finished gown on a rail outside the dressing room.

'What time do we expect Lady Astley?' I asked.

'She's due at half past eleven.'

I looked up at the clock. 'That gives us an hour. Time for a cup of tea.' No sooner had I made the suggestion when Sally entered the workroom with a tray.

'I thought you ladies might need some refreshment as you've been working since early this morning.'

'Thank you, Sally. Tilly made the same suggestion. You can leave the tray over there.'

Sally set the silver platter down on a small occasional table in the clientele area. 'I bet you're getting excited, Miss Matilda.'

'Yes, I am. I can't believe a week tomorrow I'll be Matilda Dubois.'

Sally sauntered over to Lady Astley's finished outfit. 'This is beautiful. I love the shiny material. What is it?'

'Silk.' Françoise approached the couch, adjusting her skirt as she sank into the velvet cushion. She tapped her lips. 'I believe we should make you a gown, Sally, to thank you for all your hard work.'

'No, madam, I couldn't accept that. You pay me a wage.'

'Françoise's right.' I picked up my cup and took a sip. 'Something perhaps to wear to my wedding.'

'I'm invited?'

'Absolutely.' Françoise got up from the couch and strode towards Sally. 'You most definitely deserve something new. She brushed a mousy strand of hair away from Sally's brow. 'I think a bronze shade to bring out the colour of your lovely brown eyes.'

Sally blushed. 'Oh madam, thank you. I don't know what I've done to deserve such kindness. I've never had a new frock. Thank you. Thank you both. I love working here. You're all so kind.' Her eyes filled. 'Now I must get on with my chores before you change your mind.' Leaving the room she blew her nose.

'That was very generous, Françoise,' I said.

'She is a good worker and never complains.' Françoise joined me on the couch and I poured us both a fresh cup of tea.

'I'm glad you agreed to Sir Charles staying on until after the wedding.' I dropped a sugar cube into my drink and stirred it with a spoon.

'It has been pleasant having him around but I am still not ready to forgive him.'

'I understand. He has asked if I'll allow him to give me away but I wondered how you felt?'

'It is up to you. But why him?'

'I have no one else and he's always been good to me. Sir Charles and his mother. They took me into their service when I was fourteen, taught me to read and write, and it was through them I also learned to dressmake. I've a lot to thank them for.'

'Is that a reason to have him give you away?'

'Would you rather he didn't?'

'Non. Not at all. I am trying to establish your reasons.'

'Because he has always been kind to me. Like the kindness you just showed to Sally. Sir Charles would do things like that.

He arranged staff parties with a band, an extra penny in our pay, a couple of luxuries to take home to my family at Christmas. I could go on.'

Françoise smiled. 'Then I will not stand in your way.'

Footsteps came from the hallway as I stacked the cups and saucers. After a tap on the door, André's mother entered. 'Lady Astley is here. It is a little earlier than her appointment. Are you ready or do you need a few more minutes?'

'Now is fine, Maman.' Françoise peeped her head out of the doorway. 'Do come in, Lady Astley. How are you today?'

'Good morning, Madam Françoise. Miss Matilda. Thank you for seeing me earlier than my appointment.' She glanced across at the teacups. 'I apologise, it seems I've interrupted your break.'

'Non. We have finished.' Françoise picked up the tray. 'Maman, can you take this through to the kitchen?'

'Of course, ma fille.' Maman Antoinette turned to Lady Astley. 'I will come and find you, Lady Suzanna, once you have finished in here.'

'I look forward to it.' Lady Astley's eyes were drawn to the forest-green gown hanging up by the dressing room. She made her way over. 'You've done an incredible job, ladies. I hope I don't outshine the bride.' She tittered.

I removed the frock from the rail and hung it up inside the dressing room. 'Shall we make sure it fits?'

Once in her new outfit Lady Astley glanced in the Cheval mirror, smoothing her hands down across the bodice, into her slim waist, and down the silk flowing fabric. 'The style's perfect, and the gold patterned stripe flattering.'

Françoise adjusted the puffed sleeves that set off the slim arm cut. 'You look enticing, Lady Astley. Perhaps you will meet an eligible widower.'

'I'm too old for that, Madam Françoise, but you're not. That distant cousin of yours, what's his name? Sir Charles?'

'Oui, that is his name.'

'I've noticed the way he looks at you. Don't leave him hanging too long otherwise another young maiden will claim him.'

Chapter 19

Tilly

Sally and Françoise finished dressing me in my bridal gown. I lingered at my reflection in the Cheval mirror. 'I really am a princess.' My eyes filled.

Françoise passed me a handkerchief. 'Do not cry on your wedding day. I am sure that must be bad luck.'

Sniffling, I dabbed the white linen square across my eyes. 'I think it's supposed to be good luck.'

'That's what I heard too,' Sally said. 'They say if a bride cries on her wedding day she'll shed all her tears and be free from them during her marriage.'

Françoise gave a small laugh as she positioned the veil onto my head of blonde curls. 'It is good you are crying then. Although I am sure my brother will never give you cause for tears.'

'I don't know how to thank you,' I said. 'The silver brocade bodice is beautiful and worth all the hours you put in sewing the pearls. I really am thankful.'

Françoise stood next to me at the mirror. 'Only what you deserve. Sally, please will you bring me the small boxes from my dressing table.'

'Yes, of course.' Sally left the room.

'You have been such a loyal friend to me since I first came to England,' Françoise continued, 'and in a few hours, you will become ma sœur.'

'Françoise…'

'Oui?'

'Have you decided whether you'll return to *Highwood* with Charles?'

'Non, I am not ready but that does not mean never.'

Sally returned with two gold boxes. 'These?'

'Oui.' Françoise took a sapphire pendant from one of the boxes and fastened it around my neck.

I looked in the mirror. 'It is beautiful. Are you sure?'

'Oui? The sapphire matches your eyes.'

'Have you got everything?' Sally asked. 'Something old, something new, something borrowed, something blue?'

'I have something borrowed.' Smiling, I touched Françoise's necklace.

'And here is your something old.' Françoise passed me a sixpence. 'This is the one I was given for my wedding. Now you must put it in your shoe.'

I took off my satin slipper and popped the coin in and slipped my foot back inside.

Françoise handed me a small handkerchief. 'Something blue. It is the one Maman gave to me for my wedding.'

'I just need something new.' I looked around.

'And your betrothed has seen to that.' Françoise opened up the second box and fastened a diamond bangle around my wrist.

'It's beautiful.' I wished Mam were here to see this. She'd have been so proud. My life had changed in such a short time. Today I'd become Madam Matilda Dubois and Tilly Greenwood would be gone forever. But what of Frank and the twins? Would they still want to know me? And my sisters? I didn't even know where they lived. After the wedding I'd ask André to help me track them down.

'Tilly?' Françoise waved her hand in front of my face.

'Sorry, I lost myself for a while there. I was thinking how lucky I am.'

Sally lifted the skirt of my gown. 'It's clever, Françoise, how you've managed to cover the silk material in this gorgeous lace.'

'It's very flattering.' I smiled.

'You do not need fabric to flatter that wonderful slim figure. Mon frère is a lucky man.' Françoise added the white-flowered headdress to my veil. 'Tu es belle mariée.'

'Sorry?'

'You are a beautiful bride, my friend.'

I felt myself flush.

*

I strolled down the winding staircase with Françoise and Sally behind me holding my long train. Charles and André's mother waited at the bottom. Her face showed a smile but her eyes told me it was a lie.

'You look lovely,' I said to her.

'Why thank you, ma fille, as do you. I love my gown. Merci.'

'You all look adorable. Françoise.' Charles took her hand and lifted it to his lips. He then turned to our maid. 'Is that new, Sally?'

She blushed. 'Yes. Madam Françoise and Miss Matilda made it especially for me.'

'They've done an excellent job. You look enchanting,' he said. 'How are you getting to the church?'

'Mrs Taylor has sent her carriage for me. In fact, I must hurry otherwise the bride will be there first.' She picked up her bronze skirt and ran down the hallway.

'That was a generous thing to do, Françoise.' Charles' eyes twinkled in her direction.

Maman Antoinette shook her head. 'Ma fille is far too generous at times.'

Françoise put her finger up. 'Now, Maman, have you forgotten how the Dubois family in England looked after us for all those years when we were in France?'

'I do not wish to speak about those times.' André's mother patted her false tears.

Françoise lowered the tulle veil over my face and passed me a small bouquet of white heather matching my headdress.

*

When we arrived at St John's, the driver of the carriage reined the silver-grey horses in. Maman Antoinette and Françoise were shivering at the vestibule. Charles helped me down from the Landau and took my arm as we sauntered up to meet my future mother and sister-in-law. On reaching I glanced at André's mother and smiled.

'Maman Antoinette' – Charles rested his gloved hand on hers – 'allow me to escort you inside the church as we do not wish the groom to think his bride isn't coming now, do we?'

André's mother tightened her lace shawl across her shoulders. 'Thank you, Sir Charles. I would appreciate that.' Charles took her arm and turned to us. 'Ladies, I will be back in a moment.' He led André's mother inside.

'Are you nervous?' Françoise asked, adjusting my veil.

'A little. But not about marrying André, I have no doubts about that but I'm a little worried that I may not get my vows right.'

'You will be fine and if not, it will not matter.'

'It will to your mother. She is never going to accept me.'

'Give her time. Maman will learn to love you.' Françoise picked up my train as Charles came back outside. She looked lovely in her white silk dress with its lilac sash tied in a bow at the back, and carrying a matching posy to mine.

'Are you ladies ready?' Charles asked.

I nodded.

He linked his arm in mine and as we entered the cold building the organist played the wedding march. We sauntered down the aisle with my matron of honour close behind. A kaleidoscope of butterflies fluttered in my stomach. My only regret was that I had no members of my family here with me. I missed Daisy too.

Mrs Taylor and Sally smiled as we passed their pew. Seeing Mrs Taylor in her cobalt blue outfit made me proud and Sally looked lovely in the golden satin. We stopped when we reached André who was standing at the front with Mr Astley.

Whispers in the chapel hushed as the vicar approached. He spoke out to the congregation, 'Dearly beloved, we are gathered together here in the sight of God…'

My heart pounded. It was really happening. I was soon to become André's wife.

The organist played an intro into a hymn. Choirboys dressed in red robes with white pinafores stood up and sang *Hallelujah*. My pulse quickened. The boys' soprano voices were lovely but I wanted to get on with our vows. My biggest fear was that Maman Antoinette would put a stop to our wedding but André's hand squeezing mine assured me all would be fine. He looked smart in his black tailcoat.

The vicar beckoned us closer to the altar. 'André Willeme wilt thou have this woman to thy wedded wife, to live together after God's ordinance in the holy estate of Matrimony? Wilt thou love her, comfort her, honour, and keep her, in sickness and in health; and, forsaking all other, keep thee only unto her, so long as ye both shall live?'

André brushed his hand against mine. 'I will.'

The vicar turned to me. 'Matilda Ann wilt thou have this man to thy wedded husband, to live together after God's ordinance and in the holy estate of Matrimony? Wilt thou obey him, and serve him, love, honour and keep him, in sickness and in health; and, forsaking all other, keep thee only unto him, so long as ye both shall live?'

I sensed Maman Antoinette's disapproval but turned to my soon to be husband and had no doubt at all that I was making the right decision when answering, 'I will.'

She would have to learn to love me as a daughter. Maybe when I'd given birth to our firstborn she'd accept me.

Chapter 20

Françoise

Tilly and André made a perfect couple. I was so happy that she was finally going to legally become part of our family. Maman on the other hand still showed no sign of relenting. At least now she would try to hide her dislike with a false smile but Tilly knew the truth.

As André spoke his vows to Tilly, I turned to Charles who was watching me. He mouthed the words. *To love and to cherish.* My heart told me to go back with him but my head shouted *no* louder. He had betrayed me before so what was to stop him doing that again? And then there was the question of our lives. I was happy at Sunbury, being a businesswoman and fashion designer.

When Tilly faced André to say her vows, Charles continued to watch me. I smiled back at him but did not mouth the words but said them in my head. I had been faithful. He had not.

The organist played a few bars of introduction before the congregation joined in with *Sing unto God* but my mind was elsewhere. What would happen to Tilly if I returned to *Highwood?* She was not as lucky as me with a kind mother-in-law. Maman would make Tilly's life difficult. I could not leave her.

*

Charles, Matthew Astley, and I followed the bride and groom into the vestry. Charles and Matthew were to be witnesses. Tilly

222

and André's faces glowed. I was back in Beckton as a young mademoiselle when I promised to honour and obey Charles. Such a lot had happened since then. The most important life changer had been giving birth to my beautiful boy and losing him within a matter of weeks.

Tilly handed me her bouquet as she leaned over to sign the register. I glanced up into Charles' twinkling anthracite eyes. I wondered if he was thinking back to our wedding too. He brushed his gloved hand against mine.

'Sir Charles,' the registrar said.

Charles moved forward and picked up the pen and signed his name as witness and afterwards Matthew did the same.

A bald-headed usher directed us out of the vestry and we followed the bride and groom down the aisle, keeping our eyes straight ahead.

*

Guests threw rice over Tilly and André as they headed to their carriage. The white horses whinnied, raising their heads. Maman and Lady Astley whispered to each other. *What was that about?* It looked serious. Lady Astley frowned and Maman nodded back.

Charles came up behind me and took my arm. 'May I escort you to our carriage?' He glanced over at Maman. 'Maman Antoinette, are you ready?'

Lady Astley patted Maman's arm. 'Remember what I said.'

Maman waddled over and Charles helped her into the Landau. Once I was also seated, I asked her, 'What was all that about with you and Lady Astley?'

'Nothing for you to worry about, ma fille.'

Charles clasped my hand in his but I pulled away. I did not wish to cause gossip among the locals.

*

Back inside the house Charles and I joined the bridal couple at the table while guests stood by the wedding breakfast buffet piling cold meats, breads, and salad onto their platters. André was speaking to Tilly so I took this moment to say to Maman, 'Are you going to tell me what you and Lady Astley were discussing?'

'I told you, ma fille, nothing for you to concern yourself about.'

'But it looked serious?'

She sighed. 'If you must know she was telling me how lucky I am to have such a wonderful daughter-in-law.'

'That is what I have been telling you. How did you answer?'

'I told her my concerns.'

'What did you tell her?'

'I told her Matilda was a housemaid prior to coming to *Sunbury* and mon fils deserved better.'

'How could you, Maman? What was Lady Astley's reaction?'

'She agreed with you.' Maman cut a slice of ham and pushed a piece onto her fork. 'She said whatever Matilda had been in the past, she was still a good catch for André.'

'You should not have told her, Maman.' I shook my head. 'Well, I hope now that she has reassured you, that will be the end of this nonsense.'

'I am sorry, ma filles, but with all this chatter in the room I cannot hear what you are saying.'

'I said, I hope this will be the end of you persecuting Tilly.'

'I will try.' Maman tutted. 'But your papa would be ashamed of you and ton frère. You have both brought discredit to the Dubois name.'

I raised my voice. 'That is foolish talk, Maman.'

André turned to me. 'Is everything all right?'

I pressed his hand. 'It is fine, mon frère. Nothing for you to be concerned about. Maman and I are having a little heated discussion.' I smiled. 'That is all.'

'Maybe you should save the heated discussion for later? Remember this is my wedding.'

'Je suis désolée, André.' I turned back to Maman and spoke more softly. 'What else did you tell Lady Astley?'

'If you mean have I told her about you and Sir Charles, then yes. I had to explain why you appeared disinterested in Mr Astley.'

'Maman, how could you?'

'She will not say anything.' Maman sipped her drink.

'But you knew I did not wish anyone to know.'

'Oui, that is true. However, you should be with your husband. You agreed to fulfil the oath and no matter what Sir Charles did, or did not do, he was still your husband. You should not have deserted him. Your papa would be ashamed of you.'

I took slow deep breaths to control my anger. What right did she have? What had happened to her? Not only was she ridiculing Tilly at every chance but now she was interfering with my life too. I nibbled a piece of ham from my plate.

*

André and Tilly got up from the table and the rest of us followed.

Tilly clutched her bouquet before turning the opposite way. 'Are you ready?'

The unmarried ladies giggled waiting eagerly with their hands out ready to catch the flowers.

Tilly threw the posy and it landed straight into Miss Caroline's hands. 'Blanche, look,' she said in a high-pitched voice, 'look I caught it. I'm going to be a bride.' She giggled, fluttering her eyelashes and searching the room until her focus settled on Monsieur Astley.

Everyone clapped, and continued to clap as Tilly and André made their way outside.

*

Charles and I took an early evening stroll along the river. The sky was ablaze after the warm autumn day. It was now time to say au revoir to Charles.

He took my hand. 'May I?'

'Oui.' I smiled.

'André and Matilda were lucky getting such a fine day at this time of the year.'

'Yes, they were.'

'I was thinking about our wedding. Were you?'

I glanced up at him. 'Oui.'

We meandered along the riverside. Charles stopped at a bench. 'Shall we?' He guided me to sit down. 'Is it too late for us?'

'Je ne sais pas.' A chevron of geese flew over. I glanced up and watched them disappear from our view. 'Such a wonderful sight, do you not agree?'

'Wonderful. I imagine they're off to a warmer climate. Françoise, how long will you punish me for?'

'I am not punishing you.'

'I had hoped the wedding would help rekindle our love. How long before you let me back into your heart?'

'It depends on how long it takes to trust you again.' I chewed my lip. 'I suppose…' I got up and moved to the edge of the bank and Charles followed.

'Aren't these thistles wonderful?' I bent down to smell the purple blooms.

'They are, dearest, but what is it you were going to say?'

'I suppose you could write to me, and this time I promise to write back, but I make no promise of a reconciliation. Perhaps you can visit again and in time, maybe, I will be ready to forgive.'

'I'll do whatever it takes to gain your trust again. I'm nothing without you.'

I was nothing without him. Butterflies fluttered in my stomach. 'What time will you leave tomorrow?'

'I depart at first light. So, darling, this is goodbye.' He brushed his lips against mine and I returned his kiss.

I didn't want this moment to end but I could not trust myself for it to continue. I shivered. 'It's turning cold.'

Charles slipped off his coat and wrapped it around me. 'Come, dearest, we shall return to the house and keep cosy by the fire.'

Chapter 21

Tilly

Christmas Eve 1897

André and Matthew Astley dragged a huge Christmas tree into the drawing room. They lifted it into a tub and stood it up by the window. It almost touched the ceiling. They packed coal pieces in the bucket to keep it balanced.

'Now to decorate it.' I pulled out a crimson glass bauble from the box and hung it on one of the branches. 'Your turn next, Françoise.'

She rummaged eagerly through the container and chose one of the painted ornaments we'd made together last week using papier-mâché.

Over the next hour the four of us took turns adding ribbons to baubles, sweet treats, fruit, nuts and cakes before dangling them from the branches.

André looked to the top of the tree. 'All we need now is something for the top.'

Françoise headed for the sideboard and returned with an angel. 'Here you are.'

Matthew frowned. 'Not a star?'

'Non.' Françoise frowned. 'This is Angel Gabriel. I made it specifically for this purpose.'

'And it is adorable, ma sœur. Of course, we will use it.' André pulled a chair across the room, climbed up, and stretched his arm to the top of the tree to fix the angel on top. 'There.'

I knelt down on the floor with a dustpan and brush. As I swept up the loose needles I was overcome with nausea. I got up quickly. 'Excuse me.' I dashed to the bathroom.

As I leaned over the toilet bowl to be sick, I hoped no one had been suspicious about why I had rushed off, although Françoise wouldn't have missed it. I pulled the chain. My legs trembled as I shivered. Thank goodness we had an indoor lavatory unlike poor Mam who had to go outside to the privy in all weathers when she was expecting the twins. I made my way down to the kitchen to get a drink to take away the horrid taste in my mouth.

I was sipping water from a cup when Françoise charged into the room. 'There you are. We wondered where you had gone.'

'Sorry. I felt sick. Must have been something I ate or it could be nerves due to Lady Elizabeth's visit.'

'Mais pourquoi?'

'Because she'll think I'm an upstart.'

'I am sure that will not be the case.'

'It will. She's just like your maman. Wait and see.'

'Do you really think that is why you were sick or could it be something else? You know you can tell me.'

I shrugged my shoulders. 'Well, I've missed two of my monthlies.' I grinned.

'This is wonderful news. I am so happy for you. Does André know?'

'Not yet. I thought I'd wait until tomorrow and tell him as part of his Christmas gift. What do you think?'

'I think it is a delightful idea. Do you have an idea when the child will be born?'

'June, I think. A summer baby.' I rested my hand on her arm. 'Are you all right about this?'

'I could not be happier, ma sœur. And this could mean Maman will finally accept you as her daughter.'

'I hope so. Shh, someone's coming.'

Sally entered the room with two young girls around eleven and twelve. 'Sorry Madam Françoise, Miss Matilda, I didn't realise you were in here. We've come to start the food preparation for tomorrow. These are my younger sisters. Ann and Joyce.'

'We are just leaving,' Françoise said. 'Thank you, Ann and Joyce, for helping your big sister.'

The girls giggled.

*

'It is marvellous to finally have something to celebrate. André will make a magnificent papa.' Françoise glanced at her father's portrait over the fireplace. 'I wish Papa were here. He would be so proud of his son.'

I leaned across to the mantelpiece to pick up two envelopes and passed them to Françoise. 'I almost forgot you have post.' I poked the fire and added a couple of pieces of coal from the scuttle.

Her green eyes sparkled like gems. 'One from Charles and one from Geneviève.'

'How do you feel about Sir Charles visiting?'

'A little excited. I have missed him. I hope the snow stays off until they get here as I am unsure how the horseless carriage will cope if it gets stuck.'

'Won't it be wonderful if we have snow tomorrow?' I glanced at the tree. 'It looks lovely, doesn't it? It's the best tree I've ever had. We had nothing like this when I was growing up. Da would bring in a few twigs from the woods and my sisters and I would make decorations to go on it.'

'Wait until later when we light the candles. This Christmas will be special.' She glimpsed at the portrait again. 'Although it

230

will be my third without Papa and second without Oliver. I wonder what Oliver would have been like now if he had lived.'

I put my arms around Françoise.

'Merci, ma sœur. I am all right.' She released herself from my hold and put her hands on my shoulders. 'And next Christmas you will have your baby.' She smiled.

'If you return to *Highwood* with Sir Charles, maybe you'll have a new baby by then too?'

'I am not ready to return. I rather like how we are getting to know each other. I have learned so much about him from his letters. It is rather romantic.'

'Are you going to open your letters?'

'Non. I will save them. You will adore Geneviève when you meet her. She is like a sister to me and she will be to you too.'

'I can't wait.' I turned away to hide my frown, wondering what this Geneviève was like. Would she see me as a servant like Françoise's mother? I checked the time on the clock. 'We should get ready before our guests arrive. They will be here shortly. Wear your emerald taffeta gown. Sir Charles will not be able to resist you.'

Chapter 22

Françoise

Elizabeth and Charles followed me into the drawing room. Elizabeth had aged. Her hair was ashen all over and frown lines mapped her face. She stood at the fireplace and studied Papa's portrait. 'So, this was your father?' She brushed her fingers against the string of pearls around her neck. 'He was a handsome man. I see a resemblance to Henri and Willeme. How old was your father when the painting was commissioned?'

'In his fifties, I think, but Maman will be able to advise you better. He looks distinguished, don't you think, with his greying hair and white beard?' I was so grateful that André had been able to ship the portrait from *Vue de Jardin* along with other items from home.

'Yes, I agree.' Elizabeth tapped her lip. 'Don't you think so Charles?'

'I do. Although, I see a similarity to my own father too. But then I suppose that's not surprising when they were distantly related.'

Tilly pushed a trolley with refreshments into the room. 'Do sit down Lady Elizabeth, Sir Charles. Would you like some tea?'

'Very much so.' Elizabeth lowered herself onto the chaise longue, smoothing down her cobalt blue, velvet gown.

Tilly poured tea into our new floral bone china cups and passed one to Elizabeth and Charles along with milk and sugar.

'Thank you, Tilly.' Elizabeth added two sugar cubes to her drink and stirred it with a spoon. 'Be a good girl and take my bag up to my room.'

'Excuse me, Maman Elizabeth,' I said, 'Tilly is not a servant in this house. I'm sure André or Sir Charles will be happy to carry up your bags.'

Elizabeth glared at Tilly before turning to me. 'That satin gown is rather extravagant for a maid, Françoise.' She turned back to Tilly. 'Why aren't you wearing your uniform, girl?'

'Sorry?' Tilly bent her head.

I took in a deep breath. 'I have just told you, Maman Elizabeth. Tilly is not a maid. Tilly, Matilda, is my brother's wife.'

'What? I cannot believe what I'm hearing. When you asked me to release Tilly from my service, I was under the impression she was to be your maid. I hadn't realised that this was going to happen.' She turned to Charles. 'You never told me this. You said André had married Matilda, and omitted to say she was our former housemaid.'

'I didn't think it important, Mother.'

'Well of course it is.' Elizabeth huffed. 'I can't believe it.'

André wandered in. He glanced at Tilly. 'What is going on, Matilda? Is something wrong? Are you sickening for something? Your face is ghostly.'

Tilly frowned. 'Nothing.' She bounded out of the room with André close behind her.

Elizabeth sipped at her beverage.

Maman hobbled in. 'Lady Elizabeth, my dear, welcome to *Sunbury*. Sir Charles, it is good to see you here again, young man.'

Elizabeth put her cup down. 'How could you let this happen, Madam Antoinette?'

'Excuse-moi?'

'Allow your son to marry a servant. Is this how you conducted your household in France?'

'Non. Non, it was not.' Maman shrugged her shoulders. 'I am glad you agree with me but unfortunately I had no choice in the matter.'

'I will remind you both that this is my house and I will not allow you to disrespect my sister-in-law and friend. Maman Elizabeth, you are a guest here and if we are to have a happy Christmas as we hoped, then I will ask you to cease with these derogatory comments.'

Elizabeth shook her head. 'I don't know what the world's coming to.' She glanced across at the decorated tree in the corner. 'What an adorable tree you have, dear.'

*

After dinner we retired to the drawing room to sing Christmas carols. Maman sank into her straight back armchair while Elizabeth took to the couch. 'Madam Antoinette and I will just listen,' she said.

Tilly poured glasses of mulled wine for us all while I positioned myself on the stool at the piano, fixing my gown. Tilly, André and Charles gathered around me.

'Mon fils' – Maman sipped from her glass – 'you should light the candles on the tree first.'

'Bien sûr. We must.' André strode over to the Christmas tree and lit the candles with a burning wax taper making the room glow. 'There now. I think we are ready.'

I ran my fingers lightly along the piano keys and nodded to the others to join in with *I Saw Three Ships*. Baritone sounds from André and Charles, mingling with mine and Tilly's soprano voices, created glorious harmony. Once we had finished, Maman and Elizabeth clapped.

I flicked through the music scores. 'Any requests?' I drank a mouthful of the mulled wine; it warmed me inside.

Elizabeth sat upright. '*Silent Night?* Charles can sing solo for the first verse.'

I turned to Charles and he nodded in agreement. I hovered my fingers over the notes and counted him in. His low voice made my heart race. We all joined in at the second verse. Afterwards we sang several more carols, Maman yawned. 'Mon fils,' she said to André, 'help your maman out of the chair please. I need my bed.'

'Oui. Of course, Maman.' André rushed over and offered Maman his hand.

'Time for me to retire, too.' Elizabeth stood up. 'It'll be an early start in the morning if we have church. Goodnight, all.' She kissed Charles and I on the cheek in turn.

'What next?' I asked.

'*Twas in the Winter Cold?*' Charles' black gem eyes twinkled.

André winked at Tilly and she beamed. 'I think Tilly and I will sort some refreshments,' he said.

'A hot chocolate sounds nice.' I smiled knowing this was André's way of leaving Charles and I alone for a while.

As my brother and sister-in-law left the room, I started the intro for the carol. Charles was at my side and he placed his hand over mine. I stopped playing.

'Alone at last.' He pulled up a chair beside me, leaned closer and stroked my cheek before softly kissing me. My heart pounded. I had been waiting since he arrived to feel his kiss and I was not disappointed.

Chapter 23

Tilly

I tipped boiling water from the kettle into the pan of milk and returned it to the stove. André stretched his arm up to a high shelf and brought down a tin. He flipped the lid open and laid chocolate cookies onto a plate. 'What was all that going on earlier with Maman and Lady Elizabeth?'

'Basically, that I'm not good enough to be your wife.'

He took my hand. 'Ignore them.'

'I'll try.' I pursed my lips.

'What?'

'There's something I need to tell you. I was going to wait until tomorrow but…'

'What is it?'

'Now does seem the right time.'

'Go on.'

I took a deep breath. 'Monsieur Dubois, you're going to be a papa.'

'Oh Matilda, that's the best present you could be giving me. Merci ma chérie.' He wrapped his arm around me. I glanced over his shoulder. 'Quick. The milk's overflowing.'

André grabbed the pan just in time as the froth reached the top. We both convulsed with laughter. Once we'd managed to stop laughing, André put his arm around my waist. 'Seriously, Matilda, you've made me the happiest man alive. When can we expect the arrival of our son or daughter?'

'June, I think.'

'Would it not be magnificent if he or she arrived on l'anniversaire de papa?'

'It would indeed, my dearest. We will have to see if our child will oblige.' I patted my stomach. 'We should make this hot chocolate before Charles and Françoise wonder where we've got to.'

'Do you really think they will miss us? Have you noticed how ma sœur seems much happier since Charles arrived?'

'Yes. She has her glow back.'

'Do you think she will go back home with him?'

'No, I don't, but she'll go back to him sometime, even if she doesn't know herself at this stage.'

André picked up a cookie and crunched on it. 'I suppose we need to start thinking what we will do if that happens.'

'I don't want to go back to *Highwood*, André. How can I? All they'll see is a maid.'

'We will have our own home, ma chérie. I would never expect you to return there.'

'Thank you.' My eyes filled with relief. 'Perhaps you should ask Sir Charles to have a look around for houses in the vicinity?'

'That, my darling, is an excellent idea. And then if Françoise decides to return to *Highwood*, she will know we will be close by.' André yawned as Françoise entered the kitchen.

'So, this is where you two got to. We've been waiting for you.'

'Sorry, Françoise' – André wiped crumbs from his chin – 'it seems we have been caught out.' He passed the plate to his sister. 'Cookie, ma sœur?'

'Merci, mais non.' She chuckled. 'I just came to make a hot chocolate for Maman. Her lumbago is playing up again. Pray tell me anyway, what are you two up to besides stealing all the cookies?'

I glanced at André and he nodded. 'I've just been giving André his Christmas present.'

'You have told him. Is it not the most wonderful news?' She hugged her brother.

'Absolutely. I am a happy man. We were talking about you too.'

'Moi?' She pointed to her chest.

'Yes. You and Charles. We were saying you had your glow back.'

Françoise blushed.

'What have you done with him?' André glanced towards the doorway.

'He was summoned by Lady Elizabeth.'

I stirred the milk into the cups. 'I wonder what that's all about.'

'I have no idea. She probably has some complaint too. Now I must take the hot chocolate up to Maman.'

'Let me.' André tapped my shoulder. 'It will give you and Matilda time to talk for a few minutes.'

*

Restless, I rolled over. André lay still on his back, with his mouth wide open, breathing softly. Nauseous, I leapt out of bed and grabbed the bedpan from underneath. Why did they call it morning sickness when it happened any time of the day? Mam used to say the turn was around eleven to fourteen weeks. I must be near that now. Perhaps I'd be settled tomorrow. I wanted to enjoy my Christmas dinner. André had managed to get a huge turkey from one of the farmers and it would be the first time I'd tried it so I didn't want it to be spoiled.

I padded over to the window and pulled back the curtain slightly to admire the stars. It was snowing. Trees and bushes were covered in soft ice making everything look magical. I hoped Christmas this year would be special.

Smiling, I climbed back into bed and rubbed my stomach. Soon I'd start to swell. It was exciting to think I had a new life growing inside me. I wished Mam were still here.

André turned over and whispered, 'Are you all right, Matilda?' before curling up into my back making me feel safe.

Chapter 24

Françoise

André, Charles, Tilly and I trudged through the blanket of snow to chapel. Maman, a catholic, had declined to come. 'I will not enter that place. It isn't a proper church.' Elizabeth, concerned about slipping on the ice, decided she should stay and keep Maman company.

We stopped to watch the children throwing snowballs at each other. A snowman had been erected at the side of the lane.

'Look.' I pointed. 'They have used sticks, a carrot, and pieces of coal, just like we used to, André. Do you remember?'

'Oui. Of course.' Bending down, he scooped snow in his gloved fists and shaped it into a ball. He grinned. 'Do you remember what else we used to do?'

I hid behind Charles. 'S'il te plait. Non.'

'Don't worry, dearest, I'll protect you.' Charles guarded me, stretching his hands outwards to the side.

André threw the ball at an ice-covered tree. 'I was never going to throw it at you, ma sœur, but would it not be superb if we could still play games like that?'

'Oui. It would.' We had so much fun as children. Papa would build a snowman with us and once finished, Maman would come out and admire our work, bringing each of us a beaker of mulled wine.

André faced Tilly, and with his gloved finger, wiped a snowflake away from her nose. She laughed. They were so happy. I glanced at Charles. Could I have the same happiness with him? My heart pulled. It was too soon to return with him but I was enjoying our time getting to know each other.

We joined the queue of villagers and made our way into St John's, taking a pew close to the front. The church, decorated in greenery and candlelight, took away the chill of outside and I was further warmed to see little children on their knees by the altar studying the nativity scene.

During the service, Charles slipped his hand in mine and I allowed it to stay, only releasing it when it was time to say prayers. I was glad Maman and Elizabeth had stayed at home but hoped they were not giving Sally and her sisters a difficult time in the kitchen.

*

The church had almost emptied when Charles and I strolled to the front to inspect the nativity scene. I stooped down to look inside the stable. Three wise men held out gifts, shepherds and sheep looked on at Jesus in a manger, while Mary and Joseph knelt on the straw.

'It's lovely, isn't it?' Charles put his arm about me.

'Oui. It is. I am pleased you are here.'

'I am too.' He squeezed my hand. 'Come we should go. André and Matilda have already gone outside.'

The vicar stood at the vestibule. He thanked us for coming and shook our hands. Charles passed him a velvet pouch of coins.

'Thank you, sir. God bless you.' The vicar inspected the purse.

As we plodded back home through the snow it started to rain. 'Come, let us hurry before we get too wet,' André said taking Tilly's hand. Charles and I followed them.

*

We sat around the circular rosewood table. I was next to Maman and Elizabeth, André had Tilly on one side and Maman on his other, leaving Tilly in the middle of Charles and André. I had set the table deliberately to avoid Tilly sitting close to Elizabeth or Maman. The table was decorated with flowers, evergreens and linens. Sally had done an excellent job. Even Maman or Elizabeth would not be able to find fault.

'How was church?' Elizabeth asked.

'It was a good service, Mother.' Charles flipped his napkin and placed it across his lap.

'The nativity scene was lovely.' I glanced up as Sally, her sisters, and a young waiter, came through the door. Ann and Joyce imitated little maids in black frocks and pinafores which Tilly had made.

'Madam Françoise,' Sally said, 'this is my brother Joe.'

Joe smiled and strode across to André and set the huge turkey on a silver platter down in front of him. 'At your service, Madam Françoise. Mr André.'

'Merci, Joe.' I leaned back in the chair as Sally and the girls loaded our plates with roast potatoes, cabbage, leeks, carrots and turnip.

Joe circled the table pouring the red burgundy into our goblets while André carved the turkey. Sally passed our plates, laden with vegetables, in turn to André to add the meat. He placed drumsticks on his and Charles' plate and slices of breast on ours. Sally positioned our completed meals in front of us before joining her sisters at the back of the room.

As I sipped the medium-bodied wine I caught sight of the young girls fidgeting and licking their lips. I rose from the table and went over to them. 'Sally, you do not need to stay. Pack up some of this food and take it home for your family to eat. We can manage things here ourselves.'

'Thank you, Madam Françoise. That's very kind of you.' Sally picked up some of the dishes and summoned her sisters to do the same.

Joe lifted the turkey platter from the table. 'Thank you, miss.' He left the room ushering his sisters out in front of him.

Elizabeth shook her head. 'Do my eyes deceive me, dear, or did you just dismiss the staff with all the food?'

'That is correct.' I chewed a piece of turkey. 'Mmm. It is less greasy than goose. What do you think Maman? Maman Elizabeth?'

'Maman nodded. 'Oui. I like it.'

'Charles and I have eaten turkey before but I agree this is a nice bird. It's been cooked just right.' Elizabeth shook her head again. 'But pray tell me, Françoise, why have you sent your staff home?'

'Ann and Joyce are just children and they seemed tired and hungry.'

'There are girls younger than them in service. Tilly wasn't much older when she first came to *Highwood*. Isn't that right, Tilly?'

Tilly's face turned red.

Elizabeth drank from her goblet. 'Tell them, Tilly.'

'I'd rather not talk about it if you don't mind, Lady Elizabeth. That part of my life is gone.'

'Now, Mother, leave Matilda alone. As for sending the staff home with food, it is no different to what you've done yourself many a time. You've always been generous to the staff at *Highwood*, particularly at Christmas.'

She ignored Charles. 'Gone but not forgotten, Tilly. Surely not?' Elizabeth delicately placed a forkful of food into her mouth.

'I said I don't want to talk about it.' Tilly shuffled her chair back as she got up. 'If you don't mind, I'm not feeling very well. Excuse me.' She ran from the room.

André shot up. 'I do not mean to be disrespectful, Lady Elizabeth, but you are a guest in our home and I would thank you to show my wife the respect she deserves.' He stormed out of the room after Tilly.

Charles glared at his mother. 'Why are you behaving this way? It's outrageous. You deliberately set out to humiliate Matilda. You need to apologise to her, to our hosts too.'

Elizabeth shrank into her chair, her mouth wide open.

Maman glared at her. She shook her head and tutted under her breath.

Elizabeth blinked her eyes, 'I'm sorry, Françoise. I don't know what came over me. My only excuse is I'm still fatigued after yesterday's long journey. Rest assured I will apologise to your brother and his wife.'

I rose from my chair. 'I regret my appetite is lost. If you will excuse me, I need to see how Tilly is.'

Charles was at my side. 'I will come with you.'

'I really am sorry,' Elizabeth called as we left the room. 'I didn't mean to spoil Christmas.'

Chapter 25

Tilly

Françoise and I were finishing off washing the dishes after Christmas dinner.

André tapped his fingers on the kitchen table. 'Who's for a stroll? A walk could be what we all need after that unpleasantness in the dining room. I was pleased you sent Sally home with the remaining food, ma sœur, it was the right thing to do.'

Charles rubbed his moustache. 'I really didn't understand Mother's reaction when it's the sort of thing she'd normally do herself.'

'She was making a point about me.' I folded the tea towel over the back of the chair and slipped off my apron.

André put his arm around me. 'Forget her. We shall go for a nice walk but need to hurry as it will be dark soon.'

'I'll get my bonnet and cloak. Françoise, Sir Charles, are you joining us?'

'Oui. I would like that.' Françoise glanced at Charles.

'Yes, definitely,' he said.

We collected our outdoor clothing on the way. Snores echoed as we wandered past the drawing room causing us all to laugh.

*

The rain had washed away the snow but last night's freezing temperatures had left invisible ice on the paths.

Charles took Françoise's arm. 'It's slippery. Would you prefer to turn back?'

'Non. I am all right.' Françoise glanced at me. 'Tilly, how about you?'

I held on to André. 'I'll be fine.'

As we neared the river, Françoise stopped. 'Look at these beautiful thistles. Are they not wonderful?' She leaned forward to smell them and slipped. Luckily, she didn't go right down as Charles broke her fall. She squeezed her eyes shut. 'My foot. I've done something.'

Charles swooped her into his arms and carried her back towards the house. André and I followed.

'Don't drop me.' Françoise held him tight.

'Fear not, darling, you're safe with me. André and Tilly, go ahead and heat up some water.'

'We can do that,' I said.

André took my hand. 'Be careful, Matilda, we do not wish you to slip too.'

We trod with speed back home and into the kitchen. André had the pan of water heating on the stove when Charles pushed open the kitchen door and set Françoise down onto a chair. He pulled a stool across and lifted her foot onto it. 'We'll soon get you sorted. It's lucky I know what to do.'

Françoise shivered. 'Merci.'

'I'll make you a hot cup of tea.' I filled the kettle and put it on the stove next to the pan.

Charles knelt down next to Françoise. 'I must remove your boot. This may hurt.'

Françoise tilted her head.

As Charles pulled off her boot, she winced. He rubbed her swollen ankle. 'How's that water doing?' he asked, 'it just needs to be warm.'

André scooped water from the large pan with a ladle and tested the temperature on the back of his hand. 'Parfait.' He poured the warm water into a tin bucket and passed it to Charles who carefully lifted Françoise's foot into the bucket causing her to wince again. 'This will make you feel better.' He dabbed her foot with a cloth for a few minutes. 'I need to wrap it. Madam Matilda, can you bring me something to use as a bandage?'

'Yes. I have just the thing. I darted to the workroom and pulled out a box with clean sheeting, cut into strips and rolls, surplice to our needs when we'd made bunting for the diamond jubilee. I took one roll and charged back to the kitchen. 'Will this do?' I asked.

'Perfect. Soak it in cold water.'

'Yes of course. I soaked the cloth in the sink. After squeezing it out I passed it to Charles.

He gently lifted Françoise's foot from the pail, dabbed it dry with a towel, and wrapped the sheeting around her ankle, underneath, and round and round again. 'That will do.' He tore the end of the cloth and tied it in a knot just above her ankle. 'There, dearest, that should help.'

'Merci, Charles.'

It was obvious Charles adored her. I wasn't sure how she'd be able to resist him. Would she go back to *Highwood* at the end of the holiday?

André's mother shuffled into the kitchen. Her eyes darted to her daughter. 'Ma fille, what has happened?'

'I am fine, Maman. I had a little slip but Sir Charles has been looking after me.'

'Merci, mon cher, merci.' Her mother squeezed Charles' hand. 'Oh dear, I feel quite faint.'

I moved a chair within her reach. 'Sit down, Maman Antoinette.'

'Merci, Matilda.'

I filled a beaker with water. 'Drink.'

'Merci.' She sipped the liquid and thanked me again. 'Merci.' She took a deep breath. 'Matilda, it was you I came in search of, dear. I wanted to apologise for Lady Elizabeth's behaviour. She is very sorry and has taken to her bed to rest. I am sure once she rises, she will apologise herself.'

I bit my lip.

Charles stood up behind Françoise. 'We should get ready. Lady Astley and her nephew will be here soon. Are you able to walk?'

'I will try.'

'I'll help you.' Charles lifted Françoise from under her arm and helped her from the chair. 'Lean on my shoulder.'

'Merci. I am hoping people's tempers will have ceased by the time our guests arrive.' Françoise hobbled out of the kitchen with Charles, turning back to say, 'Are you coming, Maman?'

*

André fiddled with his tie. 'Matilda, are you able to assist me with this?'

I stood away from my dressing table mirror and moved over to tie the black linen into a bow. He looked handsome in his maroon smoking jacket; the colour almost matched my silk gown.

He held his arm for me to link mine into his. 'Are you ready to go downstairs?'

'Not quite. I'd like to adjust my hair. Go down without me. I shan't be long.'

'All right, ma chérie.' He brushed his lips against mine. His moustache tickled my lips.

'I'll see you shortly.' I moved back to the stool at the mirror and piled my soft curls into a clip leaving loose ringlets brushing my cheeks. On getting up, I gazed at my reflection and ran my hand over my flat stomach. It wouldn't be like that for long and I couldn't wait. I was smiling in the glass when a tap came on the door. 'Come in,' I called.

Lady Elizabeth crept in. 'Matilda, dear.' She stopped speaking and stared at me.

'Yes, Lady Elizabeth?'

'Sorry, dear. Forgive me. You look…' Her mouth was open but she'd stopped talking.

'Yes?'

'Matilda dear, you look… you look striking.'

'Thank you.'

'I came to apologise for my behaviour earlier today. I should never have spoken to you that way. My manners were atrocious. It was a shock as I'd no idea André had taken you as his wife, but seeing you now, I understand why. Talent and beauty. Please, dear, please accept my apologies.'

'Of course. Thank you for taking the time to apologise, Lady Elizabeth.'

'I believe your other guests have arrived. If you're ready perhaps we can walk down together?'

I couldn't help smiling. Both Maman Antoinette and Elizabeth had apologised to me today. Quite a feat. I followed Elizabeth from the room.

*

The drawing room was empty but the lights were on. Where had everyone gone?

I looked around. 'I don't understand. André came down a while ago.'

Elizabeth tapped her chin. 'There's no sign of your mother-in-law either.'

'Or Françoise and you said the guests had arrived, so where are they?'

Heavy footsteps accompanied by chuckling came from the hallway and Charles, André and Matthew Astley wandered in.

'Good evening, Mother, Madam Matilda.' Charles glanced around the room. 'Where's Françoise?'

'She's not here,' I said, 'I was about to go and find her.'

Charles patted me on the shoulder. 'No need, dear lady, I shall see if she needs assistance getting downstairs.' He made his way back through the doorway.

André's cheeks looked red from windburn. 'Have you been outside?' I asked.

'Oui.' He blew into his hands. 'Matthew wanted to see Sir Charles' contraption.'

Matthew laughed. 'It was amazing. We went for a drive.'

Elizabeth frowned. 'In this weather?'

'All the snow had gone. I can't wait to tell Aunt Suzanna about the machine.' He glanced left to right. 'Where is she?' he asked as Lady Astley and Maman Antoinette came in. 'Aunt Suzanna, there you are. I've been for a drive in Sir Charles' horseless carriage. I really must get one too. They move so fast. You must get him to take you out for a drive.'

Lady Astley looked up. 'I'm not sure about that. Particularly in snow.'

Charles entered with Françoise leaning on his arm. 'It's fine out there now, Lady Astley.' He helped Françoise onto the chaise longue before rushing across by the window and returning with a footstool. 'You need to keep the weight off.' He gently picked up her injured foot and placed it on the stool.

'Thank you.' Françoise's eyes sparkled.

'You're looking a bit better than earlier,' I said.

'I am feeling much better. Maman made me a special tea which helped.'

'How are you, dear?' Elizabeth asked Françoise. 'Charles told me what happened.'

Françoise gave a small laugh. 'I feel rather foolish.'

'Not at all. It could have happened to anyone hence why I declined accompanying you all to church.' Elizabeth sank into an armchair.

'Lady Astley, forgive my manners for not greeting you properly.' Françoise said. 'Unfortunately, I have sprained my ankle.'

'You poor child, how did that happen?' Lady Astley headed over to an armchair.

'I slipped on the ice but thankfully did not fall as Sir Charles managed to catch me.' Françoise glowed with pride.

Lady Astley glanced at the bandage on Françoise's ankle. 'I see someone knows First Aid.'

'That was Sir Charles too.' Françoise beamed.

Matthew Astley was at Françoise's side. 'Dear lady, thank you for not cancelling our invitation when you're clearly out of sorts.' He kissed her hand.

'It is good to see you again Monsieur Astley. What is the weather like out there now?'

'The snow has cleared. May I pass you a drink?' he said.

'That would be nice, thank you.'

Matthew appeared mesmerised by Françoise but it was obvious she only had eyes for Charles. It would not be long before she returned to *Highwood* but maybe that wouldn't be so bad. After all, it was doubtful anyone would recognise me as Tilly the maid, and I'd be able to see my brother and trace my sisters. We could go with her. There was no reason why I shouldn't be able to continue as a dressmaker, and I'd also be able to see Daisy. I suddenly realised I hadn't had a letter from her for a while now. I promised myself I'd write as soon as the festivities were over.

Charles glanced around at each of us in turn. 'Obviously Françoise is unable to play the pianoforte so we need a pianist. How about you, Madam Matilda?'

'I'm afraid I can't, although I'd like to learn.'

'André?'

'Non. I always preferred the trumpet and unfortunately sold mine before packing up *Vue de Jardin*. How about you, Sir Charles?'

'No, my sister was the pianist in our house. Hmm, we shall have to try and sing without. It won't be the same though.' He turned to Matthew. 'Unless, sir, you can oblige?'

'I'll have a go but I need to know the tune.' He headed to the pianoforte.

I opened the storage cupboard at the back of the stool and pulled out the music sheets Françoise had used yesterday. 'You'll need these.'

Matthew waved them away. 'No good giving them to me, madam, as I can't read a word of it. It's all black dots to me.' He wiggled his ear. 'This is what I use and that's why it's imperative I know the melody.'

'I see.' I tittered, putting the music back.

Matthew took off his jacket and passed it to me as he lowered himself onto the stool. He exercised his fingers mid-air over the keys before pressing notes either end to test out the instrument. 'How about *God Rest You Merry Gentlemen*?'

Charles was next to Françoise. His eyes fixed on her. 'I'll sing from here.'

'If you don't mind,' Lady Astley said, 'I'll stay seated too as my bones are getting a little old to stand.'

'Of course, Aunt Suzanna, but you'd better make sure you sing nice and loud.' Matthew gave a hoarse laugh.

That left André and I standing either side of Matthew. Halfway through the carol I glanced across at Maman Antoinette and spotted she'd fallen asleep, her head drooping. I had to be careful not to laugh. Charles and Françoise's soprano and baritone voices carried across the room. They complimented each other well.

After *God Rest You Merry Gentlemen* had finished we moved on to sing *We Three Kings* followed by *It came Upon a Midnight Clear*. I wished I could sing like Françoise. She had such a sweet voice. Mine was lower but André didn't seem to mind. His sparkling eyes flashed at me.

Matthew spun away from the pianoforte and rubbed his hands. 'I think I need a drink after that.'

'A good idea,' André said. 'I have an announcement and once we all have a drink in our hands it will be the perfect time.' He stepped over to the sideboard, took out eight glasses from the cupboard and poured sherry into each of them before passing them around. 'Maman,' he said, gently rocking her arm.

She startled. 'Oh dear, I must have dropped off.'

'Not to worry.' He handed her a drink. 'I'm about to make a toast.'

Once everyone had a glass in their hand, he beckoned me next to him. 'We have some news.'

André's mother grinned showing off her double chin. 'Is it what I think it is?'

'Oui, Maman. My dear wife is with child.' André squeezed my hand.

Elizabeth and Lady Astley got up from their seats and came over to me. 'Congratulations,' Elizabeth said. 'You'll make a wonderful mother.'

'Congratulations, Madam Matilda. This is exciting news.' Lady Astley glanced at André's mother. 'You're to be a grandmother, Madam Antoinette.'

'Oui. This is wonderful news.' She turned to Françoise.

'It is fine, Maman. I could not be happier for mon frère and his wife.

Chapter 26

Tilly

Françoise hobbled into the workroom. 'Good morning, Tilly. You are up early. What are you working on?'

I held up a maroon velvet gown. 'What do you think?'

'You have done a marvellous job getting it finished in less than four weeks. Particularly in your condition while you have been out of sorts.'

'The sickness is passing.' I lowered Elizabeth's gown back to my lap. 'I'm just finishing the hem. How's your ankle?'

'Better than it was. I am still limping but the pain has eased. Sir Charles has asked if I am up to a short stroll in the garden.'

'Do you think that's a good idea?'

'Oui. The weather is fine with no sign of ice and it will be rather nice to spend some time alone before he sets off for *Highwood*. I shall be sorry to see him go.'

'You will miss him. I wondered if you may go back with him.'

'I have given it consideration but it is still too soon. Apart from anything else I would prefer to make the journey once the weather is fairer, and I do not wish to go until after my niece or nephew has been born.'

'When are you thinking? June? July?'

'July most likely. Sir Charles and I have spoken and he has agreed to continue to visit. He will make the visits more regularly once the better weather arrives and he has promised to come up and meet Geneviève in April.'

'That's good news.'

'It also allows André time to find somewhere for you to live. I almost forgot the reason I am here' – she held out a letter – 'this is for you. It looks like Daisy's writing. I had better go and find Sir Charles. Enjoy the news from your friend.'

I got up to hang Lady Elizabeth's gown on the rail. Afterwards I settled down into one of the armchairs we used for clients. I ripped open the envelope.

Coopers Lodge
Beckton
Kent
10th January, 1898

Dear Tilly,

Please don't contact me anymore. We're too different. You're married to a man of means while I'm still a housemaid. I'm to move away soon with the Martins and I'll not be forwarding my address.

Have a good life.

Yours truly
Daisy

'What?' I sobbed. *Why was she doing this?*

'Matilda? What is it?' André was at my side.

I handed him the letter.

He ran his eyes across the page. 'I see. I suppose you can understand her reasoning.'

I glanced up at him. 'What?'

'It makes sense that she feels you no longer have anything in common.'

'But Daisy's my friend. She'll always be my friend. I don't understand.'

André passed me his handkerchief. 'Dry your pretty eyes.'

I wiped my cheeks.

'Come' – he stretched out his hand – 'let me make you a cup of tea.'

I followed him down to the kitchen and sat at the table while he filled the kettle to boil.

'You know, Matilda, this letter may not contain all bad news. These Martins, they live in the big lodge down from *Highwood*, do they not?'

I nodded, blowing my nose.

'If *Coopers Lodge* is to become vacant, it could be our new home.'

'I hadn't thought of that, but yes, you're right. It would be perfect. It's slightly bigger than here.'

'It sounds ideal. I shall ask Charles to find out more.' He lifted the kettle from the stove, poured hot water into the teapot and stirred the tea with a spoon.

But why would Daisy want to cut ties from me? I bet it was the Martins who told her to. Surely, there was no way she'd want to break our friendship.

'Here you are, chérie.' André passed me a mug. 'A cup of tea makes everything seem better.'

Chapter 27

Françoise

Charles and I took a short meander through the garden, stopping at the bench where winter jasmine bloomed, its yellow flowers adorning the wall. Although it was the last week in January, it was warm sitting in this suntrap. A river of purple and orange crocuses waved in the flower bed facing us.

Charles put his arm around me. 'I'm going to miss you, my darling. I wish you were coming home with me.'

'We spoke about this. Remember?'

'Yes. Yes, I know, but now the time's come to say goodbye it seems so hard.' His lips pressed firmly against mine and I let them linger.

I moved my face away. 'But you understand, I must be here when the child is born?'

'I understand but it doesn't make parting any easier.' He kissed me again before gently pulling us apart. 'We should make our way back to the house before Mother becomes agitated about us getting on the road.'

*

André and Charles loaded the suitcases onto the carriage. Elizabeth hugged Maman. 'Until next time, Madam Antoinette.'

Tilly came down the steps. Already her stomach swelled, showing more as she had stopped wearing a corset. 'Have you got your new gown, Lady Elizabeth?'

'Yes, dear. It's loaded in the vehicle. Thank you for doing that for me.' She kissed Tilly on the cheek. 'I look forward to welcoming you back in Beckton, wherever and whenever that will be. And don't worry, no one will recognise you as Tilly, you are Madam Matilda Dubois and that's all people will see.'

Tilly tightened her cloak. 'Thank you, Lady Elizabeth.'

Charles opened the carriage door and helped her into the passenger seat. 'Mother, André's asked about the Martins. It seems they're moving. Have you heard anything?'

She wound down the window. 'No. I've not heard anything but I'll see what I can find out. That sounds a perfect solution for André and his wife if the Martins are selling.'

Charles slammed the carriage door closed and came over to me. He took me in his arms and kissed me on the lips. 'Until next time, Lady Françoise Dubois. I'll write to you every day.'

'And I shall write back.'

He rotated the crank to start the engine before jumping into the vehicle. As he drove down the lane, he hung his head out of the window, tooted and waved.

Tilly took my arm as we climbed the steps. 'Are you all right?'

I squinted. 'I am rather sad, but that new order for Lady Astley will keep me busy.'

When we got back inside the kitchen, Sally had a pot of tea and a plate of scones laid out on the table. 'The vegetables are prepared,' she said, 'and there's a bacon and egg pie in the oven. I'll be off now unless you need me to do anything else?'

'No,' I said, 'there's nothing else. You get off home, Sally, and thank you for tea.'

As she left the room, Maman and André came in. 'A cup of tea. Just what I wanted,' André said. 'It is going to be quiet in the house with Lady Elizabeth and Sir Charles gone.'

'Oui. It is.' I took a chair at the table and poured tea into the cups.

'I am ready for some quietness.' Maman picked up a cup. 'Lady Elizabeth is far too bossy for my liking.'

'How do you plan to cope when we move to Beckton?' André asked.

'It is obvious, mon cher, I shall live with you and Matilda.'

André twiddled his moustache. 'I see.'

Tilly glanced at me. Poor Tilly. I believe she had hoped Maman would live with Charles and I, but I could understand Maman's reasoning. She and Elizabeth together in one house would be too much for us all. I sipped my tea.

Chapter 28

Françoise

Business was quiet at *Sunbury* which made me miss Charles even more. His next visit would not be until March the earliest and that was at least four weeks away. Orders had dropped off after the mad rush before Christmas. I imagined we would be busy from March when the ladies would require new outfits for spring outings.

Flopping down on one of the armchairs in the workroom, I sighed. There was nothing left to do. Lady Astley's gown was finished and one of her footmen would pick it up today.

André burst into the room. 'Ma sœur, I have had an idea to help with your sadness.'

'Who said I am sad?'

'It is obvious. You have lost that glint in your eye when Charles is around. Can you deny that you miss him?'

'Non. I cannot. I do miss him, oui and a distraction would be welcome. What do you have in mind?'

'I have booked a table at *Bridge Tearooms* for this afternoon. We will meet with Matthew and Lady Astley. I have arranged to take her order rather than someone collecting it from here.'

'That sounds nice, André. What time shall we depart?'

'Be ready for three o'clock. The booking has been made for half past three.'

'Merci. I have not seen Tilly this morning, is she well?'

'Oui. Matilda is fine. She has not been sick for a few days now. I told her to take longer in getting up today as business is quiet.'

'You are a good husband.'

'I try.' André grinned before charging out again. He was always in such a rush. Afternoon tea did sound like fun and it would be nice seeing Monsieur Astley again. We had not seen him since Christmas.

*

André reined in the horses outside the tearooms. He stepped down and opened the door of the Landau for Maman, Tilly and I. Tilly was radiant. Her face had filled out and the cobalt velvet gown heightened the colour of her bright blue eyes. I thought back to my pregnancy with Oliver. I had looked haggard but Tilly looked exquisite. Being with child suited her.

The waitress greeted us at the door. 'Monsieur Dubois. We have missed you. And welcome to your delightful family. Mr Astley and his aunt are waiting for you. I'll arrange for someone to look after the horses.' The waitress took our outdoor wear before directing us along the parquet flooring to the table we had sat at on our last visit.

'Thank you, Ivy.' André smiled.

As we approached, Matthew Astley stood up. 'Madam Françoise, it's delightful to see you again. Please, sit here.' He pulled out the chair next to him.

'Merci, Monsieur Astley.'

'Tell me, dear lady,' he said, as I lowered myself to the seat, 'how's that ankle?'

'Much better, merci. I am now able to walk without limping.'

Once we were all seated, Ivy headed our way. 'Welcome to Bridge Tearooms. I'll be looking after you today.' She handed each of us a menu.

After we perused the list, André said, 'So, ladies, what do you think? Shall we order the special afternoon tea?'

We nodded in turn and agreed on black tea. The special afternoon tea came with the luxury of a magnum of champagne.

'Thank you, sir.' Ivy gathered the menus and disappeared into the kitchen at the back.

Matthew touched my hand. 'Madam Françoise, will you do me the honour of exploring the garden before it gets dark. This venue boasts a delightful snowdrop flowerbed.'

I glanced at André.

'Go,' he said, 'you have time. I will fetch you once the food arrives, but take care with that ankle. We do not wish you to worsen it.'

'In that case, Monsieur Astley, I'd be delighted. However, I will need my bonnet and cloak. It is far too chilly to go without.'

'Of course, dear lady, leave that to me.' Matthew disappeared to the front of the brasserie and was back in the shortest of time with my outdoor wear. He placed my cloak around me and I fixed my hat. He offered me his left arm and we ventured outside to a sea of snowdrops. I had never seen anything quite like it in my life before.

'This is parfait. Merci, Monsieur Astley, for suggesting it.'

'It truly is something beautiful. But forgive me, dear lady, that's not the only reason I brought you out here. Come.' He gestured to the adjacent wooden bench. 'Let's sit for a moment. There's something I'd like to ask you.'

It was rather chilly but I took a seat next to him anyway. He obviously had something on his mind. 'Madam Françoise, you must know how I feel about you.' He took my hand. 'Please will you permit me to court you? My aunt, I'm sure, will be happy to act as a chaperone?'

'Oh, Monsieur Astley.' I took a deep breath. 'I am sorry for I fear I have misled you. There can never be anything between us because my heart belongs to another.'

'Sir Charles?'

'Oui, Sir Charles. There is something no one in Oxhaven, apart from your aunt, knows. I did not mean or wish to deceive you, I had no idea of your feelings, but Charles is my husband. For reasons I do not wish to share we had parted but I do plan to return to him this summer. What I can tell you is that we lost a child. Oliver.' I took out my handkerchief and dabbed my tears. 'Oliver was only a few weeks when he was taken from us.'

'Madam.' Matthew squeezed my hand. 'My dearest madam. That must have been so painful for you and Sir Charles. I can understand how this would've caused a bridge between you both. Rest assured, my dear lady, your secret's safe with me.' He put his hand on his chest. 'I'll have to learn how to mend my broken heart but that's not your concern. I wish you a happy life and hope we may continue to be friends.'

'Merci.' I shivered.

'You're cold. We should go back inside.'

'Merci. And thank you for ensuring I did not miss this glorious white bloom.'

Matthew walked me back into the tearoom. 'Let me.' He slipped the cloak from my shoulders. 'If you'll excuse me for one moment, I'll return it to the cloakroom.'

'Ah, there you are, ma sœur' – André rested his palm on my arm – 'I was just coming to find you. As you can see tea has arrived.'

The table was laden with sandwiches, scones and small sponges. I eased myself back into my seat.

'Are you all right, dear?' Lady Astley asked. 'You look very flushed? Perhaps it's the cold air.'

'Probably,' I said. 'I am fine.' I felt sadness for Matthew but at least now he knew the truth.

Chapter 29

Tilly

Françoise was sweeping the floor when I entered the workroom.

I picked up the dustpan and brush. 'Here, let me help you with that.'

'Non, it is fine, I am almost finished. I do not wish to see you struggling down to the floor in your condition.'

'I'm feeling much better now.' I patted my stomach. 'Goodness knows what size this baby will be. I'm enormous. My mam wasn't much bigger than this when she had the twins.'

'Maybe you are having twins?'

'I hadn't thought about that. Do you think I am?'

Françoise shrugged her shoulders. 'Possibly. After all twins run in the Dubois family.'

I waved my hand in front of her. 'I'm not even going to think about that. Anyway, are you going to tell me what happened out in the tearoom garden with Mr Astley yesterday?'

Her face reddened. 'He wanted permission to court me.'

'Hmm, I guessed he was smitten. What did you say?'

Françoise leaned the broom against the wall and perched on a stool. 'I had to tell him everything. There was nothing else I could do.'

'How did he take it? I eased myself down on a chair opposite.

'Amazingly well. He would like us to remain as friends. What do you think you are going to have?'

'I don't know. I don't mind really so long as he or she's healthy. Are you all right talking about this?'

'Surprisingly, yes. I will never forget Oliver but I think I am ready to become a maman again and hopefully when I return to *Highwood* it will not take long.'

'I'm happy for you. It will be wonderful if our little one has a cousin of a similar age.' I pushed myself up from the chair. 'Have you heard of the ring test?'

Françoise frowned. 'Ring test?'

'Yes. A test to see whether I'm carrying a boy or girl. We need a ring and a piece of string.' I moved over to the cupboard and took out a reel of black thread. 'This will do for the string.'

Françoise shook her head. 'You will have to show me what to do.' She stepped off the stool.

I slipped the ring off my finger. 'I'll use this. We have to tie the string onto the ring.' I threaded the string through my wedding ring. 'Like this.'

'Now what?'

I laid back into one of the velvet armchairs. 'Now you dangle the ring over my stomach.'

Françoise took the ring, stood over me and let the ring hang. 'What now?'

'We have to see what it does.'

'It is moving in a circular motion. Look.'

I lifted my head and smiled. 'That means I must be having a girl.' I was pleased as I was concerned a boy would bring back too many memories of Oliver for Françoise. 'We can now start to think about names.' I laughed. 'Let's go and have a cup of tea before the Livingston sisters arrive.'

On the way to the kitchen, we bumped into André's mother. 'Where are you young ladies off to?'

'We are going to make some tea, Maman. Why not join us?'

'Merci. I was just thinking that myself. What time are your clients due?'

'Around three o'clock so we have just over an hour,' I answered.

'I will follow shortly. There is something I must attend to first.'

'We will pour you a cup ready,' Françoise said, pushing the kitchen door open. She strode in and put the kettle on the stove.

I was pleased we had a few minutes alone. 'Don't say anything to your mother,' I said to Françoise, 'I'd like to keep it between just you and me.'

She took three cups and saucers from the dresser shelf. 'It will be our secret.'

*

I gazed out of the kitchen window at the crisp grass, even the old oak at the bottom of the garden was dusted with white. It looked enchanting. The frost hadn't thawed all day, no wonder it was so cold. I moved to the stove and rubbed my hands over the heat before topping up the teapot with water from the kettle.

'Do you think we have time for another cup?' I asked collecting our mugs from the table.

Françoise glanced up at the clock. 'It is almost three o'clock. I think perhaps we should go to the workroom and get things ready.'

'I suppose so but it's so cold in there.' I shivered.

'I am sure we will be all right as Sally said she would light a fire. It may be warmer in there now than here.'

We made our way down the hallway and almost moments after entering the workroom, Maman Antoinette showed the Livingston sisters in.

'Good afternoon.' Françoise shook their hands in turn.

'I hope you're having a pleasant day,' I said. 'Do come and sit down.' I showed them to the armchairs before heading to the fireplace and poking the coals. 'It should warm up shortly.'

'Are you both having a fitting today?' Françoise asked.

'No, just my sister,' Blanche said. 'She's rather excited as Lady Astley has invited us to join her for tea next month, and her nephew Mr Matthew Astley will also be her guest. Is that sufficient time for you to get the gown ready?'

Françoise tilted her head. 'It may be difficult…'

Caroline's smile dropped.

I looked at Françoise. 'I'm sure we can manage in time between us.'

'That's very kind, Madam Matilda. My sister insists she must have something new for the occasion.' Blanche rolled her eyes.

'Do you have anything particular in mind?' I asked.

'We were rather hoping that you ladies could advise.' Blanche glanced at her sister. 'Isn't that right, dear?'

'Yes please.' Caroline laughed loudly like a horse neighing.

Françoise and I strode to the wardrobe and browsed our fabric stock. I pointed to a pink patterned stripe. 'What about this? It will bring out hints of red in her hair.'

'Oui. I agree.' Françoise picked up the roll and carried it across to our clients. 'Madame Matilda and I feel this would be quite fetching on you.'

Blanche brushed her fingers across the soft cotton.

'Please, sister. I adore it.' Caroline's eyes rounded like pennies.

Blanche patted her sister's hand. 'Then you shall have it. Do you have a style in mind, Madam Françoise?'

'I believe Madame Matilda does.'

I took the roll from Françoise and offered it up to Caroline. 'You see, the colour softens her light brown hair and brings out reddish tints.'

Blanche stood up to look. 'I see what you mean. I'd never realised she had red in her hair before.'

Françoise took the fabric and put it back in the cupboard.

'It looks perfect.' Caroline held a hand across her chest. 'Sister, I'm going to look beautiful.'

'You are beautiful, my dear.' Blanche patted her sister's hand.

'Miss Livingston,' Françoise said to Blanche, 'would you like tea while Madame Matilda measures Miss Caroline?'

'That would be nice. Thank you.'

'If you would like to come this way.'

Françoise and Blanche left the room as I picked up the small steel holder from the table, pulling out the hidden measuring tape. I wrapped it across Caroline's bosom, waist, and hips, writing the figures down in a notebook. 'I don't believe your size has changed since your last fitting.'

'Do you think I'll make Mr Astley a good wife?'

I gulped. 'Are you courting?' I had no idea if this was the case. 'I'm sure you will. Why don't we sit down and I'll go through the design I have in mind?' Holding the small of my back, I eased into one of the armchairs.

'Not yet but I think he's going to propose and that's why Lady Astley's invited us for tea.'

'I see.' I took a deep breath. 'For style I'm thinking, a fitted bodice with a pointed waist. I'll add a lace collar with matching cuffs.' I touched Caroline's arm. 'I'll make it with long, full sleeves, gathered at the shoulders, and a nice full skirt. It'll be very flattering.'

'It sounds beautiful. What's it like being married?'

Taken aback, I blinked. 'I love married life.' I sensed my eyes sparkling.

'Are you having a baby?'

I held my stomach. 'Yes. Yes, I am.'

'I'd love a baby. I must be going to marry Mr Astley because I caught your bouquet, remember?'

'Yes, I remember.' I stood up. 'Shall we go and find the others and have tea?'

'That would be nice. Madam Matilda, if Mr Astley does propose, would you mind if I came to speak to you about, you know… the wedding night, before it happens?'

I squeezed Caroline's hand. 'Of course not, Miss Caroline. Come and talk to me whenever you like. Now, let's go and find your sister and you can tell her all about your new gown.'

*

André, his mother, and Françoise were already seated at the table by the time I entered the dining room for dinner.

André pulled out the chair next to him. 'You look tired, Matilda. Come, chérie, sit down.'

'Are you in pain?' André's mother passed me a plate of beef stew with dumplings.

'Thank you. It's just my back.'

Maman Antoinette raised her eyebrows. 'Without sounding rude you are carrying a lot of extra weight.'

'Yes, I know' – I held my stomach – 'and I still have a while to go.'

'Perhaps you need to slow down.' Françoise put a forkful of food into her mouth.

'No, I'll be fine. My mam never slowed down. She used to say keeping active helped with the birth.'

Maman Antoinette sipped water from a glass. 'We have received an invitation from Lady Astley.'

'When is that?' Françoise asked.

'Next month. We have been invited to afternoon tea.' André's mother cut into one of her dumplings. 'It appears there is an announcement to be made.'

'Then what Miss Caroline told me must be true.' I moved my food around the plate not wanting to eat.

'What has the mademoiselle said?' Maman Antoinette held her stare.

'That Mr Astley is going to propose to her.'

Maman Antoinette flipped her head back as she roared with laughter. 'Foolish girl. I can assure you that is not the case.'

'How do you know, Maman?' André took the last bite from his dinner plate.

'Because…'

Françoise put her cutlery down. 'Qu'est-ce que c'est, Maman?'

Maman Antoinette sighed. 'I have been sworn to secrecy so you must act surprised. Monsieur Astley is considering a betrothal but not to the Livingston girl. The reason for the afternoon tea is to introduce the young lady and her parents to a few of Lady Suzanna's friends.'

I put my knife and fork down in the finished position. 'Miss Caroline will be so upset. She's having a new gown made especially for the occasion.'

'As I said. Foolish girl.' Maman Antoinette shook her head.

André squeezed my hand. 'Matilda, dear. You have not eaten.'

'I'm not hungry.' I rested my hand on my abdomen. 'I have no room. My stomach is stretched.'

'You must eat something, ma chérie. What can I get you?'

I stood up. 'Perhaps later. Right now, I could do with a walk if you'd like to accompany me?'

'But it is dark and cold outside.'

'I can wrap up warm. I've been squashed up all day, folded over sewing. Just a short stroll, please?'

Françoise was at my side. 'You are working too hard. You must let me take on some of your clients.'

'No. I won't hear of it. What with you returning to *Highwood* and me soon to be in confinement, we need to get through the outstanding orders. I'll be fine. I just need a bit of exercise.'

Chapter 30

Françoise

Standing by the fireplace, after reading Geneviève's letter again, I opened my mouth to say something but I was speechless.

'What is it?' André asked. 'Is it bad news? You have turned a deathly grey.'

I dropped the sheet of paper to the floor.

He picked it up and read, 'Jacques has absconded with a housemaid.' André pressed his hand to his forehead and sank into the armchair. 'How could he do this to our dear friend?'

Tilly entered the drawing room. 'Do what? Who?'

'Mademoiselle Geneviève's fiancé has run off with another woman.' André continued to scan the letter. 'Apparently, left a note. A coward as well as a despicable human being.' André sighed.

I tutted. 'What is it with these supposed gentlemen preferring women below their class?' I put my hand to my mouth. 'Sorry, Tilly. I was not inferring about you and mon frère.'

Tilly poured out the tea, adding sugar cubes into the cups, and passed one to each of us. 'I know that, Françoise.'

Jacques had betrayed Geneviève as Charles had betrayed me. Was I right to trust him? What if he was still seeing Anna, or had a new mistress, and all this wooing me was just a ruse to satisfy his mother and the terms of the oath? I only had his word. I put my cup down on the table, moved towards the window and peered out at the rain slashing on the pane. I had been so excited about Geneviève and Jacques visiting. How must she be feeling? Her letter was dated three weeks ago. I should write back straight away.

Maman padded through the doorway. 'It is almost time to leave.' She glanced around the room. 'Why do you look so gloomy? Has someone died?'

'Not died, Maman,' André answered, 'but Jacques Blanchet has jilted his bride the day before they were to wed.'

'The poor child. How frightfully awful for Mademoiselle Geneviève, but I am sure her papa will have no problem lining up another prospective husband for his daughter. There is no real loss.'

I spun around and glared at Maman. 'How can you be so heartless? Geneviève has loved Jacques since she was a little girl.'

She shook her head. 'As I said, no real loss. Are you ready to leave?'

'Non. I do not feel up to socialising. You go if you wish.' I peered back out of the window, holding my tongue, and clenching my fists. It was just like Maman to be so matter of fact, wearing that impassive expression, just like she had when Papa declared I was to marry Charles because of the oath.

André got up from the chair and strode towards me. He put his hand on my shoulder. 'Do not worry, Françoise, we will cancel.'

Tilly gathered up the tea dishes. 'Joe was outside earlier. I'll see if he's still there and ask him to take a message to the Johnstone's with our apologies.'

'Merci, Tilly.' I buried my head in my hands not knowing whether my tears were for Geneviève or for myself.

*

André pulled the Landau up outside Lady Astley's mansion. We had been here before for afternoon tea in the garden and I was looking forward to seeing the interior of this magnificent building.

The footman helped us out of the carriage and then climbed up, took the reins, and disappeared to the stables. Maman and I followed André and Tilly up the steps to the house. André tapped the large brass lion knocker. A butler reminding me of Mr Hughes from *Highwood* opened the door.

'Good afternoon, Mr Dubois, ladies. Do come in.' He showed us into the massive drawing room, almost twice the size of ours at *Sunbury*. The elaborate space was filling up with guests. I spotted the Livingston sisters on a couch over by a leaded picture window. I waved. They waved back with big smiles.

Lady Astley greeted Maman with a hug. 'Madam Antoinette, I'm so glad you made it.'

'We would not have missed it, Lady Suzanna.' Maman glanced around. 'Have the Johnstone's arrived? It was unfortunate we were unable to make their function last week.'

'Yes, they're here, and eager to meet you.' Lady Astley turned to us. 'Madam Matilda you're looking tired. How long before your time?'

'Not long,' Tilly said, 'I'm due in June and can't wait. This baby is weighing me down.'

'You poor child.' She patted Tilly's upper arm. 'Make yourself comfortable over there with the Livingston sisters and I'll come and find you once I've introduced your maman to the Johnstone's.'

I went to walk away with André and Tilly but Lady Astley touched my arm. 'Madam Françoise, would you mind waiting a moment as I understand my nephew would like a few words with you.' She turned to her right. 'Ah, here he is now. Madam Antoinette, come this way.'

I was left standing alone until Matthew Astley reached me. His greenish-blue eyes twinkled when he smiled. 'Madam Françoise, good afternoon. Might we talk?'

'Oui.' I frowned. 'What is it?'

'Not here. As a fellow botanist let me show you Aunt Suzanna's bevy of blooms in the garden.' He put out his hand. 'Through here.'

I followed him out of the French doors and down the steps to the immaculate lawn and flowerbeds. 'Is Sir Charles with you?' he asked.

'Non. He is due to visit next week.' I caught sight of the beautiful pink roses climbing up the wall. Matthew was not exaggerating about the loveliness in the garden.

'It's mild today, isn't it?'

'Oui. It is warm for April.'

We meandered along the cobbled path. I looked to the left and was amazed by the picture ahead. Forsythia in full swing bore vibrant yellow flowers on its branches but it was the purple field of bluebells that stunned me. Maman should come and see this. She adored bluebells as did I. We wandered a bit further before Matthew stopped at a bench. 'Shall we?'

I eased down next to him. 'Is there something troubling you?'

'You know my heart is yours?' He took my hand and rested it on his. His warm eyes held their gaze. He was the opposite to Charles in every way. Blond curly hair, fair-skinned, thoughtful and kind-hearted.

Butterflies fluttered in my stomach. I sneezed. 'Excuse me. I fear all these fragrances are tickling my nose.'

Matthew continued, 'My aunt believes it's time for me to take a wife. I wondered what your feelings are on this matter?'

'I do not understand.'

'I suppose what I'm asking is whether there's any hope for you and I?'

I did not try to move his hand. 'Monsieur Astley, I do not see how there can be. As you are aware, I am married to Sir Charles and must return to him in the near future.'

'Is that what you really want? Or could you, perhaps, have feelings for me, as I do you?'

I pulled my hand away. 'It is rather cold out here. We should go back inside.'

'Aunt Suzanna planned today in order to introduce a new family to the village with the hopes that their daughter will become my wife.' He gently squeezed my fingers. 'Are you sure there's no hope for us?'

I looked into his misted eyes. 'I wish you happiness, Monsieur Astley.'

*

I glanced up as the drawing room door opened. Tilly tapped my arm and signalled towards a young woman. 'Who's that with Mr Astley?'

'His future wife,' I whispered. She was older than me, by three years or more, attractive in a quiet sort of way, but her mouse brown hair piled high and low-necked, pale-yellow gown did nothing to enhance her colouring. She was in need of some stylish advice. A well-dressed gentleman and lady followed them in. He appeared to be in his mid-fifties while she, most likely, was at least five years younger.

Lady Astley coughed. 'Ladies and Gentleman if I may have your attention for one moment. Please let me introduce Lord and Lady Western and their daughter. They've recently acquired a second home in Oxhaven as a getaway from the hustle and bustle at their main residency in London. Please make them welcome.'

The chatter stopped and everyone applauded the newcomers. Lady Astley and Matthew guided the family over to a small group in the corner. Matthew glanced at me before taking a seat with Miss Western. Lady Astley patted Lady Western's hand and made her way over to join us at the Livingston sisters' table, sitting down next to Maman.

'What do you think, Madam Antoinette, do you think Miss Western will make a nice bride for my nephew?' The large sapphire on her pendant necklace sparkled as she lowered her head.

'I am sure she will. What has Monsieur Astley said?'

'Not a lot, but he's a good boy and knows it's time to settle down, and Miss Western comes from a good line.'

My heart beat fast. I did not wish Matthew to marry her. But I had no right to feel that way? I loved Charles. Or did I? I turned to the Livingston sisters for distraction. Caroline's face turned a ghastly colour before she fainted. 'I will get smelling salts,' I said to Blanche and hurried over to a young maid approaching our table. The girl rushed from the room and within moments returned. She held a small vinaigrette bottle under Caroline's nose.

Caroline squinted. 'What happened?'

Blanche held her sister upright. 'You fainted.'

'Oh, yes. I remember.' She pressed her fingers into her forehead. 'Take me home, sister. I am out of sorts.'

Blanche helped Caroline from the couch. 'Lady Astley, please accept our apologies but I fear I should take my sister home.' Blanche led Caroline from the room.

'What happened?' Lady Astley asked. 'I wasn't aware Miss Caroline was feeling unwell.'

Maman chewed her lip. 'Shock, I believe. It seems the foolish girl thought your nephew was going to ask for her hand in marriage.'

'The poor child. Excuse me, I must ensure the footman sorts their carriage.' Lady Astley bustled out.

Chapter 31

Tilly

'Grrr.' Françoise threw a scrunched paper at the basket. 'I cannot do it.' She stormed off the chair, away from the mahogany desk, and over to the long, narrow window.

'What can't you do?' I picked up the latest of the screwed-up notes and popped it into the bin.

'I am unable to find the right words.'

'Just tell her how sorry you are.'

'I have already done that in my last letter but now I need to uplift her spirits but I do not know how.' She dug her fingertips into the gold, velvet curtain. 'Just leave me alone. Please, Tilly.'

I backed away and observed her from the door entrance. I didn't want to leave her. I hadn't seen her like this since Oliver had died. Time was getting close to the birth of my baby. Was it all becoming too much for her?

André came up behind me. 'How long has she been like that?' he whispered.

'Too long. She said she's struggling to know what to write to her friend.' I signalled to the waste paper basket. 'All the letters end up in there, but I don't think it's anything to do with that…'

'What then?'

'I believe our baby getting close to being born is bringing back memories of Oliver.'

André rested his hands on my shoulders. 'Sir Charles will be here soon. Maybe he can reignite her sparkle.'

'I hope so. Look at her. She's just staring out of the window.'

André strode over to his sister and placed his arm around her. 'Françoise, are you all right?'

She turned around. 'Of course. Pourquoi?' She brushed a hand across her damp eyes.

'We are worried about you.'

'There is no need. As I told Tilly. I just need time to myself.'

'As long as you are sure?'

'I said so.' Françoise turned back to the window.

A heavy door closed and André headed down the hallway. He returned in moments with Charles at his side.

Charles kissed my hand. 'Madam Matilda.'

'Thank goodness you're here,' I said, 'we don't know what's the matter with her. I think maybe it's me.' I placed a hand over my stomach. 'With me getting closer to time.'

'Leave her to me.' Charles stepped into the study.

*

André and I meandered along the footpath towards the river.

'Ow.' I held the middle of my back.

'Are you in pain, Matilda?'

'It's nothing, I'm sure.'

'Perhaps we should turn back.'

'No, I want to see the ducklings.'

'Are you sure you are up to it?'

'Stop fussing, André. My mam had ten babies and no one fussed over her. I'm young and healthy so I'll be fine.'

André sighed. 'If you say so.'

We continued along the cobbled path but in moments I folded again. This time it really hurt. 'I think perhaps you're right. Maybe we should go back. I think our baby's coming.'

Stopping and starting I managed to hobble back up to the house. 'Fetch Mrs Taylor from the shop,' I said, 'she'll know what to do.'

'I will get you inside first and Maman can look after you while I am out.'

Taking deep breaths, I reached the back door. André pushed it open. 'Maman, come quickly. The baby's coming.'

But it was Françoise and Charles who ran into the kitchen. Françoise frowned. 'But Tilly, it is only April. It is too early.'

'I know.' I leaned over again in agony.

'Charles,' André said, 'help me get her to the couch and, Françoise, find Maman. She'll know what to do.'

*

Mrs Taylor waddled into the drawing room with André right behind her.

'What's this I've heard, young lady? Your little-un wants to make an early appearance?'

Flushed, I shrugged my shoulders. 'The pains seem to have gone.'

Mrs Taylor pressed my stomach. She shook her head. 'You're not having this baby today, Madam Matilda. It's not your time yet.'

'Then why was she in agony?' Françoise asked.

'That'll be her body getting ready.' Mrs Taylor patted my wrist. 'You need to rest up a bit, young lady.'

'I'll try.' I felt stupid. Mrs Taylor rushing round and having to leave her shop. All for nothing.

André's mother padded into the room. 'Was that Mrs Taylor I saw leaving? What was she doing here?'

'We thought Tilly had started labour but it seems that was not the case.' Françoise brushed a loose curl behind her ear.

Maman stood with her hands on her hips. 'Why did you not wake me?'

'I tried, Maman, but you were in a deep sleep.'

Maman Antoinette leaned over me. 'How are you feeling now, Matilda?'

'Fine. It was a false alarm.'

'You young women' – she shook her head – 'you will know when it is real, I can tell you.'

I gritted my teeth. 'Thank you, Maman. I'm sure you're right.'

'I remember when I was giving birth to …' she continued, but I stopped listening, curling my fingers tightly. I didn't want to hear any more of what she had to say. I wished my own mam were here. She wouldn't have mocked me for getting it wrong. A strong scent made me glance up. A bunch of daffodils bowed their golden heads in a porcelain vase. 'Where did they come from?' I asked.

'Monsieur Astley.' Françoise moved to the sideboard and sniffed the petals. 'They are wonderful.'

André twiddled his dark moustache. 'Where's Sir Charles?'

'He is in the kitchen with Monsieur Astley. Perhaps, if you do not need me, I should go and find them.'

I fixed my eyes on André and then towards his mother and back on him.

'Françoise,' he said, 'why not take Maman with you?'

'Bien sûr, bonne idée. Come, Maman, I am sure Sir Charles is looking forward to seeing you.'

I breathed a sigh of relief as Françoise took her mother's arm and led her away. 'Thank you,' I said to André. 'I was feeling foolish enough without your mother making me feel worse.'

'She meant no harm. And there is no need to feel foolish, ma chérie.' He perched next to me and stroked my cheek.

'However, we should listen to Mrs Taylor's advice, you need to rest.'

I sat upright. 'Look, there's nothing wrong with me. The pains have gone. But never mind that now, did you see that glint in Françoise's eyes? She seemed more like her old self.'

He raised his eyebrows. 'You are right. I had not noticed, mais oui, it seems ma sœur was not grief stricken but lovesick. She needed her husband.'

'Her husband or Mr Astley?'

'Non, surely not.'

I shrugged my shoulders. 'Mr Astley's certainly enamoured with her and I noticed the look on Françoise's face when Lady Astley announced she hoped he'd marry Miss Western.'

'I did not see that, but fear you are wrong. Françoise's heart belongs to Charles, trust me, Matilda.'

'We will see.' I was relieved that it wasn't our baby causing her grief. 'May we go and see the ducklings tomorrow?'

'Peut-être, ma chérie, but only if you promise to rest for the remainder of the day.'

'I'll try.' I lay back down, placing my palm across my swollen stomach and smiled. Not long now before we'd get to meet our child.

Chapter 32

Françoise

Charles should have arrived at *Sunbury* yesterday but cancelled without offering a legitimate reason. We had planned to mourn Oliver together today on what would have been his second birthday. Had he lived, he would have been running around now and most likely sporting a thick head of jet hair enhancing his almost black eyes like his father's. I smiled at Oliver's memory. I could do that now, but Oliver would never be forgotten.

I inhaled the lily of the valley bunched in my hand, their little white bells drooping from the green stem. Deep in thought, I jumped when a voice came from behind me and said, 'There you are, Madam Françoise. André said I'd find you out here. I hope you'll forgive the intrusion.'

I held my chest. 'Monsieur Astley, I did not hear you coming. You gave me rather a fright.'

'Forgive me, please.' He looked at the flowers in my hand. 'One of my favourites.'

'Mine too. I picked them for Oliver.'

'I thought you may be in low spirits today' – he took his hand from behind his back and revealed a small bouquet of lily of the valley – 'so, I brought you these, but I see I'm too late.'

'Non. Non, not at all. Merci.' I took the posy and gathered the flowers with mine. Matthew was so thoughtful. He had even remembered it was Oliver's birthday when Charles had more significant matters to attend to after promising he would come. What could have been more important than spending time with me, remembering our son?

*

Monsieur Astley offered his left arm and I linked mine with his as we sauntered down to the riverbank in the warm May heat. The sky was almost cloud free. We were greeted by quacking ducks as they tottered towards us. I pointed at the sun-rippled water. 'Look, Monsieur Astley, goslings.' The Canada geese parents lingered close to the yellow fluffy bundles.

'Enchanting.' Matthew's eyes sparkled. 'Nature is wonderful. Look, there's a bench.' He pointed. 'Shall we sit and watch the feathered creatures for a while?'

'I would like that.'

We strolled to the empty seat on the riverbank.

Once we were seated, Matthew asked, 'When do you plan to return with Sir Charles?'

'Well, I need to be here for the birth of my new niece or nephew and then, perhaps... Although...'

'What is it?'

'Nothing.'

'Please, Madam Françoise, if there's any doubt of your love for Sir Charles. Please reconsider.'

'What difference does it make when you are planning to marry Miss Western?'

'I'm not in love with her and neither is she in love with me. It's our families pushing us together. What will your life be like if you return with him?'

It was like Matthew could read my mind. I clasped my gloved hands. I had been feeling despondent about leaving my new life behind. At *Sunbury*, I was an independent woman. What would happen when I returned to *Highwood*? I obviously would not be able to set myself up in business but perhaps, with discretion, I would be able to help Tilly if she decided to continue our enterprise down south. But what if Charles betrayed me again? All this would be gone for nothing. What was I to do? And then there was Matthew, could I really ignore my feelings when he was around me?

Matthew held his gaze and leaned in closer. I allowed his soft lips to brush against mine for a moment before pulling away. 'Please, Monsieur Astley, I cannot do this.'

'Forgive me, Madam Françoise.'

I bent over to breathe in the cowslip scent when I remembered how much Matthew loved bluebells. 'André said the bluebells are blooming in the woodland. If we follow that trail' – I pointed – 'it will take us there.'

'I would like that.'

We meandered along the mudded footpath with Matthew keeping his distance. I gasped as we stepped into the wooded area. The sun blazed down between silver birch and circling their trunks was an abundance of blue.

'This is perfect.' I knelt down to pick a few stems. 'These are for Maman as she loves them but I can add a couple in the vase with Oliver's lily of the valley.' As I inhaled the light perfume I winced.

Matthew rested his hand on my arm. 'What is it, Madam Françoise?'

'I was just thinking of my lovely baby son.'

'I can't imagine your heartbreak.' Tears glazed his eyes.

I blinked. 'Come, we should return before dark.'

Chapter 33

Françoise

When I arrived at the open kitchen door, I discovered Tilly on her hands and knees scrubbing the floor. She dipped the brush into the bucket.

I squinted. 'Tilly, do you realise what time it is? What are you doing?'

She stopped, looked up, straightening her back. 'Pardon?' She tucked a loose strand of hair under a servant's mop cap.

'What are you doing?' I repeated. 'I thought we had intruders.'

She ran her tongue across her upper lip. 'Scrubbing the floor.'

'But Sally did it yesterday evening before she left and she will do it again today. There is no need for you to scrub floors anymore. And you are not a maid so why are you wearing that hat?'

'It's the best way to keep my hair free from the dirt.'

'But you should not be doing it. That is Sally's job. That is what we pay her for.'

Puffing and panting, Tilly rose from her knees. 'I woke up with an urge to do it.'

'By the looks of it you have been down here for a while. It is only six o'clock now.'

'Is it?' She shuffled over to the stove and popped the kettle on. 'Tea?'

'Merci. But you sit down. I will make it.'

'I need to keep busy. I have so much energy. Françoise, I think my time's coming. My mam told me about this renewed vigour before giving birth.'

'But it is not your time.' I tiptoed across the wet floor and took two cups and saucers from the dresser shelf.

'It is almost. And as my mam frequently told me, babies come when they're ready, not when we think they should.' Tilly poured water from the kettle into the teapot, picked up a spoon and stirred it before placing on the lid and adding a flowery patterned cosy. 'We'll let it brew for a few minutes.' She tipped soda into the sink.

'That is enough, Tilly. No more cleaning.'

'But…'

'But nothing. Come and sit down and rest or I shall have to get André.'

'Get André for what?' André stepped into the room.

'Mind the floor. It's wet.' Tilly padded back over to the dresser, reaching for another cup and saucer. 'Tea? You're up early.'

'I wondered where you had gone. Is everything all right?'

'Everything's fine.' She poured milk and tea into the cup. 'I woke up with lots of energy and came down to do some cleaning.'

'And I have told her she must rest. Tell her, André.'

André took Tilly's arm. 'Come, Matilda. Do as Françoise says.' He led Tilly towards the table.

Before reaching a chair, she held her back and leaned forward. 'You both may be right.' Her mouth gaped open as a puddle of water gushed to her feet.

Maman was at the doorway. 'L'enfant is coming.' She waddled over to Tilly. 'André, help me get her to bed.

Françoise, fetch Mrs Taylor. Tell her it is urgent. This is not a false alarm.'

*

Mrs Taylor toddled at my side as I pushed the kitchen door open.

André put both hands to his face. 'Thank goodness you are here, Mrs Taylor. Merci, for coming so promptly.'

'Where is she?' Mrs Taylor slipped off her outdoor wear. 'Here, young man, look after this for me.'

André held the cloak and bonnet over his arm. 'She is upstairs. I will show you. Maman is with her.'

'No, Mr Dubois, Madam Françoise will show me. Instead, you can bring me hot water, sheets, flannels and towels in due course.'

I headed into the hallway to the stairs. 'This way, Mrs Taylor.'

'Don't look so worried, child. Madam Matilda will be fine. She has good child-bearing hips.'

We made our way along the landing. I stopped outside Tilly and André's chambre. 'She's in here.'

'Come. She needs her sister with her, not her mother-in-law.'

Tilly was groaning and rocking on the bed as I followed Mrs Taylor into the room. She moved towards Tilly. 'Thank you, Madam Antoinette. I'll take it from here.'

'But...'

'No buts. Madam Matilda doesn't need an audience while she gives birth. She has her sister for comfort and I'll do the necessaries. I've delivered over a hundred babies. She's in safe hands with me.'

Maman opened her mouth to say something but changed her mind. 'I am outside if you need me.'

291

'You'd be better going downstairs to the kitchen and putting on the kettle.' Mrs Taylor pulled an apron out of her bag, put the loop over her head and pulled the ties together behind her large waist.

I hurried to Tilly's side and gripped her hand. 'I am here, Tilly.'

Tilly breathed normally. 'Don't worry, Françoise. I'm fine.' She smiled.

'How close are the contractions, Madam Matilda?'

'Very close. Oh no, here it comes again.' Tilly gripped my hand as she groaned a deep-throated sound.

'Madam Françoise, is that your brother I hear coming up the stairs? Fetch the items from him.'

I ventured to the door entrance, took the bucket of water and items.

'Is she all right?' André asked.

'Don't worry Mr Dubois,' Mrs Taylor bellowed. 'Your wife's in safe hands.' She turned to me. 'How early is she?'

'Err, I'm not sure. I think about three or four weeks.'

'Don't look so concerned. Babies come when they're ready not at our convenience.'

Wide-eyed, Tilly said, 'I need to push.'

'The little one's eager. Let's get some of these clothes off you. Help me, Madam Françoise.' She removed the necessary wear from Tilly and laid a sheet across her to keep her decency. Mrs Taylor made her way to the bottom of the bed and peeped under the covering. 'Now, Madam Matilda, push.'

Tilly squeezed my hand so tightly that her nails dug into my palms and I thought they might bleed.

'One more push and you're there,' Mrs Taylor re-assured.

Tilly put her hands behind her, gripping the brass bedstead and roared, relaxing as a shrill cry came as the baby was born.

Mrs Taylor picked up the infant with skill. 'It's a girl.'

'A girl.' Tilly lowered her shoulders and lay back onto the pillow. 'Can I hold her?'

'In a moment. Madam Françoise, pass me a towel. Oh, and a clean sheet.'

I rushed over to the chair and passed the linen to Mrs Taylor. She wiped the baby clean before wrapping muslin around its tiny body. 'Here.' She placed the newborn in my arms before turning back to Tilly. 'You're not finished yet, Madam Matilda.'

I glanced down at the open-eyed child who had black hair like Oliver's. 'She's beautiful, Tilly.'

Tilly's face screwed up and she let out a high-pitched howl.

My stomach churned. 'What's happening?'

'Don't panic, girl. Come out of my way, now.' Mrs Taylor lifted the sheet to examine Tilly. 'Oh lordy, Madam Matilda. You've got another one coming. A nice big push and it'll all be over.'

Grunting, Tilly gritted her teeth.

'That's it. That's it,' Mrs Taylor encouraged.

Tilly released her breath and her head fell to the pillow. 'Why isn't it crying? Is it all right?'

'It's another girl. Give her a minute.' Mrs Taylor smacked the baby's bottom causing the infant to yell. 'She's absolutely fine. They're both a good weight too. Congratulations, Madam Matilda.' Mrs Taylor wrapped the second child. 'Line a drawer with blankets,' she said to me, and turned back to Tilly. 'You're almost finished. Unless you've another surprise in there making triplets.' Mrs Taylor peered under Tilly's covering and in moments she had delivered the afterbirth. 'Fetch me the hot water and flannel so I can get our new mammy cleaned up.'

I passed the bucket and towels to her before moving back to the twins. Mesmerised, I watched the babies, one each end of the drawer, only able to move their heads as Mrs Taylor had bundled them so tightly.

'I told you she had good child-bearing hips, didn't I?' She patted Tilly dry with a soft towel. 'Now, Madam Matilda, it's time to meet your daughters. Madam Françoise, hand your sister-in-law her babies.'

I picked one child up, laid her down on Tilly, and went back for the other. 'They're identical,' I said, 'however will we tell them apart?' I tucked the second infant under her other arm.

Gazing into her daughters' eyes she said, 'Get André.'

I gulped. 'Of course.' I raced from the room onto the landing and yelled 'André, come quickly.'

He charged upstairs. 'Is she all right?'

'She's absolutely fine and she's asking for you.'

I stood back in the doorway as he made his way towards Tilly. He glanced back at me. 'Twins. I am a papa to twins.' He rushed towards his wife.

Mrs Taylor brushed her hands. 'Come, Madam Françoise, let's leave the new parents to get acquainted with their children. I'm in dire need of a cuppa.'

I watched the new family huddled together unaware of anyone else. How I longed to have that union. 'I'll be back soon,' I said but neither of them looked up.

I should tell Maman the news. She would be eager to meet her new granddaughters. Strangely, I did not feel sadness, but happiness, for mon frère and his wife.

*

We gathered into André and Tilly's chambre. Maman beamed. 'May I?'

'Of course, Grand-Mère.' André passed Maman one of the twins. 'Be careful though as she has just been fed.'

Maman cuddled the baby. 'Have you named them yet?'

André leaned over to Maman and ran his finger across the infant's forehead. 'This one is Eliza.'

'Eliza? What made you choose that?'

Tilly glanced up. 'It was my mother's name and by pure coincidence Mrs Taylor's too. So, it was a perfect choice. Eliza's the eldest. She was born five minutes before this one.' Tilly nodded to the child in her arms.

'And does that one have a name?' Maman rocked Eliza.

André took Eliza from Maman. 'Not yet, we are still deciding.' He handed Eliza to Tilly and took the other twin into his arms. 'Here, Maman, meet your other granddaughter.'

Maman looked down at the baby in her arms. 'How on earth do you tell them apart?'

'Eliza has a little mole on her chin,' Tilly said. 'Françoise, would you like to hold Eliza?'

'Oui, s'il vous plaît.' I moved to the side of the bed and took the child from Tilly. 'Hello, Eliza. I am your Aunt Françoise.' I looked up at André and Tilly. 'She is beautiful.'

'They both are.' Tilly propped herself up with André positioned next to her.

'You are so clever,' I said, 'you have managed to give birth to not one baby, but two, and so quickly.'

'I was lucky.'

'Going back to names.' Maman passed Eliza's twin back to André. 'You could do worse than name her Antoinette.'

Tilly bent her head but not before I noticed her screwed up face.

André stroked the baby's cheek. 'We were thinking perhaps Louise after Papa.' 'What do you think little miss, would you like that name?'

Tilly beamed with satisfaction.

'Parfait,' I said.

Everyone nodded in agreement.

I looked around at my family and my heart swelled with love for these babies but my stomach started to churn at the thought of Charles expecting me to return to *Highwood* now that the infants had been born. I was not ready.

*

I watched the infant opening and closing her eyes as she suckled on Tilly's breast. 'Which twin is she?'

'This is Louise.' Tilly lightly brushed her fingers through the baby's velvety dark hair. 'They look like André, don't they?'

'Oui. They do. Beautiful little creatures. Do they not hurt you when suckling?' I remembered how I'd winced when trying to feed Oliver.

'A little, yes' – Tilly passed Louise for me to put in the crib with Eliza – 'but that's not what you wanted to talk about, was it?'

'You know me so well.' I perched on the edge of her bed. 'It's…'

'Sir Charles? Is he putting pressure on you to go back with him?'

'Not yet but I fear he will.' I got up from the bed and wandered over to the window. 'There is a Phaeton coming up the drive.'

'Oh? Are we expecting anyone? Is it Mrs Taylor?'

I turned around to face my sister-in-law. 'Non, I think it is Monsieur Astley.'

'Françoise, are you in love with Matthew?'

I felt my face flush. 'Je ne sais pas.' I moved back to the bed. 'I do not know.' I held my stomach. 'I am filled with butterflies whenever he is close to me. And when I think of him with Miss Western, I feel anger. But I love Charles so how can this be?'

Tilly took my hand. 'Are you in love with Charles, or think you should be?'

I tapped a fist to my lips. 'I want what you and André have.'

'Love?'

'And trust.'

'And you don't trust Charles?'

Eliza whimpered moving her head from side to side.

'Should I pass her?'

'No, she'll go back to sleep.' Tilly leaned over and rocked the crib. Eliza closed her eyes.

'You are a natural mother. And how you managed to give birth so easily and barely making any noise, I do not know.'

'I told you. I was lucky. I'd experienced more pain in the privy whereas you…' She patted my wrist. 'You had a hard time. Hopefully next time will be easier for you.'

Chapter 34

Françoise

Tilly was at the kitchen table with one of the twins suckling on her breast. She looked radiant. Her normal rosy cheeks had returned. It did not seem possible that she had given birth only twenty-four hours earlier.

I hurried in from the doorway. 'Tilly, what are you doing up? You are supposed to be in a darkened room for at least three days.'

'Françoise, do I look like I need to be in bed?' She got up from the chair and placed the infant in the wicker perambulator. 'That's both of them fed' – she rocked the handle – 'and both asleep. You mustn't fuss. My mam never laid around for days after having her babies and I don't intend to either. I'm fine. Sit down and I'll pour you a cuppa. The girls will hopefully sleep for at least an hour.' She brought the teapot and cups over to the table and sat down opposite me.

Maybe if Elizabeth had not forced me to stay in that darkened room, giving her an excuse to provide a nursemaid for Oliver, then perhaps he would not have been so sickly. I looked under the hood at the twins lying next to each other. They looked so tiny, but healthy. 'I have brought my nieces a gift.' I passed the brown paper package to Tilly.

She untied the gold ribbons and held up one of six smocked slips. 'These are gorgeous, Françoise.' Tilly ran her fingers across the smooth white cotton. 'You must have stayed up all night making them? The girls will look so pretty. I love how you've finished the three tiers in lace. Matching bonnets too. Perfect. The gowns they're wearing at the moment are far too big. Thank you.'

I smiled. 'I was up most of the night as I was unable to sleep so I thought I would put my time to good use.'

Tilly folded up the frock and placed it on top of the other five. She poured us both a cup of tea. 'Now I believe we were interrupted yesterday when you were going to tell me something.'

'Were we?'

'You know we were. We were talking about Sir Charles. And trust.'

'Ah. Oui' – I added a sugar cube and stirred my tea with a spoon – 'I thought for a time that I would be able to trust him again but when he did not turn up for Oliver's birthday…' I took a sip of the beverage. 'What could have been more important?'

'Do you think he has taken a mistress?'

I shrugged my shoulders. 'I do not know what to think. He has betrayed me before so what is to stop him doing so again? But Tilly, what do I do if I do not go back to him? How will I ever be able to have what you and André have? I would like another child, but I am trapped and unable to remarry as it is not possible to divorce him.'

'Why not? Surely you can divorce him for committing adultery?'

'Non. The law is unfair. A man can divorce a woman for adultery but a woman can only divorce the man if she can prove not only adultery but cruelty.'

Tilly dropped an extra sugar cube into her cup and while stirring it she said, 'I would say he was cruel. Seeking comfort from his mistress while you were struggling after losing a child. He should have been with you.'

'Oui, that was cruel, but it seems he must have physically harmed me. He will never let me go because he needs a wife to provide him with an heir. And that is me. There is no other way. We are trapped together.'

'I'm sure you can find a way. It is obvious to me that you love Mr Astley.'

'He understands me. He has a love of nature like me, and he always seems to know what I am thinking.'

'Don't give up. As you once said to me, Jane Austin proved love can conquer all.'

'I hope so.'

One of the twins murmured. Tilly leaned over and pushed the perambulator backwards and forwards. The infant went back to sleep. 'Have you written to Sir Charles yet?'

'Non. I should. I shall let him know that the babies have been born but tell him I need more time.'

Maman bustled into the kitchen. 'Time for what, Françoise? You must write to Sir Charles and ask him to come and collect you. He has been patient long enough,' she said bent over, holding the middle of her back.

'I need more time, Maman.'

'Nonsense' – she turned to Tilly – 'and what may I ask are you doing out of bed, young lady?'

'I don't need to be in bed,' Tilly answered. 'Would you like me to pour you some tea?'

'Does mon fils know you are downstairs?'

'André knows better than to try and reason with me.' Tilly laughed. 'Look at me, I am the picture of health. I admit I'm feeling a little tired now but that's to be expected. I'll put my feet up on the couch shortly while the twins sleep.'

Maman leaned into the perambulator. 'Bonjour mes petites-filles.' She touched the hood. 'We will need to get a double-hooded carriage. The girls will not be able to lie side by side as they get bigger. I will speak to Lady Suzanna. She will know someone who can organise this.'

Tilly yawned. 'Actually, if you don't mind, I think I will take forty winks. Are you able to watch the twins, Françoise?'

'Oui, I shall be delighted.'

'Non, I will watch the infants. Françoise needs to write that letter to Sir Charles. And you, young lady' – Maman glared at Tilly – 'would do well to remember that you promised your husband obedience.'

Tilly looked at me and rolled her eyes. 'I do remember that, Maman Antoinette, but I am lucky that my husband allows me to be my own person.' Tilly stood up and peeped under the hood at her babies. 'Please come and find me when they wake up.'

'I will,' Maman answered, 'and in the meantime I shall write out the announcement for the newspaper to let our friends and villagers know about the new arrivals.'

Tilly marched out of the kitchen and I followed her, seething.

Chapter 35

Françoise

'May I push,' I asked Tilly as we ventured into the garden with the twins.

'If you'd like to.' She stepped aside in order that I could take the handle.

Eliza and Louise looked snug under the satin quilt. A white broderie anglaise canopy hung over the perambulator protecting the babies from the warm sunshine. We meandered along the cobble path admiring the colour of the rhododendrons' massive crimson blooms. 'These are gorgeous this year,' I said.

Tilly inhaled their high fragrance. 'Have you heard from Sir Charles?'

'Non. Nothing.'

'How did you leave it with him?'

'As you know when I wrote I told him I needed more time, despite Maman insisting I tell him I was ready to return to *Highwood*. However, I did mention he may like to visit for Oliver's anniversary in order that we could spend the day together.'

'And he hasn't answered you?'

'Nothing. Not a word.'

'Do you think he might be ill?'

I sneezed as we reached the rose garden. Beautiful fragrances but they always tickled my nose. I sneezed again.

'Non. I do not know what is going on. Perhaps he will turn up next week but it is strange how his letters have got less and less over the last couple of months. Maybe he has tired of waiting on my return. I shall not be pressured though. I love my life here and I need to be sure before I give it all up. However, as I have said before, if I do not return to him then I have no chance of a family.' I put the brake on the perambulator as we reached the bench, and peeped in at Eliza and Louise. 'I will just have to become the old aunt and make do with my adorable nieces.'

Tilly laughed. 'You make a wonderful aunt and godmother.'

I touched my chest. 'Moi?'

'Naturally. Who else would we choose?'

'Merci.' I glanced across at the flower bed filled with blue cornflowers and hyacinths. 'Joe has made a really good job of the garden. Do you not agree?'

'He has. André misses his time out here but he's so busy these days. In fact, he was saying last night that he may have to seek an apprentice to assist him with the numerous clients' books.'

'If I do return to *Highwood*, I cannot expect you and André to give up your lives here too.'

Tilly patted my hand. 'Don't worry yourself with that now. You haven't asked me who'll be godfather and the other godmother.'

'Who?' I chuckled. 'I am asking now.'

'Lady Astley for the other godmother and Mr Astley as godfather.'

My pulse quickened just at the mere mention of his name.

One of the girls tossed her head from side to side and started wailing. The next thing her sister had joined in.

'I think that's them telling us we need to move.' Tilly got up, released the brake, and placed her hands on the handle ready to push.

*

The clink of china echoed over chatter as we approached the drawing room. We pushed the door open, Tilly with Eliza in her arms and me with Louise.

Lady Astley rose from the couch. 'Good afternoon, Madam Françoise. Congratulations, Madam Matilda, I hope you don't mind us turning up unannounced but Madam Antoinette thought it would be all right. We come bearing a gift' – she turned to her nephew – 'Matthew.'

Matthew got up from the armchair. 'Madam Françoise, it's wonderful to see you again.' He nodded to Tilly. 'Madam Matilda. I'll be back in a moment.' He disappeared from the room and returned pushing a wicker perambulator similar to the one Tilly already had, only this one was double-hooded and more exquisite. 'We hope you like it,' Matthew said before returning to his seat.

Lady Astley beamed. 'I have a friend who handcrafted it.'

Maman Antoinette pushed herself up from her armchair and waddled over to inspect the carriage. 'C'est beau,' she said, 'it is beautiful. Merci.'

'Yes, thank you, it's lovely, but far too much for us to accept,' Tilly said.

'Nonsense. My friend sold it to me at a special price. It had been in his workshop for a while and he was glad to get rid of it. I will not take *no* for an answer.'

'Thank you, Lady Astley,' Tilly said again. 'Would you like to meet the twins?' With the infant in her arms, Tilly padded over to the couch. 'This is Eliza. You may hold her if you like?'

'Oh yes, please.'

Tilly passed Eliza.

'Look at that wonderful mop of dark hair,' Lady Astley said, 'and a good size for what, three weeks, four weeks early?'

'Something like that. No wonder I was so huge.'

'What time were they born?'

'Quarter-past eight. Eliza came first and Louise five minutes later.'

'What date was that?'

'May fifteenth.' Tilly smiled with pride.

'What a clever girl you are. And up and about the next day, I heard.'

Tilly shrugged her shoulders. 'No point lying in bed if you don't need to. I wasn't ill and I was lucky that I'd had easy births.'

I strode over to the couch. 'And this is Louise.'

'Oh goodness. They're identical. How on earth do you tell them apart?'

Tilly chuckled. 'If you look closely' – she placed her finger on Eliza's chin – 'Eliza has a little mole here.'

'I can see these girls are going to have fun fooling folk when they're older.' Lady Astley laughed.

Tilly took Eliza from Lady Astley and signalled for me to pass Louise.

'Meet Louise.' I passed the baby to Lady Astley.

'They're both so adorable.' Lady Astley squeezed Tilly's hand. 'Thank you for letting me be part of this.'

André strode across the room with a tray of small narrow glasses containing sherry. 'I believe a toast is in order.' He set a glass down on the mahogany occasional table. 'I shall leave yours here, Lady Astley.'

Matthew glanced at me. Butterflies beat in my stomach at his smile. 'Would you do me the honour of showing me the garden, Madam Françoise?'

I looked at Tilly and then to André. They both nodded. I ignored Maman's frown as Matthew led me out.

'Wait one moment, young lady.'

I turned around to Maman's shaking finger. 'André, you go too. Ta sœur requires a chaperone.'

André looked at Tilly and she said, 'It's all right. You go. It will give you a chance to ask that question.'

André kissed his wife and twins on the cheek in turn.

*

As we sauntered along the pathway, I pointed out the same blooms that Tilly and I had admired earlier.

'I am sorry, ma sœur, for tagging along but there was nothing I could do. I will make myself scarce.'

'There is no need,' I said. 'You adore the garden as much as we do and it is nice for you to see it in its spring glory. Joe is doing an exceptional job. Do you not agree?'

'He certainly is. I miss not being the gardener.'

When we reached the bench, Matthew asked, 'Shall we take a seat for a while and admire the bees hovering over these wonderful blue blooms?'

'A good idea,' André said sitting down and I took a seat in the middle of the two gentlemen.

'It really is quite wondrous to watch,' Matthew continued.

I loved how he cared about nature just as André and I did.

'I was wondering,' Matthew asked, 'now that Madam Matilda's given birth, does that mean you'll be returning to Beckton with Sir Charles?'

André went to get up. 'It is all right.' I pressed his knee to lower him back down. 'Stay.' I faced Matthew. 'I am not sure. I have told Sir Charles that I need more time.'

Matthew fiddled with his ear. 'Did you hear that Miss Western has found a new beau?'

'Non, I am sorry.'

'No need for apologies as I told you previously there was no love between us. She's engaged to be married before the

306

summer's out. The chap's a lord from London so a much better catch than me.'

'I am sorry,' André said, 'but here is something that will cheer you. My wife and I would like you to be godfather to the twins.'

Matthew sat open-mouthed.

'What do you say?' André asked. 'Can we count on you?'

'Yes. Yes of course. I am deeply honoured.'

'And I am to be godmother,' I said.

'That's wonderful. It means I'll get to spend some time with you.'

'I am still married, Monsieur Astley, and there is no escape for me. You should find yourself a young wife so you too can have what André has.' I wiped my moistened eye. 'I think we should go back inside. Maman will be wondering where we are.'

*

I carried a tray of refreshments into the drawing room and placed it on the occasional table. Both babies were sleeping in their new perambulator. 'Tea, Lady Astley?' I asked.

'Yes please, and then I think perhaps my nephew and I should leave you good people. We don't want to outstay our welcome.'

'Lady Astley has agreed to be our other godmother,' Tilly said to André. She then turned to Matthew and asked, 'Did André speak to you, Mr Astley?'

'Yes, he did' – Matthew picked a cup and saucer up from the table and passed it to his aunt – 'and the answer is yes. As I told André, I'm honoured. Thank you for asking me. When's the christening?'

'Three weeks today' – André bit into a biscuit – 'June 19th.'

Chapter 36

Tilly

Françoise helped me dress the twins. We'd made a gown each but, just like my girls, they looked identical. Gold linen fabric flowed down past my babies' feet. Little puffed sleeves showed off their tiny arms and the small buttons from the collar to the yoke were finished with a sash matching the lace trim giving them a luxurious look and feel.

I hugged Eliza while Françoise cuddled Louise. Eliza gave her first smile and minutes later Louise smiled too. She was like a little echo.

'They are gorgeous, Tilly.' Françoise gently brushed a finger across Louise's pink cheek.

I was amazed by the way she'd coped with the second anniversary of Oliver's death a fortnight ago. She'd stitched Louise's christening gown in-between setting up a shrine in the corner of the parlour with a posy of white lilies, Oliver's photograph, and a lit candle.

'Are you all right?' I tied Eliza's bonnet under her thin neck.

'Oui.'

'And you know what you have to do today as godmother?'

'Oui. I am looking forward to seeing Monsieur Astley again. It was kind of you to ask him to be godfather.'

'He was André's choice. They're like brothers. How are you feeling now about Mr Astley?'

'He is such a thoughtful gentleman. It was generous of him to bring flowers for Oliver when his papa could not be bothered to turn up.'

'Have you heard from him?'

'Non. I believe he is punishing me for asking for more time.'

'He doesn't deserve you.' I placed Eliza in the bassinet.

'That is what André says too. He thinks I should marry Monsieur Astley but as I told him that is not possible.'

'Yes, I know. He told me the same thing. He said if you're unable to get a divorce that you should live with Mr Astley as his wife, anyway.'

Françoise chuckled. 'Can you imagine Maman accepting that? "You need to go back to your husband and fulfil the terms of the oath." I can hear her now.'

'Forget the oath. We're almost in the twentieth century. And from what you and André have told me, the reason you had to go along with the plan initially was to prevent your mother and father from becoming paupers. That isn't going to happen now. We are financially stable and do not need to rely on the Dubois family in Kent.'

'You are right. I shall remember that argument when Maman brings it up again.'

'Have you written to Sir Charles since?'

'Non. If he could not tear himself away to be with me on Oliver's anniversary then I have no time to waste putting pen to paper. I feel nothing for him. I thought I was in love with him but now wonder whether I ever was. Whereas when I am close to Monsieur Astley I cannot think straight and I wonder what his kisses would taste like. But alas I will never really know more than a quick brush of his lips on mine. It is not possible.'

'Put Louise in the cot and I'll dress your hair.'

'Merci.' She stroked Louise's arm before settling her down in the bassinet with her sister.

'Come.' I stood by the dressing table ready.

Françoise adjusted her emerald green taffeta gown as she lowered herself down to the stool.

I brushed her thick chestnut hair. 'To think this' – I demonstrated with my arms out wide – 'all this started with me doing your hair and tending your needs.'

'Bien sûr, it did. I always knew we would become friends from the first time we met.'

I lifted strands of her hair and rolled them in big waves away from her forehead, leaving one long thick strand to brush across her neck and hang on her left shoulder. I positioned the small feathered bonnet with its white rose onto her head, finishing off her outfit perfectly.

'Merci.' The emerald stone from her choker twinkled as it caught sunlight from the window. 'If I do not return to *Highwood* then what happens about *Coopers Lodge*? I thought André was in the process of purchasing it.'

'André withdrew from the sale. He said this is our home. He's been trying to find the right time to tell you. His business is going well and he doesn't wish to leave his good friend Matthew Astley.'

'I see.' She closed her eyes.

'André doesn't trust Sir Charles. We should go down and find the others. It's almost time to leave.' I picked up Louise.

*

André was pouring a brandy as we entered the drawing room. He passed the glass to his mother. Her azure silk gown hung loose at her bosom and waist like she'd lost weight. 'Maman,' I said, 'I think your gown needs a slight adjustment.' I passed Louise to André as Françoise was holding Eliza. 'Bring your brandy if you wish.' I led Maman Antoinette into the workroom.

310

'What is wrong with my gown?' she asked.

'I just need to give it a couple of little tucks. Have you lost weight?'

Her face paled. 'Do not mention this to mon fils or ma fille.' Thick lines appeared on her forehead.

'I won't but if you're ill you should speak to them. They'd want to know.' I tucked and sewed a couple of darts so the gown fitted neatly across her bosom and into her waist. 'There that's better.'

She swayed from side to side looking at her reflection in the mirror. 'I am just tired. All this business with Sir Charles has been getting me down. Ma fille should have been back with her husband by now.'

'Supposing that isn't what she wishes? And the absence of him seems to suggest he doesn't wish it either.'

She smiled. 'All that will be fixed soon.' Her eyes glinted.

I followed her back to the drawing room and wondered what she meant by that comment. As we entered Françoise gasped.

'What is it?' I asked.

'It is Sir Charles. He is coming up the drive in his vehicle.'

I glanced out of the window. A mechanical carriage parked behind the Landau.

Françoise passed Eliza to me. She put her hand to her forehead and sank into the armchair.

'Quickly, smelling salts,' I said.

Maman Antoinette waddled over to the sideboard returning with the small bottle. She held it under her daughter's nose. Using her fan, Françoise fanned herself. 'What is he doing here? And why now?'

Her mother beamed. 'I invited him.'

Chapter 37

Françoise

I stood at the front of the church beside the vicar with Eliza in my arms. Next to me were the other godparents, Lady Astley, holding Louise, and Matthew, the godfather, at his aunt's side. My stomach was consumed with butterflies at his closeness, but at the same time I felt Maman and Charles' eyes penetrating through me. Why had Maman invited him without telling me?'

The vicar took Eliza from me and said, 'Name this child.'

In unison we godparents answered, 'Eliza Jane Antoinette.'

Laying Eliza back in his arms, the vicar dipped his hand in the stone receptacle and sprinkled Eliza with holy water as he said, 'Eliza Jane Antoinette, I baptise thee in the name of the father, and of the son, and of the holy ghost. Amen.' Eliza gave a small cry. 'We receive this child into the congregation of Christ's flock; and do sign' – he made the mark of a cross on Eliza's forehead – 'her with the sign of the cross, in token, that hereafter she shall not be ashamed to confess the faith of Christ crucified…'

Eliza screamed so much that it was difficult to hear what the vicar was saying. Once he had finished, he passed her back to me and she instantly stopped crying. He took Louise from Lady Astley and repeated the process. 'Louise Charlotte May, I baptise thee in the name of the father, and of the son, and of the holy ghost. Amen.'

Unlike Eliza, Louise offered a smile each time the water was sprinkled across her head. The vicar continued with the service but I let my mind wander. Tilly had almost convinced me earlier that there may be hope for Matthew and I, but now that Charles was here all hope had gone. Part of me wanted the ceremony to finish but at the same time I did not wish it to stop as once it was over and we were back at the house I knew that Charles would confront me. I was not going to accept it lightly. Like Tilly had said, we were almost in the twentieth century, so why should I abide by an oath that was over one hundred years old. I was more than a chattel; I was a proven successful businesswoman and had no intention of returning to *Highwood* as part of Charles' property. I deserved more.

*

'You do not appear pleased to see me, dearest.' Charles sipped sherry from his glass.

'Why now?'

'You said you needed time.'

'Mais oui, c'est vrai. Yes, that is right,' I repeated in English, 'but I also invited you to spend time with me on Oliver's birthday which you chose to decline as you had something far more important to do and did not even attempt to make up for it by coming up for the second anniversary. What could have been more important than spending time with the mother of your son at these times of need?' I strolled over to the picture window looking out on to the drive. It was nearing dark. Matthew and his aunt stepped into the carriage. I clenched my fists. Not only had Charles stolen the precious time when I needed him, but now he had stolen my time with Matthew. Maman had insisted we draw the gathering to a close in order that Charles and I may work things out.

Charles came up behind me. 'It's him, isn't it?'

'I'm not sure what you mean.'

He gripped my upper arm and squeezed it. 'Do not lie to me, Françoise, I have watched you with him all day.'

'How dare you? I have never been unfaithful. Can you say the same? What have you been up to these past months when you have chosen to ignore me? And please remove your hand. You are hurting me.'

'I apologise. I didn't mean to hurt you.' He spun me round to face him. 'You asked me to leave you alone. I did as you asked. And if I have been unfaithful these past months, who can blame me? A man has needs. You can't expect me to have gone two years without… A man's different to a woman.'

I opened my mouth to yell but decided not to give him the satisfaction.

'Your mother understands this. Why can't you?'

'What has Maman got to do with this?'

'She said you were ready to return home. Hence why I'm here. It's too far to keep driving up and down the country for nothing.'

I paced across the room to get away from him. 'For nothing. So, I am nothing now.'

'No. That's not what I meant and you know it. It was pointless driving up here all the time if you'd no intention of returning with me. Get packed. We'll leave at first light.'

'Non. I will not.' I rubbed my moist eyes. 'I am not ready to return.'

'You will return with me. You're my wife and you'll do exactly what I say.'

'Non. I will not. You cannot make me. You betrayed me, remember.'

'I gave up Anna for you.'

André strode into the room. 'You gave Anna up for ma sœur? I thought you gave her up because you could not live without Françoise?'

'That too.'

André glared into his eyes. 'You are still seeing her?'

Charles turned away.

'You are?' André grabbed Charles by the arm. 'And I would wager that the bastard is yours too.'

Tilly and Maman wandered into the room. 'Is it?' Tilly asked.

Charles sighed. 'Yes, the child is mine.'

'It does not make any difference,' Maman said, 'what is past is past. This is now and Françoise is to return with Sir Charles tomorrow. We will follow in due course.'

'We are not going anywhere, Maman' – André sighed, brushing fingers through his hair – 'and neither is she. If you think I am going to allow ma sœur to go back to the arms of that philanderer' – he jabbed Charles' upper arm with a finger – 'then you are mistaken.'

I could not believe what I was hearing. Not only had Charles continued to betray me with his mistress but he had lied about being father to the child. I took a deep breath. 'I want a divorce.'

Charles tossed his head back in laughter. 'A divorce. On what grounds?'

André answered for me, 'Adultery and cruelty.'

'I may be guilty of adultery,' Charles softened his voice, 'but I've never been cruel, Françoise. You know that.' He tipped back his glass and drank the remains of the sherry before topping it up yet again.

'You do not think it is cruel the way you have treated ma sœur?'

'No, I do not. I have always provided everything she needed and I gave her a good settlement so you could purchase this place, allowing her time to come to her senses.'

'Come to my senses?' I was seething inside. Who did he think he was? 'And I will cite you for cruelty. Only minutes ago, you gripped my arm. What is to stop me from accusing you of physically harming me?'

Tilly marched over next to me. 'And as her former lady's maid I shall back up the claims.'

'You're mad. The lot of you.' Charles threw back another full glass of the fortified wine.

Maman pushed herself between Charles and I. 'Let us all stay calm and not say things in haste we will regret. Françoise, have you forgotten about the oath?'

'I do not give a damn about that stupid oath. As Tilly pointed out to me earlier, we are almost in the twentieth century so why should I be worried about an oath that was made between two foolish brothers over one hundred years ago? And you know I only agreed to it originally because I did not wish you and Papa to end up as paupers. Well Papa is no longer here and we are not about to send you to the workhouse. Therefore, the oath is redundant.'

Tilly took my hand and smiled.

'I believe everything that needs to be said has been said.' André faced Charles. 'I suggest, sir, that you get some rest and return to Beckton alone at first light.'

Charles slammed his empty glass down on the occasional table. 'Is this your last word, Françoise?'

'Oui. You will be hearing from my solicitor.' I folded my arms.

'Françoise,' Maman yelled, 'stop behaving foolishly. This is your chance to have another child. Do you really want to end up as the old aunt?'

'I do not wish to return to a man who has betrayed me over and over again. I suggest Sir Charles that you do not contest this divorce if you wish to remarry and give your child a name.'

'Fetch my hat and cloak. I will not spend one moment more than necessary in this house. You're all mad. I always thought you French were rather strange and now you've proved it.'

'At least we are loyal,' André said. 'Tilly, get Sir Charles his outdoor wear.'

Tilly left the room.

'This is madness,' I said, 'you cannot drive in that state. Not only are you fatigued from your journey earlier, but you are inebriated. Wait until the morning' – I squeezed his hand – 'get some rest.' I did not wish him to risk his life. 'We had some good times, Charles. Please do not let this end ugly.'

Tilly returned with Charles' things.

'Charles?' I pleaded.

He snatched his hat and cloak from Tilly. 'I bid you all goodnight and farewell. You will be hearing from my solicitor, Françoise. And if you insist on continuing with this frivolous saga, I shall cite you for adultery with Mr Matthew Astley as co-respondent.' Charles stormed out of the room.

'Do you think he will carry out his threat?' I asked.

'Most likely,' André answered. 'How about you? Will you carry out yours?'

'Non. It is not possible. I cannot allow my husband to drag Monsieur Astley's good name through the courts when he is innocent of any wrongdoing.' I moved over to the window and peered out as Charles jumped up into the vehicle. The road lit up as the carriage headlights sprang to life and the vehicle sped down the drive. I glared at Maman. 'I will just have to settle with being the old aunt.'

Chapter 38

Françoise

Tilly pushed the twins in their perambulator into the drawing room.

I peeped under the hoods and glanced up at Tilly. 'Asleep again?'

'They weren't half an hour ago. I'm surprised you didn't hear them screaming.'

'That must have been when I went in the garden to try and clear my head.'

'Are you all right? I thought it was strange you didn't come to find out what was going on. Let's sit down.' Tilly made herself comfortable on the chaise longue. Before joining her, I poured us each a beverage and carried them across to the occasional table.

'Not really,' I said, 'I keep going over and over yesterday. So many bad things were said. Charles' revelation that Anna's child was his, me threatening him divorce on the grounds of cruelty, and him retaliating that he would cite Mr Astley. I cannot allow that to happen. I do not know what to do.' I took a sip of the warm drink.

'Sir Charles will cool down, I'm sure.' Tilly stirred her tea and rested the spoon on the saucer.

Maman padded into the room. 'Monsieur Astley is here. I was unsure whether you would wish to see him.'

My stomach fluttered. 'Oui, Maman, of course I would like
to see him.' I got up and wandered into the hallway catching
the scent from the pink and red sweet peas in the cobalt blue
vase. 'Monsieur Astley. How good to see you.'

'And you too, my dear lady.' He took my hand and kissed
the back of it lightly.

'Would you like to see the garden?' I asked. 'The sweet peas,
as you can see, are divine this year.'

'I would like that.'

I led him towards the kitchen and out of the back door
sensing Maman glaring at me. We meandered along the cobbled
pathway. I felt so comfortable with Matthew at my side but
saddened that the most we could ever be was friends, and once
he was wed, more than likely, our friendship would come to a
close. Should we even be friends now with Charles' threat?

We were strolling towards the mixed flower bed when
Matthew asked, 'Shall we sit for a while?'

'Oui. That will be nice.'

He looked around. 'Should we ask Madam Matilda or your
mother to be chaperone?'

'Non. There is no need.'

Matthew waited until I had lowered myself onto the seat
before sitting down beside me and admiring the multi-coloured
flower bed full of marigolds, antirrhinums and pansies, which
had replaced the cornflowers and hyacinths. 'I see what you
mean,' he said.

'They are beautiful, are they not? As are the sweet peas
behind us. Perhaps we should pick some for your aunt.'

'She'd like that, I'm sure.' Matthew tapped the arm of the
bench. 'I wasn't sure if you'd still be here.'

'If Maman had her way I would not be.'

'She seemed adamant yesterday that you'd be returning with Sir Charles. I came over on the off chance to say goodbye before you left.'

'That was her plan but I told him I was not ready.'

'I'm overjoyed that you're here for a while longer but I shall miss you once you go.'

'I will miss you too, Monsieur Astley, but I am sure it will not take you long to find a wife and then you will forget all about me.'

'Never.' He put his hand on his chest. 'I will never forget you, Madam Françoise. If only things could be different.' He blinked. 'Do you think you could find it in your heart to call me Matthew when we're alone?'

I knew I needed to distance myself from him. It did not seem fair that I should have to stop enjoying his company when Charles had betrayed me, but I could not risk Matthew's good name being dragged through the courts. I clasped my hands. 'I am not sure that would be appropriate, Monsieur.'

*

High pitched cries escalated as we approached the drawing room. 'That will be the twins,' I said to Matthew, as we entered.

Tilly was pushing the perambulator backwards and forwards trying to calm the babies.

'Françoise, thank goodness you're here. You wouldn't take one of them, would you?'

I moved over to the perambulator and lifted Eliza. 'Now, young lady, what is all this noise?'

The infant stopped crying immediately and offered a small smile but Tilly was still struggling to calm Louise. 'She can smell my milk,' she whispered. 'I'll feed her if you can take care of Eliza?'

'Oui. No problem.'

Tilly left with Louise screaming in her arms.

'You're a natural mother,' Matthew said.

I felt my eyes fill knowing I would never get that chance again.

*

I was deep in thought peering out of the window when the door knocker made me jump. I made my way along the hallway and opened the front door to a young lad standing on the step. I recognised his uniform, but why was he calling?

'Telegram Missus.' He passed me a yellow envelope.

'Merci.'

André came up behind me as I closed the door. He tapped me on the shoulder. 'Who was it?'

My hands shook as I passed him the letter. 'You open it.'

'Now, now, ma sœur, do not start worrying until we know what has happened. We will go to the drawing room and read it.'

I followed him down the passage, into the room, and took a seat next to him on the chaise longue.

He ripped the envelope open. His face whitened.

My stomach somersaulted. 'André, what is it?'

He took a deep breath. 'It is…'

I blinked. 'What?'

He coughed. It is' – he fiddled with the sheet of paper – 'it is Charles. Charles is dead. A car accident.'

I put a hand to my mouth. It must have happened after he left here. 'Surely this cannot be.' My pulse quickened. 'And it is all my fault…'

Maman shuffled into the room. 'All your fault for what? What have you done?'

'Nothing, Maman' – André passed her the telegram – 'she has done nothing.'

Maman read the words from the page out loud. 'Charles is dead. A car accident. Come quick. E.' Maman became unsteady on her feet.

André jumped up from the couch and guided her to the armchair. 'Sit down, Maman.' He rushed over to the sideboard, took a bottle from the drawer and hurried back, holding the smelling salts under her nose.

Once recovered enough to speak, she sat up and glared at me. 'This is your doing, young lady. If you had been a good wife and returned home months ago then this would never have happened. His death is on your conscience.'

'Maman. How could you?' André scowled. 'I will not have any more nonsense said like that in this house. Do you understand?'

She muttered something undecipherable under her breath.

André slammed his fist down on the occasional table. 'I said, do you understand?'

'Oui. Mon fils. I understand.'

'Bonne. Let that be the end of blame and let us concentrate on the subject in hand. Françoise, you need to go to *Highwood*.'

'It is tragic that Charles is dead, but why must I go to *Highwood*?'

'Because, ma sœur, you should be there for the funeral. And then there is a will to be read.'

'Naturally, you must be there.' Maman bit her lip. 'You are his widow.'

I clenched my fists. I did not wish to go back there. 'It must have been on the way home.'

'We cannot know that for sure, ma sœur, but we will find that out once we get there. Do not worry, you will not be alone. I will be with you. I will sort everything. We shall take the train to make our journey quicker.'

Tilly packed my bag. She pulled out a gown from the wardrobe. 'You will need this.'

'Oui.' I took hold of the black gown last worn for Oliver's funeral. At least Oliver now had his papa with him.

Tilly rested her hand on my shoulder. 'I know this is hard, Françoise, but once the funeral's over you'll be free. There'll be nothing left at *Highwood* to tie you there.'

I thought about Matthew. Would I be free of guilt in order to marry him? I was not sure. I could not think about that now.

'Françoise' – Tilly sat down on the stool with the gown across her lap – 'while you're there, do you think you could take a message to Frank?'

'Certainly, mon amie. I am happy to pass on a letter?'

'Not a letter as he can't read, that is, unless he has learned since I last saw him but I'm sure he's been far too busy with the farm and raising the twins. Will you tell him I miss him and would love to see him one day, and let the twins know that I think about them every day, and that they have twin nieces.'

I strode over to where she was sitting and squeezed her hand. 'Of course.' I sighed. 'I wish you could come with us.'

'Me too but as André said, "the girls are too young to cope with such a long journey." And, of course, he is right.'

I laughed. 'He told Maman she was too old.' I laughed again.

Chapter 39

Françoise

Joe dropped us off at the railway station. I followed André to the ticket office. He spoke through the small window. 'Two first class to Faversham.' He handed over some coins and collected our tickets.

A porter lifted our trunk. 'This way.' He trudged towards the platform. 'Your train's due any minute.'

'We are on this one for around two and half hours,' André said as we followed the porter, 'and if we are lucky our connection will be in ready when we get to London.'

The guard blew his whistle and a train pulled in with a hiss and puff of steam. André helped me up into an empty carriage. I sat down by the window and he took the seat opposite. The guard slammed the door, blew his whistle again, and the train whistled chugging out of the station.

It was strange to think that so much had happened since André and I had first arrived at *Highwood*. I had been married, but was a widow. I had been a maman, but that had been taken from me. Papa had died and our old maman had gone, replaced with a bitter woman.

'Rest, Françoise,' André said, 'we are going to be on here for a while. I plan to do the same.' He leaned back and closed his eyes.

*

I jumped as someone shook my arm.

'We are here.' André straightened his clothes.

The train pulled in. The guard whistled. André helped me down the step while a porter unloaded our trunk. We followed him on to another platform with a stationary train on the track. André opened a carriage door. 'In here, Françoise. This journey is a little shorter.'

*

The train whistle woke me up. 'Are we here?' I asked André.

He looked out of the window. 'Oui. Faversham. Mr Hughes should be here to meet us.'

We stepped out of the carriage. The porter had already unloaded our trunk. 'This way,' he said.

Mr Hughes was standing by a Landau. 'Get the trunk,' he said to the boy with him before addressing us. 'Lady Françoise and Monsieur Dubois. Delightful to see you both again. Please accept my condolences. Lady Elizabeth's waiting for you.' He helped me into the vehicle and André slid on the seat next to me. The horses trotted moving into a gallop. I did not look out of the window. I did not wish to be there. 'André,' I asked, 'where do people think I have been?'

'Fret not, ma sœur, they are under the impression you returned to France to recover from your son's death.'

'Will it not seem strange that I am here now?'

'It would be stranger if you were not.'

As we trotted past the graveyard a tear pricked my eye at the thought of my dear Oliver buried there. The Landau pulled into *Highwood.* A wreath of laurel hung on the gate. The horses slowed to a walk and Mr Hughes stopped the carriage outside the steps of the house. I looked up at the huge columns remembering how impressed I had been when we first arrived three years ago.

Elizabeth shuffled down the steps, looking years older than the last time we had seen her. Dark shadows circled her eyes. 'Françoise. André. Thank goodness you're here. Do come inside.'

A wreath of yew and boxwood with black ribbons hung from the front door. It was all too much. It was bringing everything back. We followed her into the hallway.

'You must be fatigued,' she said, 'perhaps a bit of refreshment and then rest. Mrs Jarvis has your rooms ready.'

André removed his hat. 'A cup of tea would be most welcome. Please accept our condolences. Sir Charles' death was sudden. What happened?'

'A car crash on his way home from Oxhaven. Killed outright. Thank God Françoise wasn't in the car with him.' Elizabeth led us into the drawing room. 'Sit down, please, and I'll arrange tea.' She pulled a cord to ring the bell and waited for André and I to be seated on the chaise longue, before sitting on the opposite armchair. 'What I don't understand, dear, is why you weren't with him? I was under the impression from Charles that he was bringing you home.'

'We had argued. I discovered he had never stopped seeing Anna and that her child was in fact his.'

'Nonsense, dear. That can't be right. He'd have told me.'

'It is the truth,' André answered.

My pulse quickened. I took a deep breath before continuing. 'After our quarrel he stormed out of the house and into the vehicle. I was concerned about him driving as he had been drinking heavily so I begged him to wait until first light. To get some rest first but he would not listen. I promise, Maman Elizabeth, I tried to stop him.'

Elizabeth rose quickly from the chair. 'So, it's your fault my son's dead. How could you have allowed him to drive in that state?'

'I tried to stop him' – I got up and moved next to her – 'but you are right, Maman Elizabeth, it is all my fault. If only we had not argued. But I promise I really did try to stop him from driving.' I put out my hand to console her but she pushed it away.

She shook her fist at me. 'You hoped he'd have a crash in order to set yourself free.'

'I did not. I promise.' I sobbed.

André stood up and put his arm around me. 'That is enough, Lady Elizabeth. It was no one's fault but your son's. He was the one who chose to drive in an intoxicated state.' André rubbed my arm. 'I shall let this go as you are upset. My sister is exhausted from our long journey and she needs to retire to her bed. I can assure you, Françoise did everything to stop Sir Charles getting into that contraption, we all did. I think enough has been said. We bid you goodnight.' André led me out and upstairs to my old room where I threw myself onto the bed and sobbed.

Chapter 40

Françoise

A lady's maid helped me dress into my black crepe gown. She dressed my hair and positioned a small sable hat on my head. I stared into the silk veil. I went to check in the mirror but it was hidden with black crepe.

André met me on the landing and we took the stairs together, meeting Elizabeth at the footwell. She led us to the parlour. I backed away but André held my arm and whispered, 'You can do this.'

Charles' casket was open and surrounded by white flowers.

Elizabeth took my hand. 'Come, dear, come closer and say goodbye to your husband.'

'Non, you go. I will stay here.'

She scowled at me. 'There is no discussion. You will do this.'

André nodded and came the other side of me. With small slow steps I eventually reached Charles in his coffin. He looked like he was sleeping. His head rested on a pillow as he lay on a bed of white satin, dressed in formal attire. I thought back to his mesmerising dark soil eyes which were now closed. His black hair shone emphasising his porcelain face. I had been expecting to see scratches and bruises but he was without blemish. Flowers surrounded his body. I reflected how loving he had been before our son had died and discovered my tears were for Charles as well as Oliver. I stroked my husband's cold cheek and whispered, 'Take care of our son.' Blinking my eyes to prevent further tears, I backed away, and this time Elizabeth did not try to stop me.

*

We stood around while the gravediggers lowered the oak casket into the ground. Elizabeth clung on to me as she sobbed. Charles' best friend, Arthur Alcott, looked up at me and nodded. He was next to his mother, rubbing her arm, trying to pacify her. I wondered whether Charles' friendship had continued with Arthur after Grace had brought chincough into the house, inadvertently killing our baby Oliver. Rebecca glanced at me from behind her veil. She dabbed her eyes. I had missed her company. Loose strands of fiery hair fell from her black bonnet. Her sisters, Grace and Emily, wailed making almost as much noise as their maman.

I reached for my locket which Charles had given me at Oliver's funeral and brushed my fingers against the engraved flower. The priest and his clerks approached the graveside once the coffin was interred. Elizabeth gripped my arm as the priest said, *Lord have mercy upon us* and followed with the *Lord's Prayer.*

Earth to earth, ashes to ashes, dust to dust. The priest took a handful of earth and sprinkled it on Charles' coffin. André passed me a handkerchief for my tears. I took hold of Elizabeth's hand, feeling her pain; she had lost her husband, daughter, grandson and now son. She squeezed my hand back.

*

Rebecca waited for her mother, sisters and brother to leave the house. 'Lady Françoise' – she rested her hand on mine – 'it's wonderful to see you again. When did you return from France?' Before I could answer she carried on, 'I'm so sorry

329

about Sir Charles. He was a good gentleman. You must be devastated.'

I just nodded.

'Will you be staying at *Highwood* now?'

'Non. We will be leaving shortly.' I touched her arm. 'I will write.'

'Yes. Yes, please. I would like that.'

'Rebecca,' Arthur called.

She kissed my cheek. 'I look forward to hearing from you.' Her face brightened.

*

The mourners had all gone and Elizabeth, André and I sat in the drawing room.

Elizabeth fiddled with her black sapphire pendant which was the colour of Charles' eyes. 'We'll send for your things tomorrow?'

I frowned. 'Excuse me, Maman Elizabeth, but I do not understand.'

'Naturally you'll return here. It's your rightful place.'

'Non. I do not intend to do that. Tell her André.'

André stood up and paced the room. 'There appears to have been some confusion, Lady Elizabeth, but Françoise and I shall be returning to Oxhaven directly after the will has been read.'

Elizabeth's cheeks puffed. 'This is outrageous.' She faced me. 'It's your fault my son's lying dead in his grave, the least you can do is return home.'

André marched towards her. 'Madam, I will not have you speak to my sister in that manner. Apologise immediately.'

'For stating the truth. I think not. She shames the Dubois name.'

'I shame the Dubois name? I think not.' I was trembling but carried on. 'Would you like to know whose fault it is?' I did not wait for a response. 'It is your fault, madam. Yours and that stupid one hundred-year-old oath. Your son was clearly in love with another woman but would you allow him to marry her? Non. Pourquois? I will tell you why. Because she was working class. A lady's maid would not do for a baronet. Yet Charles did not stop loving her, did he? And especially once she bore his son.'

'So you said, utter nonsense.'

'She is telling the truth, Lady Elizabeth. Sir Charles was indeed the father of the illegitimate child.'

'You are speaking lies. Lies that my dead son is unable to defend.' Her face reddened as her voice got louder. She rose from the chair. 'I'll excuse your lies this evening because it's been a difficult day for us all, but tomorrow I shall expect an apology.' Her gown rustled as she hurried from the room.

*

Mr Baines, an elderly gentleman with grey bushy sideburns matching his beard, stood away from Charles' desk. 'I'll bid you all good day now that the business-in-hand has been completed.' Swinging his brown briefcase, he left the room.

Elizabeth shook her head muttering. 'Everything left to you and you weren't even together.'

'I am happy to sign Charles' estate over to you. However, there is a condition.'

'What sort of condition?'

'Charles concealed his child's parentage for your sake, because you had enforced the terms of the oath on him, while all the time he wanted to be a good father but now, Maman Elizabeth, it is time for you to make things right. I would like you to bring the child to *Highwood* and raise him as Charles' son.'

'That is outrageous.'

'I have not finished. There is more. I would like you to set up a trust, using fifty percent of *Highwood* funds, in the boy's name for when he is older. I will sign any paperwork required.'

'Out of the question.'

'That will still leave half for Bertha to inherit on your death.'

'I can't do that.'

'If you do not then Bertha will be left with nothing when you die. The terms of the will state you will be allowed to live in the house and receive an annual allowance, but this way you will have so much more. Security for Bertha.' I got up, moved next to Elizabeth and took her hand. 'Do this for your son. Come and see the child before you say no. We shall visit Anna together. André, you will come too?'

'Naturally, I cannot allow two ladies to go unattended.'

*

We reached a small cottage in the village. André tapped on the green panelled door. A woman I hardly recognised opened it. She looked as if her hair had not been combed for days and although pinned up, straggly strands hung around her face. It was clear by the red around her eyes that she had been crying.

'Anna,' I said. 'May we come in?'

The woman wiped her eyes using the back of her hand. 'Lady Elizabeth. Lady Françoise. Sir. Please excuse my appearance.' She ran her fingers through her hair, brushing it into place. 'What can I do for you?'

'May we come in?' André asked.

She widened the door for us to enter. As we stepped in, I glanced around at the well-furnished room in disarray. Anna hurriedly picked items of clothing from the small couch and threw them into a bucket. 'Do sit down.'

I waited for her to be seated before I said, 'We are here to break some bad news.'

She patted her cheeks with a muslin square. 'If you mean about Sir Charles being killed in an accident, I already know. The whole village knows. But then I'd already lost him when he came here three weeks ago to say he was leaving me for you.' She glared at me.

'Well, she is, was his wife,' Elizabeth said.

'He'd always wanted to marry me. You knew that, Lady Elizabeth, but you still sent for her, from France.'

'Charles had a duty to fulfil,' answered Elizabeth without a smile.

'And when I was in the family way… you banned him from coming here. So why are you now at my door?'

Elizabeth perched on the edge of the couch. 'Things have changed. Back then we were under the impression that the valet was the child's prospective father.'

Anna shook her head. 'Sir Charles knew it was his. He only lied to pacify you, and her.' Once again, she glared at me.

'Just before Sir Charles had his accident,' André said, still standing and holding his top hat at his side, 'he told my sister he was the child's father.'

'I've just told you that. What of it?'

André pulled up a hard chair opposite Anna. 'Who is named as the father on the birth certificate?'

'Sir Charles. He came with me to register the birth. He was quite insistent Theo should grow up knowing who his father was.'

'May we see the child?' Elizabeth asked.

'Why? You weren't interested in him before he was born, and you haven't been interested in him since,' Anna said, as a small child toddled into the room. 'Mama.' He clambered up on her lap.

I caught my breath. He was a mini version of Charles. There could be no dispute that he was the father. The same jet-black hair, but tousled with curls, and the same anthracite eyes. This is what Oliver would have looked like if he had lived. This was Oliver's half-brother. I got up and moved to Anna's chair and held my hand out to the child. 'Hello,' I said, 'what is your name?'

The child nuzzled his head into Anna's chest. She stroked his hair. 'He doesn't talk much when strangers are around. So, what's this about?' Anna lifted the child off her lap and placed him on the floor among toy soldiers. 'Mama.' He wailed, standing up and trying to climb up her skirt. 'Shh Theo.' She rubbed his arm. 'Lady Elizabeth, would you like tea?'

Elizabeth twiddled her pearl stud earring. 'Tea would be most welcome.'

Anna rose from her chair. 'Theo.' She held out her hand to him but he did not take it, instead he tottered over to Elizabeth and patted her legs. 'Is he all right with you?' Anna asked.

'Yes. You go.' Elizabeth bent her head close to Theo.

Once Anna had left the room I said to Elizabeth, 'He is adorable, is he not?'

'He is. Charles was just like him at that age.' She scooped Theo up in her arms and I knew he had won her love.

'We are in agreement then? He should live at *Highwood*?'

Elizabeth nodded.

Anna strode back into the parlour with a tray, put it down on a small table and poured the tea.

Still with the child on her lap, Elizabeth said, 'We have a proposition for you.'

Anna passed André and I a cup of tea before sitting back down on the edge of her chair. 'A proposition?'

Theo scrambled down from Elizabeth and back onto Anna's knee, slapping her shoulders.

'As you must be aware' – Elizabeth crossed her hands on her lap – 'Theo is Sir Charles' only living child.'

Anna shrugged her shoulders. 'So what?'

Elizabeth continued, 'I'd like Theo to come and live at *Highwood* and I will raise him as Charles' son.'

Anna shook her head. 'I'm not quite understanding. You want us to come to live at *Highwood Hall?*'

'No, I'd like Theo to come and live with me. I'll grant you a fine settlement. An amount that will enable you to continue to live a decent life.'

'I'm not giving up my boy. No. You took my man away from me, and now you want my boy? No.' She held the child closer to her chest.

'Do you want your child growing up with nothing? There will be no more funds from Charles? Wouldn't you prefer that Theo had the best?'

'No, Lady Elizabeth,' I interrupted, 'you cannot take the child away from his maman. Anna must return to *Highwood* too, otherwise my offer is invalid.'

Elizabeth pursed her lips. 'But that's not possible. What will people say?'

'Perhaps,' I said, 'if you had not been so concerned about what people thought beforehand then Charles would have been allowed to marry the woman whom he had loved instead of going along with a foolish plan conjured up by two brothers over a hundred years ago.'

'Look at him,' André said. 'It is clear he is Sir Charles' son. What would he want you to do?'

'I do not doubt he's Charles' offspring,' Elizabeth said.

'It is time to put things right,' I said to her again. 'Did you not used to say how well you and Anna got on when she was your lady's maid? Perhaps she could return as your companion?'

Anna beamed.

Elizabeth bit her lip. 'I'm not sure that would work.'

'If you really want the best for your grandson…' Anna placed Theo on the floor and he toddled over to Elizabeth peering up at her with those black eyes.

'He likes you,' I said.

'One thing is for certain, Lady Elizabeth' – Anna brushed her hands – 'my son goes nowhere without me.'

Elizabeth patted Theo on the head before picking up a cup from the tray and taking a sip of tea. 'I will need time to think on the matter.'

Chapter 41

Françoise

The train chugged in the rhythm of a lullaby but I was unable to sleep. My mind was too occupied. I opened my eyes and fanned my face.

'André,' I said.

'Mmm?' he muttered with his eyes closed.

'Are you awake?'

He lifted his head with a jolt. 'What is it, ma sœur, are you unable to sleep?'

'Oui. I hardly recognised Anna, did you? She was always immaculate.'

'More than likely, she was too upset to worry about her ablutions.'

I fanned myself again. 'Are you warm?'

'Pourquoi? Are you?'

'Oui. This carriage is far too hot.'

He got up and slid down the window. 'That should help.' He sat down, leaning back into the seat.

'Merci.' The sudden breeze brushed my face. 'I keep going over things. Do you think Elizabeth will agree?'

André sat upright. 'It is clear you wish to converse.' He brushed a hand through his brown curls. 'I am sure she will once she has had time to think. She is not going to want Bertha to be left penniless. It was generous of you to suggest signing everything over.'

'Not really. I did not want it, and I believe this way Elizabeth can right the wrong she did to Charles, and hopefully it will help to alleviate my guilt.'

'You have nothing to be guilty about.'

'I cannot help it.'

'Theo is an adorable little chap.'

'He is. I think Oliver would have looked just like him.'

André leaned forward and took my hand. 'Are you all right, ma sœur? Has all this been too much for you?'

'I am fine. I am glad we had a chance to meet Theo.'

'Are you hungry?'

'I am thirsty.'

André dug deep into the bag and pulled out a flask. 'Mrs Derby packed us some of her lemonade. Would you like a cup?'

'Oui s'il vous plaît.'

He poured the liquid into a beaker and passed it to me.

'Mmm, this is lovely.' I glanced out of the window as the sun was setting. 'Have you seen this sky?'

André turned his head to the pane. 'It is the colour of orange. Beau ciel.'

'Do you remember when we buried Oliver how thunder struck and Elizabeth said that was Oliver arriving in Heaven?'

'Oui. I do.'

'I thought that might happen at Charles' funeral.'

'Perhaps he has not arrived yet unless…'

'Please do not suggest he has gone to Hell.'

André chuckled. 'He may have been bad at times but not that bad.'

I glanced out of the window again. 'It is almost dark. Will we reach Oxford soon?'

He fiddled with his pocket watch. 'Another half an hour or so I think.'

'What should I tell Tilly about Frank?'

'Hmm. Perhaps a white lie. Say he was not at home. That way it gives him the chance to change his mind in the future. She would be heartbroken to know that he wished to have no contact with her.'

I sipped the last of my drink as the train puffed and hissed into the station. A guard whistled.

'This is our stop.' André stretched his arms.

I passed my cup back to him. He fastened the lid on the flask and placed it back in his bag before rising from the seat. 'Are you ready, ma sœur?'

*

It was gone eleven o'clock when André turned the key in the front door and the horse pulling the Hansom cab trotted down the drive. We crept into the house quietly for fear of waking the others.

'In here,' Tilly called out.

We made our way down the hallway and into the kitchen.

'Ma chérie.' André took Tilly into his arms. 'I have missed you and the girls so much. But it is late. We thought you would be in bed.'

'Not until you got back.' Tilly withdrew from his hug. She put the kettle on the stove and spooned tea into the pot from the caddy. 'Françoise, you look tired. Was it very awful?'

I pulled a chair from the table and flopped down. 'Not too awful but the journey home was tiring.'

She placed a mug of tea in front of André and I. 'Did Lady Elizabeth confirm how Sir Charles came to his end?'

'Indeed it was an accident. He crashed his car on the way home from here. It was my fault. I should have stopped him.'

'I have told her that is nonsense.' André slurped a mouthful of tea. 'How have you all been while we have been away? It seems like weeks rather than days.'

'Everyone's fine. Even your mother behaved. Françoise, André's right, you didn't ask him to get into the vehicle in that state.'

'I know but…'

'No buts. Would you like a sandwich or something to eat?'

'Non, merci. Mrs Derby made us up a hamper for the trip home. She even packed her lemonade. I believe there may be some left in the flask?'

'Ooh that would be nice. How was Mrs Derby?' Tilly covered her mouth as she yawned.

'She was fine.'

'André, how about you?' Tilly asked. 'Are you hungry?'

'Non, ma cherie, I am ready for bed, as it is clear you are too. I will finish this and then we will go up.' He picked up his cup and downed the rest of his tea.

Chapter 42

Tilly

Françoise and André were chatting in the garden room looking out at the early August blooms when I entered. 'That's the twins bathed and in bed,' I said, 'and Sally's gone home. Hopefully the girls will sleep long enough for us to have a bit of time together.'

Françoise went to get up. 'I shall leave you married people to have time alone.'

'No, that's not what I meant. Stay please.'

'If you are sure. We were just admiring the summer blooms.'

I looked out at the flowering raspberry-red rose bush. 'They are rather gorgeous, aren't they?'

'I was just about to tell Françoise that we have invited Lady Astley and Matthew over next week for afternoon tea.' André got up. 'Would you ladies like a glass of lemonade?'

'Oui, merci.' Françoise licked her lips. 'I have a dreadful thirst in this heat.'

'Yes, please. I wonder when this weather will break?' I waved my fan.

André passed us each a glass.

'Merci,' Françoise said. 'Does Maman know?'

'Mais oui. She is not happy but will come around. She cannot keep blaming Matthew because you did not return to Charles. Matthew is the innocent party. Lady Astley adores you. Her wish is that you will marry her nephew, and as she is

Maman's best friend, I have a feeling it will not be too long before Maman is urging you to give him an answer.'

Françoise laughed. 'Well, he has not asked me.'

'That is because he is a gentleman and knows you need time. He will ask you though.' André's bright blue eyes twinkled.

Françoise blushed.

'And will you say yes?' I asked.

She closed her eyes momentarily. 'I do not know. I would like to but I am still torn with guilt about Charles. I am not sure I deserve happiness. Maman Elizabeth is left alone with just little Bertha. Her husband gone, her daughter, and now her son.' Françoise dabbed her eyes.

'But that's not your fault.' I took a sip from my glass. 'Kitty's lemonade is almost as good as Mrs Derby's. Françoise, you have to stop blaming yourself. It's been almost two months since the accident.'

'But Maman still blames me.'

André knelt down next to his sister and took her hand. 'Maman does not know what she is talking about. Sir Charles died by his own hand. You begged him not to drive and he ignored you. It is sad that it has come to this, but you, chère sœur, deserve happiness.'

*

'Perfect.' I beckoned Blanche out of the dressing area to look at herself in the full-length mirror.

She swayed from side to side checking her reflection. The ruby velvet gown complimented her light brown hair, and made her appear at least ten years younger.

'Is it for a special occasion?' I asked, pinning the hem.

Caroline bounced off the chair. 'She has a beau.'

'I'm very pleased for you. Anyone we know?'

'He is a gentleman from the next village. We met at the Johnstone's. A widower with three children. Two girls, seven and eight, and a lad, twelve.'

I pinned the last pin. 'We can get you out of this now and I'll finish it off this evening. I'll have it ready for collection tomorrow or Joe can deliver it.' Joe now worked for us doing odd jobs around the house and delivering clients' orders in addition to tending the garden.

Françoise came in with tea and cake. 'Miss Livingston, you look très belle. I have brought refreshments.' She placed the tray on the small table.

'Thank you, Madam Françoise. If you could deliver the gown, Madam Matilda, that would be perfect.' Blanche made her way behind the curtain and I followed. I slipped the gown from her shoulders and she stepped out of it.

'Will Miss Caroline be ordering a new outfit today?' Françoise poured tea into the cups.

'Not today,' Blanche answered from behind the curtain as I helped her back into the staid brown skirt and white blouse.

Once out of the dressing area, Caroline asked, 'May I see the twins?' She bit into a macaroon.

'I don't see why not.' I hung the new gown on a rail. 'I'll check with Sally once we've finished tea.'

Caroline patted her lips with a napkin. 'Madam Françoise, are you going to marry Mr Astley?'

Françoise's cheeks turned almost the same red as Blanche's new gown hanging behind her. 'What on earth makes you think that?'

'The villagers have been talking, haven't they, Blanche?'

'I told you not to bring that up, Caroline. Didn't I?' Blanche leaned forward on the armchair to pick up a cup of tea.

'But I'd like to know.' Caroline gave that frivolous giggle.

Françoise shrugged her shoulders. 'He has not asked me.'

Chapter 43

Françoise

I pushed the perambulator back up the path from the river with André and Tilly at my side. We had taken the girls to see the ducks. The twins were healthy, and growing quickly, although at thirteen weeks, smaller than most babies of that age.

Maman greeted us. She peeped under the hoods in turn. 'Bonjour mes belles petites-filles.' She lifted her head out. 'There is a letter for you, Françoise. I have put it on the mantelpiece in the drawing room. I think it is from Lady Elizabeth.'

'Merci, Maman.' I entered the house through the kitchen, and went down the hallway towards the drawing room. The letter was leaned up against the carriage clock. I picked up the envelope, opened the French doors, and strolled outside into the garden to take in the August warmth.

I made my way over to the bench by the dahlia flower bed. The strong scent from their burnt-orange and burgundy heads made my nose itch. Up against the wall several sunflowers stood proud at six foot tall, gently waving their huge yellow heads.

I sat down and ripped open the envelope.

Highwood Hall
Beckton
Faversham
Kent
31ˢᵗ July, 1898

Dear Françoise,

    I trust you are well. I am sorry it has taken me a time to write but I wanted to ensure I had some news first. And now I do. Life has changed at Highwood since Anna and Theo moved in two weeks ago. It's a delight to have the little fellow running around the place. He is good company for me and the staff love him. It has brought back memories to Mr Hughes, Mrs Derby and Mrs Jarvis who remember Charles at that age.

    Thank you for making me see sense. The joy Theo has brought to my life in just this short time is worth risking any disparaging comments. Anna's settled in nicely too. I had forgotten what good company she could be.

    After a lot of consideration, I no longer blame you for Charles' death. You were right, he died by his own carelessness. You were also correct in stating I should have allowed him to marry the bride of his choice. Therefore, dear child, if you wish to wed in the future, please accept my blessing.

    One more thing. Oliver's grave will always be tended well so you have no fear of neglect. If you wish to visit in the future you'll always be welcome.

    Forever yours
    Elizabeth.

I folded up the letter and put it back in the envelope. I would show it to André and Tilly. Elizabeth had given me her blessing and Theo and Anna were settled at *Highwood*. I folded my arms. The oath was behind me and perhaps now I may have the chance of happiness.

I smiled as I headed to the drawing room to share the good news with André and Tilly. Would Maman be pleased for me? Perhaps knowing Elizabeth no longer blamed me, she would change her view too.

Lady Astley and Matthew would be here later for afternoon tea. My heart beat faster at the thought of seeing Matthew again. When I entered the drawing room Tilly was polishing the furniture.

'What are you doing,' I asked. 'You should be resting while the twins are asleep, not doing housework.'

'I don't want Lady Astley thinking that we don't keep a good house.'

'Kitty only did it yesterday. Come and sit down. I have some news.' My smile widened.

'Is everything all right?'

'Oui. Very all right.' I passed her the letter.

She scanned the page with her mouth wide open. 'Well, that's it. You're free. No need to feel any further guilt.'

'Oui. That is what I thought too. I believe I am ready to move forward.'

Tilly took my hand. 'You deserve happiness.'

'Oui. You are right. I should go and get ready before our visitors arrive. Would you come up shortly and do my hair?'

'I'd be delighted.' Tilly beamed.

*

I stepped into the silk taffeta gown. Today I wanted to look my best. I fastened an emerald pendant around my neck that matched my outfit perfectly. Tilly had dressed my hair in ringlets. I positioned the small feathered hat on the side of my head and stared into the glass at my reflection. The young naïve girl who first came to England was long gone and although now only twenty, I had known far too much sadness. I was still an attractive woman and like André and Tilly had said, I deserved happiness.

Today was time for a new chapter. I stood away from the dressing table, took a deep breath and ventured downstairs.

Voices travelled along the hallway. I opened the door to the drawing room. André was holding one of the girls in the air and making her gurgle. Everyone was uttering *aw* sounds.

Matthew stood up. 'Madam Françoise. Good afternoon.' He came towards me and said in a soft voice that no one else could hear. 'You look beautiful.'

I smiled. 'Why, merci, Monsieur Astley.' I allowed him to lead me across to the others. Lady Astley was on the couch with Tilly.

'Good afternoon, Lady Astley.' I picked up a plate with a selection of cakes and offered it to her. 'Would you like one?'

'Thank you, Madam Françoise. You look enchanting.' She helped herself to a small Victoria sponge and took a bite. 'This sponge is so light. Did you make it yourself?'

'Non. Kitty did. She is our new part time help as Sally now looks after the twins while Tilly works.'

'Madam Françoise,' Matthew said, 'would you care to show me the August blooms?'

'I would be delighted.' I put the plate back down on the table. 'Would anyone like to join us?'

'No. You two young people go.' Lady Astley glanced at Maman. 'If that's all right with you, Madam Antoinette.'

Maman squinted. 'Oui. Yes, of course.'

On opening the French doors, I said to Matthew, 'You must come and see the sunflowers.'

We sauntered along the path, admiring the sunflowers, cactus dahlias and pinks until we reached the bench at the bottom of the garden.

'Shall we rest for a while?' Matthew asked.

'Oui.' I smoothed the back of my gown to sit without it getting creased. When I glanced up, Matthew was down on one knee, holding out an emerald ring.

'Dearest Madam Françoise, please will you do me the honour of becoming my wife.'

My heart banged. Butterflies fluttered in my stomach. I opened my mouth but I was speechless.

'Madam?'

This is what I wanted. I had no need to feel guilty. Elizabeth had given me her blessing and Charles' child was being taken good care of. I took a deep breath. 'Bien sûr, Monsieur Astley.' I smiled. 'I would be delighted to become your wife.' All I needed now was Maman's blessing.

Matthew sprang up from the ground and was at my side. He put his arm around me and pulled me closer and when his lips touched mine, I returned his kiss.

*

'Maman, why can you not be happy for me?'

'You have only just buried one husband and now you want another one.' She shook her head. 'Your papa would be ashamed of you.'

'Non. You are wrong. Papa would not be ashamed. He brought me up to be my own person. I honoured the oath and was betrayed. No longer is my family at risk of becoming paupers, therefore Papa would have told me to grab the chance of happiness. Before his death, you would have said the same but since his death, you have changed. Maman, you have become a bitter old lady.'

She lifted her hand to strike me.

'What on earth is going on?' André shouted on entering the room. He marched over to Maman and lowered her arm. 'When have you ever struck your children?'

Maman put her hands up to her face. 'I am sorry. I do not know what got into me.'

'We need to sit down and sort this matter out once and for all. Françoise is to marry Monsieur Astley next June and you will have to accept it. What have you got against him?'

'I have nothing against him. He is a lovely gentleman.' Maman held her back as she lowered herself to the armchair. 'It is the way this relationship has come about. If Françoise had returned to her husband, then Sir Charles would still be alive.'

I joined André on the chaise longue. 'Why are you still blaming me? Lady Elizabeth no longer does.' I passed her Elizabeth's letter. 'Please read it, Maman.'

She shook her head.

'All right, I will.' André took the note. "I do not blame you for Charles' death. He died from his own carelessness. And I should have allowed him to marry a bride of his choosing." See? It was the oath that caused all this pain. Henri and Willeme had no idea of the hornet's nest they would stir up when making that promise to each other. Or perhaps they did.' André chuckled. 'Perhaps they knew exactly what they were doing?' He got up and gave the letter to Maman. 'Read.'

She scanned the page, blinking her eyes.

'Maman' – André knelt down and took her hand – 'we would like our old maman back. When I brought you here to live with us in England, I did not think it would be a different woman to the one in France. Please' – he squeezed her hand – 'come back to us.'

Maman sobbed. 'I will try. I am sorry mes enfants, I will try. You are right, since your papa passed, my heart died with him, but he would not want this.'

'Here.' André passed her his handkerchief.

Sniffling, she dabbed her eyes.

Chapter 44

Tilly

June 1899

Eliza and Louise toddled around the furniture. At just over thirteen months they still looked identical. Big blue eyes like André's, and my brother Frank's thick brown hair.

'I've come to get the twins, Madam Matilda,' Sally said. 'It won't be long before they're walking on their own, will it?'

'Eliza stepped from the couch to the armchair yesterday before she realised she'd let go.' I chuckled. 'I finished their outfits earlier. Would you like to see?'

'Oh yes, please. That would be wonderful.' Sally picked up the girls one by one, popped them in the perambulator, and followed me into the workroom.

I held up one of the frocks. Pink lace, smocking at the yoke, overlayed cream satin. A rose silk bertha collar would show off the girls' tiny necks and puffed sleeves matched the underskirt.

'They're going to look gorgeous. I like the little pink satin roses around the yoke and sleeves. You must be so proud of your girls.'

'Thank you, Sally. Yes, I am.'

'Can I have a peep of Madam Françoise's gown?'

'Now, Sally, you know I can't show you that. You don't have long to wait. I can't believe she's getting married tomorrow.'

Louise wailed and Eliza joined in.

'I'd best take these two for a walk.' Sally gripped the perambulator handle.

As she was leaving, André popped his head in the door entrance. 'Hello my special girls. Are you off out with them, Sally?'

'Yes, Mr Dubois. I thought I'd take them to see the ducks as it's such a lovely day.'

'Don't forget the canopy,' I said, while hanging the tiny frocks back on the hangers.

'I won't.' Sally waved as she left.

André glanced around the room. 'Is she about?'

'She'll be here in a minute for a last fitting of her gown.'

'I just wanted to check how it went at Lady Astley's this morning?'

'Very well. All finished.'

'And Françoise still has no idea?'

'None. Shh,' I said, 'I think that's her coming now.'

'Good afternoon, ma sœur.' He rubbed his nose.

'Bonjour. What are you two plotting?'

'Nothing,' I said. 'André dropped in hoping to catch you in your gown.' I laughed. 'But I told him the same as I just told Sally that he has to wait until tomorrow.'

'Quite right.' Françoise playfully shoved André out of the room.

He put his hands up. 'All right. All right. I am going. I will catch you ladies later.'

'Right, let's get you into your gown. I made some final touches to it last night.'

'Merci.' She followed me over to the dressing room where I'd hung the outfit on a rail. 'It is beautiful. By the way, what were you doing at Lady Astley's again this morning?'

'Just sorting something out.'

'But that is every day this week you have gone over there. Lady Astley's taking advantage of my union with Monsieur Astley. You must tell her that we do not make home visits and she should come to the house like the rest of our clientele.'

'Do not fret, Françoise. If you must know, she's helping me with a little surprise for you.'

'Oh. Now I feel bad.' Her eyes lit up. 'What is the surprise? Please, pray tell me.'

'You'll find out soon enough tomorrow. I've said far more than I should have. Now come on. Let's get you into this.' I held up the bridal gown.

Françoise slipped off her ruby silk day robe and stepped into the gown. The rich gold fabric enhanced her chestnut brown hair and medium skin tone. She had been adamant that she should not wear white because she was a widow. We compromised by using gold silk taffeta, with a lace bodice that fitted into her small waist, flowing to the ground with layers of lace and a train. I'd finished it off with little emerald silk rosettes to match her eyes.

'Perfect.' I smoothed down the skirt. 'You look enchanting.' She was self-assured unlike when she'd married Sir Charles four years ago. Gone was the naïve teenager, instead a twenty-one-year-old mature woman stood before me. So much had changed for both of us. We had grown up together. And tomorrow when she walked down that aisle to Matthew, I knew I'd be proud of her.

'Merci. I love it.' She turned from side to side checking her reflection in the full-length mirror. 'Now we should check yours is all right too.'

I helped her out of the gown and hung it back up on the rail and she helped me into mine.

'Tilly' – Françoise frowned – 'it is a little on the tight side.' She looked at me with curiosity. 'Are you?' She beamed.

I nodded. 'I believe I am. I should've known I couldn't keep anything from you.' I placed my hand on my stomach.

'I hope you get a boy this time.' Françoise unpicked the seam to allow extra breathing space. 'There. Take a look.'

I glanced in the mirror. The gown was a lighter shade than Françoise's and less ornate. Plain silk fabric flowed to my ankles finished with a burgundy sash. The other bridesmaid would wear an emerald sash matching the rosettes on Françoise's gown.

'Parfait.' She ran her hands across the fabric. 'Does André know?' She sunk into one of the armchairs.

'Not yet. I will tell him after your wedding. I hadn't wanted you to know yet either.'

'I had my suspicions when I noticed you being sick. When can we expect this little one?'

'I think sometime around Christmas. It seems my dream is to come true to have a hoard of children around me while making gowns for rich women.' I chuckled.

Françoise rose from the chair and took me into a hug. 'I am so pleased for you. Life is wonderful. I cannot believe that tomorrow I shall be married to Matthew. It seems we are both getting our happy-ever-after.'

Chapter 45

I stepped out of the bath. Tilly had insisted on helping me bathe and dress my hair as she had done on my first wedding day. However, unlike when I had married Charles, today I looked forward to being with Matthew for the rest of my life.

Tilly patted my skin dry while shielding me behind the soft towel. The smell of lavender travelled to my nose from the oils added to the water. It was strange to think that last time we were mistress and maid, but now, sisters.

'Are you nervous?' Tilly asked.

'Non. Not at all. I feel totally relaxed. I suppose it is because I know this is the right thing. I love Matthew and he loves me. He will never betray me like Charles did.'

'No, he won't. It's clear he adores you. I think he fell in love with you from that first moment you met in the tearoom.'

I slid my satin robe on and sat at the dressing table. 'Where are the twins?'

'In bed sleeping but Sally's with them in the event they wake up.'

'Do not forget you need to get yourself ready too.'

Tilly brushed through my hair. 'Plenty of time.' She lifted up thick strands from the top and teased them into big rolls, pinning in position. For the lower part of my hair, she made a long plait and twisted it into a neat knot. 'How's that?' She held up a hand mirror in order that I could see the back.

'It is lovely.' I patted the right-hand side of my head. 'Merci.'

'And now for this.' She fixed small sprigs of orange blossom around my hair. 'There.'

'Parfait.' I had not worried about the traditional superstitions such as something borrowed or the sixpence in my shoe. They had not helped me last time.

*

Tilly and I stepped down the staircase. André stood at the bottom waiting. 'Vous êtes belles, vous deux.'

Maman and Sally joined him, each holding one of the twins. Eliza and Louise looked gorgeous in their little pink frocks. Tilly had done an amazing job on all of our gowns. On reaching the last stair, André passed me an orange blossom bouquet and handed a smaller one to Tilly. He held his arm out to me. 'Are you ready, ma sœur?'

'Oui.' And I knew I was. This time my ears would not be closed to the vows as I said *I will.*

*

A silver-grey horse pulled the Barouche. Orange blossom and green foliage hung from the carriage which was decorated with white satin sash ribbons. Joe, dressed in formal attire, took the reins. André clasped my hand in his. 'Tu es belle, ma sœur. How do you feel? No second thoughts?'

'None. I cannot wait to become Matthew Astley's wife. It seems the most natural thing in the world. I feel like I have known him all my life. We are so comfortable together. Can you understand that?'

'Oui. That is how I feel, have always felt, about Matilda. Matthew is a good man. He will take care of you.'

'I know.' I waved to the villagers as we stopped outside St John's.

356

Joe stepped down and helped me from the carriage. André took my arm as we strolled up to the church. My silk taffeta gown rustled and the train trailed the ground. Scent of orange blossom from my bouquet tickled my nose.

Onlookers cheered and clapped. I smiled. My veil shielded my eyes from the warm sun. I had no tears, and if I had they would have been tears of happiness. The cold fabric from my gown kept me cool. Church bells pealed. I squinted as I looked ahead to the vestibule. There appeared to be someone in an identical gown to Tilly's. My mind was deceiving me. I blamed it on my pounding pulse. Maybe it was Sally? But wait, this woman had dark hair. She turned to a profile position. For a moment I thought I recognised her, but it could not be so. When we reached the entrance, the dark-haired woman faced me, and I found myself speechless.

'Françoise,' she said. 'Surprise.' She gave me that affectionate smile I remembered so well.

'Geneviève.' I took her in my arms and hugged her, taking care not to squash our bouquets. 'But how? Tilly, did you sort this?' I turned to André. 'Or was it you, mon frère?'

'It was both of us.' He grinned.

I hugged him and Tilly in turn. 'Merci.' I bit my bottom lip. 'But Geneviève, I do not understand. How are you here?'

André adjusted his single stem buttonniere.

'Do you remember a while ago I mentioned my brother had married an Englishwoman?' Geneviève's brown eyes gleamed.

'Non.' I shook my head.

André squeezed my hand. 'I hate to interrupt this reunion, ladies, but there is a groom inside patiently waiting for his bride. There will be plenty of time to catch up later.'

Tilly rested her gloved fingers on André's arm. 'I don't want to worry you, but your mother and Lady Astley haven't arrived yet.'

'But they left first.' André paced backwards and forwards. 'Where have they got to?'

'Something must have happened,' I said.

Tilly squeezed my fingers. 'I'm sure there will be a satisfactory explanation.'

André took out his pocket watch. He sighed. 'We are already five minutes late.' He wandered up the path towards the lane.

'Suppose they have had a crash?' I put my hands to my face. 'We will have to cancel. André,' I called, 'you need to let Matthew know. He needs to know.' I sobbed.

André came running back. 'It is all right, ma sœur, they are coming up the road now.'

The driver reined the horse in and the carriage came to a stop. A boy jumped down and helped Maman and Lady Astley out. Maman hobbled down the path holding on to her hat, with Lady Astley at her side.

'I am sorry.' Maman chuckled. 'The driver had to pull over because I lost my bonnet in the breeze. The boy had to chase it across a field but eventually he caught it. And luckily it remained intact.'

André took a deep breath. 'Well now that you are here, please get inside without further ado.'

'Thank goodness you are both all right,' I said.

'We didn't mean to worry you,' Lady Astley said. 'My nephew is a lucky man.'

'Merci, Lady Astley.'

'Suzanna please. But your brother's right, Matthew will be wondering where you've got to. Come, Madam Antoinette, we should get in there.'

'Oui,' Maman said, 'I do not wish to miss ma fille coming down the aisle.' She shuffled into the church with Lady Astley.

André took my arm. 'Finally, ma sœur, we can get this ceremony started. The groom will fear he has been jilted.'

The organist played *The Wedding March* and my brother led me down the aisle with Tilly and Geneviève holding my train. Pews on either side of the church were filled. Maman and Lady Astley were at the front. Behind them Sally and Kitty bobbed the twins on their laps to keep them entertained. On reaching the altar, Matthew glanced at me and smiled. My heart beat faster. His greenish-blue eyes sparkled. He looked tall and handsome in the smooth vicuna black coat showing off a silk white vest and tie which fitted his medium build perfectly. Blond curls brushed his forehead. I did not recognise his best man, a gentleman with black gleaming hair. I must get Matthew to introduce him to Geneviève. It would be wonderful if they were able to build a union. I knew that was a fairy tale but fairy tale endings did happen. They had for André and now for me. My hands shook. A medley of butterflies danced in my stomach. Not from nerves but excitement. Soon I would become Madam Matthew Astley and I could not wait.

The vicar opened the ceremony. 'Dearly beloved we are gathered here today in the sight of God…'

Matthew took my gloved hand and smiled. His eyes sparkled like aquamarine gems. My skin tingled.

The vicar continued. 'We shall now sing *Glory to God.*

After an introduction from the organist the choir boys filled the church with their sweet soprano voices. The congregation joined in on the second verse.

At the end of the hymn the vicar said, 'It was ordained…'

I wished he would get to our vows.

'…Therefore, if any man can show any just cause, why they may not lawfully be joined together, let him speak, or else hereafter forever hold his peace.'

The porch door slammed shut. Footsteps crept down the aisle. *What now?* I nervously moved my head and breathed a sigh of relief when a mature gentleman with grey hair and white bushy sideburns mouthed *sorry* as he moved into the pew next to Blanche and Caroline Livingston.

*

I passed my orange blossom bouquet to Tilly. Matthew and I faced each other as the vicar said to him, 'Matthew Edward wilt thou have this woman to thy wedded wife, to live together after God's ordinance and in the holy estate of matrimony? Wilt thou love her, comfort her, honour, and keep her in sickness and in health; and, forsaking all others, keep thee only unto her, so long as ye both shall live?'

Matthew's eyes sparkled. 'I will.'

'Françoise Angélique wilt thou have this man to thy wedded husband, to live together after God's ordinance in the holy estate of matrimony? Wilt thou obey him, and serve him, love, honour, and keep him in sickness and in health; and, forsaking all others, keep thee only unto him, so long as ye both shall live?'

Without hesitation I answered, 'I will.' This time it was right. We were in love. I wished Papa were here but at least I had Maman. I held sadness in my heart for Charles. It was needless he had to die but I had stopped blaming myself for his accident. If anyone was to blame it was the Dubois brothers who had made that stupid pledge all those years ago. In a few months we would see the turn of the century. Times were changing and I was ready to move forward with Matthew and hopefully we would be gifted with children. No child would ever replace Oliver but I had plenty of space in my heart.

Matthew parted the slit in my glove. 'With this ring I thee wed, with my body I thee worship, and with all my worldly goods I thee endow: In the name of the Father, and of the Son, and of the Holy Ghost. Amen.' He slipped the ring on my finger. I glanced down at the gold band set with emerald gems and smiled. Madam Matthew Astley. I had never felt prouder.

*

Matthew took my arm as we made our way to the vestry. André and Matthew's friend, along with Tilly and Geneviève, followed behind as the congregation sang *All Things Bright and Beautiful.*

'Are you happy?' whispered Matthew.

'More than I thought possible.'

I handed my bouquet to Tilly and picked up the pen, leaned forward and signed the register as Françoise Angélique Dubois for the very last time.

*

As we stood outside the church a photographer grouped Matthew and I surrounded by our friends and families into position. André and Tilly with the twins, Lady Astley and Maman, Geneviève and Matthew's best man. I still did not know his name, but thought that Geneviève and him looked very handsome together. The photographer told us all to stay still while he backed away to his bellows camera and ducked under the cover. Once he was happy we dispersed and Matthew led me to our carriage but not before our friends and family threw rice over us. I was about to get inside the Barouche when I whispered to Matthew. 'I almost forgot. I should throw my bouquet.'

A group of guests hovered in anticipation. Most of them our clients, including the Livingston sisters standing in the front row. Sally and Kitty waited too.

'Are you ready?' I asked.

They all cheered.

I turned away and threw the posy. When I turned back Geneviève was holding it close. I smiled.

361

Back at *Sunbury* guests congregated in the garden. Mrs Jennings led them to the marquee where cold meats and salad were laid out on the table and champagne was plentiful. Geneviève came up behind me. 'I adore your gown,' she said. 'The gold is the shade of sparkling wine. What is this fabric?'

'Silk taffeta.'

'Did Matilda make it?'

'Oui. She taught me how to sew too. Not sewing like you and I used to do, but a craft. We design gowns for the ladies in the village. I love what we do and Matthew does not expect me to give it up because we are married.'

'You are very fortunate but you deserve it. When I think of what you have gone through' – she took my hand – 'I wish I could have been there for you.'

'Ladies.' Matthew came up behind me and put his arm around my waist.

'Matthew, meet Mademoiselle Geneviève, my childhood friend from France.'

'Delighted you could be here, mademoiselle.' He kissed the back of her hand. 'I noticed earlier you were getting acquainted with my good friend Mr Williams.'

'Oui. He seems very nice.'

'I have yet to meet him.' I turned my head to search for him.

'You will, my dearest, but first I thought you would like to spend a few minutes alone with your friend to catch up.'

'Merci. You are quite right. Geneviève come and sit with me, and Matthew, bring Mr Williams to meet me shortly.'

Geneviève and I found a quiet place in the garden. 'Tell me, how did you manage to get here?' I sat down carefully so as not to crush my gown.

'I mentioned earlier my brother had married an Englishwoman?'

'Pierre?'

'Oui. He is here among your guests and eager to see you again. I will take you to him and his wife shortly.' Geneviève's brown eyes gleamed.

'This day keeps getting more wonderful. What is his wife like?'

'Emma is lovely. You will adore her.' Geneviève twiddled her diamond and sapphire silver bangle. 'Your maman contacted Papa about me coming here as a surprise for you but he was not pleased about me travelling alone. It was Pierre who offered to accompany me. He said it was a good opportunity for Emma to visit her family. Papa then agreed as I would have a chaperone.' She fluttered her eyelashes.

'Have you been staying with Emma's family?' I touched her skirt. 'And how did you get this done?'

'Non. We have been staying with Lady Astley for the last week. Your good sister-in-law, Matilda, came up each day to work on my gown. She worked so hard in order to get it finished' – Geneviève giggled – 'and you had no idea what was happening.'

'Your English is perfect.'

'Oui. I am able to speak it fluently now, just like you. Emma made sure of that.'

I hugged Geneviève again. 'You look so well.'

'I am. I am over Jacques Blanchet. He did not deserve me.'

'Non. He did not. No more than Charles deserved me. You will be lucky next time as I am with Matthew.'

'I hope so. Is that not Matilda heading this way?'

I glanced up as Tilly strode towards us.

'There you are,' she said. 'We wondered where you had got to? I think you should come and meet the rest of your guests. Pierre and Emma are eager to see you.'

I got up from the seat and hugged Tilly. 'Thank you so much my dear sister for everything you have done.'

'It was only what you deserved.' Tilly held her hand out to Geneviève as she rose from the bench.

I linked arms with the two women I loved as we made our way back to the guests.

*

The garden looked magical with candles lighting up the whole area. I felt secure and loved as Matthew held me in his arms as we danced the Viennese Waltz. André and Tilly danced close. They were as much in love as Matthew and I were. Sally had offered to stay the night to take care of the twins. Pierre and his wife waltzed around the area. Pierre had not changed. Still a slim physique, moustache, beard, and well-groomed dark hair. Emma was pretty. She did not look much older than me. Blonde hair, blue eyes but shorter than me. I smiled when I caught Mr Williams dancing with Geneviève. They seemed a perfect match. It would have been wonderful if they decided to marry. Life could not have been more perfect.

*

Our guests had dispersed, the candles had been extinguished, and it was silent in the garden apart from an owl hooting in the trees. Geneviève had returned to Lady Astley's along with Pierre and his wife. Maman, André and Tilly had retired for the evening. Tilly planned to tell André her news. He would be joyful. Mr Williams had left for home but not before he had promised Geneviève he would call on her. She would be staying at Oxhaven until late July so there was plenty of time for romance to blossom. This left Matthew and I. He put his arm around me as we meandered up to the house. He stopped at the front door and scooped me up into his arms. I clung on tightly. Champagne had made my head a little fuzzy. I giggled as he carried me over the threshold.

Matthew led me upstairs and along the passage to my chambre. He pushed the door open. There was no need for a lady's maid to help me undress. Matthew did that. After he unlaced my bodice, caressing my shoulders, I stepped out of the gown.

He lifted me up and carried me to the bed. 'Françoise Angélique Astley, I have been waiting all day to be alone with you.' He smothered me with kisses from the neck down while his hands caressed every inch of my body. I had never known anything quite like it, and when we consummated our marriage he took his time.

Afterwards we lay in each other's arms and fell asleep together until dawn, and when the blackbird sang outside, it prompted me to rise and draw back the drapes. I opened the window, breathed in the morning air, and watched the sky turn orange. Matthew stirred. I slipped back into bed and cuddled up close to my husband.

Acknowledgements

Special thanks to my friend Maureen Cullen. Not only for her perceptive and thoughtful editing in *The Oath* but her continuous support, encouragement and faith in me.

A big thank you to my fabulous beta readers for their invaluable feedback, and to Margaret Royall for checking the French phrases in the manuscript to ensure translations are correct.

Additional thanks to Andy Keylock (Marketing Pace) for the cover image design, and to Colin Ward for formatting my manuscript.

Finally, a big thank you to my husband, children, family and friends for their continued support and faith in me.

About the Author

Patricia M Osborne was born in Liverpool but now lives in West Sussex. She is married with grown-up children and grandchildren. In 2019 she graduated with an MA in Creative Writing. She is a published novelist, poet and short fiction writer. Her debut poetry pamphlet, *Taxus Baccata,* was nominated for the Michael Marks Pamphlet Award.

Patricia has a successful blog at Whitewingsbooks.com featuring other writers. When Patricia isn't working on her own writing, she enjoys sharing her knowledge, acting as a mentor to fellow writers.

You can find out more about Patricia by visiting Twitter, Facebook or her website.

Twitter: @PMOsborneWriter
Facebook: PatriciaMOsborne,Writer
Website: whitewingsbooks.com

Published Books

Novels

House of Grace family saga trilogy:

House of Grace
The Coal Miner's Son
The Granville Legacy

~

Poetry

The Montefiore Bride
Taxus Baccata
Sherry & Sparkly
Symbiosis
Spirit Mother: Experience the Myth